Wayward Love:
Captain Frederick Wentworth's Story

Wayward Love:

Captain Frederick Wentworth's Story

Jane Austen's *Persuasion*
Told through His Eyes

Regina Jeffers

Cover Art
"Royal Navy" from Wikipedia,
the free encyclopedia
HMS Victory

To order additional copies of this book, contact:
Xlibris Corporation
1-888-795-4274
www.Xlibris.com
Orders@Xlibris.com
54663

Chapter 1

By day or night, in weal or woe,
That heart, no longer free,
Must bear the love it cannot show
And silent ache for thee.
—Lord Byron from "On Parting"

"I have you, Captain!" the midshipman screamed over the turmoil happening on the deck. "I need help over here!" the youth begged as he tried to support the weight of the slumped over officer clinging to his exhausted frame.

Captain Frederick Wentworth recognized the danger of having pursued the retreating French sloop, but he also recognized the need to keep the French from reaching reinforcements and from taking English secrets straight back to Bonaparte. He made the decision to take the French vessel despite the fact his wife traveled aboard *The Resolve* with him. He ordered his men to take the enemy craft. "If necessary, her crew cannot escape," he instructed, meaning the British possessed no reason to allow the French to live if they put up a resistance. The countries were at war, after all.

For two days, Wentworth's ship chased the French craft. He actually admired how the smaller French ship took to the water, trying to evade Wentworth's best efforts to overtake the ketch. Frederick initiated his favorite maneuver in stopping his enemy—full broadsides, a lesson learned from the tales of the infamous Blackbeard. *The Resolve* caught up to the French ship during the night. Dawn brought his enemy the knowledge he faced the full force of the British navy, one of the finest on Earth.

Anne watched her husband before he ordered her below deck, trying to protect her from the worst of the battle. Frederick Wentworth held a natural charisma; his men would follow him anywhere. A strong man—so formidable his intense eyes telling the world he would broker nothing but success. He made few errors in his choices, things carefully reasoned out before he made a decision. He lived for the adventure of the sea, but *her* Frederick, essentially a practical man accomplished his dreams by organizing the chaos of his mind. She drank of the weathered lines of his face with her fingertips before lightly brushing his lips with hers.

"You will be safe, my Love," he mouthed the words as he cupped her chin in the palm of his large hand.

"Of course, I am safe." Anne bit back a full smile, realizing he feared for her comfort. "You are the captain of *The Resolve*; we are all safe under your command." She took his hand in hers, kissing the palm before releasing him. "Now, do what you must do, Frederick. I will be well." With that, she left him, heading for the protection of the lower levels of the ship. Anne only shivered when she saw him load his gun, knowing the strong possibility of hand-to-hand combat when the British boarded the sloop.

Wentworth watched her go; just looking at his wife caused his heart to leap with joy. He loved her from the first time he saw her face; only her countenance brought him peace. His pulse quickened with anticipation when she came near. From that moment long ago, he set his sights on winning *his* Anne. It took them nearly nine years for him to finally satisfy his unrealistic desires for her. Anne Elliot Wentworth epitomized everything for which he aspired: society, acceptance, wealth, and love. Anne overlooked his common origins and saw the man he became. He swore to prove to her aristocratic world she took not a step down with her choice of a husband. She symbolized why he fought this war against the French emperor.

He hoped to purchase a moderate-sized estate close to the shoreline for her. They would live there when he finally cashed in his commission from the service or at the end of the war. Anne, the daughter of a baronet, deserved the best he could give her. Frederick lost her when youth demanded they make decisions not their own. Anne belonged to him now; he loved her beyond reason. Soon, they could take their place in society and start a family. Uttering an amused laugh as the image played before him, Frederick broke away and prepared to strike at his enemy.

Wentworth felt the distant vibration as *The Resolve* ran out its guns. The ship readied itself for the assault. When he placed the spyglass to his eye, he saw the French scrambling to meet the surprise designed especially for them. Older seamen shouted orders, but Frederick recognized the confusion and the dismay upon the younger sailors' faces. His men, on the other hand, stood their positions on the deck, awaiting the inevitable. His men kept a determined silent vigil throughout the night, using the darkness to overtake the French.

With a nod of his head, he ordered the attack, and the gun ports rang out, all pointing directly at the French warship. He watched with satisfaction as the enemy's sails crumbled and crashed to the deck. As the smoke cleared, he could readily see the gaping hole in the starboard tack. Although anticipating the explosion of the French powder magazines, they never came. "What the . . . ?" he muttered to himself. The sloop's mizzenmast lay in multiple pieces on the deck. With the longboats in the water, Wentworth knew the French would fight, but he also knew he successfully managed another capture to his record—the financial reward securing his future with Anne. Everything he ever wanted floated within his grasp.

Someone from beside him called to his partner, "We'll not be waiting!"

"They'll not surrender peacefully," a lieutenant tried to caution his men.

"They're daft!" a man with a knife griped tightly between his teeth hissed to the others gathering on the deck. A fierce curse sounded from the crow's nest above his head as Wentworth placed the rolled up map in his assistant's hand.

He maneuvered *The Resolve* alongside the captured ship, readying to board her officially and claim her in the name of the Crown. Then the unexpected happened. A single shot rang out, and the heat seared through his side. With an expression of surprise clearly pasted on his face, his fingers reached the bloody opening in his jacket. *How?* He wondered as he slumped forward into the arms of the nearest midshipman. He was not close enough for someone aboard the French ship to deliver such a blow. Instinctively, he raised his eyes to his attacker. The man, wearing a leather-fringed jacket and a floppy brimmed hat held a long rifle. Frederick recognized it as one American privateers used often to fight off personal attack. It had the distance the single shot volley the British carried did not. "Give that to your good King George!" he heard the man's voice clearly before the British sailors surrounded him.

Ironically, Frederick's pain came not from his French enemy but from an American assisting Bonaparte's navy. He could hear the air gurgle in his throat as he sank to his knees. The pain and the fire radiated throughout his chest as he rolled to his back on the deck, allowing his eyes to search the thin smoky air for the blue sky with streaks of sunlight opening a new day. "Anne," he murmured when the midshipman lifted his captain's head for comfort.

"We will get you help, Captain. Just stay with us," the man gasped through clenched teeth, fear coursing through him.

Shipmates rushed forward. Lifting the gigantic frame of Frederick Wentworth onto a net stretcher, they quickly carried him to his quarters. Settling him on the bed, Laraby, the sawbones assigned to the ship, rushed in, hustling various sailors from the room. "Get me plenty of rum," the doctor demanded.

"Yes, Sir," one of the lieutenants darted out the door.

Wentworth groaned deeply as another officer helped the doctor remove his jacket. They cut the shirt away from the wound as the physician began to clean away the seeping blood. "Easy, Captain," the doctor cautioned. "Let me see what we have here."

The surgeon went through a mental checklist as he examined the captain's wound. "The bullet tore a zigzag path through part of your lower abdomen, Sir. There is quite a bit of damage. The good news is the bullet exited out your side. I need to sew you up proper, but I do not need to do any cutting of my own."

"Where is my wife?" Frederick finally got the words out.

An officer moved forward. "I will get her, Captain." The sight of all the blood took its toll on the man.

"I am giving you some laudanum." The doctor eased Wentworth back onto the bed.

"Could I have some rum?" Wentworth's mouth went dry as he fell back heavily against the pillows.

The doctor half grinned. "Why not?" He supported Frederick's head while he took a large swig of the brew.

Anne rushed into the room, shoving bodies away from the bed so she could reach him. "Frederick," she whispered his name close to his ear as she brushed the hair from his eyes. "I am here, my Love." She interlaced her fingers with his.

With an effort, he squeezed her hand and opened his eyes to hers. "I need an angel watching over me," he whispered as she lowered her mouth to brush his lips lightly.

"Nothing can keep us apart—nothing ever again. I am here, Frederick. Let the doctor do his work. In sickness and in health," she murmured before kissing his cheek along the temple.

Frederick made eye contact with the doctor and nodded his assent. Then his eyes rested again on Anne's face. He felt the laudanum begin to take its effect. His lids closed, but Anne's image remained with him.

*   *   *

Commander Frederick Wentworth made his way across Somerset. The sway of the public carriage along the uneven roadway reminded him of the rolling motion of the ocean; at least, it did as long as he kept his eyes closed. When he opened them, the matronly grandmother sitting across the way questioned him about the war and about his prospects. He assumed she had an eligible female available somewhere in her family, if he wanted to pursue the offer, but Frederick had no intentions of persisting along those lines—no such futures for him. When he chose a wife, it would be a woman with whom he could share his hopes and dreams—one who would recognize his potential. So, he kept his eyes closed, feigning sleep and imagining his walking the decks of his own ship.

Crossing through Uppercross, he finally allowed himself the pleasure of looking at the rolling countryside, peppered with herds of sheep and briny cattle, grazing in the fields. His brother Edward resided as the curate at Monkford, and Frederick planned to spend part of his leave catching up. Quiet time held a pleasant prospect after some of the action he saw of late. Of course, he was not with his sister's husband, Benjamin Croft, and Nelson as they defeated Admiral Vileneuve at Trafalgar, but Frederick saw his share of battles. Like Benjamin, he expected to use the war with the French emperor to make his fortune. Thoughts of his sister brought Frederick a pang of loneliness; Sophia and Benjamin shared a rare love. "Some day," he whispered to himself. "Someday, I will turn my head . . . ."

The slowing of the horses interrupted his thoughts. "Uppercross!" the driver shouted. "Changing horses!"

Frederick debarked from the carriage, looking around at the small village. People scrambled back and forth at the posting inn. Knowing he had less than an hour to go, he chose only to stretch his legs in the inn yard rather than to waste his money on some sort of libation inside the crowded tavern.

"How much time?" he inquired of the groom as the man unhitched the horses.

"More than a quarter—less than a half hour." The driver leaned over the edge to take the mail pouch from the innkeeper.

Frederick looked at the smattering of houses and shops. "I shall take a short walk," he told the driver as he started away toward the village.

The driver called to his retreating form, "We will not wait!"

Frederick did not even look back. He just raised his hand to let the man know he heard the warning. Uppercross, a moderate-sized village, was designed in the old English style. He passed a gate, which led to what was obviously a house, substantial and unmodernized, of superior appearance, especially when compared to those of the yeomen and labourers. With its high walls, great gates, and old trees, Frederick envisioned a veranda, French windows, and other prettiness, quite likely to catch the traveler's eye.

Strolling along the wooden walkways, he paused only to look in some of the shop windows. Seeing a fan he knew Sophia would love, he smiled. On impulse, he entered the shop; he would buy the fan for his sister. He could leave it with Edward to mail to her for her birthday. It would surprise the highly critical Sophie to know even though he returned to the sea, her younger brother planned for her birthday long before the actual event.

Frederick chose the item, then turned to leave, having paid for it, but before he could depart, the shop's door swung open suddenly, and two ladies swept into the room. The first, a very handsome woman, dominated the space with her entrance. A strong, French perfume wafted over him as he allowed his eyes to assay her beauty. Her hair was nearly black, the eyes brown, and the nose, nearly eagle like, took on a distinctly aristocratic air. Belatedly, Frederick offered her a polite bow as she brushed by him, barely acknowledging his presence. "Miss Elliot," he heard the shopkeeper's voice as the man snapped to attention to meet the woman's needs.

Frederick saw the type before. Usually, he preferred to avoid women of the realm, finding most of them too consumed with their petty interests to be worth entertaining his time. Let them spend their days with their embroidery and their poetry reading; he preferred a woman with an elegance of mind—a woman with a sweetness of character.

He stepped away from the all-consuming Miss Elliot and headed for the door; his carriage would be leaving soon. The second woman remained by the entry; he started to move around her, and then she raised her eyes to his. Frederick froze. Her delicate features and mild dark eyes mesmerized him in an instant. For some reason she did not look away, and neither did he. Instead, he stood before her looking down into her doe-like eyes, watching them darken and light with sparks and wondering as if she could feel the fire burning in him. Her slim jaw, slightly square, rose a bit higher, and her ramrod-straight back made her appear taller than she was. In fact, she barely came to his shoulder. She said nothing; she simply continued to look deeply into his eyes. Frederick found himself unexpectedly amused by the situation, and his eyebrow shot up evaluatively.

"Come, Anne," the other woman demanded, and Frederick saw a flash of shame play across her face as she ducked her head, allowing her bonnet to shadow her features once again.

"Pardon me," he choked out the words, finding his throat suddenly very dry. He desperately wanted to say more to her, but she slipped away to where her companion thumbed through pages of fashion plates.

Frederick opened the door to depart, but he could not resist the urge to look at her one more time. His heart skipped a beat as she raised her head, giving him a quick smile before diverting her attention back to the bolts of material. Frederick paused; the faint smell of lavender surrounded him. He closed his eyes and inhaled deeply. Closing the shop's door and returning to the walkway, he murmured, "Beautiful." Smiling again, he headed towards the inn yard.

Within the hour Frederick found himself sitting in his brother's small cottage. "You are a sight for sore eyes," Edward teased as he handed his brother a cup of tea. "You filled out since we last saw each other. The sea is good for your constitution."

Frederick laughed lightly. "It is, Edward; it is even better for my purse. I should leave the war with a governmental position, if I so wish, and a reasonable fortune."

Sitting to join him, Edward nodded his agreement. "I know it is your wish, Frederick, to be acknowledged for your accomplishments. However, you must realize society is slow to change. Even a sizeable fortune will not allow you to live within more than the fringes of fine society. An earl one step from debtor's prison will always be accepted quicker than a commoner with accrued wealth, especially if the commoner has no significant ancestral offerings. Name is still more powerful than the quid."

"It should not be so." Frederick's words held steely determination.

Edward added another sugar to his tea. "The aristocracy is not likely to change, my Brother, but if anyone can bend it to his will, my money will be on you. Now, what would you like to do during your stay? I receive a few invitations on a regular basis. My position allows me some degree of respectability in country society, at least."

Frederick's thoughts went immediately to the darkening eyes and the slender features of the woman called "Anne." A fleeting smile turned up the corners of his lips. "Anything, Edward. I simply came to enjoy your company and to feel normal again. A taste for what I am fighting will go a long way when I must return to my ship."

"How is Harville?" Edward asked as he put his empty cup away.

Frederick chuckled. "He is in love once again. He swears this time he will marry her, but I heard such protestations before. Like me, he returned home to visit his friends and family. His sister Fanny is coming of age soon, and Harville wants to assure himself she will make no choices without his permission."

"I would hate to be in his shoes." Edward began to pick up Frederick's belongings to take them to his room. "With several females for whom he is responsible, Harville will always be caring for sisters and his mother and his aunts."

"Luckily, the man has a generous nature." Frederick rose to follow his brother. "If I ever needed someone on my side, Harville would be my first choice of all my shipmates."

*   *   *

The next evening found the Wentworth brothers at a neighborhood assembly. Obviously, Edward Wentworth earned the respect of the local gentry, and they welcomed his brother's presence in the area. Wearing his dress uniform, Frederick cut a fine figure, and more than one mother began to concoct ways to draw his attention to her eligible daughter. He relished the attention; being at sea so long, Frederick craved the attention of English society, imagining his place within the social structure of the country he called home.

He stood with Edward and several other men when he felt her enter the room. Even without turning around, Frederick knew she was there. He knew it in his heart—he knew it in the shiver, which ran down his spine. Turning slowly, he half expected "his Anne" to be standing in the doorway. Instead, he found a man of rank, self purporting his own looks, posing in the entrance and waiting to be announced. Ostentatiously attired, a young woman, the same aristocratic lady Frederick noted in the village shop, stood by his side, resting her hand lightly on his proffered arm.

A voice rang out. "Sir Walter Elliot of Kellynch Hall. Miss Elizabeth Elliot. Lady Russell. Miss Anne Elliot." A path cleared as the Elliot party walked the length of the assembly hall and took its place on the raised dais at the far end. Despite his earlier misgivings, his body was correct; she was there. Miss Anne Elliot followed at the rear of her family, a tiny little smile curving her lips. She fascinated him; a perfect lady, Frederick knew she could easily name her mate. Miss Anne Elliot, unlike the rest of her family, possessed no vanity in her looks, but as far as he could see, she should lead the group. She was, obviously, the only one of true quality among the quartet.

"Easy, Frederick," Edward whispered lightly in his ear. "Miss Elizabeth Elliot is not for you. She is to marry the heir apparent; at least, that is the accepted rumor."

Frederick's eyes never left Anne Elliot. "It is not to Miss Elliot I look."

Edward followed his brother's gaze. "Miss Anne?" he stammered. "She is the more amiable one."

"Let us get something to drink," Frederick added quickly, realizing his attention became noticeable to those around him. Retrieving lemonades, the brothers moved off to speak privately. "Tell me what you know of the Elliots."

"Sir Walter solicits the praise of the area as the only member of the aristocracy in the neighborhood. Vanity is the beginning and end of Sir Walter Elliot's character: vanity of person and of situation. He was remarkably handsome as a youth; few women could think more of their appearance than does he. He considers the blessing of beauty as inferior only to the blessing of a baronetcy."

"Where is Lady Elliot?" Frederick asked as he forced his eyes from Anne Elliot once more.

"She passed before I arrived in the area—some six or seven years ago," Edward added. "I know little about her except what I heard. She was a woman of very superior character from all reports—an excellent woman, sensible and amiable, whose judgment and conduct, if they might be pardoned the youthful infatuation, which made her Lady Elliot, never required indulgence afterwards." Frederick laughed lightly at his brother's attempt at sarcasm. "She humored, or softened, or concealed his failings, and promoted his real respectability for seventeen years; and though not the very happiest being in the world herself, she found enough in her duties, her friends, and her children, to attach her to life, and make it no matter of indifference to her when she was called on to quit them." Edward's eyes misted with the thoughts of how God often takes the best to Heaven early. "Three girls, the two eldest sixteen and fourteen, was an awful legacy for a mother to bequeath; an awful charge rather, to confide to the authority and guidance of a conceited silly father."

"Why has Sir Walter never remarried?" Frederick could not resist asking.

"Other than himself, Sir Walter is not likely to believe anyone worthy of his attention. Some thought he might choose Lady Russell; she was Lady Elliot's intimate friend, but they did not marry, whatever might have been anticipated on that head by their acquaintance. He did bring her to live close by in the village of Kellynch, where she serves as a confidante for the daughters."

The music began again, and Frederick watched as Anne Elliot took the dance floor with a member of the local gentry. The man's slightly disheveled appearance and clumsy movements did little to win Anne's admiration. She looked politely at him and offered him a gentle smile, but Frederick could easily see her eyes did not darken with anticipation as they had with him.

"Who is the gentleman?" He nodded toward the couple as Anne circled the man across from her.

"Charles Musgrove," Edward supplied the answer. "The Musgroves are the second most important family in the area. He is the eldest son and will inherit a substantial property. The Musgroves wish a match, but Lady Russell does not approve from what I hear. She wishes more for Miss Anne, whom she favors because Anne Elliot most resembles her late mother."

"I believe it is time I return to the dance floor, Brother." Frederick started forward to choose a partner and to enter the quadrille already in progress.

Edward cautioned, "If Lady Russell does not approve of Charles Musgrove, the brother of a curate will stand no chance."

"You will introduce me later," Frederick stated as he walked away toward a cluster of eligible young ladies waiting to be escorted to the floor.

"Miss Anne," Edward made a proper bow, "may I introduce my brother Commander Frederick Wentworth?"

Frederick bowed formally. "Miss Anne."

"Commander." She curtsied and then brought her eyes to Frederick's face. She spoke to Edward but looked only at his brother. "I believe, Mr. Wentworth, your brother and I met briefly several days ago, although a formal introduction was not made at the time." The softness of her voice affected Frederick's knees, weakening them and forcing him to shift his weight to maintain his stance.

"You honor me, Miss Anne, with your recognition." Frederick took her hand and lowered his head to kiss her gloved knuckles.

"What brings you to Somerset, Commander?" Anne withdrew her hand slowly, allowing Frederick the pleasure of holding it for a few brief seconds.

Frederick smiled at her. "Besides my brother's fine company, I seek the peace of the English countryside. I will be joining the crew of a new ship when I return to my duties, hopefully, my own before long."

"Then you have the prospect of your advancement?" Interest flashed through her eyes, and Frederick realized she made no pretense.

"I do, Miss Anne." He nodded toward the dance floor. "If you have not already promised the next set, would you honor me with your company?"

Anne's face glowed as she smiled up at him. "It would be my pleasure, Commander."

They danced in silence for a few minutes, but when they came back together, Frederick could bear it no longer. "Are we devoid of conversation so quickly, Miss Anne?"

"I would hope not." Her smile reached the corners of her eyes. "I was just contemplating the length of your name."

"It is quite a mouthful; is it not? Commander Frederick Wentworth. A man could expire before he could utter it in full." His laughter teased her ear as they passed each other in the dance form.

Anne's head turned to follow his progress through the twirls and turns, which would bring them back together. "Imposing," the word barely audible. "Both the man and the name."

Frederick felt his breath catch in his chest. Taking her hand as they proceeded down the line, he could not resist looking at her mouth. "Do you flatter me, Miss Anne?"

He watched as the flush of her cheeks reddened. "I . . . I apologize, Commander," she stammered.

"Please do not apologize, Miss Anne. To have the attention of such a beautiful woman would make any man puff with pride."

"It is my sister Elizabeth who is the beauty of the family. I have a mirror, Commander. Please, no false flattery." Her reprimand was the last words before they parted to circle other partners.

Frederick watched her delicate features as she wove her way through the other dancers. When the music brought them back together, he held her hand a little more tightly, and his voice dipped in decibels so only she could hear. "Miss Anne, I beg your forbearance for my words, but I must speak the truth. I traveled to the East Indies and many of the capitals of Europe, and I have yet to see a face, which instantly affected me as yours did. Please forgive me if I offend you. It is not my wish to do so."

Elongated moments passed as Frederick waited for her response. Rarely did he act so impulsively, but he thought he knew Anne Elliot instantly, and she would recognize the truth in his words. He felt the heat move through him. Even through her gloved hand, he imagined the sense of her bare one on his. "Miss Anne," he whispered again, his breath on the side of her face. "I should very much like to know what is running through your mind."

Anne lifted her chin, and Frederick fought the urge to kiss her. "I wondered, Commander, if we were to take dinner together?"

Frederick let out the breath he held. Normally, the gentleman asked the question, but Anne Elliot left him the opening he wanted. One corner of his mouth curled upward. "It would be my great pleasure, Miss Anne, but only on the condition you agree to call me Frederick."

There was a momentary hesitation before she responded. "Frederick." She smiled up at him as the dance ended. "Thank you, Commander," she said loudly for those around her to take note of the formality, but when she moved in to take his arm to go into dinner, she said softly, "I look forward to your company, Frederick."

Chapter 2

And on that cheek, and o'er that brow,
So soft, so calm, yet eloquent,
That smiles that win, the tints that glow,
But tell of days in goodness spent,
A mind at peace with all below,
A heart whose love is innocent!
—Lord Byron from "She Walks in Beauty Like the Night"

"To where are you off?" Edward gave Frederick a knowing grin, noting his brother's careful grooming this morning.

Frederick returned the smile. "I thought I might enjoy some of the countryside. A long walk perhaps."

"Would you care for some company?" his brother teased.

A laugh escaped before Frederick could hold it back. "I do not think I care for *your* company this morning. I hope you are not offended, Edward."

"Of course, I am not offended. However, do not compromise Miss Anne's reputation. She deserves the best life has to offer."

"On that fact we do agree." Frederick stood to make his exit. Anne Elliot did not agree to go walking with him this morning, but twice during dinner she told him specifically where she would be walking and at what time she would be in the area.

Making his way out the door, Frederick grabbed an older blanket. At the bakery, he bought several fresh pastries, having them wrapped to take along with him. All night he looked forward to seeing Anne Elliot again this morning. Last night during dinner he interacted with her, leaning close and feeling the heat simmering from her body. She was as alluring as a moth to a flame, and Frederick wondered if he could resist her appeal.

She seemed genuinely amazed at the stories with which he regaled her last night, but Anne Elliot was more than that. She knew about many of the more important battles; she recognized the names of some of the larger

19

ships and their skippers. Rarely did he meet a woman who would not wince when confronted with the realities of war. Frederick held little back; he spoke freely of the maneuvers a ship made, of the mechanics of boarding an enemy ship, and of the tragedies of war. Never had he known another person with whom he could share such memories. Most people only wanted to know if he was a war hero.

He strode along the road leading out of town and towards the Kellynch estate. His heart felt light as he left the main road and cut across a field leading to a secluded lake. Then he spotted her, standing there under a river birch, leaning easily against its multiple trunks. Taking a deep breath, Frederick stepped forward. "Miss Anne?" he spoke to her profile as he approached.

"Commander Wentworth." Dropping a curtsy, she turned to see him standing there.

Frederick stepped forward to take her hand before bowing over it. He studied her expression to determine if he overstepped his limits by meeting her here alone. "I hope I do not disturb your solitude; I will leave if you feel uncomfortable with my being here."

Anne Elliot seemed torn between doing what propriety told her she should do and what her mind told her she wanted to do. Finally, she spoke, "I am glad, Frederick, you listened to me last night. It pleases me you tended to my conversation so closely you knew where to find me this morning."

"I assure you, Miss Anne, there is little about you to which I did not attend." Frederick risked everything by stepping forward, tracing her jaw line with his thumb. "You are quite exquisite." His breathing became shallower. Reluctantly, he wrenched thoughts of her away from the present situation. "May I walk with you?"

"Thank you, Frederick." She took his arm. "Why do you not leave your items here? We may return for them later."

"Excellent idea, Miss Anne." He wrapped everything in the blanket and secured it high in one of the branches of the river birch. Then they took off along the hedgerows surrounding the adjoining field.

"My brother tells me you lost your mother several years ago," he began. "We share that in common. For me, I have only Edward and my sister Sophia. She is married to Benjamin Croft, another naval officer. My brother Croft will be an admiral some day soon."

Anne took in his bold gaze. "I miss my mother dramatically; Lady Russell tries to provide me some sense of family, but it is not the same." Watching her closely, Frederick judiciously realized Anne Elliot was not the type with which one had a torrid affair; she was the type a man married. "I cannot believe I am saying these things to you," she stammered. "My goodness, what sort of lady must you think I am. I rattle on about personal matters, and we are barely more than strangers."

"We are, Miss Anne, clearly more than strangers. We were from the moment our eyes met in the milliner's shop." He wanted her. Shocked at his reaction to the lovely Anne Elliot, Frederick added, "I appreciate your not making me play the courtship games others demand. My time in Somerset is short; I do not have the ability to call upon you daily for many months before I might hold your hand."

"Is this a courtship, Frederick?" The words hung in the air between them. They stopped walking, looking deeply in each other's eyes.

Frederick touched Anne's lips with his fingertips. "I stand enthralled," he whispered. "I would wish to court you properly, Anne, or as proper as one might do on a military leave. Yet, you should know I intend to win your regard."

She looked about nervously, flushing at the use of her Christian name. "I should have brought a maid with me."

"I will be the perfect gentleman, Anne; you have nothing to fear from me." He was deliberately nonchalant as he studied her through narrowed eyes.

"I do not fear you, Frederick," she said at last, but to his perceptive eyes, Anne looked rather forlorn, even a bit lonely. Instinctively, he gathered her into his arms, needing to give her comfort; she relaxed, placing her head against his chest, resting her hand on the lapel of his jacket.

Frederick swallowed hard, forcing his desire for her away. It clamored and churned in his gut, but he would not defile this beautiful woman. When she became his, it would be through an honest proposal. His head made the decision, but his body fought him on it. He wanted Anne—wanted her completely—yet, he would not act on his desire; he would do the honorable thing. "I do not wish to release you, my Dear, but I fear we need to walk once again." He lifted her chin with his fingertips and brushed Anne's lips lightly with his.

Anne blushed and moved away quickly. She froze, shame spreading through her body. Frederick stepped up to take her hands in his. "We will have none of your regret, Anne. Ours will be a different relationship. We will offer each other honesty. I will write you love sonnets, and you will tell me how much more you prefer Lord Byron or Wordsworth." That brought a smile to her lips. "I will bring you wild flowers, and you will throw out the roses of other suitors; but most of all, I will give you of myself as you will to me. Surely you must feel it too?"

"I do feel it, Frederick." Her voice brushed his heart with hope.

"Then let us return to the lake; I brought a blanket and a treat just for you, my Dear." Frederick found himself addicted to her smiles.

This time she took his hand, and they walked silently back to the water. Frederick spread the blanket and then offered her the pastries. Anne's eyes sparkled, making her more beautiful. She epitomized everything for which he yearned. He would prove to her aristocratic father he was worthy of the attentions of a baronet's daughter. "Tell me about your schooling and your friends."

"After my mother passed, my father and Lady Russell felt it best I should return to school. I do not know how I would have survived in Bath without Miss Hamilton. I went unhappy to school, grieving for the loss of a mother I dearly loved, feeling the separation from home, and suffering as a girl of fourteen, of strong sensibility and not high spirits, must suffer at such a time. Miss Hamilton, three years older than I, but still from the want of near relations and a settled home, remained another year at school. She was useful and good in a way, which considerably lessened my misery. I can never remember her with indifference."

"What happened to Miss Hamilton? I do not recall meeting her last night." Frederick broke off a piece of the pastry and fed it to her. Anne giggled like a schoolgirl, and then unexpectedly, she boldly kissed his fingertips, and Frederick brought them to his own mouth and touched them to his lips.

"Miss Hamilton was not from this area. She left school, married not long afterwards, was said to have married a man of fortune. That is all I know of her fate." Frederick's attention increased, and Anne looked away, afraid to meet the intensity growing in his eyes. "I am sorry," she stammered.

"Anne," he whispered. "Look at me." He reached out gently and caressed her cheek. She brought her eyes slowly to his. "You will never have to be alone again. I will not tolerate your feeling remorse; I want only to see a smile on your pretty face." She closed her eyes, and he leaned in for a gentle kiss, his mouth lingering over hers. He found himself breathing in warm, fragrant air, pushing it deeply into his lungs and trying to calm his thoughts. "I do not wish to say this, but I should return you to Kellynch Hall before you are missed."

Anne simply nodded. Frederick rose to his feet and helped Anne to hers. "May we meet again tomorrow?" His voice came raspy with anticipation.

"Here, at the same time." She moved into his embrace, wrapping her arms around Frederick's waist.

He rested his chin on the top of her head. "Come, Anne," he said at last. "I will not hear of ruining your reputation." With a deep sigh, he released her. "It will be a very long evening, my Love."

*   *   *

Thus began Frederick Wentworth's courtship of Anne Elliot. Unless it rained, they met daily; they walked the countryside, sharing conversations on nearly every subject possible. No drawing room chats peppered their exchanges. Instead, they spoke of the war, of crops, of family, of personal hopes and dreams, and of their growing affection for each other.

At least once weekly they spent "public" time together at a local soiree or dinner out. When in the view of prying eyes, replacing the intimacy they felt when alone with accepted propriety took on comical overtones. Often Frederick found himself reaching for her hand or resting his on Anne's back before he caught himself. Anne leaned into him when he came up behind her before realizing her error. The next day they would laugh about their actions and speculate on who might have seen them and what rumors they might face.

For well over a month, such was Frederick's life. "Do you plan to offer for Miss Anne before you return to the sea?" Edward asked suddenly one morning.

"I do." Frederick leveled his gaze on his brother. "Do you vocalize your objections?"

"Heavens, no. I will be happy to see you finally content in your life. I simply wondered what you would do if she refuses or if Sir Walter objects."

Frederick's eyebrow raised in ire. "Do you believe Anne will refuse me?"

"From what I noted of the woman, Miss Anne will not refuse you. She is obviously besotted by your charms. Yet, I do not believe she will defy her father's or Lady Russell's wishes. If they refuse, Anne may turn down your proposal. You will need to be prepared for such a situation."

"Anne loves me," Frederick said with some assurance.

"I am sure she does." Edward said no more, but concern did not leave him. He feared Frederick would suffer a broken heart.

*   *   *

Frederick shored up his confidence. He planned to ask Sir Walter's permission on Saturday. He and Edward would attend an evening at Kellynch

Hall on Friday. Knowing Anne maneuvered the invitation, he relished the idea of finally acknowledging his feelings for her. He knew many people chose a mate—part of a business arrangement, but Frederick accepted his feelings for Anne Elliot. Theirs would be a true love match.

Entering the drawing room, Frederick's eyes fell on Anne as soon as the butler announced him. He made a proper bow to the room; yet, it was to Anne he paid his attentions. Surreptitiously, they both circled the outer layers of the group, stopping to speak to honored guests and others included in the evening party. Indirectly, Frederick heard the heir presumptive, William Walter Elliot, Esq., great grandson of the second Sir Walter, was to be in attendance at the night's gathering. Miss Elliot, he noted, actually giggled nervously, almost like a schoolgirl; her eyes darted about the room in anticipation of Mr. Elliot's entrance.

The room was splendid in its décor. Antique treasures held prized places on nearly every piece of furniture in the room; rich works of art lined the walls; ornate fabrics hung from the windows. Deep shades of green and gold intertwined in the carpeting, and throughout the room freshly polished golden touches sparkled in the candlelight. It was in stark contrast to the marbled entrance foyer. For a moment before he was in her presence, Frederick realized the compromise Anne would be making by giving all this up to be his wife.

Finally, Anne and Frederick came together face-to-face. He bowed, and she returned a low curtsy. "Miss Anne," his voice held admiration, "you look very fetching this evening."

"Thank you, Commander Wentworth." Her eyes twinkled with delight at seeing him in her home. "It pleases me you were free to join us this evening."

Frederick's smile curved to the corners of his eyes. "I understand we are to be blessed with the attendance of the elusive Mr. Elliot."

Anne laughed lightly; previously, she disclosed the frustration Sir Walter and Elizabeth felt with the reception they received from William Walter Elliot. Mr. Elliot was a very fine young man, just engaged in the study of law. Elizabeth found him extremely agreeable, and every plan in his favor was confirmed. Elizabeth imagined becoming his wife and assuming her mother's position at Kellynch Hall. The estate would remain in the family. Consequently, he was invited to Kellynch to foster a relationship with Elizabeth and to meet the local gentry. "Father is all a flutter, anxiously awaiting Mr. Elliot's approval of Kellynch Hall. After all, it will be his some day. Father is not likely to remarry; even if he did, a male heir would have to be the product of any such union for him to remain in his home. The most for which he can hope is an alliance between Elizabeth and Mr. Elliot."

Frederick frowned. "The prospect of such a marriage does not appeal to one such as I." He began to search her face, hoping to find a confirmation in what he thought to be Anne's feelings for him. "I have always wished to marry for love."

She flushed with color, but his soft words caressed Anne's heart. She leaned towards him, and Frederick fought the instinct to caress her face. "I am sure, Commander," she barely whispered, "whomever you choose will love you in return."

Turning his back so others could not see, his hand sought hers. For a few fleeting seconds, he clasped her fingertips in his. "Miss Anne," he was so close his lips could feel the warmth of her breath on his cheek, "with your consent I would speak to your father tomorrow." Frederick waited, standing still, heartbeats frozen in hopeful expectation.

He watched as Anne swallowed hard, trying to make the words come. "Frederick," she murmured, "I would be pleased to entertain your entreaty." Frederick's breath rushed out with her words.

"Anne," was all he could get out, but what his mouth could not say, his facial expression spoke volumes. They both laughed nervously with the realization of the commitment they just made to one another.

When they parted in the drawing room, Frederick fought the urge to pull her into his arms and to clasp her to him. Anne Elliot welcomed his address; she accepted and honored his feelings for her and returned them with those of her own. His life grew more complete by the moment.

At dinner, Frederick could scarcely keep his mind on the inane conversations going on about him. All he could do was to fill his eyes with images of Anne. Although Sir Walter and Elizabeth Elliot barely hid their dismay at the absence of Mr. Elliot, Anne, obviously, felt none of their alarm. Frederick's heart leapt each time he detected her laugh. She sat between his brother Edward and Mr. Musgrove, giving both her attentions. With some effort, he caught her eye at last, and they exchanged a "secret smile" that would have been almost undetectable to anyone else at the table. Frederick closed his eyes and imagined his hands cupping her face, his fingers removing the pins from her hair to let it fall softly over her shoulders, his thumbs tracing the outline of her bottom lip. When he opened them again, he found both Edward and Anne staring at him. Edward chuckled lightly before turning to the squire seated on his right, but Anne held his gaze a few elongated seconds. Then she tauntingly pursed her lips before touching them with her napkin. Frederick felt the heat rush to his body. Before she could look away, he winked at her and enjoyed seeing the color increase in her cheeks. Such romantic teasing was a new sensation for him, and he discovered he quite liked the results.

Sitting quietly, waiting for the next course, he began to imagine the life they would share. Frederick chastised himself for not economizing and for spending more than he should. He earned funds each time his ship came into contact with the French. Legally, as a British officer, he shared in the "prizes" of the French captures. He could win more; he would win more for Anne. He currently held half of what he earned in the victory at San Domingo. Looking at her, he knew Anne deserved a fine home, and he would give her all she should have.

They would purchase a small estate once he left the Navy. Right now, like his sister Sophia, Anne would sail with him when he finally received his own ship. Fondly, he reflected on a conversation only yesterday morning. Her shock when he told her of the accommodations and food found on the ships surprised him. "Miss Anne," he teased her, "surely you cannot be supposing that sailors live on board without anything to eat, or any cook to dress it if there were, or any servant to wait, or any knife and fork to use?" She blushed profusely with his tease, and Frederick lightly touched her lips with his. Happiness spread through his body with such musings; Anne would be his.

Frederick hesitated as the gentlemen left Sir Walter's study; they returned to the drawing room to join the ladies. When only he and Sir Walter remained, he boldly approached his host. Totally involved in his own self-possession, Frederick did not note Sir Walter's growing anger as the evening progressed. The absence of Mr. Elliot and the man's obvious snub of Sir Walter's family took its toll on Anne's father.

"Sir Walter, may I speak to you privately?" Frederick approached the man before he could leave the room. The smell of port and half smoked cheroots drifted across Frederick's face.

Sir Walter offered his first cut. "I cannot imagine, Commander, we have anything in common to discuss."

Frederick's natural instinct told him to walk away from the pompous ass he considered to inhabit Sir Walter's body; however, the man would be his father when Anne became his wife. Instead, he swallowed his irritation and tried another tactic. "I apologize, Sir; I would not intrude on your graciousness this evening; I simply request the honor to do so tomorrow morning."

"I will be to London tomorrow morning, Commander; your request is impossible." He started to push his way past Frederick.

Instinctively, Frederick reached to stop him physically but then thought better of it. "Sir Walter, I implore you," he nearly begged. "What I have to say to you is of great importance."

"Very well, Commander Wentworth." Sir Walter's voice demanded Frederick follow him back into the study.

Sir Walter settled himself once more in his favorite wing chair facing the dying embers of the fire. Frederick began to pace, trying to right his thoughts. He planned to approach Sir Walter on the morrow, but circumstances changed, and now he found himself nearly frantic in trying to find the right words to persuade Anne's father. The clearing of Sir Walter's throat jarred Frederick from his turmoil. He forced himself to take a stance beside the fireplace's mantel. Swallowing hard, he began. "Sir Walter, since coming into Somersetshire, I have had the great honor of meeting your middle daughter Miss Anne on numerous occasions. During those times, I found my affections for Anne increasing. I am now of the persuasion to admit I think only of her, and with your consent, I wish to make Miss Anne my wife."

Sir Walter's eyebrow shot up in surprise. An amused smirk spread across his face. "You aspire to become a member of my family?" Sir Walter barely hid the sarcasm laced through his words.

Frederick stiffened with the loosely veiled cut, but he pushed back his anger, thinking only of Anne's need for family. "I aspire to make Miss Anne a worthy husband." He controlled the contempt in his words. "The fact Anne is your child was never part of my decision."

This time Sir Walter actually did laugh. "May I ask, Commander Wentworth, what you believe you could offer the daughter of a baronet?"

Frederick's starched composure felt the censure. "I assume, Sir, you mean something besides my constancy and my ardent admiration?"

"Commander Wentworth," Sir Walter's voice took on a reprimanding tone, "one cannot eat constancy nor will your ardent admiration serve as protection for my daughter."

Feeling very much like a misbehaving schoolboy being called on the carpet by the headmaster, Frederick began his protest. "I have a promising career in the British Navy; I expect to be given my own ship upon my return to my duties. As such, I foresee multiple opportunities to earn my fortune.

I will eventually be able to provide for Miss Anne in a manner in which she should be treated."

Sir Walter actually snorted in dismay. "You will pardon me, Commander, if I address my concerns over parts of your declaration." With a flippant flick of his wrist, Sir Walter motioned to Wentworth to sit in a chair across from him. He did not like giving an inferior a dominant position in a conversation, and Sir Walter refused to stand and take a stance against so formidable a figure as Frederick Wentworth. "First, I assume, you will argue the navy has done much for us at home and should have an equal claim with any other set of men."

"Defending our country has always been an acceptable occupation for many second sons of the aristocracy." Frederick did not like the turn of this conversation.

Again, Sir Walter's eyebrow incredulously shot up. "The profession has its utility, but I should be sorry to see any friend of mine belonging to it. Yes, it is in two points offensive to me; I have two strong grounds of objection to it. First, as being the means of bringing persons of obscure birth into undue distinction, and raising men of honors which their fathers and grandfathers never dreamt of; and secondly, as it cuts up a man's youth and vigor most horribly; a sailor grows old sooner than any other man; I have observed it all my life. A man is in greater danger in the navy of being insulted by the rise of one whose father, his father might have disdained to speak to, and of becoming prematurely an object of disgust himself, than in any other line. When your brother came into the area, I inquired as to your family's connection to the earls of Strafford as you have the same family name. Much to my amazement, I found the term *gentleman* misled me. Your family has no connections; you are not a man of property. One wonders how the names of many of our nobility become so common."

"Times are changing, Sir Walter, and although you may object, our country chooses to award its servants with a fortune set for the taking. I will exit the war and be able to offer Anne a place in society."

Sir Walter chuckled. "A place in society, you say, Commander? Where will Anne reside while you are off earning this so-called fortune? Surely, you do not expect her to continue to live under my roof once she becomes your wife?"

"Anne will live with me aboard ship." Frederick knew to Sir Walter this would sound ridiculous, but he and Anne previously discussed his expectations for their living quarters. "A ship's captain is given adequate quarters for himself and his family."

Sir Walter leaned forward, resting his elbows on his knees. "You expect the daughter of a baronet, who is used to living in the luxury of a house such as is Kellynch Hall, to live in rooms no larger than some of my servants' quarters? You seem to believe Anne is made of a firmer constitution than do I!" Humor bubbled from his words.

"Miss Anne is aware of the conditions under which we will reside," Frederick protested. "She expressed no qualms regarding the changes she will face as my wife." He shifted, trying to reestablish himself as an officer of the Crown.

"And my daughter agreed to such an alliance?" Sir Walter leaned back in his chair, needing to decipher what was not being said.

"She has, Sir." Frederick tried to keep his composure as he awaited Sir Walter's response.

After several infinitely long moments, Sir Walter played one more card with a sigh of resignation. "I do not expect Anne will attract someone of better consequence. Her looks are too plain, and she is too compliant to earn a suitor worthy of her position." His words shot through Frederick, and he wanted to throttle Sir Walter with his bare hands for speaking thusly of Anne. "However, I will not give my consent to such a union as you suggest, Commander." A hard thud struck Frederick's heart. He doubted Anne would defy her father's wishes. "Yet, neither will I object to your marriage." Frederick's thoughts rushed about chaotically. "If Anne chooses to marry you, I will let her go, but understand, I profess to do nothing for her. She will receive no dowry from me; even though it is only Anne of whom we speak, I find this to be a very degrading alliance. I will wash my hands of her."

Frederick started to object about Sir Walter's purposeful denial of his middle daughter's worth, but he quickly realized his protestations would fall on deaf ears and would be interpreted as his seeking Anne as his wife only because of her dowry. Instead, he forced himself to his feet. Making a quick bow to Anne's father, he started to make his leave. "I will inform Miss Anne of your decision, Sir." He took several steps before pausing. "Sir Walter, I love Anne; I will make her my wife with or without your permission and with or without your money." Turning quickly on his heels, he strode from the room.

Chapter 3

As fair art thou, my bonnie lass,
So deep in luve am I;
And I will luve thee still, my dear,
Till a' the seas gang dry.
—*Robert Burns from "A Red, Red Rose"*

He entered the music room only seconds before Sir Walter. To the others gathered to hear Miss Elliot at the pianoforte, no one took notice, but Anne knew when he stepped through the door, Frederick Wentworth felt the agitation of her father's censure. She could see it in the tension in his shoulders and the set of his jaw. She watched him slip to the back of the group enjoying her sister's performance. As the song finished, she excused herself from Mrs. Musgrove's company and made her way to where he stood.

Without saying a word, Frederick motioned to her with his eyes to follow him. As unobtrusively as possible, they turned towards the drawing room. Frederick eased the door partly closed to give them some privacy, while she took up a position in front of him. "Frederick, what is the matter? Did you speak to my father?"

Without thinking, he took her hand and brought her wrist to his lips. Keeping his eyes locked on hers, he found the peace he needed. "You are exquisite," he whispered.

A smile came across her face. "I feared you spoke to my father this evening. Lady Russell says he will travel to London tomorrow." Anne's voice caressed his being, and Frederick tried to shake off the shiver of disgust he still felt from the encounter with Sir Walter.

Taking a deep breath to calm his temper, he confided at last, "I did speak to Sir Walter."

"And?" She touched his lips with her fingertips.

Frederick turned away quickly. "Your father is a complete ass!" His fury returned without being prompted.

Anne chuckled at the familiarity of his speech. If he did not love her and trust her, Frederick Wentworth would guard his words more carefully. "My father can be difficult at times." She touched his fingertips with hers before drawing in a quick breath and lifting her chin. "He refused his consent then?"

Frederick did not turn to look at her. "Sir Walter did not refuse to allow the marriage to proceed."

"Then what is the source of your discomfort? Do you no longer wish our union?" Anne dropped her hands from his; she withdrew quickly within herself, anticipating the rejection, the same kind of rejection she knew all her life.

Angry with Sir Walter, it took Frederick several heartbeats to realize Anne shrunk away from him. Missing her comfort, he turned quickly to find her sobbing silently a few feet away. He strode to her and took her into his arms, pulling her head to rest upon his chest. "I apologize, my Dear, I attended to my own dismay at your father's words; I did not consider how it might affect you." He stroked her back as he spoke. "Sir Walter will allow the marriage although he terms it to be a poor alliance on your part." Anne started to protest, but he clasped her tighter to him. "If you choose to marry me, your father will not honor you with a settlement; you will come to me with nothing."

Anne gasped and tried to pull away from him, but Frederick held her closer still. "I do not care for myself, Anne; I am used to what is adequate for my own survival, but I fear I cannot give you what you deserve as a baronet's daughter. The only thing I can give you is my love and a promise it will not always be so. I will make my fortune, and you will look back and be able to say you knew from the beginning you would have your own estate." He loosened his hold on her, and then lifted her chin to look in her tear-stained face. "Anne, will you do me the honor of being my wife?"

"Oh, yes, Frederick." She did not hesitate. "Yes, I will marry you."

He lowered his head to kiss her lips gently. "We should return to the music room," he cautioned. "Meet me tomorrow, and we will make plans for our life together."

"Yes," she whispered and then kissed him once again.

*   *   *

Frederick waited at the river birch; he slept little, but he never felt more alive. Anne agreed to marry him; life was perfection. Finally, he spotted her coming across the field. She wore a light green muslin gown and a shawl over her ivory shoulders. Frederick found himself gasping for air just anticipating her presence. Going to meet her, he called out her name as she rushed into his arms. They stood entwined for a long time before they parted, walking back to the blanket and the stream. "I am glad you are finally here," he whispered as he helped her settle on the coverlet.

She pulled her knees up where she could encircle them with her arms, straightening her skirt first. "With father's departure, Kellynch took on a state of disarray for a few hours; I apologize if you waited for long."

"I would wait a lifetime for you." Frederick chuckled as she blushed. "Will you always blush when I tell you how much I desire you?" he teased.

"No." Her face flushed again.

He smiled at her denial. "How did I manage to win your heart, my Dear? I ask myself that every day. Providence smiled on me when my eyes first rested upon your face."

"You saw me when others could not." Anne searched his face, taking in the weathered lines with her eyes, committing them to memory.

Frederick shifted his weight to face her head on. "Then I assume you did not change your mind about our marriage?"

She smiled. "I did not change my mind. I love you, Frederick."

"And I love you, Anne." He cupped her face with the palm of his large hand. "I have barely a month left of my leave, but it will give us time to call the banns before we marry. We may start for Dover once we say our vows. I drafted a letter this morning to the Admiralty to inform them of our impending marriage so accommodations will be made, and you may travel with me aboard ship. The question is what will Sir Walter do once the banns are read for the first time?"

"I am only nineteen; without my father's permission, I may not marry. However, I was thinking about his doubts. I will speak to Lady Russell and ask her to champion our cause with my father. She knows how to deal with him better than anyone. I am sure father just tested my determination; he will see more reason once he returns from his visit to his tailor in London."

Frederick thought it ridiculous to travel all the way to London to visit a tailor for a few new clothes, but he did not express his thoughts out loud. What Sir Walter said about Anne's chances of making a good marriage disturbed him more. The man spoke of his own daughter as if she had no merit. "Will Lady Russell help us? I truly do not care for myself; your father's money is of little significance to me."

"It is my inheritance, Frederick. It should not . . . he should not withhold it. If he does not object to our union, then I deserve the same consideration my father would give to Elizabeth or to Mary. That is what I will have Lady Russell argue."

"Then let us finish our plans," he said softly. "We have much to decide."

*   *   *

Each day they met added depth to their future plans. All his sanguine expectations, all his determination, all his confidence would make him successful. He would prove it to her and to her family; he would distinguish himself and early gain another step in rank. Those were his guarantees to Anne.

The day after Sir Walter's return, Frederick waited, a rose in hand, expecting a change, but he never anticipated what occurred. As usual, he met Anne by the lake. The moment he saw her coming across the field, he knew to expect trouble. Normally, Frederick went to meet her, but today something told him to wait—to wait for what was to come. A shiver of cold shot down his spine as she approached. Tears tugged at the corners of her eyes, and he could see she cried recently.

"Anne?" his voice came out barely more than a whisper. His breath stirred the wisp of hair dislodged from her bonnet as he took her into his embrace.

She slid her arms around his waist, loving his strength, hearing his heart beat as she rested her head on his muscular chest. "I love you," she murmured. "Please remember I love you." She buried her face in the folds of his jacket, trying to stop the tears.

"Will you tell me?" he said at last.

She shook her head in the negative. "I cannot." Hauling in a breath, her lips trembled with the effort.

"Lady Russell was unable to convince Sir Walter?" He assumed the baronet resisted her friend's entreaties. "We knew it was likely your father would not relent, but we will continue without his support."

"I cannot." She said again, but this time he knew the words spelled doom.

"You cannot what, Anne?" he demanded.

Tears sprung to her eyes as she lifted her chin to his gaze. "I cannot . . . . I cannot marry you, Frederick." One lone tear trickled down her face.

"No!" He grabbed her and pulled Anne tightly against him, vowing never to let her go. "I will not allow you to change your mind."

She looked up at him, craning her neck. "Do you not see?" she pleaded.

"See what?" he taunted—his voice cold—shoving her from his embrace. "I see a woman who breaks my heart with her words. I see a woman who promised to remain constant in her affections for me, but who turns away to the comfort of her four-poster bed as soon as she meets resistance. Is that not what I am supposed to see, Miss Anne?"

His return to the formality of his address struck her forcibly, knocking the air from her. Looking at the despair she caused, Anne collapsed to her knees in supplication. "Please, Frederick," she begged. "I love you; do you not see how much I love you? I would only hold you back if I went with you."

He wanted to drop to his knees too and plead with her—to convince Anne she did not know him if she thought he needed protection. Instead, he stepped away from her, turning his back on the woman he loved. "Do not lie to me, Anne; you simply do not care for me enough to give up your fine society." The words sounded bitter; he could not disguise the betrayal he felt. "Is there someone else?" he accused. "Has your father allowed you to accept Charles Musgrove—he can offer you the security I cannot?"

"Surely you know that is not true." Nestled tight in a ball of shadows, she tried to look into his eyes. The truth lay in their eyes, but something she did not recognize flickered there.

His jaw tightened in annoyance. Taking a deep breath at last, he slowly rested his gaze on her. "Anne, I will ask you once again to come with me—this day—this hour. We will travel to Gretna Green; we will marry, and I will love you with every ounce of my being."

He paused, waiting for her answer, but she would not raise her face to him. Instead, she rocked herself for comfort, letting the sorrow seep from her. "I love you, Frederick," she sobbed. "Go with God." The words suffocated her, and Anne collapsed completely on the dusty bank.

She could see the toes of his black Hessians as he stepped up beside her. "You do not know love," he said softly. He bent to lay the rose beside her head. "Go with God, Anne." Then he left her there, taking the devastation with him.

Walking away from her was one of the hardest things Frederick ever did. Part of him wanted to take her in his arms and kiss her until Anne changed her mind. Part of him wanted to shake her like a rag doll driving sense to her head. He could hardly breathe. Climbing the last incline before the town road, and reaching the summit, he shouted first one curse and then another at the open sky as tears cascaded down his face.

God gave him life when He gave him Anne, and now she was untimely ripped from him. Five weeks of happiness was not enough; he wanted more of Anne Elliot. A guttural cry escaped his throat as he sank down in despair. *How could she turn on him so quickly? How could Anne allow her father and Lady Russell to persuade her to give him up? Nothing—nothing could convince him to love anyone but her.* Another cry of anguish filled the air before he began to recapture his composure, but anger and frustration still reigned.

Frederick sat for hours on the hillside, looking out over the land, but he saw none of it. His mind replayed every moment he spent with Anne Elliot from her entrance in the village shop to her crumpled form on the lake's bank. Every nuance of every word—every gesture—every dream he held of their life together—everything he ever wanted—he could not ask for more. *Except—he wanted more—he never wanted the time to end.*

Trancelike, he made his way back to his brother's home. "I was beginning to worry," Edward called from the kitchen. "How is Miss Anne today?"

"Miss Anne returned to Kellynch Hall." Those were all the words he could share with Edward at the time. Nothing else made sense except for the fact Anne returned to her home. She would never be his bride—his wife; she did not love him enough. "I have some correspondence of which I need to attend. Please excuse me, Edward." He walked right past his brother, never seeing anything but the darkness of his mind.

"Certainly," Edward looked on in concern. "I will be here if you need anything."

Frederick did not answer; he could think of nothing but the image of Anne Elliot shriveled and weeping along the lakeshore line—a place which once held pleasant memories of a growing courtship. He collapsed across the bed, seeking a pillow to cover his face—to black out the picture of the woman he loved.

The room was clothed in deep shadows when he heard his brother's voice and the light tap on his door. "Frederick, may I get you something to eat?"

"Nothing, Edward, thank you; I just need some time." Frederick could not consider talking to anyone about Anne Elliot. The light in his life disappeared.

"I will leave some fresh bread on the table." Edward left the portal of the guest room. Frederick did not answer; he was lost once more to his pain.

*   *   *

For three days he refused to leave the room; he did not eat. If he slept, Frederick could not remember doing so. All he knew was the desolation he felt every time he replayed her words in his head. The restless ache in his chest jarred him. Edward's appraisal of the aristocracy was correct; even a successful naval officer would never be good enough for a daughter of the realm. He could die for England, but he could not aspire to marry into one of its annointed families.

The ache of emptiness ate at him. He would show them all. Frederick Wentworth would become wealthy—he would win the praise of the King, and he would make them all—Anne and her family—regret the day she turned from him. By that time, he convinced himself Anne would no longer mean anything to him. He would forget her as quickly as she forgot him. Yet, even as he told himself those things, Frederick knew he would never stop wanting Anne Elliot; she was his other half.

Finally, he appeared at the morning table. His brother noted the dark circles under Frederick's eyes and the sharp angular cut of his cheekbones, but Edward chose not to comment on his obvious weight loss. "Good morning," he greeted as Frederick reached for a plate.

Frederick did not answer, but he did nod in his brother's direction. Filling his plate with fresh fruit and toast, he joined Edward at the house's butcher-block table. They ate together in silence for several minutes. Noting the packed bag sitting in the doorway, Edward began carefully, "So, you are to leave me today?"

"I find it to be for the best." Frederick did not raise his head when he spoke. Instead, he seemed mesmerized by the action of spreading apple preserves on another piece of toast.

Edward hid his concern. "You have more than three weeks of leave remaining."

Frederick decidedly placed the knife beside his plate and let his hands drop to his side. "I will stay with Harville; he and I can return to our ship together. Forgive me, Edward, but I need the silence of a noisy household."

"Of course, Frederick—I understand; Harville is a good choice for you right now." Edward leaned back in his chair and seriously looked at his brother's demeanor. "I assume you would have the vicar delay the reading of the banns."

Frederick finally looked at his older brother. His lip trembled, but he forced steadiness into his words. "If you could attend to that duty for me, Edward, I would be most appreciative."

"Consider it done." Edward returned to his food. After an elongated silence, he ventured, "Will you take your leave of Miss Anne?"

"Miss Anne took her leave of me several days ago; I see no reason to revisit what must be." Frederick's steely countenance told the story.

"I see." Edward swallowed hard, fighting back the remorse. "I will walk with you to the posting inn when you are ready to leave."

"Thank you, Edward, for your hospitality." Frederick tried to show his softer side. "You are more than a brother, and for that I am eternally grateful."

"Family is our greatest wealth." Edward knew Frederick suffered. "Men in our family generally choose to wait for marriage until we secure our future. Then we marry for love." Edward stood to look down at his younger brother's dejected stature. "Possibly you need to question whether you were ready. Look at me; I am three years your senior, and I have yet to complete either of those tasks."

"Possibly," Frederick mumbled, "but it seemed so right." He laid the napkin on the table. "Now it is inconceivable to me the woman I thought Anne Elliot to be ever existed."

"You looked for perfection in Miss Anne," his brother added. "Yet, you should know by now perfection is rather boring. Frederick, you always were a bit willful—a lot willful, in fact. Do you really envision yourself as being able to tolerate Sir Walter's inane views of society? Those of the Elliots' world would never understand the overwhelming responsibility you assume each day in your position."

"I know in my mind what you say is correct, Edward; however, it will take my heart some time to reconcile those truths. My heart, unfortunately, knew only her."

Later that day as Frederick boarded the carriage to take him to Portsmouth to spend the rest of his leave with the Harvilles, Edward stood silently by. Frederick embraced his brother before stepping up into the carriage. "I should tell you," Edward offered a soothing smile, "I applied for positions in Herefordshire and Shropshire. When we next meet it will not be here."

"I do not believe I ever wish to return here." Frederick leaned out the coach's window to shake his brother's hand. "I saw all of Somerset of which I care to see. It will be my pleasure to visit you in your new home. It is time for you to complete the tasks: build your future and marry for love. It would please me to see both you and Sophia well settled."

"As it would I you." Edward looked around, making sure no one overheard him.

Frederick looked discerningly at the surrounding buildings. "It is a pleasant village—quite perfect, in fact."

"Quite boring," Edward added quickly as the coach began to roll forward.

Frederick smiled and waved. "Boring perfection!" he shouted as the carriage pulled out of the inn yard and onto the main road.

*   *   *

"His fever is worse," the doctor placed another cooling cloth on Captain Wentworth's forehead. "We have to find a way to break it soon. If not, he likely could die of his wounds."

"Tell me what else to do for him." Anne's voice held her exhaustion. She had been by Frederick's side for over six and thirty straight hours.

"You will make yourself a patient, Ma'am, if you do not get some rest," he cautioned.

"I will not leave him." She spoke with resolve. "And I will not tolerate anyone considering my husband's demise. Is that understood, Sir?"

"Certainly, Mrs. Wentworth," the man self-consciously stammered. "We could try a bath of cold water. Submerging the captain could be risky, but it could be worth trying."

"Then let us do it." Anne moved to take over the cold cloths for her husband's care.

"I will have the men bring in the tub; we can haul in some of the sea water. It will be cooler than anything we have on board. I want to make sure his bandages do not become too wet. We cannot let the sea water get into the wounds." The doctor motioned for a midshipman as he opened the door to the captain's quarters. After relaying his orders, he returned to the officer's bedside. "I shall have several men help me strip the captain and support him in the water as we lower his body into the coolness. You, Ma'am, should use the opportunity to freshen your own clothing and get something more substantial to eat. It would embarrass the men to handle your husband as such with you in the room."

"I understand," Anne whispered. "I will tend him until you are ready." She soothed the hair away from his forehead.

The doctor moved away as several sailors brought in the low tub. Men hauling buckets of icy seawater to fill the vessel followed them. Several glanced furtively at their commanding officer outstretched on his bed, unresponsive even to his wife's tender ministrations.

"Will he make it?" one of the men whispered to the doctor.

"We are doing everything we can to assure that he does." The physician motioned for another man to dump his bucket into the waiting tub.

When the cooling waters filled the vessel, the doctor turned to Anne. "It is ready, Mrs. Wentworth." He reached out his hand to help her to her feet. "The officers and I will tend your husband in the waters. It is likely you will hear the captain scream in pain, but you must not come back in here until I send for you."

"Yes, I understand." She leaned forward to kiss Frederick's feverish lips before she left the room. "Please take care of him." She allowed her hand to linger on his chest; finally, the doctor led her to the door.

"The captain is strong; he will be fine." Although not totally convinced, Anne nodded at his words and left the area.

Four of the lower officers entered immediately. Lieutenants Harwood and Avendale began to strip the clothes from the captain's body. "Be careful of opening up his wounds again," the doctor cautioned. "You two, take off your jackets and your shirts. We are all likely to get soaked during this endeavor." Mastermates Langdon and Shipley began to remove their own clothes.

When all five men were bare to the waist, they lifted Wentworth's limp body from the bed. Positioning him as they might a body to lower it into a grave, they began to immerse Frederick's form into the cooling seawaters. "Hold him steady," the physician demanded. "He is likely to fight you when the heat of his body hits that icy water. Do not let him go under completely. We want the water around his form, but we do not want it to cover his body."

The men all nodded, tightening their holds on Frederick's limbs. The doctor's estimation of what would happen played out immediately. Still out of his mind with a fever, Wentworth twisted and turned, trying to break the hold his men enforced on him. Cries of pain filled the cabin as Frederick cursed their deceit and threatened their safety. Yet, they held him with their combined strength.

The doctor dipped a cup in the water and poured it over Frederick's body. His backside floated—suspended in the drenching coolness, supported tenuously by his officers. The doctor continued to stream water over his head and chest and legs, carefully avoiding the bandages around his abdomen. "Aaahh!" Wentworth gasped. "I will see you rotting in hell for this!" Once again he wrenched his arm, trying to free himself, but his men held him in vise-like grips. "You will hang for attacking an officer of the British Navy!"

And on it went for nearly three quarters' hour until the tub water became closer to room temperature. Finally, they lifted him from the water. Drying him quickly, they pulled a nightshirt over his head and placed him back onto the freshly made bed. During this time, Frederick continued to fight them and to mutter curses while emitting moans of pain. The doctor considered all these good signs. He knew the shock of the cold water on the captain's feverish body could cause an apoplexy; Wentworth's fighting it meant his body had not given up.

Finally, with the tub and water removed and the bandages checked, only the doctor remained by his side. He watched as Wentworth wrestled his way to consciousness; his eyes fluttered and fought for focus. "Where is Anne?" he mumbled.

"I sent her away so we might tend you. She has been here at the risk of her own health. I will have someone find her now that your fever is down." The doctor checked his forehead and looked into Frederick's eyes for signs of recovery.

Flashes of memory came to him—thoughts of what a senseless act brought him to this point. Now, he knew the answers to all those questions with which Anne bombarded him. His favorite place of all he had seen was Italy. He preferred French wine to British; he hated it when she tickled his feet, but loved when she kneaded the muscles of his back. So close to losing his life, Frederick could see it all plainly—how to analyze the sum of his experiences and know what mattered. "Will I live?" He licked his lips trying to bring moisture to his mouth.

"You have a long recovery." The doctor purposely did not answer the question.

A light tap on the door brought the doctor's attention away for a moment. "Enter," he called.

"Excuse me, Sir," a midshipman offered, "Mrs. Wentworth reports she will be here in a moment. She is writing to Captain Harville; she wants word to be sent to him and to Captain Wentworth's family as soon as we make port."

"Thank you, Rogers." The doctor turned back to his patient. "Did you hear, Wentworth?"

"Captain Harville is a long time friend," Frederick whispered.

"I remember him well; we all sailed together back in '07 and '08." The physician adjusted the blanket across Wentworth's body. "Too bad his leg wound drove him from the service; we could use a man like him right now." The captain gasped with pain as he tried to move in the bed. "Let me give you some laudanum." He supported Frederick's head as he administered the dose. "Rest now," the doctor cautioned.

Chapter 4

Each lover has a theory of his own
About the difference between the ache
Of being with his love, and being alone.
—W. H. Auden from "Alone"

"Rest now, Wentworth," Harville reassured him. "You have a ship at last."

"She sure is not much, is she?" Frederick looked around at the condition of the sloop *Asp*.

"She may not be the largest ship on the sea, but she was found fit to form part of the line in action, if necessary. She has thirty guns, Frederick." Harville moved up beside his friend as they surveyed Wentworth's new command.

"What say the orders?" Wentworth drew his attention away for a few seconds as he motioned his assistant to store the captain's belongings in his cabin.

When he delivered the news, Harville's smile held an amused smirk. "His Majesty desires our attention in the West Indies."

"Who is the new lieutenant?" Wentworth gestured again, this time to his right.

"Harold Rushick." Harville returned the salute offered by the first rung commissioned officer. "He has much experience with gun divisions in battle and in dangerous boardings and is rumored to be most observant in overseeing the watch. We are lucky to have him on board."

"Then I shall extend an invitation to dine with me." Wentworth noted the man's demeanor. "I want him on my side."

The two started to stroll along the deck, each noting the ordinary seamen and landsmen as they loaded the *Asp's* storage. "Have I told you I asked Milly to wait for me?"

"She is a fine woman, Thomas." Wentworth's thoughts immediately went to Anne Elliot. At least ten times a day he found himself momentarily lost in thoughts of her. Even after two months, the pain still pierced his being. He never told Thomas Harville about his close encounter with love; Frederick could not bear to speak of the hurt aloud. Each night she came to him in his dreams; Anne professed her love, and they walked hand-in-hand together into the vision. He swallowed hard and forced Anne's image into the recesses of his mind. "Milly will make you a fine wife. When do you plan to ask her?"

"I need to make my fortune before I can take a wife." Harville paused along the railing, looking out over the activities along the dock.

Again, Frederick thought of Anne; his potential was not enough to make her place her trust in him. Literally, her betrayal sucked the air from his lungs. *God, I love her!* He would still win his fortune; he would show her someday what she missed with her choice. "You will have your chance, Thomas; we will both have our chance." Wentworth stepped up beside his friend. "Then let us prepare for our journey. The *Asp* is our future."

*   *   *

After nearly six months in the West Indies, Frederick received notice he was to join Higgins and others in an effort to forestall Napoleon's taking of the Danish fleet. "The British forces will be under the command of Admiral Gambier and General Cathcart." Frederick walked over to refill his glass of brandy. His officers were gathered around the small table in his quarters.

"And our mission's purpose would be?" Harville asked nonchalantly. After serving with Frederick for many years, he recognized the nuances of the captain's assessment of their new orders.

"The Danish fleet is superb, but the British high command worry whether it might fall under Bonaparte's hands if Denmark can no longer defend its southern border against French attacks. My guess is we will be attacking Copenhagen by mid July."

"Will that be all for now, Captain Wentworth?" Lieutenant Rushick steadied his resolve. "If so, Sir, I will see to the men."

"Certainly, Rushick." Frederick caught the all-knowing look Thomas Harville offered. "We will lift anchor when all the supplies are aboard."

Once the room emptied, Frederick turned his attention to his long-standing friend. "And your point is what, Thomas?" he remarked as he topped off his drink.

"Something about this mission bothers you, Frederick." Harville took a seat, stretched his legs, crossing them at his ankles while folding his arms across his chest.

Wentworth waited, measuring his words and his thoughts. "I feel a need to weigh my remarks," he began at last. "In '01 we had a legitimate reason to go up against the Danish. The Armed Neutrality of the North treaty threatened British trade in the Baltic Sea. But this time the Danish are on our side; we are reduced to the point of attacking our allies. The war makes strangers out of compatriots. Sometimes I wonder if I have a stomach for it." He crossed the room to sit opposite his friend.

Harville leaned back, nearly slumping out of the chair, maintaining an easy relationship. "I, too, would like to go home; I do not relish being a pawn in some high-ranking officer's chess game. We came close to counting our own deaths at San Domingo. Duckworth was determined to catch those Frenchies."

"We paid a high price with some seventy casualties and nearly three hundred wounded. I admit I enjoy the spoils of war—men of my rank have no other way of making our way unless we turn to trade—but the loss of life bothers me. It seems now we are asked to endanger the lives of good men in a futile battle."

"What is really bothering you, Wentworth?"

"Maybe I am just feeling my own mortality." Frederick took a mouthful of brandy, letting it trickle down his throat.

Harville turned his full attention on his friend. "What happened in Somerset?"

"What makes you believe something happened in Somerset?" He felt his breathing constrict as he tried to maintain a disinterested countenance.

"I cannot say for sure, but you are different since before you took command of the *Asp*."

He put down his glass, trying to control the emotions shooting through him. "Nothing really—just seeing Edward struggle as a curate made me realize how little I have to offer anyone. Our parents left us with nothing—being the children of the third son in a family . . . ." He could not finish his thoughts without thinking of Anne Elliot; he would never be good enough for the Elliots. "I suppose I should be thankful of the opportunity the British navy gives me; I should leave the war with my fortune."

"Once I have myself a nice coffer, I am headed home to Milly, and King George can go hang himself. I plan to go home in one piece and raise myself a crop of children." Harville chuckled with his own words. "That is what you need, Wentworth—you need a woman to bring out the best in you. Men were meant to heel to the whims of women," he teased.

"Maybe someday." Frederick tried to sound as uncommitted as possible. He realized he would eventually need to find a woman he could marry, but what woman would want a man with only half a heart to give? He tried to cover up his loneliness. "Right now, my life belongs to Admiral Gambier and the British navy."

*   *   *

As Wentworth predicted July found his ship among those gathering along the Danish coastline. Warily, the men waited, playing cards to pass the time. Frederick lurked on the periphery, listening to snippets of conversations. He learned over the last few years to judge his men's readiness by how they handled the long hours before the battle actually began.

"You be with Sir Duckworth at Alexandria?" one of the carpenters asked as he shuffled the cards.

The gunner picked up his hand and began to rearrange the cards. "We carted infantry back and forth for days."

"Me hears it was something to see." Both men held warranted ranks aboard ship, but they had limited opportunities to commissioned posts. Along with the pursur and the boatswain, they were part of the standing officers appointed to a ship by the Navy Board.

The gunner turned his cards over. "We took care of the landies; that be for sure. Despite high surf, Lieutenant Boxer disembarked almost seven hundred troops, five field guns, and fifty-six seamen. They breached the palisades entrenched sometime after nightfall. The spirits and old Neptune himself be with them that day; I see no way they survive that landing. Britain must be the chosen people; Bony may as well give up."

"Chosen people?" Mackenzie, the carpenter laughed lightly. "I imagine the chaplain might disagree with those words."

"He cannot disagree," the gunner smiled as he readied his hand to play. "He be an Englishman also."

Frederick smiled as he moved on. When they spoke of the invincibility of England that was a good sign. He passed a small group of able seamen, most of whom good-naturedly teased one of the new landsmen. "You should have been with us in '01 with Nelson," they told him. Wentworth watched them from a position along the railing. "We had twenty-six battleships and seven frigates in the line. The Danes stood no chance. The only thing they had was a sixty-six gun battery and dangerous shoals, but none of it could stop Horatio Nelson."

Keats, one of the men with the most experience at sea and currently serving as a mast captain, handed the landsman a cup of rum. "Parker panicked when we lost a floating battery and a few other key ships to the shoals, but Nelson had balls. Do you remember what he said Woods when old Malcolm told him Parker ordered a withdrawal?"

Woods guffawed, nearly choking on the spirits they drank to steady their nerves. "Nelson, you see, Lad, was blind in one eye. Nelson looked at old Malcolm, his one eye dancing with humor and said, 'I have only one eye—I have a right to be blind sometimes. I really do not see the signal.'" Woods gave the group his best imitation.

"It was a bloody one," Keats whistled lightly in exasperation.

The landsman looked a bit afraid. It was, after all, his first confrontation. "How bloody?"

"Do not ye be a worrying, Lad. Our captain is nothing like Nelson. The Vice-Admiral did not care how many we lost as long as we won the battle. Nearly one thousand left us that day. Of course, the Danes lost more than twice that many. We learned something in those days. Ye will not be exposed to such carnage."

Frederick purposely strode towards the men. They started to scramble to their feet to acknowledge his presence, but he motioned for them to remain seated. "I just wanted to say I am proud to serve with you men. We will engage with the Danish by early tomorrow morning. Relax as much as you can, but stay alert to changes happening along the line. You each know your jobs well. If we all do what is in our domain, we will come through this with little problem. Right now we are in transport mode for the foot soldiers needed by General Wellesley. I just wanted you to know where we stood. Good night, men."

"Good night, Captain," a chorus of voices called as he walked away. "A good man." He heard one of them mutter before he went below deck. Those who were at sea for many years knew how unusual it was for the commanding officer to address them thusly.

The smell of gunpowder drenched the air; the British fleet continued to bombard the city of Copenhagen. "How much longer can they hold out?" Harville growled as he surveyed the damage with his spyglass.

"Only the Lord knows." Wentworth took the glass from his friend and raised it to his eye. "We sent in at least five thousand rounds last night." He walked to the other side of the upper deck to get a better look. "There are three battleships and one pram setting dead in the water directly in front of us."

"We have men boarding them as we speak. Lieutenant Rushick is leading our contingent." Harville oversaw the lowering of the small boats off the side of the ship.

The appearance of the British transports coming towards Copenhagen, obviously, came as a surprise to the Danish command. Early on, they took a frigate and two brig-sloops. Unlike the last siege of the city, high surf and seas calmed right before the attack. "The last message from Gambier says the Danish General Peymann turned down offers of capitulation." Harville handed Frederick a message just delivered by the communications officer.

"Then we will fight on," Wentworth offered with a shrug of his shoulders, forcing the tension he felt from his upper back. "There is something rotten in Denmark. At least, the Bard would agree with the Prince Regent." A slightly amused smile turned up the corners of his lips. "At this rate, Thomas, you may marry Milly by year's end."

The night brought no relief from the battle. Frederick made only one trip below in the hours since the battle began. He constantly checked on the conditions above and below deck, assuring himself his men and his ship came to no harm. "Get some rest, Frederick." Harville came to check on him. His voice came softly off Frederick's right shoulder. "The men will be fine; they know their jobs."

"Just a few minutes more," Frederick mumbled, searching the horizon for any changes in the siege. The constant bombardment lit up the skyline with explosions followed by puffy clouds of black smoke as the fires sprang up. "The Congreve Rockets appear to be doing their job; look at the number of fires; the city will never be the same." He still stood, riveted to the spot along the railing; he never even turned to acknowledge Harville's presence.

"You feel the pain of each battle too intensely, Frederick," his friend concluded with a shake of his head.

"There ought to be a better way of solving differences. I know I should not want to bite the hand that feeds me, but such destruction—such destruction should not occur. Sometimes I wonder how a God of love can let it happen." Frederick lowered the glass from his eyes.

"Maybe we should let our women folk run the wars." Harville laughed with the thought.

"It would be a kinder, gentler way." Wentworth turned his attention to his friend. He let down his guard—Harville's unaffected easy kindness of manner, which denoted the feelings of an older acquaintance.

Captain Harville's countenance reassumed the serious, thoughtful expression, which seemed its natural character. "It is not in the nature of women; they dote on their loved ones. They never forget the men they love."

His words brought Frederick pain although Thomas Harville was perfectly unsuspicious of inflicting any peculiar wound. "I am sure women might argue we men have always a profession, pursuits, business of some sort or other, to take us back into the world," Frederick reasoned. "Yet, I will not allow it to be more man's nature than woman's to be inconstant and forget those they *do* love or *have* loved. I believe the reverse. I believe in a true analogy between our bodily frames and our mental; and that as our bodies are the strongest so are our feelings—capable of bearing more rough usage and riding out the heaviest weather."

"Maybe we are saved from such musing." Thomas took the spyglass from Frederick's hand and began to search the shore for results of their siege. "Songs and proverbs, all talk of women's fickleness. I suppose women could not attend to such grand ideas as domination and submission."

Frederick could not totally abandon the ideas; he spoke of more than the battle. "Both men and women—we each begin probably with a little bias towards our own sex and upon that bias build every circumstance in favor of it which occurred within our own circle; many of which circumstances, perhaps those very cases which strike us the most, may be precisely such as cannot be brought forward. I suspect in life men and women are very much alike although we see the world from different perspectives."

"Just listen to us." Harville laughed lightly. "Since when are we students of philosophy? Since when do we digress in the midst of battle?" He took a step forward. "I, for one, need a few hours sleep; if you refuse to take time in your quarters, I will take time in mine." He patted Frederick's shoulder as he handed back the glass. "I will see you with the dawn unless you send for me before then."

"Hopefully, with the dawn this will all be over," Frederick mused. Then his friend moved away into the night, and he was left all alone. Staring out into the darkness, his thoughts rested once again on Anne Elliot. He doubted he would ever find a woman he could love the way he loved Anne. He wanted a home with her—wanted children with her—wanted to live out his days with her. Now, his hopes—his hopes died when Lady Russell convinced Anne Elliot to break their engagement. Silently, he pushed the hurt deeper, feeling it in his gut—in his soul. Surprisingly, the hurt lessened over the past year. Now he could only compare it to having a knife plunged deeply into his heart and then someone turning the handle, or maybe it was more like a wild animal ripping off his leg at the joint. Swallowing hard, he turned back to the task at hand—trying to leave his love behind. Sometimes he wondered if he should write her—see if she realized the foolishness of her decision. However, he knew he could never risk rejection again. Somehow it was better not to know. Yet, some day he wanted to hear Anne say, "I am sorry." Those words could go a long way in covering everything that went wrong.

* * *

Anne Elliot sat dutifully by his bed; seeing his gaunt figure scared her. The doctor assured her repeatedly his recovery seemed inevitable; yet, used to the image of the strong, viable man she loved, standing feet braced against the swell of the ocean, she could not now leave the vision of his crumpled body lying haphazardly across his bed.

"Anne?" The soft pleading of his voice brought her attention back to his face. Frederick strived to open his eyes. "Anne," he murmured again. Struggling to overcome his laudanum-induced somnolent mind, Frederick felt limited connections to his world. Trying to concentrate for more than a few moments at a time, he found himself constantly drifting back into the dreams, which haunted him. He dreamed of losing her—*his Anne*—and now he needed to know she was here with him—in this room—guaranteeing the nightmares no longer plagued him. He licked his lips, forcing moisture to his mouth. A flash of memory jolted through his head, and he grimaced with the thought. He spoke her name a third time, and he felt someone sit beside him on the bed.

"I am here, my Love." Eyes still closed, he felt warm lips linger enticingly over his, but after a brief fleeting kiss they pulled away.

"So nice," he mumbled, and a smile tried to make its way to the corners of his mouth.

Anne's voice held relief. "You are incorrigible," she teased. She felt calmer at hearing his tremulous words, reaching out to take his hand for assurance. "May I get you anything?" She spoke close to his ear.

Frederick forced his eyes to flutter open and to focus on his wife's face. "Only you," he managed to say as he searched her countenance for recognition. A stray strand of hair hung down loosely along her face. Frederick wanted to reach out and push it behind her ear, but he could not yet will his hand to respond.

She rested one arm across his chest and leaned over him to be close. Frederick felt the warmth of her body radiate through him; he found it ironic that even though he was injured, Anne still had that effect on him.

She smiled at him, up close and personal. "I need you to concentrate on your recovery," she whispered close to his lips, kissing first the corner of his mouth, then his cheek, his temple, and his ear. Frederick demanded his body answer as he turned his head to the side to properly kiss her. Anne responded instantly, happy to have him reacting to her at last. "You have been here for nearly four days," she explained, and he nodded that he understood. "Rest." She stroked along his cheekbone with her fingertips.

Frederick could only nod once more as he took in her features—features others might find nondescript—but features, which beset him for years. At first glance, a person might think *his Anne* unexceptional, but on closer observation a man would be a fool not to see her elegance. Her hair changed color with the lamp lighting from a dark chocolate to strands of gold mingled with red within a mahogany forest. Her skin remained a smooth ivory although she spent the last six months at sea with him, and her eyes sparked with intelligence and amusement. "Your eyes mesmerize me," he choked out. "Pools of strong coffee—a man could get lost in your eyes. I thank God every day they rest only on me."

He watched with delight as Anne's smile overtook her face. "You flatter me," she whispered as she kissed him lightly on the lips.

"Honesty and flattery rarely mix." An amused—nearly wicked—flash crossed his eyes. Anne had a presence he could not define—something utterly feminine, but hiding a strength of will learned from years of self-denial. With the words spoken, Frederick found himself suddenly very tired again. Knowing Anne would watch over him allowed him to relax back against the pillow. For eight years he took responsibility for everything around him; now, he could give up that answerability. She would tend to him without fail, an intoxicating sensation to say the least. He felt Anne reach to pull the blanket up to his shoulders, careful not to disturb him as he drifted back to the oblivion. Frederick forced his eyes open, wanting to imprint her image on the back of his eyes. He learned the lesson to treasure *every* moment they shared.

She bent to kiss him on the forehead. "It is not flattery I seek from you, Frederick." Anne's voice pierced what was left of his consciousness. "I wish you to rest and to recover. You promised to cherish me, and I, to love, honor, and obey you. It took us too long, my Love, to find each other again. You promised me constancy, and I do not wish to terminate our agreement."

Frederick made his hand respond to her physical closeness. He interlaced his fingers with hers. "I have missed you." His eyelids drifted closed with the words.

"And I you—more than words can express." She squeezed his hand, and he never felt so totally loved.

"You are mine," his voice barely audible.

Anne touched his lips with hers. "As you well know."

*   *   *

"As you well know, Frederick," Sophia's letter left him shaking as he read the words out loud, "Benjamin has long wished to return to Somersetshire and to settle in his own country. Last month we came down to Taunton in order to look at some advertised places in that immediate neighbourhood, which, however, did not suit him. Upon accident, we heard from a local innkeeper the possibility of Kellynch Hall being to let. It took Benjamin no time to introduce himself to Mr. Shepherd, as the man serves as Sir Walter Elliot's solicitor. My husband made particular inquiries, and had, in the course of a pretty long conference, expressed as strong an inclination for the place as a man who knew it only by description, could feel, and gave Mr. Shepherd, in his explicit account of himself, every proof of his being a most responsible, eligible tenant."

Frederick took a seat; Sophia's news dredged up memories he thought long since to be dead. "Benjamin did not quibble about the price as he should have. He let Mr. Shepherd know he only wanted a comfortable home and to get into it as soon as possible—knew he must pay for his convenience—knew what rent a ready-furnished house of that consequence might fetch—should not have been surprised if Sir Walter had asked more. Of course, I asked more questions about the house and terms and taxes than the Admiral himself. I even explained to the solicitor my connection to Somersetshire—Edward having lived in Monkford a few years back.

"Several weeks later we toured the manor, and I met the infamous Miss Elizabeth Elliot. I found I often had to keep my tongue in my cheek in order not to offend her sensibilities; yet, we parted with each of us well disposed for an agreement. Benjamin's hearty good humor and open, trusting liberality could not but influence Sir Walter. The house and grounds and furniture were approved; Mr. Shepherd's clerks were set to work, without there having been a single preliminary difference to modify of all that 'This indenture sheweth.' The Admiral, with sympathetic cordiality observed as we drove back through the Park, 'I thought we should soon come to a deal, my Dear, in spite of what they told us at Taunton. The baronet will never set the Thames on fire, but there seems no harm in him.' The long and the short of it is, my dear Brother, we take possession of Kellynch Hall at Michaelmas. When you come to us in October, you must return to the area where you spent a half-year with Edward in '06. You are probably more familiar with Kellynch than either the Admiral or I at this point. I am sure after having spent six months in the neighborhood, you already understand what I do not say about Sir Walter and Miss Elliot. He must be to Bath to save his reputation and to keep his creditors at bay, but Sir Walter's inability to manage his life gives Benjamin and me a fine home to share with you.

"Until then, I remain your loving sister."

SC

Frederick let out the breath he did not realize he held. He already made a commitment to visit his sister, but how could he go to Kellynch Hall? For many years the place hounded his dreams. What excuse could he give? Bonaparte was banished to Elba, and as the war dwindled down, he let it be known repeatedly, barring any new uprisings, he would take his newly made fortune and return to civilian life. Now, Sophia expected him to come to her. How this news trifled with his feelings! He left his heart in Somersetshire; his match to Anne Elliot would not have been the most advantageous match imaginable, but marriage was not impossible for them. Anne acted dishonorably by breaking off her engagement to him.

"How can I return to Somersetshire?" His mind asked the question his lips did not. He searched the letter again, wondering why Sophia did not mention Anne. Could it be she no longer lived in the area? Had she married at last? It was eight years after all. How soon had she married once she broke their engagement? Did Anne have children of her own? Some part of him wished her happy while a more dominate urge wished some form of revenge on her. A sarcastic laugh escaped his throat. "Is it not revenge that my sister will take possession of Sir Walter's estate house? My family was never good enough; now it is Anne's family that is found wanting." The thought consoled him. "Even if Anne Elliot is still in the neighborhood," he shored up his own resolve, "she will soon learn she is nothing. I have long since forgotten her hold on me."

Chapter 5

No, the heart that has truly loved never forgets,
But as truly loves on to the close,
As the sunflower turns on her god, when he sets,
The same look which she turned when he rose.
—Thomas Moore from "Believe Me, If All Those
Endearing Young Charms"

"Frederick, you are here at last," his sister called as she met him in the entrance hall. He handed his hat and greatcoat to the butler before taking her hands in his and lightly kissing her proffered cheek. Seeing her at last eased the chaos his stomach endured from the moment his public carriage entered Somerset. "You look well, my Brother." She embraced him again. "Come," she took his arm. "Benjamin awaits us in the front parlor."

Sophia Croft, though neither tall nor fat, had a squareness, uprightness, and vigor of form, which gave importance to her person. She had bright dark eyes, good teeth, and altogether an agreeable face; though her reddened and weather-beaten complexion, the consequence of her having been almost as much at sea as her husband, made her seem to have lived some years longer in the world than her real five and thirty. Her manners were open, easy, and decided, like one who had no distrust of herself, and no doubts of what to do; without any approach to coarseness, however, or any want of good humor.

Frederick fought the urge to look around for remnants of Anne Elliot in the furnishings. From the time he entered the Park, he felt her presence—could nearly visualize her moving through the gardens—entering the house—walking towards the lake to meet him. He shook his head to chase the images away. "You must be exhausted," his sister added as she tightened her grip on his arm. Looking over her shoulder she turned to the butler. "Mr. Steventon, please have someone bring us fresh tea and some refreshments."

"Right away, Mrs. Croft."

"Look at you," Frederick teased, "acting the fine lady of the estate."

Her eyes twinkled with anticipation. "Who says I am acting?"

Frederick laughed lightly. "Being the mistress of the house looks well on you, Sophia. I am pleased to see you well situated."

"It is pleasant to finally have roots rather than sea weeds upon which to stand. Of course, do not tell the Admiral I made such a bold statement." Her eyes pleaded for his discretion.

He cupped her hand with his. "Your secret is safe with me," he whispered close to her ear as he turned his attention towards his brother in marriage and in service. "Admiral," he acknowledged the man rising to his feet, "I am so pleased to see you, Sir."

"None of the formality here, Frederick." The elder seaman extended his hand in warm welcome. "We have both left our ships behind. I am no longer your superior officer; here at Kellynch Hall, I am Sophia's husband and your brother."

"Thank you, Sir." Frederick took the seat to which the Admiral gestured. "Although I must admit old habits will be hard to break." His sister took the seat next to him on the settee while the Admiral sank back into the wing chair. "How are you feeling, Benjamin?" He noticed immediately the man sat with his leg propped on a close-standing ottoman.

"I am having a bit of difficulty getting my land legs," the older man nearly moaned. "Your sister tends me well, though, and I am sure I will be up and about soon."

"How do you like Kellynch Hall?" Frederick allowed his eyes to circumnavigate the room. Visions of the last time he sat in this very room flooded his senses.

"It is a fine estate," Sophia mused. "Of course, we are still trying to accustom ourselves to all the room. Benjamin and I are used to much smaller quarters. Were you ever here when you visited Edward years ago?"

"Only once." Frederick's jaw twitched with the strain of not allowing Sophia to see his reaction. "Edward and I dined with some of the local gentry just a week before I left the country."

"Was the master of the house his usual pompous self?" Benjamin looked about amused.

"It was the only evening Sir Walter and I had a private conversation in the many months I resided with Edward." He bit the inside of his jaw to distract himself from the pain of remembering that conversation. "I am afraid Sir Walter did not approve of my bettering my lot in life through the navy. He was most persuasive in his opinions."

The admiral "Hurrumphed" with disgust. "You have no idea how many mirrors I removed from the walls!"

Frederick chuckled. "The man radiated vanity as I recall."

"That would be an understatement if I ever heard one." The Admiral shifted his attention to the maid bringing in a fresh tray of tea and cakes. "Thank you, Hilda. We will ring if we need anything else."

"Yes, Sir." She curtsied and left, closing the door behind her.

Sophia poured each of them a fresh cup of tea. Frederick took several sips as he built the courage to ask what he knew he must. "Then the family—the Elliots, that is—all removed themselves to Bath?"

Sophia settled herself next to him again. "Sir Walter and the eldest daughter, Elizabeth, are there on Camden Place; I believe I heard Mr. Shepherd say. His widowed daughter Mrs. Clay is Miss Elliot's traveling companion." Frederick waited, his heart thumping so loudly in his chest he thought surely Sophia would hear it. "The younger daughter married Charles Musgrove and is living at Uppercross. We met them recently. Mrs. Charles is quite insipid, would you not say, Admiral?"

Frederick did not hear his brother's response. All he could do was force himself to take steady breaths. *So, Anne married Charles Musgrove; he always suspected as much. More than once he replayed scenes of Musgrove dancing with her at the assembly.* "Mrs. Musgrove's children," the Admiral's voice penetrated Frederick's musings, "are high-spirited enough; she certainly cannot control them." *Anne had children! What did he expect? Certainly she could not remain celibate if she were married.* Yet, the thought of Anne Elliot loving anyone but him seemed a crack in the natural order of things.

"Did you meet the Musgroves when you were here before?" Sophia asked casually.

"Just briefly—I would not recognize the man, I am sure. I am surprised, however, Anne Elliot married him. From what I remember, he did not have the same elegance of mind as Miss Anne." It hurt him deeply to even utter Anne's name.

"Oh, I must apologize, Frederick, when I said the *younger* daughter married Charles Musgrove," his sister interrupted. "Mrs. Charles was once Mary Elliot; Miss Anne remains unmarried." A lightning bolt shot through him. *Anne, too, never married. Surely, it had nothing to do with him. It could not be. Obviously, his bachelorhood held no basis in their failed engagement. If he chose not to marry, logically, she could make a similar choice. Miss Elliot never married. Why should Anne? Sir Walter probably dashed her every offer as he dashed his hopes. It would be just like the man to refuse viable suitors to keep his daughters' affections focused purely on him.* A twinge of sympathy, centered on Anne's lost dreams, wormed its way into his heart. "I assume you knew Miss Anne?" his sister concluded.

"We were in each other's company upon several occasions." He forced himself to control his facial expression.

"I never suspected as much," Sophia replied. "I knew from our conversation when we returned the call at Uppercross some fortnight ago Miss Anne was familiar with Edward; yet, I did not realize you also met her acquaintance. If so, I could have shared your recent success when I told her about Edward's marriage. I am sure she would be interested to know of your moving up in the ranks. You were not given your first command when you visited Edward those years ago."

"I assure you Miss Anne could not be interested in my calling," Frederick reiterated, trying to keep the bitterness out of his words. "Then I assume Miss Anne is at Uppercross with her younger sister." The statement came out as a question.

"Mrs. Charles is of a delicate nature, or so she prefers to tell anyone who might listen. I suspect Miss Anne is the only one in the family with common good sense; she appears to be the only one who may placate Mary Musgrove."

"My wife has immersed herself in the neighborhood's gossip." Benjamin Croft teased her although Frederick noted Sophia did not seem offended by his chastisement.

She brushed away his rebuke before continuing her story. "Miss Anne travels with Lady Russell to Bath before Christmas. Lady Russell is away in Hertfordshire at the moment. Although she lives in the estate lodge, we have not met the woman. She left the area before we took possession of the house. It is common knowledge she serves as a confidante to the Elliot family, but I suspect you know that already."

Frederick stiffened noticeably with mention of Lady Russell's name. As much as he blamed Anne for succumbing to Lady Russell's advice, he blamed the woman herself more so. He always considered her his nemesis. The knowledge of her absence from the country came as a pleasant surprise; he did not think he could face her without animosity. "Sophia, I suddenly feel very tired; if you would show me to my room, I believe, I would like to freshen up before dinner."

"Of course, Frederick." She rose to lead the way.

"Until dinner, Sir." Frederick offered the man a slight bow as he stood. Not even considering getting up, the Admiral gave him a jovial smile as Frederick headed towards the door.

"Mr. Steventon arranged for his nephew to serve as your valet while you are here, Frederick. I know you are quite adept at handling your own ablutions, but the man is available if you need him."

"Thank you, Sophia; you are the perfect hostess." He followed her up the staircase to the private quarters. He wondered as he passed each of the closed doorways, which one belonged to Anne. For years, Frederick saw her everywhere he looked; now those images loomed larger than life.

He sat on the edge of the bed, waiting for his heart to stop pounding, the blood coursing through his veins, making him light headed. He cursed himself for still being susceptible to thoughts of Anne Elliot. Being in Anne's house might prove overpowering, after all. It certainly increased the memories bombarding his senses. Why in bloody hell did she still have such a hold on him? "I thought I rid myself of feelings for her long ago," he muttered, catching an image of his demeanor in the reflection of the window and trying desperately for a coherent thought. He moved to take in the view of the garden below, veiled in the last strands of sunlight.

"How foolish am I?" he spoke the words out loud, chastising his recent behavior. When Harville wrote of his latest child, Frederick found himself wondering about what life with Anne would have held. When his friend James Benwick lost his love Fanny, Thomas's sister, he grieved for his friend, but he also grieved for his own loss. When his brother Edward finally married the love of his life, he fantasized about life with Anne Elliot. Each remembrance brought him new pain. "Maybe this is what I need to finally be rid of her—to move on with my life. We will meet, and I will see she really has no hold on me. I wasted my time loving her. Anne Elliot betrayed me; she ill-abused me." Saying the words, he began to frantically pull at the knot in his cravat. "I will be her puppet no longer. Today I am cutting those strings that once bound me to her." He jerked the shirt over his head and tossed it on the bed. "Yes," he paused before pouring water into the basin. "This is exactly what I need—my chance to finally bid Anne Elliot farewell on my own terms."

*   *   *

With a new resolve, Frederick threw himself into the companionship of his sister and the Admiral. He rode out with them as they took pleasure in examining their lands and holdings. "It is beautiful here," Sophia sighed.

Frederick chuckled; he took her hand in the crook of his arm as they strolled through the gardens. "You appear content, Sophie."

"I admit I could become accustomed to the serenity that life at Kellynch Hall offers." She smiled up at him. "Benjamin served Britain long enough; it is time he takes care of himself. I wish for the peace to last; I am weary of war."

"Will the Admiral accept his half pension?" Frederick directed her to a bench upon which they could sit.

Sophia glanced furtively towards the house. "I will try to persuade him to do so. My husband will want to return, but I fear fate and luck could be against him. My instincts tell me he should not return. One cannot sail successfully as often as the Admiral without listening to the voice in his head. Of late, that voice seems to be saying enough is enough. I will use all my powers of persuasion to get him to adhere to what his inclinations tell him."

Frederick reached out to pat her hand, but before he could respond, a servant interrupted his thoughts. "Pardon, Mrs. Croft," the footman stammered. "Admiral Croft asks that you and Captain Wentworth join him in the front parlor. Mr. Musgrove attends your husband."

"Which Mr. Musgrove?" Frederick asked before he could stifle the words. Only a few days ago he imagined Anne married to the younger Musgrove.

"The father, Sir." The footman made a slight bow. "The Admiral said to tell you Mr. Musgrove was most interested in meeting you, Sir."

"Thank you, Landon," Sophia acknowledged.

"Yes, Ma'am." He left the area, exiting through the back garden gate.

"Well," Frederick said as he stood and offered her his hand. "Let us meet Mr. Musgrove."

Frederick followed Sophia into the room as Benjamin and Mr. Musgrove both struggled to their feet to acknowledge her. "My Love," Croft's eyes lit up when she accepted his hand and moved to sit beside her husband on an ornate settee.

"Mrs. Croft." Mr. Musgrove bowed to her before turning his attention to Wentworth.

Sophia ventured the appropriate introductions and ushered everyone to seats before the conversation began again. Musgrove was in the old English style—a very good sort of person—friendly and hospitable, not much educated, and not at all elegant. The man cleared his throat, attempting to stall before speaking, "Captain Wentworth, I cannot tell you how pleased I am to finally make your acquaintance."

"Thank you, Sir." Frederick inclined his head to acknowledge Musgrove's wording.

"As soon as your sister told us of your return to England, my wife, Mrs. Musgrove, has thought of little else. It appears, Captain, our second son Richard once served under you. Mrs. Musgrove found in his letters where he spoke of his commander Captain Wentworth. She is beside herself with joy to thank you for your kindness to our poor Dick when he served you on the *Laconia*." The words gushed from him, nearly leaving him breathless and quite reddened in the face.

Wentworth searched his memory for an image of Dick Musgrove. Doing so, he draped a countenance of concern, displaying it for all to see. "And how is Midshipman Musgrove?" Frederick feigned any real interest. He remembered Dick Musgrove well, having the ill fortune of adding Musgrove to his crew when he set in at Gibraltar in '09. Never had he met with such a troublesome, hopeless man. Obviously, he was unmanageable on shore, and upon reaching his twentieth year, he was sent to sea. Wentworth despised anyone who did not pull his own weight upon board, and in his estimation "poor Richard" was nothing better than a thickheaded, unfeeling, unprofitable Dick Musgrove, who never did anything to entitle himself to more than the abbreviation of his name.

"Unfortunately, we lost our poor son two years ago, Sir," Mr. Musgrove sounded very out of spirits.

Frederick looked around and caught the Admiral's eye. "Forgive me, Mr. Musgrove, I had no idea."

"It is of no consequence, Captain; we have many other children to fill our home, but we maintain a place in our hearts for Richard. I came here today to invite you to our house to share our table. Mrs. Musgrove insists she owes you a debt of gratitude for your personal attention to our dear boy."

Frederick fought the urge to roll his eyes. "I assure you, Mr. Musgrove, I did nothing to earn such praise."

"I am afraid, Captain, I will surely have a difficult time convincing my wife of such modesty."

"Then I will meet Mrs. Musgrove and convince her myself; however, I am committed to previous engagements for the next week. Will Mrs. Musgrove be kind enough to accept me at that time?" Frederick offered up his best "captain" smile.

Musgrove beamed with delight. "Mrs. Musgrove will be sorry to have to wait so long to make your acquaintance, but the anticipation will enhance the experience. May we say dinner at Uppercross for you, the Admiral, and Mrs. Croft in one week hence?"

Frederick conceded the response to his sister. As much as he pretended pleasure in meeting someone outside his family's circle, his thoughts drifted elsewhere. If he called upon the Great House at Uppercross, he would likely come face-to-face with Anne Elliot. How could he bear it? As much as he tried to convince himself he wanted nothing to do with her, a curiosity still loomed. His sister's words penetrated his thoughts. "It would be our pleasure, Mr. Musgrove."

The man scrambled to his feet before the group might withdraw their consent. "I must hurry home," he began, "and give Mrs. Musgrove the good news. She and my daughters will be thrilled." He edged closer to the door. "Thank you for receiving me, Admiral. Mrs. Croft, please know how anxious we at Uppercross were to have you at Kellynch Hall. This is a most pleasant circumstance, indeed."

He was nearly out the door before Sophia could interlace her arm with his and show him to the entranceway. When left alone, Frederick laughed lightly at the absurdity of the scene.

"Mr. Musgrove is an amiable man," the Admiral observed.

Frederick could not hide his amusement. "To think the Elliots aligned themselves with the Musgroves is a delightful diversion. I would definitely prefer the company of the Musgroves, however."

Croft's eyes danced with humor. "So, how bad of a sailor was Dick Musgrove? I saw how you bit your lip when his father spoke kindly of the man."

"He was several years at sea, and had, in the course of those removals to which all midshipmen are liable, and especially such midshipmen as every captain wishes to get rid of," he answered tongue-in-cheek, "quite nugatory. Dick Musgrove spent six months onboard the *Laconia*."

"May you find something positive to say about the man?" Croft forced himself to his feet. "You have a week to think of something." He chuckled as he patted Frederick on the shoulder. "I will see you at dinner; I want to take a look at the ledger book for the last month on the estate. I will be in the study if Sophie is looking for me."

"Later, Sir," Frederick mumbled.

*   *   *

"Captain Wentworth," Mr. Musgrove laughed happily at seeing the man, "it is so good of you to return our call. May I present my wife, Mrs.

Musgrove, and our daughters Miss Louisa and Miss Henrietta Musgrove?"
Frederick noted the Musgrove parents made a fine pair, both jovial—both
well rotund.

Frederick bowed politely. "I am proud to make your acquaintance,
Mrs. Musgrove." He saw tears mist her eyes as she took a close look at his
countenance while he tried to mask his real feelings. "Misses Musgrove."
He bowed formally to the women.

Henrietta and Louisa Musgrove were young ladies of nineteen and twenty,
respectively, who were brought from a school at Exeter—they possessed all
the usual stock of accomplishments, and were now, like thousands of other
young ladies, living to be fashionable, happy, and merry. Their dress had
every advantage, their faces were rather pretty, their spirits extremely good,
their manners unembarrassed and pleasant; they were of consequence at
home and favorites abroad.

"Captain, oh dear Captain, you have no idea how pleased we are to
receive you. We were anticipating the arrival of our daughter Mrs. Charles
and her sister Miss Anne Elliot. Please have a seat; they will be with us in the
next few minutes. You will be able to meet our son's wife; she and her sister
are two of Sir Walter's children; Miss Anne is newly come from Kellynch
Hall." Mrs. Musgrove seated herself on the sofa across from him.

Hearing Anne's name and realizing within a few minutes he would
see her once again, Frederick steeled his composure, trying to appear as if
everything was normal. After eight years, she would be in the same room
with him. Sweat formed on his forehead, and, he unobtrusively, wiped it
away with his handkerchief. Yet, before he could think further on what he
would say or do, a servant rushed into the room. "Oh, Mrs. Musgrove," the
woman gasped, "dear me."

"What is it, Jemina?" Mr. Musgrove rushed forward. "Is it Charles?"

"Lord, no, Mr. Musgrove," she gulped for air. "It is Little Charles; he fell
from a tree. The whole house is at sixes and sevens—alarmed with the idea
of some such injury received in the back. Miss Anne sent for the apothecary,
informed Master Charles, kept Mrs. Charles from hysterics, and sent me
here to inform you. She begs you to forgive their not attending you."

Mrs. Musgrove forgot all about their honored guest. "Father, we need
to go immediately."

"Of course, my Dear. Retrieve your wrap. I will have the carriage
brought around at once. Forgive us, Captain Wentworth; we must attend
to the disturbance at Uppercross Cottage. You will call upon us again on the
morrow? Please, Sir. Right now I must see to my heir—to Little Charles."

"Naturally, Mr. Musgrove; have no doubt. I will see myself out." Frederick rose quickly to leave. "As far as our engagement, I will wait until I hear from you on your grandson's progress before I call upon you again. Your attention needs to be there, Sir, not with me."

"Thank you, Captain. Now we must leave you. Hurry girls. Your mother is without." So saying, he led Wentworth to the hallway and shook his hand before turning towards his approaching wife.

On the walk back to Kellynch Hall, Frederick did not know what to think. He came so close to seeing Anne again. Looking down, he noticed his hands balled into fists; without thinking, he wiped his sweaty palms on his breeches. He cursed under his breath, realizing how flushed he felt—a band constricted his chest, and he could barely breathe. "Damn it," he murmured. "What am I to do? I must see her to rid myself of Anne Elliot, but how will I survive looking on her at last? Look at yourself, Frederick," he cursed again. "You fall apart with anticipation." Forcibly, he straightened his shoulders and took deep breaths, trying to quiet his troubled heart. "Tomorrow then," he thought out loud. "One more day will see us together." With a new resolve, he continued his walk towards Kellynch Hall.

*   *   *

Frederick called on the Musgroves the next evening, having received word earlier in the day of the continued progress of the child. "I must tell you, Captain, I experienced great uneasiness about my heir." Mr. Musgrove took a deep drink of port.

"I was a bit surprised to receive word regarding tonight's entertainment." Frederick let his eyes drift to the others at the table. It amused him to see the Miss Musgroves hang on his every word; he experienced such "adoration" from daughters of his fellow officers, but this gave him a heady sensation. If only Anne could see him now!

From the tidbits of conversation he gleamed about the table, Frederick determined Mary Elliot Musgrove possessed much of the Elliot pride. She was often unwell and out of spirits although she appeared quite animated on this particular evening. It took him only moments to realize Mary had not Anne's understanding or temper. While well, and happy, and properly attended to, she possessed great good humor and excellent spirits; but, evidently, any indisposition sunk her completely; she had no resources for solitude. She inherited a considerable share of the Elliot self-importance and was prone to add to every other distress that of fancying herself neglected and ill-used. In Frederick's opinion, she was inferior to both sisters.

Charles Musgrove was civil and agreeable; in sense and temper he was undoubtedly superior to his wife, but not of powers of conversation or of grace. In Frederick's estimation, a more equal match might greatly improve him, and a woman of real understanding might give more consequence to his character, and more usefulness, rationality, and elegance to his habits and pursuits. Musgrove was single-minded in pursuit of his sport; it appeared he did nothing with much zeal, but sport; and his time was otherwise trifled away, without benefit from books or anything else. Frederick could not imagine such a life of indolence. Yet, the man had very good spirits, which never seemed much affected by his wife's occasional lowness; bore with her unreasonableness; and, upon the whole, though there was very often a little disagreement, they passed for a happy couple.

"The child had a good night," Charles Musgrove confided to Frederick, "and Mr. Robinson found nothing to increase alarm so I saw no necessity for longer confinement. What can a father do?" Frederick thought if it was his child nothing could make him leave his son; yet, he hide his thoughts behind his wine glass.

"I agree, Boy," Mr. Musgrove added quickly. "This is quite a female case, and it would be highly absurd of you, who could be of no use at home, to shut yourself up. Besides I wished you to make the captain's acquaintance."

"Then your sister is with the child?" Frederick was disappointed when Anne made no appearance at the gathering. He would like to know how she felt as to a meeting. Perhaps indifferent, if indifference could exist under such circumstances. She must be indifferent or unwilling—unwilling to face him.

Mary joined the conversation. "I told Charles, to be sure, I may just as well come as not, for I am of no use at home—am I?" She turned to her husband for confirmation of what she said. "And it only harasses me. My sister Anne has not a mother's feelings and is a great deal the properest person. She can make Little Charles do anything; he always minds her at a word. It is a great deal better than leaving him with only Jemina."

Anne possessed a way with children! Her sister said it in an off-handed remark. He always imagined it to be so but suspected he would be the disciplinarian in their family. How often he saw her with a babe in her arms—her child—his child? The pain crept into the pit of his stomach, focusing on the drama of which he was a part.

"It was very kind of Anne," Charles assured everyone in ear shot. "I wanted her to join us in the evening when the child might be at rest for the night. I urged her to let me come and fetch her, but she was quite unpersuadable."

"I am sorry Miss Anne could not join us. We met when I was here before, and I wanted the opportunity to acknowledge that acquaintance formally." Frederick felt the necessity of escaping an introduction when they were to meet.

"I never realized you knew my sister!" Mary exclaimed.

"I believe you away at school when last I came to Somerset," was all the explanation he offered before turning his conversation back to Louisa Musgrove.

The evening continued with music, singing, talking, and laughing; Frederick found it all most agreeable. He forced himself to be charming, leaving his pensive thoughts of Anne in the deep recesses of his mind. He and the Musgroves took to each other quickly; they seemed all to know each other perfectly. "Then you will come for breakfast before we go shooting?" Charles Musgrove said his good-byes.

"Not at the Cottage," Frederick decided against seeing Anne. If she chose not to let Charles bring her for the evening's end, she, evidently, did not want to see Frederick. He would not force himself upon her. "I would not wish to be in Mrs. Charles's way on account of the child."

"Then we will meet here at the Great House." Charles moved to allow his parents to bid their own farewells.

"Tomorrow," Frederick added, making his bows first to the ladies and then to the Musgrove men. He mounted the horse he borrowed from the Kellynch stables and headed towards his sister's home.

Chapter 6

When we two parted, in silence and tears,
Half broken-hearted to sever for years,
Pale grew thy cheek and cold—colder thy kiss;
Truly that hour foretold sorrow to this.
—Lord Byron from "When We Two Parted"

"So beautiful." The words brought Anne Elliot's attention to the figure reclining lazily against the pillows. She sat reading a book of poetry. "Did you know I fell in love with you the first time I saw you in the mercantile. Your delicate features and mild dark eyes enthralled me from the moment I set mine upon you."

She smiled tenderly at him. Moving to sit on the edge of the bed, she reached out and pushed the hair away from his forehead. "You did not look away." Anne leaned forward and whispered in his ear. "I saw your eyes darken with something I did not understand at the time." She kissed his temple and his cheek.

Frederick's breath caught in his throat—a true indication of his desire for her. "I saw the sparks in yours, my Dear, and suddenly I wanted to be the only man you ever saw; I wanted to be the one who made those sparks reappear in those doe-like eyes."

"I am thrilled you are feeling better, my Love." She nibbled on his lower lip." I feared I might lose you."

"Never again," he said more emphatically.

Anne chuckled lightly before pulling back, but before she could respond to his taunt the physician burst through the door. "Ah, Captain," he called as he strode across the room. "It is time to get you up out of that bed." He immediately started checking Frederick's wounds.

"Are you sure, Doctor Laraby?" Anne looked concerned. "Will that not injure my husband further?"

"Of course not," Laraby stood firm. "He needs exercise, or he will get weaker. Trust me, Mrs. Wentworth. Besides, you need to get out of this room for a while. Look at her, Captain; see how pale she is. Your wife has done nothing but tend you night and day for nearly five days now. Order her, Wentworth; she ignores me."

Frederick turned his eyes on Anne's countenance. Laraby was right; she was pale and gaunt, and, if possible, she lost weight. "Anne," he stammered, "I am sorry I never noticed."

"You were in dire straits; it is of no consequence. You needed me," she protested.

"I did; I do," he corrected. "But because I need you, my Love, I want you to take care of yourself. Please leave, Sweetheart; go do something special for you." He took her hand in his, bringing her fingertips to his lips for a lingering kiss. "Do not make me give you a direct order, Sweetling." His eyes lit up with amusement.

He watched as she playfully raised an eyebrow in mocked contempt. "Can you spell mutiny, my Love?" she teased.

"M-u-t . . ." Her laughter cut off the end of the word.

She conceded, "I will go, but please note it is not with a willing heart."

"So noted," he quipped. "Now get out of here."

"Aye, aye, Captain." She offered a half-hearted salute before dropping him a quick curtsy.

As she left, Laraby ushered in Avendale and Harwood once again. "We need to get the captain on his feet; I want him walking about this room."

His men supported his every move, allowing him to lean his weight on their shoulders. Halting steps and gritting teeth painted the scene, but Frederick wove a path to and fro across the room. Each movement was dizzying, holding his body so tight he could barely breathe. Pausing, when it became too intense—too much—he tried to organize his thoughts as he traversed the short distance from one side of his cabin to the other.

"That is good," Laraby motioned for the sailors to help Frederick back to his bunk. "We will have you up again a little later today."

Frederick collapsed to a seated position on the side of the bed. "Thanks for the warning, Laraby," he hissed through the settling pain.

"You know it is best, so quit your complaining." Laraby supported Frederick's shoulders as the captain pivoted on the bed, swinging his long legs up and over the edge. He gasped audibly as he lay back against the pillows. "Do you need more laudanum?"

"Could we wait a while?" Frederick pushed himself up on his pillows.

Laraby pulled the blanket over Frederick's long frame. "Sure. How about I get a man in here to shave you? That might make you feel better."

"I think I would enjoy that." Frederick smirked. "Mrs. Wentworth would appreciate not seeing my scruffy face when she returns."

Laraby sent for Wentworth's assistant before saying, "Your wife is a fine woman, Sir. You are fortunate to have earned her regard. Not wishing to seem rude, Sir, I am surprised some man did not claim her attentions long ago."

Frederick laughed lightly. "Some man did—me." He looked off in space visualizing Anne as he first saw her. "I wooed her in '06, but we were young, and things were not to be. I assumed I lost Mrs. Wentworth until I returned to her home country to visit with my sister Sophia and the Admiral. Then we were thrown together through mutual acquaintances."

"Then you are truly a lucky man," Laraby acknowledged.

Frederick smiled, the corners of his lips turning up in anticipation. "Bringing Mrs. Wentworth back into my life is the only good thoughts I ever had for Dick Musgrove."

"Musgrove! That worthless piece of . . ." Laraby checked what he wanted to say, not knowing Musgrove's connection to Mrs. Wentworth.

"I agree," Frederick added. "Dick Musgrove was useless in my estimation, but his parents thought the world of him—at least, he was scarcely at all regretted once the intelligence of his death abroad worked its way to Uppercross. His parents came to thank me for the letters I insisted he write home, and I was presented with the pleasant situation of finding *my Anne* in residence with the Musgroves. Mrs. Wentworth's youngest sister is the eldest son's wife. The rest is history."

The assistant entered at that point and began setting up the shaving tools. Laraby moved to the chair before continuing the conversation. "It sounds as if God meant for the two of you to be together."

"I like to think so," Wentworth added, "although the Devil provided us several twists and turns along the way."

"You will tell me of them some time?" Laraby asked. "For now, I will remain quiet while Yates takes care of your ablutions."

The assistant moved up to cover Frederick's cheeks and jaw line with a soapy lather. A few minutes later, the captain was clean-shaven once again. Rubbing his palms along his smooth skin, he looked at his reflection in the mirror Yates offered. "I am glad Anne chose me before I lost all this blood and the weight. She may consider herself at a disadvantage. Look at the dark circles under my eyes." Frederick shook his head in disbelief.

"You were never handsome, Captain," Laraby taunted.

Frederick rolled his eyes. "I am getting as bad as my wife's father in thoughts of my own appearance." He laughed at his touch of vanity. "More sleep will rid me of the circles, I suppose."

Laraby assured him, "More sleep and then more exercise."

"Oh, good," he added sarcastically. "Pacing a room is one of my least favorite things."

*   *   *

Frederick paced the morning room, waiting for Charles Musgrove to finish his breakfast. The Musgroves thought him anxious for the sport of the day. In reality, his thoughts fell once again on Anne. He and Charles were to return to the Cottage for the dogs; more than likely Anne would be in attendance. They would meet at last.

"Let us go," Charles called, picking up the gun to which the elder Musgrove pointed.

Louisa Musgrove strolled into the room. "We would join you if you have no objections? Henrietta and I wish to call at the Cottage regarding Little Charles."

Frederick recognized the ruse, but he chose to ignore it. After all, the Miss Musgroves were two of the most genial young ladies of his acquaintance. "I would be pleased for your company."

They walked to the Cottage, animated conversation springing from the Miss Musgroves. Frederick, on the other hand, felt as if he might be attending his own execution. He steeled his nerves and cleared his countenance as he approached the house. Within seconds, he would face her after eight years.

"The morning hours of the Cottage are always later than those of the Great House," Louisa explained as they approached the door. "With the late hours of the party, I suspect Mary and Anne are just beginning their breakfasts."

"Then we will not intrude for long," Frederick insisted, thinking this would give him a legitimate reason not to tarry in Anne's presence.

The door opened to the Cottage, and Frederick followed Louisa and Henrietta into the room. Air rushed from his lungs as he stepped forward to greet Mrs. Charles. He made his bow, not allowing his eyes to rest on either woman standing by the breakfast sidebar. Although he had not looked at her, his body told him Anne Elliot finally stood before him.

"Mrs. Musgrove," he began, "excuse the intrusion. I came with your husband to inquire on the progress of your son. I pray the morning brings him continued peace."

Mary, very much gratified by his attention, was delighted to receive him. "Oh, Captain Wentworth," she gushed. "You do so honor us . . . ."

He heard nothing else; his eyes rested purely on Anne's face although he tried to give the impression of attending to her sister's effusions. They were the same features he remembered; yet, she was somehow changed. She nearly blended into the woodwork; Anne appeared used up—defeated by life. What happened to the woman he loved so dearly all those years ago? She allowed life to consume her rather than her consuming it. It angered him she never learned to take up her own cause. In some ways, he believed she deserved serving her inane sister and never having a life of her own. He once thought she would be adventurous enough to sail with him around the world; now, he saw her as nothing more than an accessory to her family's whims. How could he have pined for such a woman? How could he believe she could live the life of a sailor's wife?

A self-conscious silence engulfed him; Mary Musgrove looked at him expectantly. Frederick realized he did not attend to her ramblings; he was just about to make some sort of excuse when her husband appeared at the window. "Come, Wentworth, I have the dogs." He held the leashes of several beagles and pointers.

"If you will excuse me, Ladies," he said with a bow and then turned towards the door, needing to escape the room.

"Let us walk with them to the end of the village," Louisa encouraged her sister.

Mary grabbed her shawl from the back of a chair. "I will go too."

Frederick paused at the door to allow the women to precede him. Reluctantly, he glanced at Anne to see if she would join them also. Instead, she stood fixated on a spot on the floor, never raising her eyes to him. *Join us* he wanted to say to her. *Take your life in your own hands* he tried to will her to move. But she did no more than drop a quick curtsy. Disgusted with her inability to respond, he strode out the door, never looking back.

He walked silently beside Charles Musgrove, lost in his thoughts. He replayed the scene—her eyes half met his; a bow, a curtsy passed; he talked to Mary, said all that was right; said something to the Miss Musgroves—the room seemed full—full of people and voices—but a few minutes ended it.

"It is over! It is over!" he repeated to himself, and again in nervous agitation. "The worst is over!" He had seen her. They had met. They were once more in the same room! Eight years, almost eight years passed, since all was given up. How absurd to be resuming the agitation which such an interval had banished into distance and indistinctness! What might not eight years do? Events of every description, changes, alienations, removals—all, all must be comprised in it; and oblivion of the past—how natural, how certain too! It included nearly a fourth part of his life.

Alas! With all his reasoning, he found, that to retentive feelings eight years may be little more than nothing. Frederick wondered how were her sentiments to be read? Was this like wishing to avoid her? Irritation flooded him—only a few moments in her presence, and he felt discomposed.

He turned from his thoughts reluctantly when he heard Henrietta address him. "Captain Wentworth, what did you think of Miss Anne?"

Without realizing her sister would carry round his words to her, Frederick responded in a defensive manner, afraid to betray his real thoughts about Anne Elliot. "I am sorry to say I found Miss Anne altered beyond my knowledge—so altered I should not have known her again!"

He thought her wretchedly altered, and, in the first moment of appeal, spoke as he felt. He realized he had not forgiven Anne Elliot. She used him ill; deserted and disappointed him; and worse, she showed a feebleness of character in doing so, which his own decided, confident temper could not endure. She gave him up to oblige others. It was the effect of over persuasion. It was weakness and timidity. He assumed maturity would absolve her of those tendencies; instead, Anne Elliot presented a "ghost" of the woman she should be.

He had been most warmly attached to her and had never seen a woman since whom he thought her equal, but he had been wrong. Now, except from some natural sensation of curiosity, he had no desire of meeting her again. He swore her power with him was gone forever.

*   *   *

Later that evening, he sat in the drawing room with Sophia and Benjamin. They sipped on a fine wine. Staring at the glowing fire in the hearth, Frederick, despite his earlier vow, remained consumed by his continual thought of Anne. "The Miss Musgroves are attractive." Sophia roused him from his musings.

Frederick smiled, knowing where this conversation would lead. "They both offer pleasant company," he said at last.

"Do not play coy, Frederick," the Admiral admonished. "Does either of the young ladies interest you? Your sister and I would like to see you as well settled as is Edward."

"I know, Admiral," he conceded. "You two will be pleased to know it is now my object to marry. I am rich, and being turned on shore, fully intend to settle as soon as I can be properly tempted. I am actually looking round, am ready to fall in love with all the speed which a clear head and quick taste will allow. I have a heart for either of the Miss Musgroves, if they can catch it; a heart, in short, for any pleasing young woman who comes my way." *Anyone except Anne Elliot,* he thought. This was his only secret exception to his sister's suppositions. "Yes, here I am, Sophia, quite ready to make a foolish match. Anybody between fifteen and thirty may have me for the asking. A little beauty and a few smiles, and a few compliments to the navy, and I am a lost man. Should not this be enough for a sailor who has had no society among women to make him nice?"

"You just wish me to contradict you," she reasoned. "No woman could ask for a kinder man than you, Frederick."

His mind instinctively returned to the newest images of Anne Elliot. "If I were to more seriously describe the woman I should wish to meet," he hesitated, remembering his initial assessment of Anne, "she would possess a strong mind, with a sweetness of manner." He paused again, considering his own words. "This is the woman I want," said he. "Something a little inferior I shall, of course, put up with, but it must not be much. If I am a fool, I shall be a fool indeed, for I have thought on the subject more than most men."

* * *

From this time Captain Wentworth and Anne Elliot were repeatedly in the same circle. They soon dined in company together at Mr. Musgrove's, for the little boy's state could not supply his aunt with a pretense for absenting herself; and this was but the beginnings of other dining and other meetings.

Frederick no longer feared being in the same room with her. He treated Anne as everyone else did; she was a nonentity—she did not exist other than being part of the room decoration. In this manner, he could deal with her presence. Yet, as often as he tried to not let himself think of her, he foolishly succumbed nevertheless. It irritated him to see her treated as an afterthought in the minds of her family. It irritated him to think she accepted her life as it was. It irritated him that despite her betrayal, he still had moments when his eyes rested on her and her alone.

"Do you mean to say sailors have private accommodations on board ship?" Louisa gushed with surprise.

"Miss Musgrove, we are not barbarians. We officers live quite comfortably. My sister," he nodded towards Sophia, "travels with the Admiral. Obviously, she could not be expected to live in substandard conditions."

"Did you ever hear of such a thing, Anne?" Henrietta turned to her for confirmation.

Frederick, too, turned his attention to Anne. He suspected, like him, she remembered a similar conversation; the thoughts of those pleasant hours with her beside the lake turned up the corners of his mouth with a smile; he noted she held his gaze for a few elongated seconds before looking suddenly away. "I assume, Henrietta, the Crown would not send men off to fight wars in row boats; it would not be practical. What man would make a career of the Navy if he had to suffer long periods of deplorable conditions." Her voice painted pleasant ridicule of the Miss Musgroves' flirtations, and it pleased Frederick to see her assert herself.

Frederick started to respond directly to her, but Mrs. Musgrove whispered what appeared to be fond regrets of Dick Musgrove. He watched as Anne suppressed a smile and listened kindly. It was a quality he once admired in her. He considered joining their conversation, but then thought better of it. It was a seductive illusion to which he wanted to succumb; yet, Frederick knew the folly of it.

"Oh, Captain," Henrietta kept her eyes exclusively on him, "we sent off for a Navy List. Will you help us find in it the ships you commanded?" She rushed to the mantelpiece to retrieve the book.

"I am sorry, Captain," Mr. Musgrove apologized, "they made me send for it."

Frederick smiled broadly with their regard. "It is quite all right."

"Anne has her own Navy List. Do you not, Anne?" Louisa told him in passing.

Frederick's eyes darted to her face; he watched the flush overspread her countenance. "I am interested in many things, Louisa," she stammered before dropping her eyes to her hands resting on her lap.

"When did you get your first command, Captain?" Mr. Musgrove asked as he motioned for a servant to refill the wine glasses.

Admiral Croft answered instead. "It was in '06, was it not, Frederick?"

"It was, Sir, shortly after I left Somersetshire. Yes, I was here in '06 visiting my brother Edward." He watched Anne withdraw into herself with his words.

"Your first was the *Asp,* I remember; we will look for the *Asp.*" Louisa poured over the listing.

"You will not find her there.—Quite worn out and broken up. I was the last man who commanded her.—Hardly fit for service then.—Reported fit for home service for a year or two—and so I was sent off to the West Indies."

The Musgrove girls looked all astonishment.

"The admiralty," he continued, "entertain themselves now and then, with sending a few hundred men to sea in a ship not fit to be employed. But they have a great many to provide for; and among the thousands that may just as well go to the bottom as not, it is impossible for them to distinguish the very set who may be least missed."

"Phoo! Phoo!" cried the Admiral, "what stuff these young fellows talk! Never a better sloop than the *Asp* in her day—for an old built sloop, you would not see her equal. Lucky fellow to get her." He leveled a look of command at Frederick. "He knows there must have been twenty better men than himself applying for her at the same time. Lucky fellow to get anything so soon, with no more high placed connections than his."

"I felt my luck, Admiral, I assure you." He looked about seriously, planning to make a point with Anne. "I was as well satisfied with my appointment as one can desire. It was a great object with me at the time to be at sea—a very great object. In '06, I wanted to be doing something."

The Admiral got up to stretch his legs, trying to ward off another attack of gout. "To be sure you did." He spoke more to himself than he did to Frederick. "What should a young fellow, like you, do ashore, for half a year together?—If a man has not a wife, he soon wants to be afloat again."

Frederick eyed Anne once again. He put special emphasis on the beginning words. "In '06, I had no wife to keep me on shore." The words served their purpose; Anne turned a bit away from the rest of the table. He relished the idea he could make her think of him; he knew how often over the last eight years he thought of her. It was gratifying in some small way to see his words affect her.

"But, Captain Wentworth," cried Louisa, "how vexed you must have been when you came to the *Asp* to see what an old thing they gave you."

He smiled at her when she lightly laid her hand on his arm to retrieve his attention. "I knew pretty well what she was before that day. I had no more discoveries to make, than you would have as to the fashion and strength of an old pelisse, which you had seen lent about among half your acquaintance, ever since you could remember, and which at last, on some very wet day, is lent to yourself." He tried to make his analogy one the Miss Musgroves would understand. All eyes at the table now rested on him. Although he did not look at her, he felt Anne's eyes glued to his face. "Ah! She was a dear old *Asp* to me. She did all I wanted. I knew she would.—I knew we should either go to the bottom together, or she would be the making of me. In reflection, I never had two days of foul weather all the time I was at sea in her, and after taking privateers enough to be very entertaining, I had the good luck, in my passage home the next autumn, to fall in with the very French frigate I wanted. I brought her into Plymouth, and here was another instance of luck."

He focused his attention on Anne's end of the table. He knew she had not looked away during his tale; it was his chance to let her know how successful he had been and how the luck he knew he would have was there as he predicted. "We were not six hours in the Sound," he continued in a voice that mesmerized his audience, but Frederick's attention rested purely on Anne Elliot, "when a gale came on, which lasted four days and nights, and which would have done in the poor old *Asp,* in half the time; our touch with the Great Nation of France not having much improved our condition. Four and twenty hours later, and I should only have been a gallant Captain Wentworth in a small paragraph at one corner of the newspapers; and being lost in only a sloop, nobody would have thought about me."

Louisa and Henrietta gasped and declared how awful such thoughts were, but Frederick watched Anne for her reaction. She openly shuddered—a shiver shaking her body. Her bottom lip trembled, and although she made no open exclamation of pity and horror, as did the other ladies, he noted tears misting her eyes. Her reaction stunned him—his heart skipped a beat. He only watched her to gleam an idea of whether she regretted her decision in light of the fortune he won, but her obvious distress over his words made him question what to do about her. She was moved by his description of how close he came to death—the indication of the fortune he won brought only looks of admiration for his successes, but his near demise affected her in a way he did not expect. He never considered renewing his addresses to Anne Elliot, but it seemed they would always be connected—their pasts bound him with silver threads to her.

He heard Mrs. Musgrove say something to her son Charles about Dick Musgrove. Frederick knew he would have to think of something positive about "poor Dick" soon. He would find a way to ease her pain.

"Come, Captain," Henrietta pulled on his left sleeve. "Help us find the *Laconia* on the List."

He could not deny himself the pleasure of taking the precious volume into his own hands to save them the trouble and to read aloud the little statement of her name and rate and present non-commissioned class, observing over it, that she too was one of the best friends man ever had.

"Ah! Those were pleasant days when I had the *Laconia*! How fast I made money in her.—A friend of mine and I had such a lovely cruise together off the Western Islands. You remember Harville, do you not, Sophia? You know how much he wanted money—worse than myself. He had a wife.—Excellent fellow! I shall never forget his happiness. He felt it all, so much for her sake. I wished for him again the next summer, when I had still the same luck in the Mediterranean."

His words of the *Laconia* brought Mrs. Musgrove's thoughts back to her son. The time came for him to console her. She rested on the same sofa, as did Anne. Making his way to her, he allowed himself an indulgence of self-amusement at how many pains he went through to be rid of Dick Musgrove. Now, he would hide his real feelings from the man's mother. He sat on the same upholstered seat; Mrs. Musgrove separated them. Even her girls did nothing to keep Frederick's reaction to Anne in check. Although he fought it, as he entered into the conversation with the elder woman, his real thoughts lay with the petite lady seated to her right. He offered sympathy and attended to Mrs. Musgrove's large fat sighs over the destiny of a son he suspected for whom nobody cared when he was alive. She patted Frederick's hand and thanked him profusely for his kindness. He allowed her to prattle on while he noted the delicate curve of Anne's neck and the slight lift of her chin when she spoke to his sister. A strand of hair worked its way loose from her chignon, and he fought the urge to reach out and touch it. It would be so simple to do . . . .

The Admiral, after two or three refreshing turns about the room with his hands behind him, being called to order by his wife, now came up to Frederick and without any observation of what he might be interrupting, thinking only of his own thoughts, began with, "If you had been a week later at Lisbon, last spring, Frederick, you would have been asked to give passage to Lady Mary Grierson and her daughters."

Lost in thoughts of touching Anne's neck, Frederick sarcastically turned on his brother. "Should I? I am glad I was not a week later then." The tone of Frederick's voice set the Admiral on guard as the Captain continued to explain to the others around him, "But, if I know myself, this is from no want of gallantry towards them." Suddenly realizing the spectacle he was making, Frederick softened his tone. "It is rather from feeling how impossible it is, with all one's efforts, and all one's sacrifices, to make the accommodations on board, such as women ought to have. There can be no want of gallantry, Admiral, in rating the claims of women to every personal comfort *high*—and this is what I do. I hate to hear of women on board or to see them on board; and no ship, under my command, shall ever convey a family of ladies anywhere, if I can help it." Frederick had not always felt this way about women aboard ship; obviously, at one time he planned to share his quarters with Anne, but now he could not bear such intrusions into his domain. If Anne could not travel with him, Frederick wanted *no* woman on the ship.

Typically, Sophia took offense with his words. "Oh, Frederick!—But I cannot believe it of you.—All idle refinement!—Women may be as comfortable on board, as in the best house in England. I believe I have lived as much on board as most women, and I know nothing superior to the accommodations of a man of war."

"Nothing to the purpose," Frederick protested. "You were living with your husband and were the only woman on board."

"But you, yourself, brought Mrs. Harville, her sister, her cousin, and the three children round from Portsmouth to Plymouth. Where was this superfine, extraordinary sort of gallantry of yours then?"

"All merged in my friendship, Sophia." Frederick's voice rose in volume, realizing where his sister's argument lay, but he could not concede his *need* to keep women from his ship—a *need* vested in his hurt at Anne's refusal. He knew it was not rational, but reason and love do not always lie together. "I would assist any brother officer's wife I could, but I might not like them the better for that. Such a number of women and children have no *right* to be comfortable on board."

Sophia's ire also rose; his stubbornness riled her. "But I hate to hear you talking so, like a fine gentleman and as if women were all fine ladies, instead of rational creatures. We none of us expect to be in smooth waters all our days." He resisted the urge to look at Anne at that moment. Could she have survived on a ship—survived with him?

"Ah! My Dear," the Admiral came to sit beside his wife on the settee, "when he has a wife, he will sing a different tune. When he is married, if we have the good luck to live to another war, we shall see him do as you and I, and a great many others, have done. We shall have him very thankful to anybody who will bring him his wife."

Sophia nodded. "Aye that we shall."

Frederick could take no more—Anne sat nearby—the Miss Musgroves and their cousins, the Miss Hayters fawned all over him—and all he wanted to do was retreat to the privacy of his room and recoup his composure. "Now I have done!" he exclaimed. "When once married people begin to attack me with 'Oh! You will think differently when you are married.' I can only say, 'No, I shall not.' And then they say again, 'Yes, you will.' And there is an end to it." He got up and moved away to the window, studying his reflection in the candlelight.

Frederick swallowed hard, trying to steel his nerves. Between him and Anne, they had no conversation together, no intercourse but what the commonest civility required. Once so much to each other! Now nothing! There *had* been a time when of all the large party now filling the drawing room at Uppercross, they would have found it most difficult to cease to speak to one another. With the exception, perhaps, of the Admiral and Sophia, there could have been no two people so in love. Now they were as strangers—nay, worse than strangers, for they could never become acquainted. It was a perpetual estrangement.

Lost in his thoughts, Frederick barely heard his sister telling Mrs. Musgrove about all the places to which she traveled. "Cork and Lisbon and Gibraltar."

Anne's soft lilt caught his attention, and he felt his body stiffen with interest. "Did you never suffer, Mrs. Croft, from your time at sea?"

Sophia went into her usual spill of her devotion to Benjamin Croft. He did not have to hear the words to know she spoke of her undying love for the man. "The only time I ever really suffered in body or mind, the only time I ever fancied myself unwell, or had any ideas of danger, was the winter I passed by myself at Deal, when the Admiral, Captain Croft then, was in the North Seas. I lived in perpetual fright at that time, and had all manner of imaginary complaints from not knowing what to do with myself, or when I should hear from him next; but as long as we could be together, nothing ever ailed me, and I never met with the smallest inconvenience." Was that the reason? Had Anne been afraid to follow him to sea? It was something he never considered; he always assumed she did not love him enough to face the hardships together. She was but nineteen in '06. She was larger than life in memory, and he never thought of her as afraid of what he offered. Would she survive the separations, living alone in a seaport? Sophia was young when she married Benjamin, but she had not led a sheltered life, and a woman of four and twenty was different from a girl of nineteen. He needed to think; he needed to decide where Anne Elliot fit into his life.

Louisa Musgrove moved up beside him. "Have we said something to offend you, Captain Wentworth?" Her soft eyes told him she would eagerly receive his attentions. Even if he considered renewing his regard for Anne, he could not be sure she would receive him willingly. He would not allow Anne the opportunity to humiliate him again; his heart could not survive such censure. Why not accept what was in front of him? *Why not accept a sure thing?*

"Of course not, Miss Musgrove. I was just taking in the splendor of the evening." He offered her a genuine smile.

"Anne offered to play for us." Louisa leaned in a bit too close for propriety, but no one, except him, seemed to notice her forwardness. "I hoped you would dance with me, Captain."

"Should I not be asking you rather than your asking me to dance?" He half chuckled with her flirtations.

"As long as we dance, does it matter who asked whom?" She pursed her lips in a pretend pout.

"No . . . no, Miss Musgrove, it does not." He automatically offered her his arm.

Chapter 7

He and Louisa moved to the area in the music room cleared for dancing; furtively, he shot a quick glance at Anne as she settled herself on the bench behind the pianoforte. She withdrew from the party again. *"Again,"* he thought, *"again, she desires nothing but to be unobserved."*

Louisa Musgrove enthusiastically twirled about him in the quadrille, and Frederick could not help but laugh, watching her smiling up at him. Obviously, in her young romantic heart lurked the secret desire to capture his interest. "You seem quite happy this evening," he said as he passed her in the form.

"Do I?" She actually giggled as she tilted her head up to him as they came together. "I would assume it is the company I keep."

Frederick moved away, circling Sophia and Charles Musgrove. When they joined hands to move down the line, he leaned toward Louisa and spoke to her hair. "You are very bold, Miss Musgrove."

Her eyes lit up with excitement. "I am sure of what I want in my life, Captain Wentworth."

"Interesting, Miss Musgrove." Yet, his looks never betrayed his real thoughts. He was thirteen years her senior, and he certainly did not know what he wanted in his life.

After the dance, they joined Henrietta and the Hayter sisters, all awaiting patiently for their turns to dance with him. "Do you know how to waltz, Captain Wentworth?" Miss Hayter asked with a gulp of air.

"I do, Miss Hayter. Most officers are familiar with the more popular dances. We find it quite useful when we are required to attend Naval functions."

"I wish Mamma would allow us to waltz." Henrietta sighed with regret. "She believes it to be a quite scandalous dance. What do you think, Captain?"

Frederick did not know how to answer. Waltzing with the right woman in his arms could be very *stimulating,* but a gentleman could never say such things to a cluster of young virginal ladies. Instead, he tried to divert their imaginings. "In London, before a lady of the *ton* may waltz she must be presented at Almack's and receive permission from one of the patronesses there—Lady Jersey, Princess Lieven, or Lady Castlereaugh. The three are quite content to control Society from their lofty perches. It is even rumored they once turned away the Duke of Wellington himself for wearing trousers instead of knee breeches." The girls all giggled nervously at his description of life in London's best parlor rooms. "Will any of you experience a Season this year?"

"Oh, no," Louisa assured him in serious tones, "we will never experience the *ton* and its wicked ways. The Elliots and Lady Russell are the extent of father's tolerance for the nobility. We will all find matches in the country. Living in London sounds exciting, but Papa would never tolerate the number of soirees and balls of a Season."

Frederick found this to be a merry, joyous party, and his spirits were high. How could a man not enjoy an evening where four young women vied for his notice and his deference? The Miss Musgroves and the Miss Hayters did all they could to see to his pleasure of the evening. They hung on his every word—his every gesture. At a pause in the music, he moved to the instrument bench to pluck out a tune of which the young ladies were not familiar. They crowded around, eager to tease him with his inability to play well.

"Oh, Captain," Miss Hayter gushed, "you are perfectly awful!" They all laughed heartily.

"It is true, my Ladies. Playing the pianoforte is not in the domain of most sailors." Yet, he continued to stroke the keys aimlessly searching for the right one as he spoke.

"Would there be room aboard a ship for my new harp?" Henrietta questioned.

"Of course, room could be had for such an extravagance, although I am not sure how the sea air might affect the instrument."

Suddenly looking up, he saw Anne approaching the bench. Not wishing her presence to intrude on the vignette he created in his mind where he received the notice of women purely because he was an eligible prospect and where he had no history with Anne, he stood to move away from the bench. He wanted to do more than move from the instrument; he wanted to "move" on with his life and leave the specter of Anne Elliot behind. "I beg your pardon, Madam, this is your seat." He bowed quickly to her.

"No, Captain, please, do not let me disturb you." Anne's soft voice demonstrated her embarrassment at his studied politeness. She immediately drew back with a decided negative, but he was not to be induced to sit down again.

"I insist, Madam." He offered his arm to Henrietta, and the five of them walked away from her. Frederick seemed calm on the outside, but that short intercourse changed his reality. When the music began again, he shared the floor with the younger Hayter sister first, and then with Sophia, and finally with Henrietta. Throughout, his gaze sought Anne; it was impossible for him not to notice her eyes would sometimes fill with tears as she sat at the instrument. He observed her altered features, trying to trace in them the ruins of the face, which once charmed him.

"Miss Henrietta," he asked against his will, "does Miss Elliot never dance?"

"Oh! No, never, she quite gave up dancing. She had rather play. She never tires of playing."

The words shot through him. Anne never danced! How had that happened? Everything she loved about life was gone! Frederick shook his head in disbelief. His vivacious Anne took enjoyment in being employed for her family's pleasures—her life held no greater promise. Having loved him cost her in ways he never suspected.

∗   ∗   ∗

"It appears, Frederick, you no longer intend leaving for Shropshire," Sophia teased.

Frederick's eyebrow shot up in amusement. "Do you wish to be rid of me, Sister Dear?"

"You know better. Stay as long as you like. Benjamin enjoys your company; you remind him of his fond memories of his time at sea." She handed him a cup of tea. "Do you call at Uppercross today?"

He took a sip of the strong brew. "I have a standing invitation to do so daily."

"What occupies your time with the Musgroves?" Frederick knew Sophia wanted to know if he considered one of the Musgrove ladies as marriage material, but he made no such decision. For right now, he simply enjoyed the attractions of Uppercross. There was so much of friendliness, and of flattery, and of everything most bewitching in his reception there; the old were so hospitable, the young so agreeable, that he could not but resolve to remain where he was, and take all the charms and perfections of Edward's wife upon credit for a little longer.

"Charles enjoys his sport; we often hunt or shoot. I walk out with the Miss Musgroves; we walk into the village or visit at the Cottage. One sunny day we spent the afternoon at croquet—another at archery. The days are pleasant with like company." He paused before adding, "Their cousin Charles Hayter of Winthrop joined us for dinner last night."

"Really?" Sophia mused. "How did you find the curate?"

"His disquiet seemed out of place on such a homecoming. From what I understand Hayter was away a fortnight. The Musgroves seemed pleased he might discharge his curacy duties soon at Uppercross itself as Dr. Shirley's assistant. I wish Edward experienced such opportunities early on."

"Our brother paid the price of his choice of occupations, but now he seems well situated." Sophia refilled her tea. "Then I suppose you dine at Uppercross again this evening?"

Frederick smiled to himself. "I believe I will. He stood and returned his empty cup to the tray. "I take my leave now, Sophia, as soon as I change my waistcoat." She tilted her head up to receive the kiss he bent to bestow upon her cheek. He tapped her nose tenderly with his index finger. "And when I choose one of the Musgroves or another for my wife, you will be one of the first to know, my Love." He winked at her and then strode from the room.

*   *   *

"The ladies are all at the Cottage," Mrs. Musgrove told him when he presented himself at the Great House. "You are welcome to wait, Captain, but if I know my daughters, it will be some time. Mrs. Charles received a new book of fashion plates. I am sure Henrietta and Louisa are making plans for creating the latest fashions for their holiday dresses."

"Perhaps, Ma'am, I will walk to the Cottage and offer my services upon their return." He made a bow to excuse himself.

"That is an excellent idea, Captain Wentworth," she chucked as she picked up her embroidery. "Your presence will delight Henrietta and Louisa, I have no doubt."

Less than a quarter of an hour later, Frederick presented himself to the servant who answered the door at the Cottage and was immediately shown into the drawing room. Yet, he came up short, finding only Anne and Little Charles in the room. As he lay on the sofa, she tended the child, still recovering from his fall.

"Fred . . ." she caught herself. "Captain Wentworth, welcome, Sir." She offered him a quick curtsy.

Her near use of his Christian name deprived his manners of their usual composure: He started and could only say, "I thought the Miss Musgroves were here—Mrs. Musgrove told me this is where I might find them." Surprised at being almost alone with Anne Elliot, he walked to the window to recollect himself and to feel how he ought to behave. He braced his hands on the sill and focused his attention on the withered flowers of the garden.

Anne too stammered in embarrassment. "They are upstairs with my sister—they will be down in a few minutes, I dare say."

"Aunt Anne," Little Charles's voice called her to his side. "May I have some water?"

She busied herself with bringing the boy his water, cradling his head as he held his lips to the glass. "Let me rub your arms and legs; lying still so long is nearly as tiring as being outside, is it not, Sweetheart?" She began to gently massage his arms, working her way slowly down his limbs, offering the comfort of her touch and her attention.

Frederick remained at the window, but he knew good manners demanded he say something. "I hope the little boy is better." His words brought Anne's eyes to his; she smiled and nodded with his sincere sentiments. Anne continued her administrations to the child. He watched her caress the boy's cheek with the palm of her hand. The picture of the two of them together brought images of Anne with her own children—with their children. It was a likeness, which haunted him for years.

The sound of some other person crossing the little vestibule made Frederick pray to see Charles Musgrove. Instead, Charles Hayter stepped briskly into the room.

Anne looked up from where she tended the child. She stood briefly to offer the visitor a welcoming greeting and a curtsy. "How do you do?" she mumbled. "Will not you sit down? The others will be here presently." She looked tentatively at Frederick. "I believe you know, Captain Wentworth." She gestured to where Frederick stood and then knelt once more to the child.

It did not take Frederick long to determine Charles Hayter was probably not at all better pleased by the sight of him, than Frederick was by the sight of Anne. However, Frederick forced himself away from the window, apparently not ill disposed for conversation. He offered a quick bow and extended his hand to the man. "How do you do, Sir? It is pleasant to see you again."

Hayter just looked at Frederick's extended hand and made a curt bow. Instead, he spoke to Anne. "Miss Elliot, is Little Charles better?"

"I believe so," she answered from her seated position.

Then Hayter strode to the wing chair beside a waiting table and picked up the newspaper laying there, ignoring everyone else in the room. Frederick found Hayter's actions amusing in an offensive way. Having lived for many years in close quarters with other men, he sometimes forgot how rude landlubbers could be. He shrugged his shoulders and returned to the window, wondering how much longer he would have to wait for the Miss Musgroves. He suspected the ladies would make the gentlemen wait at least a quarter hour. It seemed to be the way of ladies, and secretly, Frederick enjoyed the ploy.

Deep in such thoughts, the addition of the youngest Musgrove child took him by surprise. Evidently, someone without opened the door for the boy. He scrambled to where Anne sat beside young Charles. "Aunt Anne," he called as he ran towards the sofa, "I am hungry."

"I am busy with your brother," she explained in an even voice. "Please ask Jemina to prepare you something, Walter."

The use of her father's name for the child peaked Frederick's curiosity, and he turned to take a look at the boy, Sir Walter's namesake. He was a remarkably stout, forward child of two years, and Frederick thought the boy would never be handsome. *"How ironic that will be for Sir Walter!"* he thought, chuckling with the idea. *"The man will blame the mix of the Musgrove heritage for any inadequacies the boy possesses."*

"But I want you to get it, Aunt Anne." The child began to pull at her hands and to try to get her to leave his brother.

She worked his chubby hands free from her sleeve. "You must wait then, Walter, until I finish helping Little Charles."

"I want to play," the boy whined. "Come play with me." Again, he latched onto her arm and pulled with all his might. Anne had to catch her weight with her hand or be pulled over.

"Walter, that is no way to get me to play with you. If you wait until your mother comes down with Aunt Henrietta and Aunt Louisa, I will happily take you outside to play, but I cannot leave your brother unattended." She spoke close to the child's face, trying to entreat him to be reasonable.

The boy stamped his feet, demanding she do as he said. Frederick thought the child looked like Sir Walter after all. "I want to play now!" he ordered while hopping onto her back.

"Get down, Walter," she insisted, pushing him successfully away.

Just as she turned back to the invalid, Little Walter had the great pleasure of getting upon her back again. "Get up, Horsey," he called close to her ear as he kicked Anne in the side. His arms clutched about her neck.

"Walter," she said more determinedly, "get down this moment. You are extremely troublesome. I am very angry with you." Anne tried to separate herself from the child.

"Leave her alone, Walter," Little Charles warned from his position. "Papa will be mad at you if you do not get down."

"Walter," cried Charles Hayter, "why do you not do as you are bid? Do you not hear your aunt speak? Come to me, Walter; come to cousin Charles."

Frederick waited for Charles Hayter to take some sort of action; after all, he was family and could step in to discipline the child if necessary. The boy, obviously, hurt Anne, as he continued to kick her in the side, pretending she was a pony to be ridden. She pushed at the boy, begging him to let her go. Hayter watched her struggle for a few moments and then returned to the paper. Frederick wanted to throttle the man. He did not know who needed a thrashing more—the child or Charles Hayter.

Anne bowed with the boy's weight upon her back and the strength of his grip about her neck. She struggled to remain upright, but the child's continued high-spirited wrangling forced her to her hands and knees. Frederick could take no more; he would not stand and watch her fight the humiliation of what her life held for her.

Before he thought what he did, he caught the boy by the nape of the neck with one hand, while prying away his arms from Anne's neck with the other. He spun around and forcibly placed the boy in a nearby chair. A warning stare told the child not to even consider moving. Then he advanced quietly to where Anne rested on her knees and forearms. Without saying a word to her, he leaned down and offered his hand. Unsteadily, she placed her delicate fingers in his gloved hand and rose to her feet. She never raised her eyes to him nor did she thank him; it was not necessary between them. He witnessed her mortification; Frederick would not amplify that with his words of concern. She nodded slightly and returned to her place by the boy on the sofa. A silence as thick as stuffed upholstery hung between them.

Frederick moved a chair next to Little Walter. Using the tone he might use to demand obedience from his crew, he leaned down to look in the child's face. "A gentleman *never* hurts a lady."

Hayter lowered his paper and reprimanded the boy also. "You ought to have minded *me*, Walter; I told you not to tease your aunt." With an obvious look of regret that Frederick did what he ought to have done himself, he buried his face behind the paper once more.

Frederick saw the boy's face twist in a pretense of crying. Whispering to the child, he kept up his warning. "Do not cry, Boy, unless you are truly sorry for what you do. A man must protect the women in his house; they will love and protect you in return. Never . . ." he leveled a cautionary look at the boy. "I will be most displeased to know you hurt your Aunt Anne again. Do you understand me, Walter?"

"Yes, Sir," the child's lower lip trembled, and he squirmed uncomfortably in his chair.

"Before you go to bed this evening, you will apologize to your aunt. Do I make myself clear, Child?" His words were spoken so softly anyone watching them would think he shared secrets to a buried treasure with the boy.

"Yes, Sir."

Clearing his throat audibly, Frederick took the child's hand. "Let us find your nurse," he said loud enough for the room to hear. "She will find you something to eat while you wait for your mother to come downstairs." He walked the child to the door and motioned for his nurse to take him. That done, Frederick returned to the silence of the window. Anne's singing softly to the child as she massaged his legs underlined the regret they all felt.

A few minutes later, Mary Musgrove and her husband's sisters swept into the room. "Oh, Captain Wentworth," she called as he made them a proper bow, "we did not realize you waited upon us, did we Henrietta?" She pushed the girl towards him when she spotted Charles Hayter rising from the chair in the far corner of the room. "Cousin Charles," she flicked a wrist in his direction, "you are here too." He gave them all a courtesy greeting while eyeing Henrietta suspiciously. "Please have a seat, Captain. Let me send for tea." Mary seated herself close to the hearth where she could rule over the room. Henrietta looked divided—she knew not to whom she should show her notice. "Henrietta, tell the Captain about what we decided to do for the holiday wardrobes."

Henrietta turned to speak to Frederick. As she did, Hayter moved forward to interrupt. "Henrietta, might I speak to you privately?" She looked up at him with second thoughts.

"Of course, Charles," she stumbled through the words. Then she turned to leave the room, and he followed her towards the garden.

"Well," Mary said with disgust. "I never saw such rudeness! But what is one to expect from those at Winthrop! He did not even pay proper due to those of us in the room."

"Mary," Anne broke the tension. "I will leave Little Charles in your care and check on Walter." Without waiting for her sister's agreement, she slipped from the room after offering them all a quick curtsy.

Frederick's eyes followed her. Like a child picking at a sore place, he needed to know she did not suffer from her predicament. "I came to walk you back to the Great House, Miss Musgrove." He forced a smile to his face as he finally turned to Louisa.

"Thank you, Captain." Louisa stepped forward to take his proffered arm. "That would be perfect." She smiled up at him with anticipation. "You will join us for dinner, will you not?"

"It would be my honor, Miss Musgrove." After the histrionics of the last few minutes, Frederick allowed his body to relax into the quickly developing familiarity of Louisa Musgrove's flirtations. "If you are ready, we will set off."

"I am thrilled, Captain."

*   *   *

"Should we let him stretch his legs?" Doctor Laraby swung into the cabin, making his morning call on Frederick Wentworth.

Anne Wentworth laughed lightly. Her husband hated the way they coddled him although he was still too weak to do anything for himself. "I am not sure the man appreciates our efforts." She reached out to bring Frederick's hand to her lips.

He turned his hand over in hers, letting his fingertips trace the line of her cheekbone. "I appreciate everything about you, Mrs. Wentworth." He let his eyes caress her face and mouth. "Have I told you today how much I love you?"

She turned her head to kiss his palm. "A few minutes ago, you spoke to Louisa in your dreams." An amused smile flitted across her face. She watched distress creep into his demeanor.

"I never thought of Louisa like that," he whispered so only she could hear. Anne moved to sit on the edge of his bed, leaning close, their lips only inches apart. "I love only you, Anne."

"I know that, Frederick. When I heard you call her by name in your sleep, I never thought you regretted our union. You are a man who allows me to be me—all my insecurities—all my strengths. You accept them all and love me for them. A man who gives such freedom to a woman does not dream of another." She kissed him tenderly, totally forgetting the doctor was in the room.

"I dreamed of finding you again; that is why Louisa was there, but she and James were meant to be as were you and I." He looked lovingly in her eyes, and a spark of desire flashed through them.

"In that case, Captain Wentworth," she brushed his lips with hers, "then you may dream of Louisa if it means you do so in pursuit of me."

He pulled her closer, letting her head rest on his chest. "You are unbelievable."

Anne closed her eyes and drank in his maleness. After a few infinitely long seconds, she swatted at his chest and sighed loudly. "Let us get you up, My Love. I want you strong and energetic once again." She leaned back from him and motioned to the doctor. "I will return soon; I want to freshen my things."

"Do not be gone long." He grabbed at her hand as she started away. "I miss you when you are not near."

"You cannot be rid of me that easily," she teased again. "You may count on that, my Love."

"I always count on your affections, Anne." He leaned back heavily against the pillow.

"Then do what the doctor suggests. Come back to me; I need you as you need me." She squeezed his hand before slipping out of the room.

Laraby took her place by his bed. "Let me see this wound," he stated as he moved Frederick's nightshirt aside. "I believe we might need to drain this one—the exit wound on the side. Infection seems to be a possibility." He worked the bandage loose. "You must be rubbing it somehow as you sleep; it looks raw." He pushed against the opening, forcing the skin together and squeezed the pus from around the stitches while Frederick gritted his teeth in pain. "I will clean this with soap and water when we are finished. A tincture should heal it up soon enough. We could use leeches if we need to—if the circulation becomes a problem."

"None of those nasty things if you please," Frederick protested. "How uncivilized are you, Laraby?"

"You may think the use of some ancient ways uncivilized, Wentworth, where I see medicine from the ancient cultures the basis of civilization. I have seen the healing ways of leeches and snake venom and Chinese ginseng and many other folk remedies. I will use any restorative that cures my patients without regard to what propriety says is proper." Laraby began to rebind the wound, making sure the bandages were tighter than before. "I do not want you pulling this open when we walk you today. Now let me get Avendale and Harwood. They are becoming quite adept at handling your great bulk as you maneuver across this room."

"When might I go up on deck? This room and this bunk seem to have shrunk since my men carried me in here." Frederick pushed up on his forearms before pivoting his legs to hang off the edge of the bed.

"Not for a few more days," Laraby cautioned. "Let us be rid of the infection first, and getting a pair of breeches and boots on would probably be best. You would look rather odd walking the decks in your nightshirt and bare feet."

"I hate it when you are right, Laraby; you know that, I suppose." Frederick planted his feet soundly on the floor and stood on his own. Yet, he waited for his crewmen before he attempted a step forward. He no longer clung to their shoulders or dragged his feet along the worn boards. Now, he used their arms for balance, and he lifted his feet gingerly, stepping higher than necessary each time he placed one foot in front of another.

"Making progress, I see," Anne stood posed by the door of his cabin, smiling beguilingly at him.

"I weave about almost as much as Benjamin driving a gig," he bemoaned.

She laughed lightly as she stepped into the room. "I recall your placing me in Benjamin's gig and leaving me to his care." Anne straightened the bed linens as he made his last tour of the room.

He looked over his shoulder at her. "You, Mrs. Wentworth, were exhausted. You staggered very like what I am doing at the moment. It was either Benjamin's gig, or I would have had to carry you the last mile to Uppercross Cottage, and at that time, we had no understanding between us. It would have been most improper to lift you into my arms in front of all your family and friends." She laughed at his teasing; it was a good sign, in her estimation, that he let his guard down in front of his men and the doctor.

She moved the blanket back as he made his way to the bed. Moving to the far side of the room, she pretended to straighten the items along his dresser while the men helped him prop himself up in the bed.

"We will see you later, Wentworth," Laraby called as he followed the men from the room.

"Tomorrow," Frederick said while leveling a look on the doctor.

Laraby nodded, shooting a quick glance at Anne's back. "Tomorrow morning." Then he was gone.

She remained still, running her fingers over his brush and the leather strap. "Anne?" His voice came softly behind her.

She did not turn to look at him. "Yes, Frederick?"

"Lock the door, My Love, and come lay next to me." His words sent a shiver down her back, and her palms began to sweat.

Anne turned to face him. "Frederick, we cannot. It is too soon."

"It is never too soon to hold my wife—the love of my life—in my arms. I need you next to me, Anne. I will rest better with your lying alongside of me, feeling the heat of your body radiating through me."

"Frederick," she gasped, blushing profusely.

He laughed lightly. "How nice it is to see my words still effect you, my Dear." Then he suddenly quieted, revealing his lack of confidence. "You will lay with me, Sweetling?"

She moved to lock the door. "I will lay with you, Frederick." Her eyes darkened with a passion he recognized only as being for him.

"Only your chemise, Anne." She reached back to undo the buttons of her gown, never taking her eyes from him. She let it drop from her shoulders to the floor before stepping out of it. Then she slipped under the blanket and turned into his embrace. He kissed the top of her head as he reached for the pins holding her hair. "You are so incredibly beautiful, my Love." He cupped her chin and brought her mouth to his for a long, lingering kiss.

"I should chastise you, Frederick." She snuggled in closer to him. "You accused me at not being supposed a good walker. I am offended." Her voice taunted, but her fingertips stroked his jaw line.

"But I never said any such thing," he defended before recapturing her mouth. "I simply wanted to protect the woman I love."

Chapter 8

When in disgrace with fortune and men's eyes,
I all alone beweep my outcast state,
And trouble deaf heaven with my bootless cries,
And look upon myself and curse my fate.
—William Shakespeare from "Sonnet 29"

"Why do you suppose I am not a good walker?" Mary bemoaned the obvious ruse of Louisa and Henrietta to be rid of her for the day.

"We will take a *long* walk—a very *long* walk."

"I should like to join you very much; I am very fond of a long walk." Mary insisted, always afraid they would experience some deference of which she may not be a part. Anne tried to dissuade Mary from going, but in vain; and that being the case, thought it best to accept the Miss Musgroves' much more cordial invitation to herself to go likewise.

Frederick and Charles returned from their hunt at that time. They took out a young dog, who spoilt their sport, and sent them back early.

"I wonder of what Mary complains now," Charles grumbled upon hearing her shrill voice from the entranceway.

"I cannot imagine why they should suppose I should not like a long walk!" She nearly stomped up the stairs. "Everybody is always supposing I am not a good walker! And yet they would not be pleased if we refused to join them. When people come in this manner on purpose to ask us, how can one say no?" She continued to lament to Anne as Charles and Frederick entered the passageway leading to the private quarters.

Frederick watched as Charles and Anne turned to each other and rolled their eyes before moving away to their own diversions. Surprisingly, Frederick found himself jealous of the private moment and of the intimate understanding they shared.

"Captain Wentworth," Louisa spotted him through the Cottage's open window. "It is such a very fine November day," she said as she approached, "that Henrietta and I propose to take a long walk. Would you consider joining us?"

"What say you, Charles? Do you have the time and the strength and the spirit to accompany the ladies on their journey?" Frederick noticed Anne's countenance changed, as if she wished to retract her agreement to walk out with them. *Did she wish not to be in his company?* He tired to read her reaction; he wanted to see her eyes; they spoke the truth when her words did not.

"I believe I am exactly ready for this walk," Charles added quickly. With that, the whole six set forward together in the direction chosen by the Miss Musgroves, who evidently considered the walk as under their guidance.

Frederick walked with Louisa and Henrietta, but his thoughts dwelled on Anne Elliot. As always, she lagged behind the others, placing herself in a subservient position, allowing the others to take precedence over her. In reality, he should be walking with her; she was the highest-ranking woman in the party and should assume her rightful place. His hand still burned from touching her; it was a week, but he could still feel it in his fingertips and his palm. Instinctively, he started to raise his arm to look at his hand, to discover the source of the sensation still lingering there, but, instead, he clenched it, fisting it at his side. To him, the fist represented the pain of their separation and the anger he felt from his perfidy. It also represented his anger with her for allowing her own degradation. Heaven help him, he could not stand by and see her suffer so.

Louisa, especially, prattled on as she walked beside him. He remarked to himself how quickly they all moved to an intimate footing. He wondered whether he should continue to pursue these relationships. Obviously, other women occasionally tempted him, but Frederick considered himself damaged goods. If he would choose one of the Musgrove girls as his wife, he would periodically be thrown into Anne's company. Treating one of the Miss Musgroves with respect and regard as his wife while Anne looked on no longer seemed a proper revenge. *Could I hurt her that way? Could I bring myself to touch another woman with Anne still so prominent in my life?* Maybe if she chose another, his conscience would be clearer, but now he thought better of it. Of late, he planned to move up the date when he would leave Kellynch and move on to a visit with Edward and his new wife. He felt a need to remove himself from Anne. He felt a need to be away from her and to decide what he must do about her. *Sorry* was the hardest word he knew, and, lately, *sorry* was all he felt. They were beyond talking about their situation. Neither of them could muster the desire to examine what they once had.

Louisa put forth for his notice once again. "It is a beautiful day, is it not, Captain?"

He looked about, forcing his attention to the scenery and to the girl walking beside him. "What glorious weather for the Admiral and my sister!" he said in passing conversation. "They meant to take a long drive this morning; perhaps we may hail them from some of these hills. They talked of coming into this side of the country. I wonder whereabouts they will upset today. Oh! It does happen very often, I assure you—but my sister makes nothing of it—she as lieve be tossed out as not."

"Ah! You make the most of it, I know," cried Louisa, "but if it were really so, I should do just the same in her place. If I loved a man as she loves the Admiral, I would be always with him, nothing should ever separate us, and I would rather be overturned by him, than driven safely by anybody else." She spoke with enthusiasm, trying to capture Frederick's exclusive attentions.

He knew she only said what she thought he wanted to hear; women placated to men in such a way. *"Yet, why not continue the flirtation?"* he thought. *"What else is there for me here?"* "Had you?" cried he, catching the same tone. "I honor you!" Unfortunately, his words brought him back to Anne; she allowed others to separate them. *Drat!* He could not even flirt with another woman without images of Anne playing across his memory. She treaded too close; he definitely needed distance between them, and he was not simply thinking of her current proximity to him on this walk.

"Is not this one of the ways to Winthrop?" he heard Anne ask, but nobody else heard, or, at least, nobody answered her. Her insignificance reigned; no one, except him, attended to her musings, and he held no idea whether Winthrop was near or not. At the time, he knew not whether Winthrop was the predetermined destination of the Miss Musgroves. But after another half mile of gradual ascent through large enclosures, where the ploughs at work, and the fresh-made path spoke the farmer, counteracting the sweets of poetical despondence, and meaning to have spring again, they gained the summit of the most considerable hill, which parted Uppercross and Winthrop, and soon commanded a full view of the latter, at the foot of the hill on the other side. Winthrop, without beauty and without dignity, was stretched before them—an indifferent house, standing low, and hemmed in by the barns and buildings of a farmyard.

He heard Mary exclaim in disgust. "Bless me! Here is Winthrop—I declare I had no idea!—Well, now I think we better turn back; I am excessively tired."

A family drama was about to play out in front of him, and Frederick was not sure he wanted to be a party to it. He turned his back on the scene, trying to divorce himself of the group's dynamics. He noticed out of the corner of his eye Anne too held back. He could tell she wanted to say something sensible to her younger sister, but she, literally, bit back her words.

"No," declared Charles Musgrove to his wife's avowal.

Louisa pulled Henrietta aside before she added her own, "No, no."

"We are this close," Charles continued, "and I will do what is proper—what is my duty—and call upon my aunt. Mamma would be terribly upset if I did not. You will accompany me, Mary." The statement came out as a plea for her acquiesces.

"I will not go, Charles." Her resolve strengthened by the audience watching their interplay.

"You may rest at Winthrop for a quarter hour while I pay my respects," her husband reasoned.

Mary took on a regal bearing. "Oh! No, indeed!—Walking up that hill again would do me more harm than any sitting down would do me good. I will not go."

After a little succession of these sorts of debates and consultations, it was settled between Charles and his two sisters, that he, and Henrietta, should just run down for a few minutes to see their aunt and cousins, while the rest of the party waited for them at the top of the hill. Frederick disapproved of how easily Charles Musgrove gave into his wife's lamentations. He wanted no such life for his own marriage; he would not tolerate such silliness from the woman he married.

At first, it appeared Louisa would accompany her siblings to the estate house, but she soon turned back to where he stood. Frederick allowed himself a moment of relief, having panicked at being alone with Anne and her sister and having to make conversation in the absence of the others. Along with Mary and Anne, he watched Louisa shoring up Henrietta's composure.

Despite the tension she caused, Mary was oblivious to how the others saw her, especially Frederick. Finally settling herself on a comfortable seat on the step of a stile, she took the opportunity of looking scornfully around her and saying to him, "It is very unpleasant, having such connections! But I assure you, I have never been in the house above twice in my life!"

Did she seriously believe he would consider her actions acceptable? Mary Musgrove treated the Hayters the way Sir Walter treated him—to a certain extent the way she—the way they all—treated her own sister. All he could offer her was an artificial assenting smile, followed by a contemptuous glance, as he turned away. If he spoke to her now, Mrs. Charles Musgrove would earn his wrath.

Luckily, Louisa reached him at that time. "Captain, may we gleam some nuts in the hedge-rows while we wait?" Walking away, he heard Anne try to pacify Mary's need to take precedence over them all. How he hated Anne being in such a position! It gnawed at him excessively.

Yet, he tried to give Louisa the attention she deserved. Forcing his conversation, he acknowledged, "That was quite a scene of *domestic tranquility!*"

"My brother Charles is too kind to his wife," she noted as she reached for a low hanging branch. "Mary lords her heritage upon all of us. It riles me to see her trying to supplant Mamma within her own house."

"I assume you sister planned to come here today." Thoughts of Charles Hayter's dislike of him became apparently clear.

"Henrietta and my Cousin Charles have held a long standing affection for each other. There was some doubt on both their parts of late. We resolved today that she would speak to him." Frederick smiled; it seemed Henrietta Musgrove gave him over to her sister; now he understood the lay of the land.

They walked on in silence for a few minutes, pausing occasionally to pick at the hazelnuts still remaining on the trees. Frederick finally noted, "It appeared for a few minutes your sister would acquiesce to Mrs. Charles's demands."

Louisa looked on incredulously. "I made her go, you know. I could not bear she should be frightened from the visit by such nonsense. What!—Would I be turned back from doing a thing I was determined to do, and I knew to be right, by the airs and interference of such a person?—Or, of any person I may say. No,—I have no idea of being so easily persuaded. When I make up my mind, I make it. And Henrietta seemed entirely to make up hers to call on Winthrop today—and yet, she was as near giving it up, out of nonsensical complaisance!"

Frederick remembered how Anne turned to Lady Russell for counsel, and that woman destroyed his hopes for a happy marriage. Would his life be so different if Anne had a sister possessing Louisa's sensibilities? He mused aloud, "She would have turned back then, but for you?"

"She would indeed. I am almost ashamed to say it." Louisa met his eyes and gave him a bold triumphant look.

Moved by his thoughts of what might have been with Anne, he spoke from his heart. "Happy for her, to have such a mind as yours at hand!—After the hints you gave just now, which did but confirm my own observations, the last time I was in company with him, I need not affect to have no comprehension of what is going on. I see more than a mere dutiful morning visit to your aunt was in question—and woe betide him, and her too, when it comes to things of consequence, when they are placed in circumstances, requiring fortitude and strength of mind, if she have not resolution enough to resist idle interference in such a trifle as this. Your sister is an amiable creature, but *yours* is the character of decision and firmness, I see. If you value her conduct or happiness, infuse as much of your own spirit into her, as you can. But this, no doubt, you have always done. It is the worst evil of too yielding and indecisive a character, that no influence over it can be depended on.—You are never sure of a good impression being durable. Everybody may sway it; let those who would be happy be firm." He was wrapped up in his fervor—all the memories of how Anne dashed his plans by succumbing to Lady Russell's advice occupied his mind. It never occurred to him his words would encourage Louisa's regard. He praised her for her resolve, not for herself, but for an example of what he wished for Anne.

He was on a bandwagon—he kept these thoughts secret for so long—he could not hide his passion. Frederick finally spoke his regrets out loud. "Here is a nut," said he, catching one down from an upper bough. "To exemplify—a beautiful glossy nut, which, blessed with original strength, outlived all the storms of autumn. Not a puncture, not a weak spot anywhere.—This nut," he continued, with playful solemnity, "while so many of it brethren fell and was trodden under foot, is still in possession of all the happiness a hazelnut can be supposed capable of." Then returning to his former earnest tone: "My first wish for all, whom I am interested in is they should be firm. If Louisa Musgrove would be beautiful and happy in her November of life, she will cherish all her present powers of mind."

Finished, he waited for Louisa to respond—waited for her confirmation or her refutation of what he said, but he remained unanswered. Louisa Musgrove did not possess the depth of intelligence, as did Anne; she could not conceive such advanced thoughts. She reacted to the serious warmth of his tone, but Frederick realized she did not understand the analogy he made. Choosing Louisa as his companion would mean a life where no one would challenge him—no one would see *him*—she would see only his wealth. Could such an existence bring him satisfaction? Realizing she could not offer a proper response, he dropped the nut to the ground, and knowing not what else to do, Frederick offered her his arm.

Relieved at his acceptance of her misunderstanding, Louisa gave him a full smile and then joined Frederick as they circled the hedgerow. They walked on in silence before they spotted Mrs. Charles sitting under a shady tree. Louisa nodded towards her brother's wife, letting her dismay show through her words. "Mary is good-natured enough in many respects, but she does sometimes provoke me excessively, by her nonsense and her pride—the Elliot pride. She has a great deal too much of the Elliot pride." Frederick nodded in agreement. "We do so wish Charles married Anne instead.—I suppose you know he wanted to marry Anne?"

Her words shot through Frederick. Nightmares where Anne and Charles walked away hand-in-hand haunted him for years after the separation. He swallowed hard, and after a moment's hesitation, said, "Do you mean she refused him?"

Loving gossip, Louisa chattered on. This was a subject upon which she could speak with authority. "Oh! Yes, certainly!"

He did not want to ask the question, but he could not resist the temptation. "When did that happen?"

Louisa smiled up at him, happy to have a conversation in which she could participate. "I do not exactly know, for Henrietta and I were at school at the time; but I believe about a year before he married Mary. I wish she accepted him. We should all like her a great deal better; and Papa and Mamma always think it was her great friend Lady Russell's doing, that she did not—they think Charles not be learned and bookish enough to please Lady Russell, and that, therefore, she persuaded Anne to refuse him."

"Lady Russell again," Frederick thought. Single-handedly, she twice ruined Anne's chances of happiness all in the name of love. How could the woman refuse Charles Musgrove as a legitimate suitor? He was amiable and kind, and more importantly, he could give Anne a fine estate in the country. The Musgroves lacked the Elliot lineage, but they were still a dominant element in the local society. Although he hated to admit it, Charles Musgrove would be a caring husband for *his Anne. His Anne!* Perhaps—an idea ricocheted through him—perhaps it was not Lady Russell's decision. Perhaps—Anne—*his Anne*—refused Charles Musgrove because of him. She would have been one and twenty by then. She would have been of age. *Was it possible?* He often wondered if he came to her in '08 before he took the *Laconia,* would she leave with him then? These facts suggested perhaps—perhaps she would.

He needed time alone to consider this possibility so Frederick was happy to see their whole party being immediately afterwards collected and once more in motion together. Charles Hayter, as expected, returned with Musgrove and Henrietta. This time he shook hands with Frederick—evidently, there was a withdrawing on the gentleman's side and a relenting on the lady's, and they were now very glad to be together again did not admit a doubt. They were devoted to each other almost from the first instant of their all setting forward for Uppercross.

Frederick noted all assumed Louisa was now marked for him. *Nothing can be plainer to everyone, including Anne,* he thought. How could he renew his addresses to her if she thought he favored another? And did he want to renew his addresses? He walked beside Louisa, but his heart took another path. Suddenly, every fiber of his being became aware of Anne. She was tired enough to be very glad of Charles's arm, and Frederick wished it was he to whom she turned. He hated when Charles abandoned her rather than ignoring Mary's lamentations of being ill-used.

They crossed a long strip of meadowland—forming distinct parties: Hayter and Henrietta, he and Louisa, Anne and Mary and sometimes Charles. Louisa continued to chatter on about the things that interested young girls, but her words meant little to him. He responded automatically, allowing her to think as she would. He should distance himself, but that was impossible now; it would have to wait until the next time.

"Help me down," Louisa demanded once she climbed to the top of the stile. He did so, but tried to set her some distance away from him when her feet touched the ground again. She purposely clung to his lapels longer than necessary, and he gently removed her hands before offering her his arm. Before he welcomed her interest, but now he saw how he must find a way to curtail her ardor.

The long meadow bordered a lane, which their footpath, at the end of it, was to cross. When the party all reached the gate of exit, they heard a carriage advancing in the same direction and looked up to see Admiral Croft's gig. Benjamin and Sophia took their intended drive and were returning home.

"How far did you walk, Frederick?" his sister inquired once they stopped.

He added casually, "The nearly two miles to Winthrop and back, I suppose."

"Two miles," Sophia gasped, "please let us offer one of the ladies a ride back to Uppercross."

"My sister will share her seat with any lady who might be particularly tired," Frederick announced to the group.

Henrietta looked about nervously; she would not leave Charles Hayter after the fuss she caused earlier. "It is less than a mile," she mumbled.

"I am not tired in any way," Louise offered, and to prove her point, she skipped in circles around her brother and Mary.

"I am fine," Mary protested.

Frederick knew enough to recognize Sophia offended Mrs. Charles by not asking Mary to ride before any of the others. He overheard Louisa whisper close by to Hayter, "Mary would not make a third in a one horse chaise. It is not grand enough for her."

At that moment, Anne stumbled up the stile to make her way across to the next field. He watched her delicate form struggle to maintain her balance. Without thinking, he motioned for the Admiral to stop his horse. Walking quickly to the carriage, he leaned in to speak to his sister before he could change his mind.

"What is it, Frederick?" Sophia looked around at the walking party crossing the lane and clamoring over an opposite stile.

"Take Miss Elliot," he whispered in her ear.

Sophia shot him a look of concern. "Are you sure, Frederick? You will center your attention on her?" She spoke so softly no one could hear.

"I have never been more sure of anything." They kept their counsel close and secret.

Sophia nodded and then raised her head to cry out, "Miss Elliot, I am sure *you* are tired. Do let us have the pleasure of taking you home. Here is excellent room for three, I assure you. If we were all like you, I believe we might sit four.—You must, indeed, you must."

Anne was still in the lane and instinctively began to decline. "I assure you, Mrs. Croft, I am well."

"Please, Miss Anne, humor an old man. You must let us be of service to you," the Admiral's kind urgency came in support of his wife's.

"That is very kind . . ." Frederick heard Anne begin, but he did not let her finish. He turned to her and quietly obliged her to be assisted into the carriage. One hand rested at the small of her back, and the other held hers tightly as he directed her to the gig. Beside it, he turned her to him and placed his hands at her waist.

"Frederick?" her mouth moved to say the word, but no sound came out.

A slight smile turned up the corners of his mouth. "Anne," he whispered close to her hair as he lifted her to the seat. Quickly, he looked away to lessen the attention of his actions. He watched his family compress themselves into the smallest possible space to leave her a corner. He did it. She was in the carriage, and he placed her there; his will and his hands did it. He recognized her fatigue when the others did not, and he resolved to give her rest. This little circumstance seemed the completion of all that went before. He understood her. He could not forgive her—but he could not be unfeeling.

Though condemning her for the past, still he could not see her suffer without the desire of giving her relief. It was the remainder of former sentiment; it was an impulse of pure, though unacknowledged, friendship. Emotions of compounded pleasure and pain still prevailed, but he still possessed a warm and amiable heart where Anne was concerned.

"Walk on," the Admiral clucked his tongue to encourage the horse before tapping its rear with his whip. Frederick stepped to the side to let them pass, and then he walked back to where the others stood. He chose not to turn around and acknowledge the pull Anne's presence had on him. If he looked back, he would likely chase down the gig, take her in his arms, and demand she love him once again. Instead, he fell into place beside Louisa to finish their walk back to Uppercross Cottage. Maybe when they got there, he would see Anne again before he returned to Kellynch. Maybe he could speak to her at last without the hurt crowding his heart.

*   *   *

"Do you want to explain what happened today?" Sophia asked as they sat together in the library after dinner. He knew she would ask eventually and wondered why she waited so long.

"There is nothing to explain; Miss Elliot was exhausted; I recognized her need." He tried to turn his attention back to the military history volume he grasped loosely in one hand.

Sophia paused for a long time before adding. "I observed your exchange with Miss Elliot. The others could not see because they were on the far side of the road, but I saw, Frederick."

"Leave it, Sophia," he warned.

"Benjamin and I thought you to be interested in the Miss Musgroves," she mused. His only response was a raised eyebrow; otherwise, he did not even raise his head. "The Admiral told Miss Elliot of our abbreviated courtship, claiming that is the way of sailors."

That captured his interest. "What was Miss Elliot's opinion of your conjectures?"

"In reality, she spoke very little, but that does not mean she did not make herself clear. The woman holds you in some regard. How long have you loved her?"

He frowned before finally answering, "I shall not honor that question with a response." He gritted his teeth and clamped his jaw shut.

Sophia laughed out loud. "That long, heh?"

"Please do not vocalize your unfounded accusations even to the Admiral, Sister Dear. Rumors spread too quickly in a country society." Frederick closed his book and walked to the fireplace, leaning his arm and forehead on the mantel as he stared into the flame.

"I will leave your heart to your own devices, Frederick, but, beware; I do not wish to see you hurt."

"Then you need to look the other way, Sophia. My heart is fairly bruised and battered already." With that, he strode from the room, leaving her to imagine the worst.

*   *   *

Mr. Steventon, the estate butler, tapped on the door of the morning room. Upon entering, he presented a silver salver to Frederick. "A letter for you, Captain."

Frederick's head snapped up as he took the thickly folded missive from the tray. "Thank you, Mr. Steventon," he stammered.

"Who is it, Frederick?" the Admiral called from his end of the table.

Frederick turned the bundle over in his hand, looking at the post. "The letter has been to Plymouth and back," he acknowledged out loud. "It is from Captain Harville."

"Open it, open it, Man; tell us where he has settled," the Admiral encouraged.

Frederick broke the wax seal to open the three closed drafted pages from Harville but written in Milly's hand. He sat quietly for a few minutes, perusing the first page. "Thomas has settled with his family at Lyme for the winter."

"Really?" Sophia added. "That is not far from here."

"How far, do you suppose?" Frederick spoke his thoughts aloud.

Sophia looked to Benjamin for specifics. "I would say a little short of twenty miles—by the sea—Lyme is a great port; Harville will like it there."

Frederick's eyebrows contracted in a frown. "What is it, Dear?" Sophia asked.

He still held the letter in front of him. "Milly Harville snuck in a few lines regarding the continuation of Thomas's deteriorating condition. He has not been in good health since receiving that severe wound to his leg two years ago." His jaw took on a hard line. He stood quickly and announced, "I believe I will go upstairs and pack a small bag; I will ride to Lyme today if neither of you have an objection to my borrowing one of the horses again."

"Of course not, Frederick," the Admiral assured him. "Stay a day or two with your old friend."

"Friends," Frederick corrected. "It seems Captain James Benwick has taken up residence with the Harvilles. He still grieves for Fanny Harville, no doubt, and finds solace in her brother's home."

Sophia caught his hand before he left the room. "Being away from Uppercross for a few days—placing distance between you and those in attendance there—is probably for the best—give you time to think."

"I know you mean well, Sophia, but it will be what it will be. I cannot manipulate it for my own will." He leaned down to kiss her cheek gently. "I will see you in a few days, my Dear."

Chapter 9

He who binds himself to a joy
Does the winged life destroy
But He who kisses the joy as it flies
Lives in Eternity's sunrise.
—*William Blake from "Eternity"*

Milly Harville rushed into the little room, wiping her hands on her apron as she came. "Frederick Wentworth, as I live and breathe," she called lightly as she embraced him. "Thomas will be delighted to see you; he bemoans the lack of your company. You received his letter?"

"I did." Frederick shot a quick look about the room, taking in its sparse offerings.

She followed his eyes with hers. "It is not much, but I insisted we economize until Thomas can find stable work." She gestured towards a comfortable chair while taking his hat and greatcoat.

"I am sorry, Milly; I did not mean to judge." Frederick took the seat to which she indicated.

"You do not judge, Frederick. You are Thomas's closest friend." She seated herself across from him. "I should not rush our greeting as such, but Thomas will arrive any moment, and I want to preface things for you before he comes."

"I am your servant, Milly." Frederick took a second longer look at their surroundings. "Tell me what I need to know; you must not stand on ceremony with me."

"Things have gone poorly for Thomas; a bad investment took a large chunk of his savings, plus his leg injury keeps him from productive work." Her words struck Frederick as if something sucked the air from his lungs. "Of course, Thomas's generous nature did not keep him from denying family and friends their loans. We are not destitute, but unless things change we could soon be."

"But Thomas took nearly ten thousand pounds with him when he left the service!" The concept of his friend losing so much astounded Frederick.

"I understand your dismay," she added softly. "Thomas never admits his weaknesses."

Before they could say more, they heard male voices in the entryway. Both stood to greet the men. "Thomas," Milly rushed forward to take her husband's hand and to discretely offer him steadiness as he stepped into the room, "look who came to visit!"

"Wentworth!" he exclaimed. "You were in my thoughts lately, and now you are in front of me." They shared a typical male hug, lightly embracing each other and pounding the other's back.

"Your letter found me, at last." Frederick grinned. "Actually, I am with Sophia and the Admiral in Somerset—twenty miles from here."

"You are so close!" Milly grabbed at his hands. "I did not realize."

Harville stepped to the side to allow the other man access to his guest. "Hello, Frederick," James Benwick stepped forward to take Thomas's place.

"Benwick, I did not realize you were with Thomas until I received his letter."

James Benwick shot a quick glance at Harville. "Thomas shows me a great kindness."

They shook hands as Milly began to hustle them into the room. "Come now," Milly encouraged, "let me find us all some tea and cakes. Thomas, would you check on the children before you sit down?" She rushed towards the kitchen.

"I will see to the children," Benwick nodded. "Join Wentworth by the fire, Thomas."

"Thank you, Benwick."

Thomas Harville slowly lowered his bulk into the nearby chair, balancing his weight on the cane he held in his left hand. Frederick waited before he resettled in an accompanying chair, anticipating Thomas's need for support. "I am so pleased to see you at last, Wentworth." An explosion of air escaped as he settled his limbs into the comfort of the cushions. "I have missed your dry wit. Benwick is not much of a conversationalist; what attracted my sister Fanny to him I will never understand."

"Love is not to be understood," Frederick mumbled in response. "Benwick has an intellectual attractiveness, and as I recall your dear Fanny could masquerade as a bluestocking if she came from more austere roots. She read voraciously; she and James found a companionable peace in each other."

Harville looked off as if seeing Fanny's face in his memory. "She possessed such a joy for living. Sometimes it is hard for me to believe she is no longer with us." With a slight shake of his head, he slowly returned his attention to his friend.

"How goes it with Benwick?" Frederick asked, letting his voice drop in case the man was close at hand.

Thomas glanced towards the door leading to the second story. "He grieves deeply." Harville searched for the right words. "He was always so bookish—depending on someone else's words to express his emotions so he does not say much. Milly and I agreed he needed to be with us. Truthfully, I feared, at first, he might try to find a watery grave so he might join Fanny for an eternity. I see some improvement since he came to us—I think, the children bring him a quiet joy—but, he needs so much more than what we can give him. He needs to find an occupation or a hobby or an interest to distract his mind—something besides the volumes of poetry he reads and rereads."

Frederick nodded, taking it all in. "When I delivered the news of Fanny's passing, I never saw such anguish in a man's face—I fully expected an apoplexy. For days, Benwick sat at that table—he did not move, literally. Often I walked to him and touched his shoulder to make sure he still breathed. No words—no tears—no anger—no nothing! I prepared myself for him to rail against the gods for dealing him such a fate—such irony, but he turned everything inward—his grief filled him, and then one day he took a step back to life. James returned to his duties, but even a casual observer could see he did so out of routine; his passion was gone."

"He occasionally comments on how he would not have survived the news if you were not with him. One day last week out of the blue, he up and says, 'If Wentworth were not there to watch over me, I could not let Fanny go.' Then he quoted some Shakespearean sonnet." Harville shook his head as if he did not understand the workings of James Benwick's mind.

"A man like Benwick—a reading man—does not soon forget the woman he loved." Wentworth whispered, as images of Anne Elliot crept back into his psyche. Even with all the years, he could not erase her from his mind.

"Nature surely played a foul trick on him and my sister." Harville stretched out his leg to relieve the stiffness seeping into his joints. "Just as Benwick earned enough money to give her a life of leisure, the good Lord took our Fanny away."

"Money cannot buy us happiness." Frederick thought about the fortune he now possessed and realized he, like Benwick, knew not the love of his life. Anne would always own his heart. Could he consider moving on with someone else? Should he try to rekindle what they once held in their hands?

If he knew for *sure* she would welcome his attentions, he would forgive her previous immaturity and build a life with Anne, but he could not survive if she turned him away again. Maybe he should begin to show her his true feelings in little ways, like he did with the Admiral's gig the other day, and see how she responds. If positive, he would risk it all—he would make Anne his.

"You seem well, Wentworth." Thomas attempted to change the subject.

Frederick smiled. "Sophia and the Admiral are excellent hosts. Except for the occasional hints towards marriage, it has been a pleasant sojourn. I still plan to visit Edward and his new wife in Shropshire soon."

"Your sister believes all naval men to be like the Admiral." Thomas chuckled. "Not all are as needy as he."

Frederick laughed lightly. "The Admiral is an astute military man, but he concedes other points in his life to Sophia. They complement each other well."

"Does Sophia wish you to return to the love you left behind in Somerset?" Harville watched Wentworth's face for a reaction.

"I have told you for years, Thomas, nothing happened in Somerset eight years ago!" Frederick said with a little more frustration than he cared to show to his best friend. Yet, he *might* still have a chance to right his shipwrecked life.

"That is what your words always say, Wentworth, but your face tells another story." Thomas gestured as if he would dismiss the subject. "How long can you stay? Please tell me it will be an extended visit."

"I am to disappoint you then; I have previous engagements at the end of the week, but your letter compelled me to come immediately. I return to Kellynch Hall late tomorrow."

Thomas looked dissatisfied. "I suppose we will make due."

Milly Harville entered the room at that instant, carrying a tray of teacups and a plate of finger cakes. "I hope you stay for dinner, Captain Wentworth," she offered as she placed the tray on a low table.

"I believe I will, Milly," Wentworth smiled up at her. "But I insist you all be my guests at the inn. That way you and the children can enjoy the evening along with us men. Let me give you an evening away from the kitchen."

"That will not be necessary, Captain," she started to protest.

"Milly, I did not say it was *necessary*," he insisted. "I said it would be my *pleasure* to entertain you for a change." Frederick turned to his friend. "Tell her, Thomas—remind your wife how often over the years she took care of you and me when we were deep in our cups. She deserves an evening without waiting on the two of us."

Thomas Harville let his eyes drift slowly over Milly, caressing her with his smile. "The man is right, my Love. You deserve more than life gave you." A note of sadness entered his words. "Let our friend thank you for being the most compassionate woman God ever created."

Milly leaned across him as she handed Thomas a cup of tea. Even with Wentworth looking on, she did not hesitate to show her husband affection. She cupped his chin with her free hand, raising it every so slightly so their eyes met. "Life gave me you and the children, Thomas. I would never ask for more."

Wentworth watched as Harville's eyes misted over. The man knew real love; as sparse as his surroundings might be, in many ways he was far richer than Frederick. Wentworth clapped his hands together as if finalizing a major transaction. "Excellent! We will be a lively party. I imagine at this time of the year in Lyme there is little of note. Am I right?"

"You are, Captain," replied Milly as she turned her attention away from her husband.

"Then the innkeeper will be happy to accommodate our reunion this evening. Let me send him word so he will prepare for us properly. I shall be right back." Wentworth stood and quickly moved to the door. Uncharacteristically, he looked back just in time to see Thomas Harville intertwine his fingers with his wife's, pulling her onto his lap for an embrace. The domestic picture increased Frederick's loneliness—what he would not give to know Anne as his friend knew Milly.

Returning to the Harvilles' dwelling after dinner, Frederick sat up late with Thomas, sipping weak ale, which he found only tolerable because of the company. "You have been quite industrious in making this place feel of home." Wentworth offered up a compliment. "Benwick pointed out the shelves you fashioned for his volumes of poetry; he praised you profusely for it. I see fruits of your labors spread throughout the house—a chair, a table, new netting needles and pins, the fishing net in the corner, toys for the children." Unconsciously, he picked up a Jacobs Ladder left behind by Harville's daughter when Milly carried the child to bed. Instinctively, he looked at the workmanship—the way the wood segments turned within the colorful grosgrain ribbon strips in an inexplicable illusion of simplicity. "I never understood how these things work," he said as he shoved the toy across the table to his friend.

Harville laughed lightly. "You no longer possess a child's imagination, my Friend. Here try the Bilbo Catcher instead." Thomas playfully tossed the ball attached to the string and adeptly caught it on the end of the spindle, balancing it there before releasing it to spin once again.

"You made all these?" Frederick moved to the wooden crate in the corner of the room. He took out toy after toy, laying them on the floor in front of the box, displaying a variety of cup and ball toys, dice games, tabletop ninepins, a whip top, solid wood grace hoops, a hammered lead musket ball whirligig, and several peg games.

"I spoil my children the only way I can." Harville offered up a sheepish grin. "I take scraps of wood and give them a new life."

Frederick spun one of the wooden hoops on his finger before placing everything carefully back into the box. "They are incredible!"

"The joy on my children's faces when I finish another design is priceless. Children are God's hope come to life—something set free—a fledgling—a seed drifting and taking roots." Harville saluted his friend with his tankard as Frederick returned to his seat. "Some day I hope to see you so blessed, Wentworth."

Frederick picked up his drink and gulped down the last of the bitter brew. "With that," he began as he wiped his mouth with the back of his hand, "I will bid you a good night." Wentworth turned to find his greatcoat and beaver.

"You will break your fast with us before you return to your sister's home?" Harville struggled to his feet to show Frederick to the door.

"It would be my honor, Thomas." Having donned his outerwear, Frederick turned to his friend. They clasped hands. "I will see you early, my Friend."

"Until the morrow, then . . . ."

Frederick reflected on his brief visit with Thomas Harville as he rode for Somersetshire. "He is blessed," he mumbled as he envisioned the happiness he saw in the faces of his friend's family. A sense of contentment spread through him as he thought of finally having his own home—his own wife—his own children. Where would Anne fit into that picture? He never imagined anyone else but her in his bed—at his side when he entered a room—taking meals at his table. Even after eight years, only she stirred his soul. "I must first distance myself from Louisa Musgrove. Anne must see my withdrawal for herself; otherwise, she will think I ill-used the girl to make her jealous. Anne would never tolerate such abuse," he reasoned aloud.

His thoughts returned to Harville's financial straits. A seed of an idea began last evening as he lay across the lumpy mattress of the inn's four-poster bed. Frederick purposely played with Thomas's children this morning; he wanted a closer look at the toys his friend made. The craftsmanship was evident in each piece. He had a plan, but he would tell no one until everything was in place. If he was right, Thomas could make a fair living with his hands. Frederick would send off a letter of inquiry as soon as he reached Kellynch.

*   *   *

"Wentworth," Charles Musgrove exclaimed as he entered the drawing room of the Great House, "you were missed, Sir!"

"I am sorry if I caused anyone at Uppercross a moment's concern." He offered his new friend a polite bow.

"It is of no consequence," Musgrove added quickly. "I am sure the ladies will be pleased to see you as well. They are all at the Cottage. Come along," he hastened the captain towards the door. "They will have my head if I let you get away without their receiving your call."

They walked the quarter mile to the Cottage with Musgrove prattling on about a new gun he hoped to purchase soon from a dealer in Bath. Frederick only half listened to the man. Truthfully, as much as he enjoyed Charles Musgrove's company, some days the man's obsession with hunting bored Frederick's sensibilities.

Obviously, someone in the Cottage noted their approach because the Miss Musgroves met them in the foyer. "Captain, for shame," Louisa chastised as she helped him remove his coat. "You sent us no word of your withdrawal."

"I apologize for any offense, Miss Musgrove." He moved past her in an urgency to see Anne again. He could not explain it even to himself, but after viewing Thomas Harville's domestic bliss, Frederick needed to see Anne was still here at Uppercross.

"Mrs. Musgrove," he acknowledged Mary, realizing not to make Anne feel her sister's ire for turning to her first. Then his eyes fell on her. "Miss Elliot," he said huskily as his gaze bid her eyes to meet his. "It is pleasant to see you still at Uppercross." He could say no more, but Frederick relished the slight blush overtaking her face as she stammered her thanks.

"Have a seat, Captain." Mary gestured to several chairs encircling the fireplace.

Frederick paused just long enough to determine where both Anne and Louisa planned to sit, and then he purposely took up one close to Anne. He forced his attention to everyone in the group, even when he would prefer to speak only to her.

"Will you tell us where you have been?" Louisa demanded as she poured tea for him.

Wentworth laughed lightly. "My manners were questionable, and I ask all of you to forgive me." He took the cup passed to him by Anne, allowing his fingers to briefly touch hers and relishing in the light flush of her cheeks. "My closest friend sent me a letter, and I rushed off to greet him."

"One of your Navy friends?" He heard Anne's soft voice ask the question before she looked away in embarrassment.

Frederick did not address her directly, but he responded to her prompt. "Captain Harville served with me for nearly eight years; he was my second in command on both the *Asp* and the *Laconia*. His letter tracked me to Plymouth and then finally to Kellynch. He is living in Lyme with his family and with another compatriot, a Captain James Benwick, who some time ago was first lieutenant of the *Laconia*. You may remember my mentioning them the night we dined with the Admiral and my sister."

Charles rolled his eyes up as if recalling the conversation. "Was it not Harville's family who sparked your sister's rebukes about women aboard a ship?" he teased.

"It was indeed." Wentworth made a point of catching Anne's attention. "I once believed women should not travel aboard a ship, but I thoroughly understand a man needs his wife with him." He hoped she honestly recognized his sentiments; he also hoped Louisa did not misinterpret his words as being meant for her.

"So you went to Lyme?" Henrietta added as she reached for one of the apple tarts brought in by a servant.

"I did, Miss Henrietta." Frederick purposely turned towards her. "You see Thomas Harville suffered a leg wound in a skirmish two years ago; he continues to languish from his wound although he never complains about his fate. I went to see for myself what I could do for my friend. He lost part of the fortune he accumulated along the way; I will not allow him to withdraw from society, and I will not tolerate his decline."

"Really, Captain Wentworth, you are to be praised for your loyalty," Louisa lauded. "Yet, you must realize what happens to Captain Harville is not your responsibility."

Frederick bristled at her words; she did not understand him at all. He started to respond, but Anne found her voice first. "Louisa, I believe, Captain Wentworth conveys the feelings of many men in the military. As we would rush to help someone in our own family, so would most soldiers and sailors. In times of war, they learn to depend upon each other—very much like a family. Besides, as the ship's commander, and as he did with your brother, I am sure Captain Wentworth feels responsible for all those who served under him." Frederick forced the smile from his lips. He always knew Anne would comprehend his need to serve others. God! He wasted so many years hating her when he could have been building a family with her.

"What is Lyme like, Captain?" Henrietta captured his attention away from Anne.

"It is a port city although the season and the weather is turning. Holiday travel to the shale beach slacks off this time of year, but I found the Cobb breathtaking in its wildness—its control of nature. It makes one feel very insignificant in the scope of things."

"I would love to walk along a beach," Louisa interjected. "It would be very adventurous to have the sea roll in around my feet." Frederick grimaced at her ploy to flirt with him. However, before he could dampen her forwardness, she turned to her older brother. "Charles, why do we not go to Lyme for a day trip? All of us could go, could we not?"

"How far is it to Lyme?" Henrietta questioned.

Charles Musgrove seemed to like the idea. "It is only seventeen miles—a few hours travel—we could go in the morning and return at night. What do you say, Wentworth? Should we all go to Lyme together?"

"We would be honored to meet your friends, Captain," Louisa looked hopeful, obviously thinking his friends could be her friends some day.

"I do not like the sea," Mary squelched their plans with her protest. "I am sure the sea air will exasperate my recent head cold."

"Then remain at Uppercross." Louisa's boldness silenced Mary for the time. "I am ready for a holiday; are you not, Anne?"

Anne looked away quickly. "I should remain behind," she stammered. "Lady Russell shall return soon, and we travel to Bath after Christmas."

"That is nonsense, Anne," Henrietta insisted. "Tell her, Charles; she must come with us."

"Of course, you must, Anne. You have done nothing but to help Mary and to tend to Little Charles since you came to visit. We owe you a day trip for all your kindness, and I will not hear of your remaining behind."

"It is not necessary . . ." she began, but Charles Musgrove would broker no withdrawal on her part. Frederick let out a jagged breath. If Anne did not go to Lyme, neither would he. He would not leave with Louisa and the Musgroves.

"I will arrange to use Papa's carriage for you ladies, and Wentworth and I may use the curricle." Charles took charge of the arrangements.

"When shall we leave?" Louisa looked pleased with how she manipulated the situation.

Musgrove thought about what his days might hold. "I plan to shoot with Anderson tomorrow; he has a new bitch, and he wishes to see how she trees. The season is nearly over, and I do not wish to miss the chance to go with him. We could go right after an early breakfast the day after tomorrow. How does that sound?"

Henrietta and Louisa loved the idea; however, Frederick showed less excitement. The only good thing would be a chance to speak to Anne more privately. He needed to gauge her reaction to his renewal. Sophia seemed to think Anne held him in some regard; he wanted to see that for himself. He would exploit every opportunity on this trip to approach Anne—to determine if she could accept him this time. If not, Frederick would be leaving for Shropshire soon; he would not offer for Louisa Musgrove.

*   *   *

Their first heedless scheme was to go in the morning and return at night, but to this Mr. Musgrove, for the sake of his horses, would not consent; and when it came to be rationally considered, a day in the middle of November would not leave much time for seeing a new place, after deducting seven hours, as the nature of the country required, for going and returning. They were consequently to stay the night there and not to be expected back until the next day's dinner. This was felt to be a considerable amendment; and though they all met at the Great House at rather an early breakfast hour and set off very punctually, it was so much past noon before the two carriages, Mr. Musgrove's coach containing the four ladies and Charles's curricle, in which he drove Captain Wentworth, were descending the long hill into Lyme.

"Will we never reach this God-forsaken place?" Mary bemoaned as they drew up beside her husband's two-wheeled carriage and paused before descending into the city.

Frederick heard Anne reassure her. "Not much longer; I could see the city as we circled around that last bend in the road."

Entering upon the still steeper street of the town itself, it was evident they would not have more than time for looking about them before the light and warmth of the day were gone.

"Finally," Mary grumbled as Charles helped her from the coach.

Luckily, for Frederick, he accepted first Henrietta and then Anne on his arm as they entered the inn. The innkeeper rushed forward, seeing Frederick again so soon. "Captain," he called and making a low bow, "you returned and brought friends."

"I did, Mr. Morris. I assume you can accommodate us for the evening."

"It will be my honor, Sir. How many room might you require, Captain?"

Frederick quickly conferred with Charles. "Four rooms, Mr. Morris. Let us register, and then you may send your man to bring in the luggage and to tend to the horses."

"Excellent, Captain." The man ushered them forward. "If you desire anything else you have only to ask."

"We will walk down to the beach before we lose the light, but first, we shall order dinner for later. Possibly, we could have a light supper before our walk. I am sure the ladies would enjoy some tea." Frederick beamed throughout this exchange. In reality, Mr. Morris should placate to Charles and Mary, but, he, obviously, saw Frederick as the superior member of the group. Even better, both Henrietta and Anne rested on his arms throughout the exchange. He could feel his chest fill with pride as he glanced down at Anne's soft lashes, shadowing the crest of her cheeks. Did she realize how much he still admired her and how right she felt on his arm?

After securing the accommodations and ordering their dinner, the next thing to be done was unquestionably to walk directly down to the sea. They were come too late in the year for any amusement or variety which Lyme, as a public place, might offer; the assembly rooms were shut up, and the lodgers almost all gone, scarcely any family but of the residents left—and, as there is nothing to admire in the buildings themselves, the remarkable situation of the town, the principal street almost hurrying into the water, the walk to the Cobb itself, its old wonders and new improvements, with the very beautiful line of cliffs stretching out to the east of the town, are what the stranger's eye will seek; and a very strange stranger it must be, who does not see charms in the immediate environs of Lyme, to make him wish to know it better.

The scenes in its neighborhood, Charmouth, with its high grounds and extensive sweeps of country and still more its sweet bay, backed by dark cliffs, where fragments of low rock among the sands make it the happiest spot for watching the flow of the tide, for sitting in unwearied contemplation—the woody varieties of the cheerful village of Up Lyme, and, above all, Pinny, with its green chasms between romantic rock, where the scattered forest trees and orchards of luxuriant growth declare that many a generation must have passed away since the first partial falling of the cliff prepared the ground for such a state, where a scene so wonderful and so lovely is exhibited as may more than equal any of the resembling scenes of the far-famed Isle of Wight: these places must be visited, and visited again, to make the worth of Lyme understood.

The party from Uppercross passing down by the now deserted and melancholy looking rooms, and still descending, soon found themselves on the seashore.

"It is so windy and so damp," Mary complained as they walked to the sea's edge. She refused to go near the water.

Louisa and Henrietta chased the tide in and out, just as small children might do. They giggled and laughed with joy of the novelty. Charles Musgrove walked out on one of the rocks littering the shoreline and pretended to cast a line from a rod into the sea. His sisters encouraged him to pull in a great whale on his imaginary line, and he bent to indicate the weight of the catch. The waves lapped about his high boots, keeping him safe from the water.

Frederick watched with some amusement; a person's first view of the sea spoke volumes about his personality and what he valued. With that in mind, he turned to find Anne. Like Musgrove, she stood alone on a rocky promontory, but she did not "play" with the sea. Instead, Anne Elliot closed her eyes and inhaled deeply; she leaned into the power of the ocean—allowing it to draw her into its grasp and hold her with its potency. Unlike the rush of water surrounding the others, the waves lapped at Anne's feet, never touching her slippers, but kissing her feet, nevertheless. She opened her eyes, and a smile captured the corners of her mouth, until, instinctively, she pursed her lips and offered the scene a gentle kiss, a caress—a gesture of pure awe.

Frederick stood mesmerized by her beauty and by her demonstration of the effect the sea had on her. He knew the feeling well, having experienced it on more than one occasion. The sea became a part of a person's soul, taking him into its depths and bringing him once again to the land. He saw that on Anne Elliot's face when he looked at her, and he knew, without a doubt, she could survive as his wife, accepting the dangers the sea offered, but never fearing them. Frederick found himself swallowing hard, trying to quiet the thud he heard resounding from his chest. "Not yet," he mumbled in warning as he pushed the desire away. "Soon," he mouthed the word as he turned to the others.

"Let us walk to the Cobb before we lose the light completely," he called to gather them once more and to quell the anxiety building in his chest.

They proceeded towards the stone breakwater wall bordering the harbor. "The sea will claim the wall one day," he added as they gaped wide-eyed at the structure. "It will allow nothing to stop its flow."

"May we walk along the top, Charles?" Louisa nearly whined.

He easily conceded, wanting to experience the power of the ocean himself. "At least part of the way." He led the group to the steps leading to the top of the sea wall.

"Charles, if you do not mind, I will leave you for a few minutes. I wish to let Captain Harville know I returned."

"Of course, Wentworth, take as long as you need. If we finish before you complete your visit, we will meet you back at the inn."

"I shall not be long." With that, they watched as Frederick turned into a small house near the foot of an old pier of unknown date. The others walked on with the assurance he was to join them on the Cobb.

Chapter 10

I ne'er was struck before that hour
With love so sudden and so sweet
Her face it bloomed like a sweet flower
And stole my heart away complete.
—John Clare from "First Love"

"Wentworth, you returned," Harville called out to his friend as he hobbled into the room, having been summoned by his wife.

"I have, Thomas." They shook hands. "My new acquaintances upon hearing my description of Lyme wished most profusely to partake of it on their own. We came for a day trip, which will extend into tomorrow morning so we might properly rest the horses."

"And where are these *new* acquaintances?" Thomas tried to peer over Frederick's shoulder, expecting to see strangers on his doorstep.

"They are walking along the Cobb."

Milly joined the two of them, having checked on the children first. "How many are in your party, Captain?"

"There are six, counting myself. Four ladies and two gentlemen."

"Ladies?" She looked happy with the news.

"My Milly misses the companionship of other women," Thomas informed him. "I fear Benwick and I bore her with tales of the *Laconia.*"

Milly Harville slapped him on the arm, feigning being insulted. "That is so untrue," she protested, but a grin quickly overspread her face. "I love hearing you two speak of your time together—even if you share it for the twentieth time."

"I believe you wound me, my Dear." Thomas caught her hand and brought the back of it to his lips. "Come, Wentworth." He chuckled as he turned back to his friend. "I must find an audience for my retellings who would more appreciate them."

"We will all go." Milly reached for her cloak.

Wentworth asked, "You too, Benwick?"

"Of course." James Benwick rose to join them.

The Uppercross party walked nearly to the end of the Cobb before turning back towards the inn. They discovered Captain Wentworth leading three companions, all well known already by description. Meeting at last, Wentworth made the appropriate introductions. Everyone talked over each other, trying to extend the acquaintances. Milly bubbled with excitement, especially enjoying the enthusiasm of the Miss Musgroves.

Frederick watched carefully as the group interacted. All three Musgroves gushed with meeting the Harvilles and Benwick. Less affected by class, they welcomed the connections because of Wentworth's warm praise of each of them. Mary Musgrove acknowledged the trio but made little effort to create an accepting atmosphere.

Frederick noted all their exchanges, but it was upon Anne his attention rested. She seemed to struggle against the meeting, and that bothered him. Of course, he expected Mary to disdain the group, but he did not anticipate a like action from Anne. Yet, as she stood there, Frederick watched her withdraw from the group. *Why?* he thought. If they married, these would have been all her friends. Anger crept into his bearing. *How dare she judge them?* Less than an hour ago he considered renewing his attentions, but now he wondered could she adjust. He started to turn away from her, but, unpredictably, Anne lifted her chin, and Frederick gazed into her eyes—pools misted over—eyes blinking back a lone tear cascading down her cheek. Anne dropped her chin, letting her bonnet hide what only Frederick saw. He froze, his heart fighting for air. *Why did she cry?* Did Anne, like him, realize this could be their life—a seaport—his comrades—other naval wives? Frederick swallowed hard, fighting to keep his emotions in check.

"Please, you must come to our home." He heard Milly Harville offer the invitation.

"That would be most pleasant," Anne said before turning to Musgrove. "I am sure Mary would like a few moments to warm up, do you not agree, Charles?" Wentworth smiled at how she manipulated both sister and her brother-in-law, not allowing Mrs. Charles to speak disparagingly about the arrangement.

"Of course, Anne—an excellent idea." Charles began to usher everyone along. "Follow Mrs. Harville."

Stepping into the space, Frederick wondered what the others must think. Only those who invite from the heart could think rooms so small capable of accommodating so many. Yet, he listened as Anne, Louisa, Henrietta, and Charles all commented on the pleasanter feelings, which sprang forth from the sight of all the ingenious contrivances and nice arrangements of Captain Harville to turn the actual space to the best possible account, to supply the deficiencies of lodging-house furniture. Milly praised Thomas's ingenuity in the varieties in the fitting-up of the rooms, where the common necessaries provided by the owner, in the common indifferent plight, were contrasted with some few articles of a rare species of wood, excellently worked up, and with something curious and valuable from all the distant countries Frederick and Harville visited.

"One would not believe how talented my Thomas is!" Milly Harville gushed as she set up a tea tray for everyone.

"Look at these," Wentworth indicated the toy chest. "Harville made all these." He handed a few of them to Anne and Louisa.

Louisa immediately tried to catch the ball in the cup while Anne examined the craftsmanship found in the Jacobs Ladder. "These are exceptional, Captain Harville," she added as she returned the toy to the box.

Thomas looked a bit uncomfortable with all the praise. "My injury prevents me from taking much exercise, but I have a mind of usefulness, and a bit of ingenuity furnishes me with constant employment. If I find nothing else to do, I set down to that large fishing net in the corner."

Several of the group giggled at noticing the items he pointed out. "I wish I were as talented," Charles Musgrove noted.

The group enjoyed their tea, but time came for them to return to the inn. "Are you sure, Captain, we cannot convince you to join us for dinner?" Milly Harville busied herself by collecting the teacups and plates.

"We could not so impose, Mrs. Harville," Mary added with polite disdain.

Frederick forced himself to not show his own contempt for Mrs. Charles's behavior. "We ordered dinner, Milly. Mrs. Morris would be upset if we declined to eat at the inn after putting her to so much trouble."

"Of course." Her disappointment showed.

Frederick touched her hand. "We will see each other tomorrow before we leave for Uppercross."

"I shall come for a visit after dinner," Thomas added, "if that is acceptable to all. I still have all those stories to tell about Frederick, after all."

"Please do, Captain," Louisa encouraged. "We all want to be regaled with tales of Captain Wentworth." She batted her eyes as she looked up at Frederick. At first, he pretended not to notice, but she walked to where he stood and took his arm as if he offered it to her. "The Captain quickly became one of our favorite people."

Frederick felt his skin crawl with Louisa's touch. He wanted to put distance between them—to reestablish a connection to Anne. He forced a smile to his face; he would walk with Louisa to the inn, but he would take more care not to be caught in her attentions again.

"So tell us, Captain, what is the story with James Benwick? He is so melancholy." Louisa nearly snarled her nose in remembrance.

Frederick put down his knife and fork. "I believe I told you previously Captain Benwick lost his fiancé. He was engaged to Captain Harville's sister and now mourns her loss. They were a year or two waiting for fortune and promotion. Fortune came, his prize-money as lieutenant being great—promotion, too, came at *last,* but Fanny Harville did not live to know it. She died last summer while he was at sea. I do not believe it possible for a man to be more attached to a woman than poor Benwick was to Fanny Harville or to be more deeply afflicted under the dreadful change. His disposition is as of the sort that must suffer heavily—uniting very strong feelings with quiet, serious, and retiring manners and a decided taste for reading and sedentary pursuits. The friendship between him and the Harvilles seem, if possible, augmented by the event, which closed all their views of alliance. Captain Benwick now lives with them entirely. I believe the quiet solitude of Lyme in winter exactly adapted to Captain Benwick's state of mind."

"Oh, the poor man," Henrietta spoke her thoughts aloud.

Louisa conceded, "I suppose he has a right to his sadness."

Frederick nodded in agreement. "He is young, and, I believe, Benwick will rally again and be happy with another, although it will be some time. Because he never had an opportunity to renew his addresses to Fanny, he will eventually seek another, but I cannot imagine his doing so at the moment." His attention rested on Anne's face. *What would he do if he returned to Somerset to find her passing?* He often thought of losing Anne to another, but Frederick never considered she would not survive something as common as a fever. A shiver ran down his spine as he reflected on the time he wasted.

Anne acknowledged to everyone's agreement, "I doubt the good Captain will join us: Captain Benwick has all the appearance of being oppressed by the presence of so many strangers."

The words no more escaped her lips when the Captains Harville and Benwick appeared in the doorway of the private dining room. "Well, look who is here," Charles called out rather loudly, assuring no one else would speak of Benwick within his hearing. The group split, allowing the two newcomers a chance to take center stage.

At first, both men sat with the entire group, but as the evening progressed Frederick watched James Benwick withdraw both physically and mentally from the gathering. To Frederick's chagrin, the very good impulse of Anne's nature obliged her to begin an acquaintance with Benwick, seating herself beside him and devoting her conversation to him. Frederick instead wanted her to hear of his exploits—his successes—to appreciate how close he came to death and how hard he worked to achieve respectability.

"Did you tell them about Copenhagen?" Captain Harville asked as he launched into another story of their service together. Frederick shook his head in the negative, but his eyes and ears still searched the corner where Anne sat with Benwick.

He strained to hear what they shared. Their heads bent together in tight conversation; Frederick noted Benwick's shyness and his disposal to abstraction faded as the engaging mildness of her countenance and the gentleness of her manners soon had their effect, and Anne was well repaid the first trouble of exertion. Despite twinges of jealousy coursing through his veins, Frederick could not help but to smile with the knowledge *his Anne* could reach the unreachable. Frederick picked up snippets of what they said to each other.

"You have no idea, Miss Elliot, how pleasurable it is to speak to someone as knowledgeable as you." Benwick's shyness existed on a different level now.

Anne smiled briefly at him. "I, too, am a connoisseur of good poetry, Captain, but I remind you of the duty and benefit of struggling against affliction."

"Oh, Miss Elliot, a man could not feel such remorse in your presence." Benwick said the words with such passion that Anne blushed. That jealous pang shot through Frederick again, and he forced the ache from his throat. Looking back at them, Frederick took some delight in watching the redness spread even if it came from another man's attention. A woman in a full blush was exquisite, and he recalled speaking words of endearment to Anne simply to achieve that same reaction. The thoughts brought him an "unusual" contentment.

"Did you really eat caviar three times a day?" Louisa's words pulled him into the conversation at hand.

"I was not about to turn over such delicacies to Prinny," he declared, and the group laughed lightly. "Every man on board developed a taste for fish eggs. The French love the dish, but, personally, I quickly tired of its novelty."

"What other French foods have you tasted?" Louisa inquired.

Harville answered for him, and Frederick only half heard the gasps as Thomas described escargot.

"Snails!" Mary Musgrove reacted before she could recover her composure.

By dividing his attention, he filtered out the Musgrove conversation and concentrated once more on what Benwick said to Anne. "Do you prefer Sir Walter Scott's 'Marmion' or 'The Lady of the Lake'?"

Anne laughed lightly. "Obviously, the Lady."

"A true romantic at heart." Benwick's gentle gaze rested on Anne's face, and Frederick felt the green-eyed monster all over again. The tenor of his friend's voice softened as he began to repeat Scott's words:

> Hark! As my lingering footsteps slow retire,
> Some spirit of the Air has waked thy string!
> 'Tis now a seraph bold, with touch of fire,
> 'Tis now the brush of Fairy's frolic wing.
> Receding now, the dying numbers ring
> Fainter and fainter down the rugged dell;
> And now the mountain breezes scarcely bring
> A wandering witch-note of the distant spell—
> And now, 'tis silent all!—Enchantress, fare thee well!

How dare he? Frederick thought with an unspoken degree of incredulity. The man repeated love poetry to *his Anne,* the only woman he ever loved. He once saved Benwick's life, and he was the one who gave the man comfort when Benwick found out about Fanny Harville. *And what of Fanny?* Would he push her memory to the side and welcome Anne into his heart?

"You captured Scott's tenderness, Captain." Anne offered him an enchanting smile. "And what of Lord Byron? Do you prefer 'Giaour' or 'The Bride of Abydos'?"

Again, Benwick fell into the rhythm of the poem.

> Burst forth in one wild cry—an all was still.
> Peace to thy broken heart, and virgin grave!
> Ah! Happy! but of life to lose the worst!
> That grief-though deep—though fatal—was thy first!

Anne looked concerned. "Captain, you must not let the hopeless agony consume your thoughts. May I recommend a larger allowance of prose in your daily study?"

"I loved Fanny Harville, Miss Elliot. You cannot know my pain—my despair," he offered, trying to justify his preoccupation with poetry.

Anne pulled herself upright. "I preach patience and resignation, Captain, because, I, too, suffered the pains of lost love, and I wish most desperately someone offered me such solace."

Had he heard her correctly? Frederick felt his heart would break; his departure hurt Anne as much as it hurt him. He knew she spoke of their love, for without a doubt, Anne once loved him. When he left that day eight years ago, she still desired him as much as he desired her. After that, Frederick heard nothing either group said. He was lost to his own thoughts. Finally, Louisa Musgrove and the others demanded his undivided attention. For once, Frederick was happy to divine her with his tales; he did not want to think anymore about Anne Elliot and their lost love. All he really wanted was to escape to his own room and replay every word spoken and not spoken today.

"Captain, you really must go with me." Louisa snuggled into his arm. "I thought we might take a stroll before breakfast."

"Should we not wait for the rest of our party?" Frederick purposely stepped away from her, pretending to look towards the stairway to see if Anne or the others might be about.

Louisa sashayed towards him, deliberately swaying her hips in an exaggerated manner. "Henrietta wanted to speak to Anne privately about pleading for Lady Russell's help in securing a position for our cousin Charles. They left a quarter hour ago, and, of course, Mary will not be up for, at least, another hour."

"Then maybe we should find them." Frederick started towards the door, avoiding offering her his arm. He would walk with Louisa, but he would not encourage her. During the night, he thought it best to make Anne aware of his constancy. Somehow he must find a way to speak again of his love.

They walked less than a quarter mile down to the sea where they met Henrietta and Anne returning. The women went to the sands to watch the flowing of the tide. Frederick regretted he did not join them. He would like to tell Anne about the tide—how a fine southeasterly breeze was bringing it in with all the grandeur, which so flat a shore admitted. He would teach her to praise the morning, to glory in the sea, to sympathize in the delight of the fresh—feeling breeze—and to be silent, just as she was yesterday—silent, and let the world come to her.

Breaking his concentration—his thoughts of Anne—he heard Louisa nearly squeal, "I wanted to buy a new fan for Mamma. We must go back towards town. After breakfast we will be leaving, and there will be no time."

"Certainly," Anne added quickly. "Mrs. Musgrove will be quite pleased with your thoughtfulness."

Frederick watched as Louisa beamed with praise, playing the grown up role bestowed upon her by Anne. Crossing the last of the shoreline, they prepared to climb the steps leading upwards from the beach to the top of the seawall and the path into town. Just as they reached the steps, a gentleman at the same moment preparing to come down, politely drew back and stopped to give them way. They ascended and passed him, and as they passed, Anne's face caught his eye, and he looked at her with a degree of earnest admiration.

Frederick, having gone up the steps first, stood braced near the top, waiting to help each of the ladies over the last step and to safety. Louisa, always taking precedence, waited for the others, and Frederick held Henrietta's hand to steady her footing when he saw the look in the man's eye as he beheld Anne. Frederick allowed himself to look at Anne, something he tried not to do when they were so close to each other. She still held a magical charm where he was concerned, and he could not resist the urge to take her in his arms and kiss her until she remembered only him. More than once over the past fortnight images of tossing Anne in a private carriage and taking her directly to Gretna Green played through his mind. Now he realized she was looking remarkably well; her very regular, very pretty features, having the bloom and freshness of youth restored by the fine wind, which had been blowing on her complexion, and by the animation of eye, which it also produced.

It was evident that the gentleman, completely a gentleman in manner, admired her exceedingly. Realizing the man's intent, Wentworth looked around at her instantly in a way that showed his noticing it. *First Benwick and now a complete stranger!* Frederick quickly summed up the situation. If he did not make a move soon, Anne might assume he was intended for Louisa and take up with someone else. She had a right to happiness, but only if her happiness came through him. *I cannot lose her again!* he thought, although as quickly as the thought came, he amended it—knowing at the moment Anne Elliot was not his to lose. What was worse was Anne noted the man's interest, and she gifted him with a beguiling smile. Frederick wanted to grab the cad's cravat and throw him from the steps like a rag doll into the sea. Finally, Anne reached him, and as Frederick took her hand to steady her way as he did the others, he could not resist giving hers a gentle squeeze and stroking the inside of her wrist with his index finger. A slight blush radiated from her, and Frederick basked in her heat. She refused to make eye contact with him, but he did not care. He elicited a response from Anne and was repaid for the effort.

After attending Louisa through her business and loitering about a little longer, they returned to the inn. Frederick noted upon their return that the gentleman in question was also staying at the inn. A well-looking groom strolled about the area, and like the man on the steps, the servant was in mourning. The knowledge Anne might see the stranger again vexed Frederick; he could not risk their forming an acquaintance. Feeling a bit overwhelmed with how quickly things changed and how little control he had over the situation, Frederick resolved to make an immediate move. He would ask to speak to Anne privately, and he would explain he was foolish in thinking he could forget her. He would explain he would not want to hurt Louisa Musgrove or affect Anne's relationship with the Musgrove family, so he would travel to Shropshire and spend time with Edward in order to weaken the girl's expectations. He would reason that with Anne's returning to Lady Russell's home, it might not be best for him to call upon her at this time, but he would seek her permission to do so when she retired to Bath with her family. He would let her know he hoped to regain her regard.

Happy with the decision, Frederick waited impatiently in the main hallway for Anne to come down to breakfast. Finally, he heard her light tread on the landing. Blood rushed to his ears, and he could briefly hear only the beat of his own heart. Then a heavy thud—one of a door closing nearby—mixed with the approach of Anne's footsteps. Frederick did not mean to eavesdrop, but the voices rang clear as he moved instinctively into the shadows.

"Pardon me," the man responded automatically to Anne's small gasp of surprise. Then an elongated silence told Frederick they partook of each other's countenances. "It seems, Miss, I am to plague you with my presence." Frederick knew instantly it was the man from the beach, and he stifled a moan of disbelief.

"It is perfectly all right, Sir," Anne's voice danced with excitement. "You simply frightened me momentarily; my heart you gave a start." Frederick realized Anne did not flirt with the man; she told him the truth: He startled her. Yet, the tone of the words might make the stranger think otherwise.

"My apologies, my good Lady." Frederick imagined the gentleman doffed his hat with these words. "I will not have you fear me in any way, and, confidentially, the fact I affected your heart pleases me."

Frederick waited for Anne to give the man the proper sit down he so rightfully deserved for being so forward, but to his amazement, she did not do so. "You are too bold, Sir," she replied automatically. "Now, if you will excuse me." With that, Frederick heard her step away from the unfamiliar guest. He could not approach Anne now; the unknown gentleman over spoke; Frederick could not follow that man's interests with those of his own. Anne would find his words an imposition. He would wait until they prepared to load the coaches; in the midst of the chaos of packing so many bags, he would take her into the private dining room and plead his case. Before she could see Frederick there in the shadows, he moved quickly away. He was at the sidebar filling a plate when Anne entered the dining room.

They nearly finished with breakfast when the sound of a carriage, almost the first they heard since entering Lyme drew half the party to the window. Henrietta called out, "It is a gentleman's carriage—a curricle—but it is only coming round from the stable yard to the front. Somebody must be going away.—Look, it is driven by a servant in mourning."

"A curricle, you say?" Charles Musgrove jumped up, hoping to compare the one outside to his own.

By now, they all stared out the window at the carriage. Frederick had no intention of spying on the personage, but when Anne moved to see what was without, he moved too. He knew the curricle belonged to the stranger. There could not be two gentlemen in mourning staying at the same inn. He would make it a point to stand close to Anne when she viewed the stranger again. So the whole six were collected to look by the time the owner of the curricle was seen issuing forth from the door amidst the bows and civilities of the household and taking his seat to drive off.

Wentworth half glanced at Anne. "Ah, it is the very man we passed." He waited to see Anne's reaction, but she turned away to the sidebar once more before he could ascertain her feelings.

"I believe you are right, Captain," Henrietta confirmed and then kindly watched the man as far up the hill as she could.

"I wonder who he was," Mary Musgrove mused as she refilled her plate.

At that moment, the waiter came into the room. "Pray," said Wentworth, "can you tell us the name of the gentleman who is just gone away?"

"Yes, Sir, a Mr. Elliot, a gentleman of large fortune—came in last night from Sidmouth—dare say you heard the carriage, Sir, while you were at dinner—going on now for Crewkherne, in his way to Bath and London."

"Elliot!" Louisa gasped.

Charles returned to the window for a second look. "Did he say Elliot?"

"Bless me!" cried Mary. "It must be our cousin—it must be our Mr. Elliot; it must, indeed!—Charles, Anne, must not it? In mourning, you see, just as our Mr. Elliot must be. How very extraordinary! In the very same inn with us! Anne, must not it be our Mr. Elliot, my father's next heir?" Turning to the waiter, she continued, "Pray, Sir, did not you hear—did not his servant say whether he belonged to the Kellynch family?"

"No, Ma'am, he did not mention no particular family, but he said his master was a very rich gentleman and would be a baronet some day."

"There! You see!" cried Mary, in an ecstasy. "Just as I said! Heir to Sir Walter Elliot!—I was sure that would come out if it were so. Depend upon it—that is a circumstance, which his servants take care to publish wherever he goes. But, Anne, only conceive how extraordinary!" Mary nearly pulled Anne from her seat. "I wish I looked at him more. I wish we had been aware in time, who it was, that he might have been introduced to us. What a pity that we should not have been introduced to each other!—Do you think he had the Elliot countenance? I hardly looked at him; I was looking at the horses, but I think he had something of the Elliot countenance." She now paced the floor, trying to organize her thoughts. "I wonder the arms did not strike me! Oh!—the great-coat was hanging over the panel and hid the arms; so it did, otherwise, I am sure, I should have observed them and the livery too; if the servant had not been in mourning, one should have known him by the livery."

"Of course, we all would," Charles assured his wife.

"We saw him briefly on the steps to the beach," Louisa added, trying to draw the attention back to her.

When she could command Mary's attention, Anne quietly observed, "Mary, Father would not wish us to renew an acquaintance with Mr. Elliot. Father and Mr. Elliot have not for many years been on such terms as to make the power of attempting an introduction at all desirable."

Frederick wondered if Anne now regretted her interaction with the stranger. Obviously, she did not intend on sharing her recent conversation with Mr. Elliot with anyone else. With the competition out of the way, Frederick felt secure—a return of his regard for her would now be warmly welcomed. Therefore, when he spoke next, he did so with some sarcasm in his voice. "Putting all these very extraordinary circumstances together, we must consider it to be the arrangement of Providence, that you should not be introduced to your cousin."

Mary Musgrove ignored Frederick's remark. "Of course," said Mary to Anne, "you will mention our seeing Mr. Elliot the next time you write to Bath. I think my father certainly ought to hear of it; do mention all to him."

"Mary, I will not bring such news to our father; you may write him if you choose, but I shall not be the bearer of such tidings. You were away at school through much of Father's dealings with Mr. Elliot. I know the offense offered our father, and I suspect Elizabeth's particular share in it. The idea of Mr. Elliot always produces irritation in both."

"Do not be silly, Anne." Mary disregarded her sister. "Prior to the man's arrival at an assembly or a holiday soiree, Father would want news of Mr. Elliot's appearance in Bath if our cousin truly plans to travel there."

Anne avoided a direct reply. Everyone in the party knew arguing with Mary would be fruitless.

"Well, all that can be decided when we return to Uppercross," Frederick stepped into the melee. "We promised Captain and Mrs. Harville a final walk about Lyme. We ought to be setting off for Uppercross by one."

Chapter 11

Are flowers the winter's choice?
Is love's bed always snow?
She seemed to hear my silent voice,
Not love's appeal to know.
—John Clare from "First Love"

Breakfast was not long over when they were joined by Captain and Mrs. Harville and by Captain Benwick. As a group of nine, they started to take their last walk about Lyme. Frederick noted how quickly Benwick sought Anne's attention; evidently, their conversation the preceding evening did not disincline him to see her again. He walked beside her, talking as before of Mr. Scott and Lord Byron.

"Your Miss Elliot was most kind in speaking so long to James," Harville confided as he and Frederick walked along together. "She did a good deed in making that poor fellow talk so much. I wish he could have such company oftener. It is bad for him, I know, to be shut up as he is, but what can we do? We cannot part."

"Then you should tell her so," Frederick nodded in Anne's direction. "It does not surprise me, though; Anne Elliot is the kindest woman I ever knew. The man who receives her affection is blessed indeed."

Frederick's words sparked Thomas's interest. "How long have you know Miss Elliot?" His curiosity flamed into being.

Frederick still watched Anne as she spoke to James Benwick. "Nearly eight years," he mumbled.

"Eight years?" Thomas's voice rose with anticipation. "When you were in Somerset with Edward?"

Frederick's attention snapped back to his friend. "I understand the implications, Thomas, but you are mistaken. Miss Elliot's family is the only aristocrats in the area. Of course, my brother would be familiar with them."

"Anything you say, Wentworth." But his tone told Frederick Harville did not believe him.

"Get on with you." He laughed lightly as he shoved Harville in Anne's direction.

They continued on for some time, each pair engrossed in their conversations. Eventually, Milly Harville became concerned for her husband's leg injury, and she insisted they return home. The group would accompany them to their door and then return to the inn and set off themselves. By all their calculations there was just time for this; but as they drew near the Cobb, there was a general wish to walk along it once more.

"We really must," Frederick heard Louisa beg Charles to let her have her way once more.

"Louisa," he tried to reason with his sister, "we must be off. Late November days are short of light, and Mamma will worry so if we do not return home by dinner."

"Be patient, Charles," she nearly whined. "How long would it actually take us to walk the length of the Cobb? You know I may never get a chance to see the ocean again. Do not deny Henrietta or I that pleasure."

Her words soften Musgrove's resolve; the man had little backbone when it came to making decisions regarding his family. Frederick thought it ironic Louisa spoke so poorly of the manipulative ways of Mrs. Charles; from his point of view, Louisa incorporated the same techniques into her dealings, as did Mary Musgrove. She whined and cajoled until she got her way, and Louisa always "demanded" to be the center of attention. Poor Charles! He was to live a life of constant compromise! "What is a quarter hour give or take?" he assured the others in a loud voice.

"We depart from you here, Wentworth." Harville turned to take his leave of his friend. "You will no longer be a stranger to us; we insist you return soon."

"Wild horses could not keep me from seeking your hospitality," Wentworth guaranteed his sentiments. He took Milly's ungloved hands and brought each to his lips. "You are charged with keeping this rascal in line," he teased as he lightly kissed her knuckles. "I leave him in your able hands." With those words, he took Harville's hand and placed Milly's in it.

Automatically, Thomas interlaced his fingers with hers. "Only my Milly could have such control over me. As you recall, Wentworth, I do not take orders very well."

"Neither of us does, my Friend." He bowed to Milly. So with all the kind leave-taking and all the kind interchange of invitations and promises, which may be imagined, they parted from Captain and Mrs. Harville at their own door, and still accompanied by Captain Benwick, who seemed to cling to them to the last, proceeded to make the proper adieus to the Cobb.

"My, it is very windy today!" Mary noted as she grasped her bonnet to keep it from blowing away. "Should we not turn back, Charles?"

"What do you think, Anne?" Like everyone else in the group, Charles constantly sought Anne's confirmation when it came to dealing with her sister.

Anne's cloak whipped around her. She stood steady, allowing the wind to dance about her rather than to fight its force. Frederick relished in the image of her welcoming Nature's force. Anne offered her brother-in-law a secret smile, knowing Charles would suffer if the group did not agree with Mary's request. "I suspect Mary is right; the wind seems especially powerful today. I am sure now you know the beauty of this place, you may return in the spring when it is more lively in its entertainments."

"I agree." Charles nearly laughed with having the decision taken from his hands. He would neither want to disappoint his sisters nor to meet his wife's wrath. "Let us turn back."

"May we, at least, walk along the shoreline?" Henrietta asked quietly.

Charles jumped at the idea of appeasing everyone. "What a good compromise, my Dear." He turned to the others. "Let us get down the steps to the lower."

As he did previously, Frederick preceded the others down. That way, he could offset the women's movements on the narrow steps. Charles and Benwick remained at the top as Mary, Anne, and Henrietta descended the tapered path. All were contented to pass quietly and carefully down the steep flight.

"I need no one's help," Louisa assured her brother, pulling her hand from his. "I would prefer to stay up here; the wind is of no consequence to me."

"Please, Louisa," Charles Musgrove begged in mumbled tones. "You know I will have no peace if . . ."

She hissed, "You give in to Mary too often!"

Charles gave her a knowing nod. He whispered, "I made my bed years ago, and although you do not understand now, soon you will realize a man must pick his battles. This is not one I choose to fight."

"Then go on," she admonished him. "I will make my own way."

Frederick remained at the bottom of the steps, waiting for Louisa's descent. The others on safe footing began to regroup and move away. Charles came past Frederick, offering up a sheepish grin for his part in the disagreement.

Louisa was nearly three-fourths of the way down the steps when she called out to Frederick, "Catch me!" In all their walks, he had had to jump her from stiles; the sensation was delightful to her, and Louisa remained determined to make the walk memorable in one way or the other. She lost her power to Anne with Charles's decision to turn back, and Louisa did not like that feeling.

"Louisa, be careful," Frederick cautioned, as he quickly moved to prepare for her leap. The hardness of the pavement for her feet made him less willing to play her game upon the present occasion; he did it, however. Catching her at the waist, Frederick sat Louisa decisively away from him.

Louisa gifted him with a flirtatious smile; then she broke away from his grasp, and, instantly, to show her enjoyment, ran up the steps to be jumped down again. "Once more," she teased as she climbed several steps higher than before.

"Louisa, no!" he warned her. "It is too high! The jar will be too great!"

Having let her go, Frederick turned momentarily away to pick up his hat and gloves, which he discarded to catch her the first time. But before he could turn back to properly station himself, she smiled and said, "I am determined. I will."

He put out his hands; she was to precipitate by half a second. Louisa's body floated through the air in slow motion; her skirt tail and cloak spread out like angel wings. Frederick saw the horror overtake her face when she realized he could not catch her, and her body fought to brace for the impact. The thudding sound reverberated as she fell on the pavement on the Lower Cobb and was taken up lifeless.

"Oh, my God!" Frederick's words, as well as the sound of Louisa's crash turned the rest of the party in their direction. Frederick hovered over her. "Louisa—please, Louisa!" He reached for her hand. There was no wound, no blood, no visible bruise; but her eyes were closed, she breathed not, her face was like death.—The horror of that moment froze all who stood around. Wentworth, who caught her up, knelt with her in his arms, looking on her with a face as pallid as her own, in an agony of silence.

"She is dead! She is dead!" screamed Mary, catching hold of her husband, her words contributing to his own horror and making Charles immoveable. In another moment, Henrietta, sinking under the conviction, lost her senses too and would have fallen but for Captain Benwick and Anne, who caught and supported her between them.

"Is there no one to help me?" Frederick cried out in a tone of despair, as if all his own strength left him.

"Go to him. Go to him!" cried Anne. "For heaven's sake go to him. I can support her myself. Leave me, and go to him. Rub her hands; rub her temples. Here are salts—take them, take them!"

Captain Benwick obeyed, and Charles at the same moment, disengaging himself from his wife, were both with Frederick. They raised Louisa up and supported her more firmly between them. They did Anne's bidding—rubbing her extremities and placing the smelling salts under her nose, but in vain.

In horror, Frederick staggered backwards, clinging to the wall for support. He exclaimed in the bitterest agony, "Oh, God! Her father and mother!"

"A surgeon!" said Anne.

Frederick caught the word; it seemed to rouse him at once, giving him hope and a purpose. "True, true, a surgeon this instant!" he called and started to dart in the direction of the town.

"Wait!" Anne's words caught him in mid stride. "Captain Benwick! Captain Benwick! Would not it be better for Captain Benwick? He knows where a surgeon is to be found."

Everyone, including Frederick, capable of thinking felt the advantage of the idea, and in a moment—it was all done in rapid moments—Captain Benwick resigned the poor corpse-like figure entirely to Charles's care and was off for the town with the up most rapidity.

"Louisa, talk to me." Charles patted her face gently, trying to coax his sister back to consciousness.

Mary kept up her laments. "Dead—she is dead!" a continuous stream of wailing. "Oh, what will we do? Help me, Charles, I feel so weak!"

Charles looked up from his sister to witness the hysterical agitations of his wife calling on him for help, which he could not give.

"Mary, be quiet!" Anne ordered. "You are not helping." Then she turned to the sagging Henrietta. "Louisa will be fine; she just took a bad spill. The surgeon will be here in a moment." To emphasize her words, Anne grabbed Henrietta's chin, forcing the girl to meet her eyes; Henrietta gave a reassuring nod.

Frederick looked on—the dreaded tableau playing out before his stare. The only thing he could comprehend was Anne would make it right; she would know what to do.

"Anne, Anne," cried Charles, "what is to be done next? What, in heaven's name, is to be done next?"

Wentworth's eyes also turned towards her. Her shoulders shifted as if shrugging off the weight of the situation. "Had not she better be carried to the inn?" she said with all the calm possible. "Yes, I am sure, carry her gently to the inn."

"Yes, yes, to the inn," repeated Wentworth, comparatively collected and eager to be doing something. "I will carry her myself. Musgrove, take care of the others."

By this time the report of the accident spread among the workmen and boatmen about the Cobb, and many were collected near them, to be useful if wanted, at any rate, to enjoy the sight of a dead young lady, nay, two dead young ladies, for it proved twice as fine as the first report. To some of the best-looking of these good people Henrietta was consigned, for, though partially revived, she was quite helpless; and in this manner, Anne walking by her side, and Charles, attending to his wife, they set forward, treading back with feelings unutterable, the ground, which so lately, so very lately, and so light of heart, they passed along.

They were not off the Cobb before the Harvilles met them. Captain Benwick flew by their house, with a countenance, which showed something to be wrong, and they set off immediately, informed and directed, as they passed towards the spot.

Shocked as Captain Harville was, he brought senses and nerves that could be instantly useful; and a look between him and his wife decided what was to be done. "Take her to our house!" Harville ordered.

Without a second thought, Frederick trusted his old friend's advice. He turned in at the Harville's door, and the others followed. "Upstairs!" Milly directed him. "Place her in my bed."

"Oh, no, we cannot take your bed," Charles protested, although it was a weak effort on his part, having his attention divided by his still sobbing wife and the need to care for both of his sisters.

"Nonsense," Milly admonished. "Do as I say, Frederick." He quickly disappeared through the entranceway and just as quickly conveyed Louisa's limp body to the waiting bed. "I will tend her until the surgeon arrives. Go back down and help Thomas."

"Thank you, Milly," he stammered, trying to grasp the severity of the situation. "You and Thomas . . ." he began, but he could not finish the words. Ducking his head to clear the doorframe, he made his way slowly down the stairs, needing to digest the ramification of what just happened.

At the bottom, he met the surgeon scurrying up the steps, two at a time. "I guess we wait," Anne said softly as she helped Captain Harville pour restorative drinks for all who needed them.

After a quarter of an hour, the surgeon reappeared in the Harville's sitting room. Both Charles and Frederick rushed forward to meet him. "Tell us, Doctor," Charles pleaded. "Will my sister live?"

"Your sister will likely recover. Her head received a severe contusion, but I have seen people recover from greater injuries. I do not deem the situation hopeless. In fact, the young lady opened her eyes momentarily although she did not regain consciousness, but I take that as a good sign." A collective sigh of relief rang out in the room. "I do not regard your sister's condition as desperate, but I cannot say how quickly she will convalesce; the brain has its own time table to recuperate."

"Thank God," Frederick heard himself say. Then he collapsed into a nearby chair, leaning over a table with folded arms and face concealed, overpowered by the various feelings of his soul. Silently, he offered prayers for Louisa's speedy recovery and words of thanks for protecting her as God did.

It now became necessary for the party to consider what was best to be done, as to their general situation. They were now able to speak to each other and consult. That Louisa must remain where she was, however distressing to her friends to be involving the Harvilles in such trouble, did not admit a doubt. Her removal was impossible. The Harvilles silenced all scruples, and, as much as they could, all gratitude. They looked forward and arranged everything, before the others began to reflect. Captain Benwick must give up his room to them and get a bed elsewhere—and the whole was settled. They were only concerned the house could accommodate no more; and yet perhaps by "putting the children away in the maids' room or swinging a cot somewhere," they could hardly bear to think of not finding room for two or three besides, supposing they might wish to stay; though, with regard to any attendance on Miss Musgrove, there need not be the least uneasiness in leaving her to Mrs. Harville's care entirely. Mrs. Harville was a very experienced nurse; and her nursery-maid, who lived with her long and gone about with her everywhere, was just such another. Between those two, Louisa could want no possible attendance by day or night. And all this was said with a truth and sincerity of feeling irresistible.

Charles, Henrietta, and Frederick were the three in consultation, and for a little while it was only an interchange of perplexity and terror. "Uppercross—the necessity of some one's going to Uppercross—the news to be conveyed—how it could be broken to Mr. and Mrs. Musgrove—the lateness of the morning—an hour already gone since they ought to have been off—the impossibility of being in tolerable time."

At first, they were capable of nothing more to the purpose than such exclamation; but, after a while, Wentworth, exerting himself, said, "We must be decided and without the loss of another minute. Every minute is valuable. Some must resolve on being off for Uppercross instantly. Musgrove, either you or I must go."

"I cannot leave my sister," Charles added quickly. "I will sleep in a chair if necessary, but I cannot, ought not, leave Louisa in such a state."

Henrietta declared, "I need to stay, too."

Charles reached for his younger sister's hand. "I love your resolve, my Dear, but we both know you are not even able to be in the room with Louisa without crying."

"But I must, Charles," she protested.

"Miss Henrietta," Frederick wanted her to make a decision, "you could help Louisa more if you bring comfort to your mother and father. Neither I nor Miss Anne nor Mrs. Charles could offer them what you can."

"Wentworth is right, Henrietta."

"You are correct. I need to be with Mamma; she will need me, will she not? When do we leave?"

"Then it is settled, Musgrove," cried Frederick. "You will stay, and I will take your sister home. But as to the rest—as to the others—if one stays to assist Mrs. Harville, I think, it need be only one.—Mrs. Charles will, of course, wish to get back to her children; but, if Anne will stay, no one is so proper, so capable, as Anne!"

Charles added quickly, "I concur."

Henrietta nodded her agreement. "If not for Anne, where would we be now?"

Frederick's eyes rose to greet her countenance as Anne entered the room. It was as if they took a step back into time—hers was the face he saw when she entered the mercantile eight years ago. "You will stay; I am sure; you will stay and nurse her." He turned to her and spoke with a glow, and yet a gentleness, which seemed almost restoring the past. He watched as she colored deeply, and readily realizing where his thoughts drifted, he recollected himself and moved away. Standing and watching her, another thought ricocheted through his head. He asked the woman he loved to tend the girl with whom he flirted outrageously for a time.

"I would gladly stay with Louisa," she began with a gentle assurance. "It is of what I was thinking. If Mrs. Harville would make up a bed on the floor of Louisa's room, it would be sufficient for me."

"In all probability, Musgrove, we should leave your father's carriage here. You will need it in the morning to send an account of Louisa's night to your parents. I will rent a chaise or a curricle at the inn to take your wife and sister home."

"Agreed," Charles turned immediately to the task of informing the others, and Frederick hurried off to make the arrangements.

Less than a half hour later, Frederick looked up to see Charles attending his sister and Captain Benwick walking beside Anne. "Why?" Frederick's question burst forth, but he soon stifled it. Obviously, Musgrove once again gave in to his wife's protestations; the man put peace in his household above peace of mind for his sister. In that instant, Frederick lost much of the respect he once held for the man. If it were Sophia lying in the Harville's bed, nothing and no one would sway him. He would want Anne to nurse her.

Without delay, he handed Henrietta and Anne into the carriage and placed himself between them. Full of astonishment and vexation, Frederick maneuvered the curricle out onto the road.

Through the early part of the drive, Frederick devoted most of his energy towards Henrietta, trying to support her view—raising her hopes and her spirits. In general, his voice and manner were studiously calm. To spare Henrietta from agitation seemed the governing principle. Frederick knew not what to say to Anne. He knew what he wanted to say to her—for weeks he wanted to renew his attentions. Now, it was too late. He could not speak words of affection for Anne with Louisa lying unconscious in Harville's house.

Henrietta leaned against his shoulder as he guided the carriage towards Uppercross. She looked up into his face before speaking. "I wish we never went to Lyme—never saw the Cobb." Her voice came out flat and unemotional.

"Please—do not talk of it—do not talk of it!" he cried. "Oh, God! That I had not given way to her at the fatal moment! Had I done as I ought! But so eager and so resolute! Dear, sweet Louisa!" As he said the words, Frederick recalled all the conversations he had with Louisa about universal felicity and the advantage of firmness of character. Now, he wished he encouraged her to realize, like all other qualities of the mind, independent thinking should have its proportions and limits. He now felt a persuadable temper, like the one he used to curse about Anne, might sometimes be as much in favor of happiness as a very resolute character.

As they neared Uppercross, Henrietta slumped against him, having succumbed to the rhythmic swaying of the horses' gait. "Take the reins for a moment," he leaned down to whisper in Anne's ear. One of her curls teased his cheek, and Frederick felt a rush of desire shoot through his veins.

Trusting him, she lightly took the straps he laid in her palm. "Hold them easy," he instructed, and she nodded her understanding. Turning slightly, he eased Henrietta's limp form back against the seat. "Thank you," he spoke quietly as he reached once more for the reins. Their fingers intertwined for a few elongated seconds, and Frederick knew real regret. "Anne, I need to tell you . . ."

"Do not say the words, Captain," she interrupted.

Frederick knew he had no right; Anne could not be his now no matter what he desired. He swallowed his words, and gently released her hand from the leather. "We will be at Uppercross soon." In a low, cautious voice, he continued, "I was considering what we had best do. Henrietta must not appear at first; she could not stand it. I was thinking whether you had not better remain in the carriage with her, while I go and break it to Mr. and Mrs. Musgrove. Do you think this is a good plan?"

"That seems prudent," she said thoughtfully. "Mrs. Musgrove will be distressed and would likely send Henrietta into new hysterics. You calm down the mother, and I will instruct Henrietta on what to do to be of service to her parents."

They rode the rest of the way in silence, both deep in thought of what could be. As they turned into the gates leading to the Great House, Anne placed her hand on top of his and gave it a little squeeze. "You will do the honorable thing," she whispered, "because that is the kind of man you are."

"I will return to Lyme tonight as soon as the horses are baited." He did not turn to look at Anne; his heart would stop if he did, but Frederick concentrated deeply on the feel of her hand on his—memorizing the beauty of the moment.

He disembarked as soon as the carriage came to a halt, and without looking back at Anne, he strode to the door. After rapping twice, a servant finally bade him to enter. Frederick waited impatiently for Mr. Musgrove in the yellow drawing room. He reflected on how often over the last month he sat in this same room, making small talk with the Miss Musgroves, but especially with Louisa. He cursed the fact he could have instead been calling on Anne at the Cottage. "How foolish I was," he chastised himself. "Anne was there for the taking, and all you wanted was revenge."

Mr. Musgrove interrupted his musings. "Captain Wentworth," the man's voice held pure agitation. "Is something amiss? You return without my family."

"Your son and Mrs. Charles are still in Lyme with Louisa," Frederick began. "I fear I bring you bad news."

Mr. Musgrove demanded, "Tell me quickly, Man!"

"Louisa—Louisa fell from the seawall. She has a severe contusion and is at present unconscious. The surgeon feels strongly she will recover, but there are no guarantees. Your son remains behind to help tend her."

"Where is Henrietta?"

"Miss Henrietta is in the carriage with Miss Elliot. I wanted the opportunity to speak to you and Mrs. Musgrove first; Henrietta is a bit distraught. I did not want to upset her further."

Mr. Musgrove stepped past Frederick and reached for the brandy decanter. He poured himself one and tossed it off before refilling another. "How did it happen? I need to know everything before I tell Mrs. Musgrove." He stood with his back to Frederick, shoulders hunched, trying to ward off reality.

"It was my fault, Sir. I encouraged Louisa to be adventurous. She jumped from the seawall. I tried to catch her, but I was too late. It was purely my fault. I know not what else to say, Sir."

Mr. Musgrove started past him. "I will tell Mrs. Musgrove—if you would be so kind to bring Henrietta in. I am sure Mother will want to assure herself of Henrietta's safety." He patted Frederick's shoulder.

"I will return to Lyme this evening, as soon as I refresh the horses and retrieve some clothing from Kellynch. If you wish to send anything to Charles or Mary or for Louisa, I will gladly take it with me." Frederick stood in supplication. "I beg your forgiveness, Sir."

"There is nothing to forgive, Captain. Now if you will excuse me." Mr. Musgrove moved dejectedly towards the stairs.

Frederick turned to go back where Anne waited in the carriage with Henrietta. "Your parents need your help, Miss Henrietta," he said without emotion as he helped her from the carriage.

"Thank you, Captain." She rushed up the steps and through the door, still being held open by the footman.

Frederick turned to help Anne. "If you could see that the Musgroves gather some items for your sister and Charles, I would appreciate it. I will look to the horses."

"I shall take care of it." She paused, obviously, not wanting to part from him; Frederick, too, lingered.

"Thank you, Anne. If not for you, today could have been a disaster. It was to your good counsel each of us turned in our need."

"There is nothing for which to offer gratitude. I prefer to be of service."

Again, silence prevailed. So much needed saying, but neither of them had a right to speak the words. Finally, Frederick forced himself into action. "I suppose, then, this is farewell," he said as he took the bridle of the nearest horse to lead it away.

"Good-bye, Captain." She gave him one last look and then scurried up the steps and into the mansion.

"Good-bye, my dearest Anne," he whispered to her retreating form.

Frederick stopped at Kellynch to give Sophia and Benjamin the news and to gather some of his belongings. He sent Ned Steventon to prepare his clothes, anticipating a lengthy stay in Lyme.

Reluctantly, he entered one of the bedrooms in the east wing. He knew exactly which one it was, having innocently asked Ned several weeks ago. Sophia refused to use this wing of the house—it was where the Elliots lived. Frederick closed the door quietly behind him, before taking the candle and holding it high. This was Anne's room, and although most of her personal items were no longer evident, Frederick felt he needed to be here, where she once slept. After today, the chance to return to her would be slim, and he needed to feel close to Anne once more.

Setting the candle on the nightstand, he sat gingerly on the edge of the bed. He looked about him, envisioning Anne moving about the room—dressing behind the screen—writing letters at the desk—standing by the window—observing the garden below. He groaned with the knowledge she would never be his. Lying back, he stared up at the canopy above his head. *His Anne* slept in this bed, and Frederick found himself grasping the pillow to his chest, trying to smell the lavender she always wore. A pain shot through his heart—happiness—fleeting happiness—would never be his.

Lying as such for, at least, a quarter-hour, finally, he shook off the despondency filling his whole being. "I best return to Lyme," he said out loud. "I must finish what I started."

*   *   *

Returning to Harville's house and the inn, Frederick joined those gathered in the downstairs sitting room. As expected, Charles took the latest news of

Louisa's recovery to his parents the next day. Frederick barely arrived in Lyme before Musgrove was on his way to Uppercross. He told Frederick upon his arrival, "Mrs. Harville is exceptional. She really left nothing for Mary to do. In fact, Mary and I returned early to the inn last night. Mary was hysterical again this morning, but Captain Benwick was kind enough to walk out with her. I wish I heeded your advice and sent her home last night. She is of no use to Mrs. Harville; at least, Anne would be of service to the family."

"Anne is uncommon," is all Frederick could get out before Charles took his leave.

When Musgrove returned in the early evening, he brought with him the family's old nursery-maid. Mrs. Musgrove thought having their old nursery-maid in attendance would speed Louisa's recovery; the woman held a reputation for coddling her charges, and she was of little use to the family since young Harry Musgrove went off to school.

For the next two days, Frederick sat quietly in the Harville's parlor. Everyone assured him the intervals of sense and consciousness were believed to be stronger; Louisa's recovery began in earnest, but still he could take no solace in the news. God answered his prayers—at least, his prayers for Louisa.

*   *   *

Frederick seemed thankful for the assignment of returning to Uppercross to bring some of Louisa's personal belongings to Lyme. At least, it got him out of Harville's house; he did not know how much longer he could sit in that room and wait. As a man of action, such indolence drove him mad.

Riding into the circle at Kellynch, he slid easily from the saddle as the groom took the animal towards the stables. Sophia was out the door before he could reach the steps. "Oh, Frederick," she touched his face. "You look pale. You are not sleeping, and I can tell you are not eating properly. Look how much weight you lost!" She wrapped her arm through his. "You must spend the night."

"I should return to Lyme," he said automatically.

"You will not," she insisted.

Frederick looked at her with hollow eyes. "I have no choice, Sophia. I came here first to pick up some more of my own clothes. I am to call at Uppercross and have the Musgrove maid gather some of Miss Musgrove's trinkets and personal belongings. There is hope such remembrances will speed her recovery."

"Then the girl is doing better?" The Admiral joined his wife and Frederick in the front foyer.

Frederick seemed lost in his thoughts. "Miss Musgrove is awake for longer periods each day. She converses with Milly Harville and the family's nursery-maid." He headed towards the staircase, needing to take care of things quickly.

"Have you not spoken to her?" Sophia followed him up the first few steps.

He turned back to her. "Sophia, it would not be proper for me to enter Miss Musgrove's bed chamber." A part of Frederick thanked the rules of propriety for such behavior. He had no desire to encourage Louisa's affections any more than they might already be in place.

"Of course, I should have thought," she added quickly. "It is just learning everything second hand; it must be maddening."

"That is an understatement." Frederick took several steps before casting a glance over his shoulder at her. "Would you ask the groom for a fresh horse while I take care of a few things in my room?"

"Naturally, Frederick. I shall see to it right away, and I will send a tray up for you." His sister headed towards the servant's entrance, and, in haste, he took the steps two at a time.

Less than an hour later, he reappeared in the front drawing room, a satchel under his arm. "You are off again?" Sophia asked with some regret. "When will we see you next?"

"At present, I have no intention of quitting Lyme until this is settled." Frederick seemed resolved to his fate. He walked to the window, not really seeing the garden view. Pausing, he debated before asking his next question. "Sophia, have you seen Miss Anne? I assume she returned to Kellynch Lodge with Lady Russell."

"I have not seen her, but she and Lady Russell sent a note with an intention to call here tomorrow."

Frederick swallowed hard; he could not turn around and look at his sister. He would give anything just for a glimpse of Anne. "Would you convey my respect to Miss Anne and tell her I hope she is none the worse for what happened at Lyme. She was the stalwart throughout those initial moments. The exertions were great, and I pray she did not suffer unduly." He would love to leave her word of his constancy—to tell her how much he still admired her, but those words would never be spoken.

"Perhaps you would like to leave Miss Anne a note. I am sure she is anxious to receive information on Miss Musgrove's progress," Sophia suggested.

"That is an excellent idea, Sophia. I will do so before I leave." Frederick crossed to the desk; taking out a piece of foolscap, he scribbled Anne a message. He did not allow himself the liberty of saying anything personal or even to sign the paper. He knew Sophia would convey that information directly to Anne. In an impetuous move, he kissed the corner of the folded page before he sealed it with wax. His kiss would touch her fingertips as she unfolded the paper to read his message. Closing his eyes, he envisioned his lips caressing Anne's fingertips in a playful seduction. It was all he could do not to groan as the vision played across his mind.

"I believe that is it," he said before placing the note on the side table where Sophia would remember it to Anne. "I am back to Lyme once I retrieve Miss Musgrove's belongings. I shall send you word every few days to let you know how things progress."

Sophia walked out with him. "You are in my prayers, Frederick."

"I know, Sophia. Pray for us all, please." He swung up into the saddle and rode away.

*   *   *

Thomas Harville slid into the chair next to him. Frederick sat at the table for the last three hours, shuffling a deck of cards he did not play—staring off in space, lost in his thoughts. "The girl will recover," Harville said as a way to get his friend's attention.

"Yes—yes, I suppose she will with time. It has not been a fortnight, after all." Frederick sipped on the tepid tea, now several hours old.

Harville hesitated, "Louisa Musgrove will make you a fine wife, Frederick."

Frederick rolled his eyes heavenward in supplication. "Do I have a choice?"

"Her family expects a proposal when she recovers. Mrs. Charles, and even the nursery-maid, indicated as much. I understand her mother and father and sister will arrive tomorrow in Lyme." Thomas leaned back in the chair to watch carefully his best friend's reaction.

"I was so foolish, Thomas. I allowed Louisa Musgrove the liberty to think I would choose her when my heart belonged to another for many years. Now, if she recovers, I feel obligated to ask for her properly." Frederick stared off once again, as if reading his sentence written on the air. "What else can I do? I must do the honorable thing." In the back of his mind, he heard Anne telling him the same thing the last time they were together.

"I was thinking maybe you should withdraw and see how things go once Louisa recovers. She is young and possibly out of sight—out of mind will prevail. Should you not go to visit with Edward, after all?"

Frederick's eyes fell on Thomas's face. What his friend suggested gave him hope. "I would only be in the way here, would I not?" he said slowly, as if he needed to digest the idea himself. "Louisa has her whole family to tend her, and you could send me word if I need to return because of her illness. I should be off to Plymouth for a time to oversee the dismantling of the *Laconia,* and Edward has a new wife I must really meet." He searched for permission to leave.

"If absence makes the heart grow fonder, I will send you word immediately, but I see no reason for you to be underfoot any longer. I suggest you take your leave early tomorrow morning."

"How can I thank you, Thomas?" Frederick lowered his voice to share his despair. "You saw what others did not."

"Go with God, Frederick." With that, he pushed away from the table and went to find his children. Good friends—old friends did not need such gratitude among them.

Chapter 12

Nothing in the world is single,
All things by a law divine
In one another's being mingle—
Why not I with thine?
—Percy Bysshe Shelley from "Love's Philosophy"

"Is that better, Sir?" Avendale asked as he helped Frederick to a chair. It was the first time he was on deck since the fateful day they overtook the French sloop.

Frederick took a deep breath, filling his lungs with sea air. "It is near perfect—thank you, Lieutenant Avendale." The journey from his quarters to this chair propped against an outside wall took nearly ten days of his life, but, at last, he felt the mist grazing his freshly shaved face.

"I am to wait with you until Mrs. Wentworth comes. I believe she went back for a blanket." The officer transferred his weight from one foot to another.

Frederick chuckled. "My wife fears my demise." He rolled his eyes in a way to say, *What can I do?* "Women are the practical ones, are they not Avendale?"

"I believe they are, Sir. At least, my Maggie seems to always know what is best." The man smiled with his recollection.

"Is Maggie your wife?" Frederick asked, glad to hold a normal conversation with one of his men.

Avendale bent down where he could speak to his captain on a more personal level. "I hope to make her my wife when we put into port. My term is up, and I will be going home."

"We shall be losing a valuable part of the crew when you leave us." Frederick's tone held real respect for the man kneeling in front of him.

"Thank you, Captain." Avendale dropped his eyes. "The sea is not my life; I thought it would be, but I am not meant for this constant pull of Nature."

"What will you do?" Frederick asked before he checked his words. Seamen did not normally discuss private matters.

Avendale stared off for a moment. "I would like to take my orders; I studied at the university. My father wished me to begin a military career, but the life of a country curate would serve me quite well. My father will be disappointed, but a man must define his own life. Do you not agree, Captain?"

"For those not first born or for those whose family can offer their sons little, I am a firm believer in the power of choice. My brother Edward chose the clergy and is very happy, where I could think of little but the sea and the adventure. The Navy gave me opportunities I would never have otherwise."

"Does your brother have his own parish?" Avendale seemed interested in what to expect from his career choice.

Frederick realized this was the man's purpose all along. Rumors told Avendale of Frederick's family, and the lieutenant wanted his captain's opinion on his change in occupations. "My brother toiled for many years as a curate, but he, at last, took a position in Shropshire near Shrewsbury. He married and welcomed his first child recently."

"Then he is happy?"

Frederick smiled and nodded. "When I saw him last he was. His calling serves him well as I am sure it will you."

"When we reach Plymouth, I will meet Maggie there; she travels from Bristol. I will make her my wife—then I hope for a position near Hull." Avendale stood as he saw Anne Wentworth approach. "Here comes your wife, Sir. When you are ready to return to your quarters, it will be my honor to help you."

"Thank you, again, Avendale. I will send for you."

Anne took the seat next to Frederick, but only after spreading a light blanket over his lap. "Is not the sea air glorious?" she whispered.

Frederick turned his head to look at her. "You love it as much as I."

"A ship is nothing like what one would imagine. When a person sees the sails from a distance, he would think a ship moves silently upon the waves; but, in reality, the canvas sails roar and snap in the wind, the hull breaks water like an explosive thunderclap, and the guns roll with a volcanic eruption. Yet, in the mix of all this noise, there is a peace—a faceless gentleness that creeps into a person's soul—into his veins." Her voice trailed off, and she stilled. Finally, Anne came full circle, out of musings. "You seem deep in thought," she half teased.

"I was thinking of Plymouth. The last time I spent more than a few days there I was trying to forget the mess I made with Louisa Musgrove's fall and trying to justify my undying need for your love." Frederick reached out and took her hand in his. He traced circles on the inside of her wrist with his index finger. "I prefer it when you do not wear gloves," he whispered to her.

"It seems foolish to do so while onboard," she reasoned. He placed a kiss on the pulse of her hand.

Anne's eyes flashed with an unspoken desire, and Frederick felt his body harden in response. Instinctively, she leaned towards him half expecting him to kiss her, yet, knowing he could not as they sat openly on the deck. Finally, she stammered, trying to recoup her composure. "Why do you not tell me about your time in Plymouth? I know so little about what you did before you came to Bath."

He taunted, "Do you mean before I threw myself at your feet and begged you mercilessly to marry me?"

"First, you did not beg," she began to protest, but then stopped suddenly. "Why do you enjoy teasing me so?"

"Because I cannot live without that spark of passion I see in your face when your emotions are engaged." He traced his fingertips from her temple to her jaw line. "You mesmerize me; when you are near, I am spellbound—enthralled—captivated—just pick a word because none of them completely describe what I feel." Love and need held them as they memorized each other's features. After longing moments only those who truly love understand, he cleared his throat, needing also to clear his thoughts of Anne's heat-laden eyes. Looking straight ahead, he began, "I have been to Plymouth many times."

*   *   *

Walking along George Street, Frederick mused at the many changes he witnessed in the Plymouth landscape over the years. When he first made port here, back before his sailing to the Americas, George Street stretched beyond the West Gate in rows of independent houses. Now, the Theatre Royal II anchored a development, which also included the Royal Hotel. From 1811 to 1813, every time he sat into port, he made a special trip to the area, intrigued by the construction.

Boasting a special vestibule, private boxes, a pit, and a gallery, the theatre was once isolated, but now the town met the site. Frederick was in attendance for the opening program, consisting of *As You Like It* and a farce entitled *Catherine and Petruchio*. He recalled how, much to his chagrin, some of the unruly audience interrupted portions of the performance. The building itself was something of an anomaly, using cast and wrought iron for fireproofing. Seeing the structure from a distance, he smiled with the remembrance.

He took room at an inn on Cornwall Street. In actuality, Frederick had no real reason for this trip to Plymouth other than the fact he wanted to escape the scenario playing out in Lyme. If Louisa Musgrove did not recover completely, he would be obligated to make her an offer of marriage. She placed her trust in him, and he could not turn from her if she continued to suffer from her fall. He prayed daily for her full recovery. Frederick hoped with the distance, she would forget her dependence on him and place her affections elsewhere. It was an act of a desperate man—one of which he was not proud, but he could not control the dread he felt when he considered making Louisa his wife.

In town for just three days, Frederick spent his time walking the streets of Plymouth, visiting with clothiers and auctioneers. He purchased a new watch as a gift for Edward and several packets of seeds and bulbs for Christine, Edward's wife.

He stood along the shore one day and watched for hours as barge after barge made its way from the Quay at the Breakwater Quarry out to drop stones and cable into the sea to form the Breakwater. It would eventually be one thousand yards in length and ten feet above the low water and be located at the mouth of Plymouth Sound, between Boyisand Bay on the east and Cawsand Bay on the west.

He recalled coming into the Sound the first time. The port was dangerous because Plymouth Sound was open to storms from the southwest, creating anchorage problems. On that particular entrance, he stood on deck as a lieutenant, gritting his teeth as the crew navigated past a previous wreckage on the Boyisand coast.

One late afternoon, he drifted towards the shipyards in hopes of meeting some former crewmates. Shipbuilding and repair establishments sprinkled the shores of Hamoaze, and Frederick sought familiar faces. Amazingly, he had been in town for nearly a week, and he saw no one whom he knew, a testament of how much the war changed this port city. As he turned towards the harbor off of Exeter Street, he heard someone call his name. "Wentworth! Say Wentworth!"

Frederick rotated in the direction of the sound, seeing a man broad of shoulder, but also broad of hips scurrying towards him. Although anxious to catch up with Frederick, the man's iron-jawed expression reflected alarmingly intense eyes. "It that you, Hawker?" Frederick asked as the man drew near.

"What brings you to Plymouth?" The man shook Frederick's hand in greeting. "Is not your ship already in dry dock?"

Frederick could not explain his real reasons for being in town. "I came on business on behalf of Thomas Harville. He is struggling a bit right now."

"I see." John Hawker turned to acknowledge another acquaintance. In 1810, although it was apparently drying out at every spring tide, John Hawker took over the Sutton Pool. When the Prince Regent miraculously gave a ninety-nine year lease to the Sutton Pool Company, Hawker went from fool to astute businessman. "Do you have plans for dinner? I would enjoy catching up."

"I have no definite plans." Frederick hesitated before accepting the offer.

"I would be obliged if you could join our party," Hawker pleaded.

Frederick knew something was amiss. "Who else will be in the group?"

Hawker looked up sheepishly. "Several business investors, of course, and Lord Grierson will be in attendance."

Frederick rolled his eyes in exasperation. "I assume Lady Mary Grierson and her daughters will be part of the group."

"I would imagine," Hawker tried to sound innocent.

"I thank you, Hawker, for the invitation, but I will decline."

"Must you? I am sure her Ladyship would approve of your company."

"Although her Ladyship is most pleasurable company, I will still decline. You might mention to her Ladyship I intend to make an offer of marriage soon." It was not a lie; if Louisa did not recover, she would receive his offer; and if he was fortunate enough for Louisa to look elsewhere, he would seek out Anne once again.

Looking about as if he suddenly remembered a prior appointment, Hawker questioned, "Marriage? Really? Well, I will tell her Ladyship, and I will wish you happy, Wentworth. I would be honored to meet your future wife some day." With that, Hawker made a quick bow and took his leave.

Frederick laughed at the obvious anxiety found in the man's walk. It was an oddity that the Griersons often "hinted" for Frederick to pursue one of their daughters, while Sir Walter Elliot denied his offer. The irony caused Frederick to shake his head in disbelief. If worse came to worse, he could turn to the Griersons in order to squelch Louisa's plans. If he must marry someone he did not love, having Lord Grierson as a relative would, at least, would be a financial advantage, and no one would criticize his withdrawal from Louisa Musgrove for such a prestigious alliance. *What was he thinking? He did not want what Lady Grierson offered nor did he want Louisa; he wanted Anne—for eight years Frederick wanted Anne Elliot.*

On the seventh day of his stay, his mail caught up with him, being forwarded by Sophia. Actually, Frederick nearly forgot about sending the letter of inquiry on Thomas's behalf. It seemed a lifetime ago when he sent it off—in reality, only a little over three weeks. He opened the reply and read what he expected. "Well, I guess I will call at Lyme, at least, long enough to speak to Milly and Thomas. If only I can find a way not to see Louisa or her family," he said the words out loud.

*   *   *

The public carriage rolled into Lyme in the late afternoon. Instead of seeking out the better accommodations Mr. Morris offered at the Wooden Lion, he took a substandard room at the posting inn. It was out of the way, and he was less likely to meet any of the Musgroves along the post road. They stayed in town close to the Harvilles' home. He planned to only stay the one night; he would be on his way to Shrewsbury and Edward's new home tomorrow.

"Say, Boy," he called to one of the stable hands hanging around the inn. "Would you take this message to Thomas Harville. I wrote the directions on the back. Do you read, Boy?"

"Yes, Sir." The youth looked about him. "Should I wait for a reply, Sir?"

"No—that will not be necessary." He slipped two shillings in the boy's hand. "Give the message only to Thomas Harville or to Mrs. Harville—no one else. Do you understand?"

"Yes, Sir—it will be done, Sir." The boy disappeared across the road, heading along an open orchard on his way to the town's center.

Frederick waited, knowing it would be after dinner before his friend would appear. He took his meal in his chamber, avoiding the public rooms in case someone recognized him. It was well after dark when he heard the light tap on the door, opening it to find both Thomas and Milly.

"Welcome," he said as he hustled them into the room. "Did you have any trouble getting away?" He carried another chair to the table, bringing a bottle of brandy and two glasses with him. "Let me send for some tea, Milly." Frederick stepped to the hallway and, luckily, found one of the maids, giving her the order before returning to his friends.

"How was Plymouth?" Thomas asked as he poured himself a drink.

"Tolerable." Frederick seated himself across from them. "I saw Hawker; he tried to hook me up for dinner with Lord and Lady Grierson."

"I am sure the daughters were not far behind," Harville said sarcastically. "If they want to rid themselves of those two mousey women, they will need to increase the size of their dowries." He laughed at his words. "Neither has any personality—no redeeming qualities whatsoever."

"They are amiable and biddable if a man was so inclined," Frederick added without looking at either of his friends. He would not let them know that just yesterday he briefly considered the Griersons as a way out of his current situation.

Milly reached for his hand. "I am sorry, Frederick, that you feel you must hide from the Musgroves; I find them to be very pleasant people."

"And I would thoroughly agree with you." He patted the back of her hand before reaching for the brandy decanter. "I just do not choose to become part of their family if I can avoid it."

"So, do you wish to know the latest on Miss Musgrove?" Thomas became his second in command again—a role with which they were both familiar.

"Please."

"Miss Musgrove is able to sit up for significantly longer periods of time; although more subdued, she has no problem in recalling details. In fact, Charles and Mary Musgrove return to Uppercross tomorrow. Mrs. Charles thoroughly enjoyed her holiday—she walks about the town with Benwick, she shops, she reads—just about anything besides tending her sister."

"That does not surprise me; at Uppercross, she pawned off her boys on Miss Elliot or on their grandmother." Just the mention of Anne caused Frederick to flinch. "How long do you expect to tend Miss Musgrove?"

Milly answered this one. "Mr. and Mrs. Musgrove leave at the end of the week; they take our children with them—the youngest Musgroves will be home for the holidays at that time—the children will be able to celebrate together. Miss Henrietta remains with us as long as it takes. The doctor says at least another month."

"That long . . ." Frederick sighed.

The maid brought the tea tray, and all conversation stopped until she exited the room. When she left, Thomas turned to Frederick. "Your note said you had something of importance to discuss; I assumed it was more than a health update for Miss Musgrove."

Frederick nodded, trying to figure a way to bridge the topic. "Actually, Thomas, I bring some news for you. In fact, if I did not deem it important, I would never stop in Lyme on my way to see Edward."

"Then tell us," Milly encouraged.

"When I was here the first time, if you recall, your craftsmanship, Thomas, impressed me.

"I know that, Frederick. What of it?

"When I returned to Kellynch, I sent out a letter of inquiry. Do you remember Harold Rushick?"

"Certainly, he was a damn fine lieutenant; I hated when he left us to return to civil life." Thomas took a sip of his drink. "What does he have to do with all this?"

"On the ride home, I remembered something important about Rushick. His family owned a novelty and furniture business outside of Brighton; he left us to take over the business when his uncle died. I wrote him about the toys and the chairs and the hammock. Here is his response." Frederick slid the letter across the table to his oldest and dearest friend.

Thomas picked it up and read it quickly. "What does it say?" Milly questioned. Her husband passed the note to her, his pride warring with his need to support his family.

"Oh, Thomas," she gasped. "This is like a prayer come true." Tears misted her eyes as she turned to Frederick. "Bless you." She shook her head in disbelief.

"Why?" Thomas looked questionably at Frederick.

"Why did you help the Musgroves, people you did not know? Because we are friends, Thomas. We served together in a brotherhood no one else can understand. I found you an opportunity—you must take advantage of it. It is not charity; Rushick will expect you to perform at the best of your abilities. That is how he approaches work, and you know it."

"Thomas," Milly pleaded, "you can make furniture, and Lieutenant Rushick will sell your items on commission for you. He shall out and out buy the toys to sell. The letter says wooden toys are selling quickly in the Americas. You can create your pieces. In May when our lease is up, we can move closer to Brighton; you will still be near the sea there."

"Brighton is quickly becoming the new Bath. Visitors will be most anxious to buy something of quality," Frederick encouraged. "Think about it; I will say no more. If you want to deal with Rushick, his directions are on the letter."

Thomas let a smile turn up the corners of his mouth. "Milly and I will discuss it and see what is possible. Thank you, my friend."

Frederick allowed himself to breathe at last. He knew Harville's pride, and he feared his friend would reject the idea before hearing it out. Thankfully, his need to provide for his family overpowered his misplaced conceit. "Some day I will say I was one of the first to own a Harville original," Frederick teased.

"We should get back." Thomas took the lead, after shaking Frederick's hand. "I borrowed Musgrove's curricle; we told everyone Milly needed to call on a sick friend."

"Should I take on a coughing fit to keep you from having to tell a lie?" Frederick stood to bid them farewell.

"We will keep your secret." Milly gave him a quick hug of gratitude. "I will write to you in care of Edward and keep you abreast of Miss Musgrove's progress."

"I do not wish Louisa ill—in fact, I wish her happy. I just wish her happy with someone else." Frederick tried to make her understand.

*   *   *

Three days later, the public carriage rolled into Shrewsbury, and Frederick alighted at last. It was a bone-jarring ride, plagued by snow and rain for two of the days. The driver tossed down his bag, and Frederick spun around, trying to get his bearings, but found himself in his brother's happy embrace. "Thank God," Edward offered prayers of appreciation. "I am so glad you are here; I thought you would never come."

A smile moved across Frederick's face; he forgot how much he needed Edward's solid nature in his life. His brother served not only as a loved one, but also as a trusted friend. Frederick always could count on Edward not judging him.

"You changed, Edward." Frederick took a close look at his brother. "You look more contented," he mocked.

"When you meet my Christine, you will understand why. Come." He pulled Frederick towards a waiting chaise and four. "Lord Calderson loaned me his carriage to bring my brother home—no more poorly sprung carriages for you today."

"Thank Goodness for that." They stored his gear in the luggage compartment and climbed in. "I am thrilled to be here, Edward; I need your counsel when we find time for some privacy."

"I would be pleased to help you. Let us return home, and later we will sit together—just like old times."

"Christine, he is here," Edward called as they entered the vicarage bestowed upon Edward Wentworth as part of the Calderson's living. Frederick looked around, taking in the simple décor. Some of the furniture showed wear, but the house offered large rooms, a great improvement from what Frederick encountered previously.

Christine Wentworth came quickly to answer her husband's call. Frederick took in her presence—tall and thin and aristocratic in her posture, she, at first glance could make a man think haughty, but her fair hair framed a face sporting a faint smile and a demure downward glance at her messy apron. She evidently was cleaning one of the fireplaces and was now covered in soot.

Edward laughed, "My cinder maid." He bestowed a quick kiss on the end of her nose and used his fingertips to try and remove a smudge from her cheek before pulling her close to him. "Meet my own version of the Cinderella story," he told Frederick as she tried to free herself from his grasp. "This is your new sister—my wife Christine."

Frederick watched as a full blush made the black splotches more evident. He gave the woman a quick bow and then tried to ease her embarrassment. "Christine, welcome to the family. Do not let this cad tease you, my Dear. He is just jealous. Edward was always more of a frog than a prince." He shot her a knowing smile.

She returned the smile, and he noted how amusement flashed through her eyes. "We are pleased you are finally here, Captain. I apologize for my appearance; I foolishly tried to clear the flue in the guest room—something I asked my 'prince' to do yesterday, in fact." It was Edward's turn to look embarrassed. "Now, if you will excuse me, I will freshen my clothing. Thank you for understanding." She looked at Edward as if to tell him she would make him pay for her discomfiture. "Please have Sadie bring in some tea. I will ask Cal to finish sweeping out the ashes before you show your brother his room."

"I am at your beck and call, my Lady Love." Edward gave her an exaggerated bow.

"Get out of here," she waved her hand at him before she curtsied and made her exit.

"I never saw you so carefree," Frederick added as he took the seat to which his brother gestured.

"Christine is remarkable." Edward looked lovingly at the doorway through which his wife exited. "She gives me a new purpose; Christine brings me contentment. The woman actually knows me better than I know myself sometimes. I really cannot explain it."

"Love." The word hung in the air as if it explained everything.

Edward smiled again. "Marriage to Christine has been the exciting—the satisfying—experience God intended it to be."

"Now I am jealous." Frederick seemed amused, but, in reality, he did feel the pain of not knowing such happiness. "Both you and Sophia placed the bar high. How will I ever measure up?"

Edward's countenance sobered. "I assume it is of such to which you wish to speak to me. Did your heart survive its encounter with Somersetshire? I cringed when I realized Sophia and the Admiral planned to take over the Elliot estate. Obviously, you never told her about Anne Elliot."

"No one knew about Anne—no one but you." Frederick shifted his weight, uncomfortable with having to acknowledge his shortcomings.

Edward noted his reluctance. "Is Miss Anne still in the area? Have you seen her?"

Frederick laughed at the question. "I saw Miss Elliot repeatedly over the past month. She stays with her younger sister at Uppercross Cottage."

"Yes, I recall now. Mary Elliot became Mrs. Charles Musgrove only a few months before I left the area. There were rumors Musgrove asked for Miss Anne first, but she refused him. I relished in the news on your behalf although I dared not tell you at the time." Edward began to pour them both some tea, having taken the tray from the housekeeper.

"It was quite a revelation when I innocently discovered the news. I became friends with the Musgroves when I arrived in the area. Ironically, one of Musgroves' sons served under me."

"Dick Musgrove?" Edward exclaimed. "I should have made the connection. Oh, Frederick, he was a trouble to his family; I hope he served you better than he did them."

"Unfortunately, no," Frederick chuckled, "but his parents now have fonder memories of their son's worth."

Edward nodded as if to say such was a common occurrence. "How did you handle seeing Miss Anne after all these years? I know how you suffered with the parting."

Frederick paused, reflecting on how the foolishness of his actions gave him little amusement. "At first, I relished the idea of seeing Miss Anne treated poorly by her family; they speak of her as an afterthought. I wanted to see her brought down—see her Elliot pride dragged through the dirt. But she does not deserve that, Edward. Anne is still the kindest, most intelligent woman I ever knew. She possesses a silent strength most men would be blessed to hold in their hands. I was a fool, Edward. I should have returned to Somerset and renewed my offer to her in '08. She would have been of age by then, but I feared rejection."

"Why not renew your proposal now? Do you believe Miss Anne still indifferent to your standing?" Edward leaned back in the chair. In years of dealing with Frederick, Edward knew to let the information come to him. Pressing forward bristled Frederick's defenses; a more relaxed position served him better.

"I created a quagmire. When I first went to Uppercross, I purposely entertained the attentions of the Miss Musgroves. I needed Anne to see how others wanted me when she did not. My conceit played games for which I must pay. Lately, I decided I still wanted Anne, but I knew I must distance myself from Louisa Musgrove, in particular, before I could plead my regard for Miss Anne."

"That seems a logical sequence. Am I to assume that was the impetus for your visit?" Edward looked amused.

Frederick frowned, bringing the lines of his brows together. "Oh, Edward, I wish it was that simple. I was in Lyme with Harville, and the Musgroves, as well as Anne; we traveled there together."

"I see." This time Edward's voice held the caution he sensed he needed.

"Throughout my relationship with Louisa Musgrove, I encouraged her to demonstrate her independence. I did it as part of my revenge on Miss Anne; I was always of the opinion she possessed a too persuadable nature. Louisa flirted with me by climbing on stiles and high steps and having me catch her when she jumped. In Lyme, she jumped from the seawall steps. The first time I caught her and set her apart from me. My thoughts were on Anne at the time. Captain Benwick and an unknown man, whom we later realized was her family's estranged cousin, both found her attractive. How to foil their plans with those of my own absorbed me. Louisa must have sensed my withdrawal for she climbed the steps a second time, taking on a greater height. Although I tried, I could not reach her in time. She sustained a blow to her head and was unconscious for a prolonged period. In short, her family expects an offer because I showed her so much attention. If she does not fully recover, I cannot in good conscience withhold that proposal. Yet, my heart does not belong to Louisa Musgrove. Even if I marry her, she will never be Anne—no one will."

Edward seemed confused. "What do you do now? Should you not be in Lyme?"

"Harville suggested I put distance between me and Louisa Musgrove. He believes she is young and will forget the flirtation. If she does not, then I will do the honorable thing and make her my wife."

Edward let out a low whistle; he finally leaned forward. "What if Miss Anne moves on before this is resolved? Did you not say she attracted the attention of two men in less than a day? What of her cousin? Is this the same cousin—the future baronet?"

"Evidently." Frederick grimaced, remembering Mr. Elliot's forwardness in speaking to Anne at the inn.

"If I recall the man snubbed the Elliots' advances previously, but if he is older, he may see the advantage of such a marriage. Sir Walter wanted Mr. Elliot for his Elizabeth, but I am sure he would be just as pleased if the heir apparent chose Miss Anne. If so, her father's family keeps control of Kellynch Hall, and our family will be looking for another residence."

"For me, it could be no worse. Back in Lyme, when we discovered who Mr. Elliot was, the waiter mentioned the man's servant bragged about going to Bath soon. Obviously, Sir Walter and Miss Elliot are in Bath, and Anne is to travel there with Lady Russell. I hoped to renew my attentions to Anne once she arrived in Bath. Now, I must wait for my fate back in Lyme while Mr. Elliot is likely to move in the same circles as the Elliots and have free access to Anne." Frederick nearly growled with thoughts of such a development. "Even if Louisa recovers and chooses someone else or chooses to end the relationship, I may be too late to earn Anne's regard again."

"You are right—a quagmire is an appropriate term." Edward shook his head in disbelief. "So I am to entertain you while you wait. Great! A caged animal in my house! Does Sophia know what she sent me? If so, I will plot my retaliation."

"I am afraid our sister is innocent this time." Frederick laughed lightly, recalling their years of teasing and tormenting each other. "Sophia discerned my regard for Anne about a week before our fateful trip to Lyme, and her concern flared to the point of my acknowledging my interest in Anne. Assuming Louisa Musgrove to be my choice, it shocked her."

"Our sister thinks she understands us," Edward joined in Frederick reminiscences. "Unfortunately, she thinks you and I would choose someone like her. Obviously, my Christine is not like Sophia."

"Oh, I do not know about that; I can easily see Sophia as a cinder maid." Frederick taunted. "Of course, now that she is the mistress of a fine house, she might consider herself above such things."

"We Wentworths are not afraid of hard word," Edward asserted.

Frederick agreed with his older brother. "It is not in our nature; that is for sure."

"I am glad you think so," Edward added quickly. "I plan to toughen you up, my Brother. I have a long list of projects that need more than two hands."

"The Wentworth men together again! Look out Shrewsbury, you are in for a treat." Frederick gave his brother a full smile. "Thank you, Edward—thank you for understanding my need to be here."

"You are my brother. No matter what your troubles, you may always find a home under my roof. Now, let us get you settled. Tomorrow, we begin your visit in earnest." Together they climbed the stairs, laughing and jostling all the way.

Chapter 13

"Let us not speak, for the love we bear one another—
Let us hold hands and look."
She, such a very ordinary little woman;
He such a thumping crook;
But both, for a moment, little lower than the angels
In the teashop's ingle-nook.
—Sir John Betjeman from "In a Bath Teashop"

Over the next few weeks, Frederick became Edward's shadow. Rarely separated from his brother, he willingly did all the things necessary to ease Edward's way in the community. He helped Edward prepare the land for Widow Leverton's garden, removing rocks and weeds despite the hardness of the winter soil. Frederick spent a night in one of the estate Cottager's main rooms, tending to the family's small children, while Edward administered to the needs of a dying parent. He used his physical strength and natural agility to make repairs around the vicarage, and he sat with pride beside his sister Christine as Edward delivered soul-searching sermons to a packed village church.

Regularly, he received reports from Harville as to Louisa's recovery. Evidently, the Musgroves returned to Uppercross, and as Milly indicated earlier, they took the Harville children with them. The last letter revealed the fact Louisa would return home before her brothers and sisters left for school, presumably right after the start of the new year. Frederick nearly panicked with the news; his fate awaited him. Would Anne be a part of his future? Nightly, he dreamed of her—the dreams more real now than they were when they first parted years ago. In his favorite dream, Frederick played out the many ways he would greet her if Anne should appear before him again—everything from dropping to his knees immediately and begging her to accept him to taking her in his arms and kissing her until she could think of nothing but him to clasping her hand in his and slowly bringing her delicately gloved fingers to his lips. He preferred the kissing her crazy idea best, but, no matter what, Frederick knew he would never walk away from her again. He would stay in her life until Anne Elliot accepted him. Thoughts of such pleasure brought a warm smile to his face.

Luminaries led to the Christmas Eve service at the church. Frederick helped Christine down from his brother's open carriage, having escorted her to the program. Entering the vestibule, she lightly placed her hand on his arm. "Frederick," she hissed, as they started up the aisle. He turned his head to look down at her, noting how she glowed. "How do you feel about being an uncle?"

Frederick froze, pulling her to a quick halt and nearly causing the family behind them to crash into their backsides. Christine smiled up at him and forced him to continue their entrance. He leaned down and whispered as he braced her hand and helped her to a seat on the far end of the pew. "Did I misunderstand you, my Dear?"

She leaned so close their heads nearly touched. "You did not. I was just thinking what a great uncle you will be to our child."

"Does Edward know?" He nearly laughed with the secrecy she shared.

Christine's eyes drifted to where her husband stood greeting parishioners. "Not until tonight." She blushed and looked away quickly.

"Edward will be ecstatic!" Frederick's grin spread as he took her hand in his.

"Do you believe it to be so?" Suddenly, his self-assured sister in marriage seemed to ask for advice on how to handle his brother.

Frederick's gaze found his older brother in the throng gathering at the back of the church. "Edward says Wentworth men wait for the women they love; he waited for you, Christine. Next to the day he made you his wife, I would venture to say the birth of his first child will be the happiest among his memories. It would be mine if I were in his shoes." He turned back to her and brushed his lips across the knuckles of her hand. "Thank you for loving my brother as you do." Then he chuckled. "Should I go tell him now? We could watch him float up the aisle in happiness. It would be a perverted justice for me to see how flustered such news could make my always-in-control brother."

"I have it planned for when I will tell him this evening. You will keep my confidence?"

"You know I will, my Dear, but I want to be at the breakfast table tomorrow morning before Edward comes down. I want to be jealous of the look on his face. You will be giving him the ultimate gift."

Christine squeezed his fingers. "May the upcoming year bring you recompense, Frederick. I pray you find the love you seek at last."

"Edward has told you?" He dropped his voice, unable to think of Anne without feeling every muscle in his body tighten.

"Edward did not need to tell me. A woman sees such things in a man's eyes, and your eyes, Frederick, say you have an unrequited love."

Frederick swallowed hard. "I have but one prayer on this Christmas Eve: Some day I will know the happiness my brother found in you."

Listening to Edward's word regarding a child being born and bringing happiness to the world took on special meaning that evening.

*　　*　　*

After six weeks in Shropshire, the weekly reports from Harville became redundant; and when the one came late in the afternoon, he nearly tossed it in the fireplace without reading it. Reluctantly, Frederick brought it to the table for the mid-day meal, leaving it lying conspicuously next to his setting while he filled a plate from a sidebar piled high with food.

"You have another letter from Harville?" Edward noted as he filled Christine a plate; he took a protective stance since learning of his wife's first pregnancy. Christine adopted several unusual eating habits of late; for example, she seemed to desire herring and chocolate, not always as separate dishes. Frederick tried not to observe what might be her latest culinary concoction.

"I am sure it is very much as it always is, filled with praises for the Musgroves' continued kindness. Louisa improves but nothing of merit happens—at least, nothing of merit as far as I am concerned." Frederick dug into the boiled potatoes as soon as Edward offered his blessing for the meal.

Christine encouraged, "You must read it, Frederick; I have a feeling about this." She shrugged her shoulders, indicating she could not explain her words. "It will—I know it will—give you what you want."

Frederick smiled at her; since the onslaught of her pregnancy, his very sensible sister had become a watering pot—a pool of emotions. "For you, my Dear," he placated her by breaking the seal on the letter. Harville addressed the note, but Milly wrote this one, and Frederick relaxed, expecting a more detailed accounting of the situation.

1 February 1815

My dear Frederick,

Both Thomas and I pray this letter finds you well. As your last missive brought us the news of Edward's upcoming arrival, we know that all is happy for you in Shropshire. Your brother must be beside himself with the love he has for Mrs. Wentworth.

We are still in residence at Uppercross although Thomas insists we return to Lyme; we will do so on Friday. Thomas says he must refocus on creating pieces for Mr. Rushick, but I know otherwise. My husband does not choose to be at Uppercross now that others join our party.

I suppose I need to tell you, Frederick, things with Louisa Musgrove have changed dramatically. Although I know what transpired, even I cannot reconcile the difference in our relationship.

Frederick's hand began to shake, and Christine ungraciously kicked her husband's ankle to get his attention. "What is it, Frederick?" Edward's voice rose in concern.

As he thumbed to page two, Frederick pushed the apprehension he felt down by wiping his forehead with his linen. "Mrs. Harville says things have changed."

"What things?" Christine gasped before she could stifle the words.

Edward touched his brother's shoulder. "Why do you not read it out loud, Frederick? We would like to share whatever it is."

Frederick nodded and shuffled the pages in his hands. He cleared his throat, trying to stall for as long as possible, before reciting the lines.

As you know, while in Lyme, Miss Musgrove spent several weeks with us. We tried as your friends to care for her, as we knew you would if you were here. Once the young lady began to recover, we all—including her loving family—spent hours reading to her and trying to entertain Miss Musgrove—to help her remember what she might have forgotten.

However, as her family felt the need to return to Somerset, the extended hours assisting Miss Louisa fell completely in our laps. You know Thomas never was a reading man and sitting quietly for hours would certainly not appeal to him. Plus, he felt the need to provide Mr. Rushick with multiple offerings to prove his worth and to secure our children's futures.

So when James Benwick offered to sit with Miss Musgrove, we were thrilled to relinquish some of our duties to him. After all, he has lived with us since leaving the service; it would be the least he could do. Captain Benwick recited beautiful verses to Miss Louisa; I often heard his resonant tones as I completed my household tasks.

That said, now, here is the catch. Captain Benwick comes to Uppercross today for he asked Miss Louisa to marry him. The good captain sent a letter to Mr. Musgrove via Thomas, and his plight was accepted. The happy couple will make a formal announcement with his arrival. Thomas does not know how to respond to all this; he is relieved for your benefit—it is as he predicted: Your withdrawal led Miss Musgrove to pay her attentions elsewhere. Yet, he feels betrayed on Fanny's account. Deep down, my Thomas knows Captain Benwick could not be expected to never find another love, but the immediacy of Benwick's suit and the fact Fanny's death came less than a year ago creates a quandary for him. Therefore, we will wish the couple happy and then return to our home.

I am sure this brings you relief, and that is its purpose. Both Thomas and I pray you will be able to return to us soon; I believe my husband could use your sensibility in dealing with the change in our home's dynamics. As always, we remain your friends—

MH

Frederick looked up in disbelief to see tears streaming down Christine's face. "You were right," he whispered, not sure his voice could respond.

"Oh, Frederick!" she exclaimed.

Edward half laughed. "I suppose this is the end of your visit?" He slapped Frederick on his shoulder. "You are one lucky man, my Brother!"

"Can it be true?" Frederick still held the letter, afraid if he moved all his hopes would be dashed. "I must write Sophy." He turned wide-eyed to stare at his brother.

Edward's smile grew by the moment. "Yes, write Captain Benwick and offer him your congratulations. Send Thomas Harville words to ease his consternation, and then write our sister. By the way, you do recall Sophia and the Admiral traveled to Bath so he might take the waters for his gout?"

The significance of what Edward said dawned on Frederick. "Benjamin's gout? They are in Bath!" He started to laugh hysterically. Getting up and dancing around the room, he swept Christine out of her seat. "Sophia is in Bath," he chanted as he twirled her around the furniture.

"Easy, Frederick," Edward cautioned. "Those are my goods you swing about the room."

Frederick spun his brother's wife once more before depositing her in Edward's lap. "I have so much to do," he called as he headed towards the door.

"What about your meal?"

"I will take it with me." Frederick grabbed his plate from the table. "I can breathe again, Edward!" he nearly shouted on his way out of the room. "I can breathe at last!"

Christine snaked her arms around Edward's neck as he adjusted her in his embrace. She laid her head on his shoulder. "Some day," she said dreamily, "you will explain to me what just happened?"

"If things go the way I suspect, the next time we see my younger brother, he will introduce you to the love of his life." He lifted her chin before taking her lips. "Frederick's love will meet my love." Then he deepened the kiss.

*   *   *

Frederick Wentworth strode down the busy street, secure in the knowledge he would see Anne Elliot soon. He arrived in Bath yesterday, nearly a week from the day he received Milly Harville's note—the longest week of his existence. In his letter he had not told Sophia he planned to join her in Bath; Frederick knew she would be thrilled he returned to her household. He simply told her of the developments at Uppercross.

Today he would meet some acquaintances; if he were fortunate, he would learn the latest gossip about the Elliots. Later, he would ask Sophia to help him meet Anne again. Sophia and the Admiral called on the Elliots previously, and Benjamin spoke of how often they saw Anne about town. In fact, the Admiral escorted her home only three days ago. If nothing else, he could make a call of "respect" on her to see how she fared. After spending so much time in each other's company at Uppercross, such an act would be appropriate.

A little below Milson Street, he met his party, having agreed last evening to spend time with Lieutenant Harding, the younger son of the Marquis of Brookstone; his sisters, the Ladies Amelia and Caroline; as well as their cousin Lady Susan Lowery. Yesterday morning, Frederick encountered Buford Harding quite unexpectedly at a posting inn twenty miles north of Bath. They agreed to meet for today's outing. Frederick might have declined the offer, but he knew Harding's family would move in the same circles, as did Anne's. He hoped to stumble upon Anne Elliot quite innocently.

"Ah, Wentworth," Harding called out as he approached. Frederick offered the group a proper bow. "Let me introduce you, Captain," he said, clarifying the connections by explaining to his family Captain Wentworth was the personal friend of Captain Benwick, under whom Harding recently served.

"Our brother tells us Captain Benwick recently became engaged." Lady Amelia's statement became a question.

"Only a fortnight ago," Frederick assured her, "if my source was reliable." They started walking toward Molland's, a fashionable confectioner's shop, often patronized by members of the *ton*. Frederick assumed he could ask his companions about the Elliots soon enough.

"Are you familiar with his betrothed?" Lady Amelia seemed interested for some reason.

Frederick guarded his words, unsure what she might have heard. "The young lady is quite pleasant; Miss Musgrove should soften Captain Benwick's need for solitude, and the Captain should allow Louisa Musgrove to develop a deep love of learning. They are well matched."

"My brother admired Captain Benwick," Miss Amelia added quickly. "I do not believe I know the Musgroves."

Frederick thought, *Now here it comes. The lady will want to know the latest gossip.* He paused before answering. "The Musgroves are a wealthy family in Somerset. Their son once served under me, but Richard Musgrove passed away several years ago."

"Ah, so they have no title?" Lady Amelia showed the usual disdain for the lower gentry.

Frederick could not resist, having felt the sting of such rebukes before. "Then maybe I should withdraw. You should not be seen in my company, Lady Amelia. Like the Musgroves, I am among the unwashed and the untitled."

"Oh, Captain," she gushed, "I meant no offense."

"None taken," he mumbled, but his partner's words so incensed him that when he stepped into Molland's and found the one person in the world he most wanted to see, every word he planned to say upon finding Anne Elliot flew out of his mind. He stood there transfixed, feeling himself turn quite red. God! She was more beautiful than he remembered, and it was all he could do not to shout for joy at being in her presence once again. Obviously equally struck by seeing him, Anne took a slight step back, and Frederick, instinctively, reached out to steady her. Just touching her sent a shock through him. All the overpowering, blinding, bewildering, first effects of strong surprise were over for her, but Frederick still could not conquer his sensibilities. It was agitation, pain, pleasure, a something between delight and misery.

"Miss Elliot," he stammered, his muscle memory offering her a bow he did not realize he completed.

Still a bit confused by the sight of him, Anne managed a quick curtsy. "Captain Wentworth." A smile turned up the corners of her mouth, as Frederick searched her face for the truth of her reaction.

"Miss Elliot," Lady Susan interrupted his thoughts, "it is pleasant to see you again. May I inquire as to the health of the rest of your family?"

Anne cleared her thoughts and responded automatically, breaking the gaze she held with Frederick. "My father is well, thank you, Lady Susan." Then she gestured towards one of the tables. "My sister and her companion, as you may see, are with me. We took refuge from the weather." Lady Susan and Elizabeth Elliot acknowledged each other with an aristocratic nod.

"I assume with Lady Dalrymple's patronage, your family will be in attendance for Madamé Tresurré's premiere?"

Anne shifted her weight, allowing other patrons to step around them. "My family shall share in the performance."

"Then we shall see you there." Lady Susan and her cousins started to move away, and with a quick bow, Frederick followed suit. He neared the table Harding located for them before he realized he just walked away from Anne—the one thing he swore he would never do again. For nearly two months he prayed daily for the opportunity to rekindle Anne's desire for him, and he just walked past her to sit with Lady Amelia, a woman who not three minutes ago made him so angry he reacted in a very ungentlemanlike manner. "Excuse me," he said to his group and came back to where Anne still stood looking out at the street.

"Miss Elliot," he spoke softly as he stepped up beside her, "I am happy to see you well."

"Thank you, Captain, and are you well? I understand from the Admiral you were with your bother in Shropshire?"

"I could do little in Lyme to help the situation so I took the opportunity to visit with Edward and his new wife. He took a living with Lord Calderson and is very productive." Frederick spoke the words automatically; he did not care of what they talked; he simply wanted to be here in her presence and to look into Anne's eyes.

"Then Mr. Wentworth has his own congregation? I am ashamed to say I lost track of him after he left the country. It gives me pleasure to know he found completion." Anne lifted her chin to better address him, while Frederick fought the urge to lower his head and kiss her.

"My new sister Christine gave Edward the ultimate gift; they will welcome their first child in late spring." His hands itched to touch her—to take her hand in his. Anne's face flushed with color at the mention of a child, and Frederick watched as she bit her lower lip. He wondered if he embarrassed her by speaking of such intimacy. Having always felt at ease in her company, he never hid his thoughts from her. "I am sorry if I embarrassed you, Miss Anne."

"I am not embarrassed, Captain. I was just thinking how blessed your brother is to find such happiness at last."

Frederick wanted to guarantee her she too would know such love; he would see to it personally, but it was too soon. He prayed "soon" was the right term—*too late* would be unbearable. "I have not asked of your own family, Miss Anne. Are they in health?"

Anne motioned towards where Elizabeth sat. "My family does well in Bath, Sir." Frederick made a point of starting to offer Elizabeth Elliot an acknowledgment, but the woman turned away with unalterable coldness. Anne flinched with the act.

Frederick stammered, trying to recover his composure, not accustomed to such snobbery—such a social cut. "I was—I was concerned—concerned for how the situation at Lyme affected you." He brought his eyes back to the comfort of Anne's face; only in looking at her did he feel contentment.

"I knew agitation for several hours when Louisa first suffered her injury, but I cannot compare my angst to what you endured."

Her words spoken so softly he strained to hear them told him they now spoke of their relationship. His next words would lay the groundwork for their future. "I am deeply sorry to be a part of any affliction Miss Musgrove met that day; I fear in some ways she misinterpreted my intent. Yet, I am thrilled Miss Louisa found happiness with Captain Benwick and he with her. He has known grief at its lowest depth, and if Louisa Musgrove gives him a new focus for his life, I relish the fact I played some part in bringing them together, although at the time none of us could think of such an end."

"I wondered if the change would affect your relationship. I hoped you would not feel ill-used by your friend. I should be very sorry that such a friendship as has subsisted between you and Captain Benwick should be destroyed, or even wounded, by a circumstance of this sort."

Anne went straight to the crux of the situation; Frederick must convince her with his next words only she could touch his heart. "Miss Musgrove is a pleasant companion, and any man would be blessed to have her in his life, but I believe she chose what is best for her. With her just leaving the schoolroom, she will easily adjust to learning poetry and philosophy from James. Her affectionate nature, demanding constant attention and giving it in return, will heal James Benwick, as is proper. I hope most sincerely they will be happy together." Frederick watched with delight as a glow grew in Anne's eyes. Feeling some relief from the agitation he felt from the moment he walked through the shop's door, he added quickly, "My time at Uppercross taught me I should set my cap elsewhere." He prayed Anne would understand his intentions.

A servant bedecked in the Dalrymple's livery interrupted their exchange. "The Lady Dalrymple's coach for the Miss Elliots," he called in a clear voice.

Elizabeth Elliot donned her best haughty pose as she stood to make her leave, letting everyone know her connection to the Dalrymples. Meanwhile, her companion scrambled to retrieve their packages. Miss Elliot walked right at them, and Frederick stepped back from Anne to give her older sister her way. After the two passed him, Frederick remembered his manners. "May I?" He offered Anne his arm and reached for the door closing behind the Dalrymple servant.

Anne dropped her eyes in embarrassment. "I am much obliged to you, but I am not going with them. The carriage would not accommodate so many. I walk." She added quickly, "I prefer walking."

Frederick realized nothing changed for Anne; her family still treated her worse than a poor relative. He looked out the window and exclaimed, "But it rains!"

Anne smiled with his defense of her. "Oh, very little. Nothing that I regard," she assured him.

After a moment's pause he said, "Though I came only yesterday, I have equipped myself properly for Bath already, you see." Frederick pointed to a new umbrella. "I wish you would make use of it, if you are determined to walk; though, I think, it would be more prudent to let me get you a chair."

"Please, no, Captain. I am much obliged for your kindness, but I need no cover from the elements, and the rain will come to nothing." Again, Anne's nervousness came to the forefront, and looking away, she added, "I am only waiting for Mr. Elliot. He will be here in a moment, I am sure."

Anne's words shot through Frederick, and a thud easily sounded from his chest, but before he could react, Mr. Elliot walked in. Frederick recollected him perfectly. There was no difference between him and the man who stood on the steps at Lyme, admiring Anne as she passed, except in the air and look and manner of the privileged relation and friend. He came in with eagerness, appeared to see and think only of her, apologized for his stay, was grieved to have kept her waiting, and anxious to get her away without further loss of time, and before they walked off together, her arm under his, a gentle and embarrassed glance, and a "good morning to you," being all she had time for, as she passed away.

Frederick stood frozen for a few elongated moments, confused about how quickly Mr. Elliot whisked Anne away. He nearly reached out for her, but realized how foolish that would seem, even to him. He returned to his party and reluctantly joined them as they watched Anne and Mr. Elliot make their way across the busy street. As soon as they were out of sight, the ladies of his party began talking of them. "Mr. Elliot does not dislike his cousin, I fancy?" Lady Caroline said dreamily.

Lady Susan leaned across the table as if to share a prime piece of gossip. "Oh! No, that is clear enough. One can guess what will happen there." Frederick fought the shiver shooting up his spine. "He is always with them—half lives in the family, I believe. What a very good-looking man!" Frederick could not breathe. *Too soon* might really be *too late,* after all.

"Yes, and Miss Atkinson, who dined with him once at the Wallises, says he is the most agreeable man she ever was in company with." Lady Amelia motioned for the wait staff to bring another pot of tea to the table. She poured a cup for Frederick and refreshed the others' cups before adding, "She is pretty, I think; Anne Elliot—very pretty, when one comes to look at her." Lady Amelia shot Frederick a knowing glance, but he barely registered the words she spoke. "Of course, it is not the fashion to say so, but I confess I admire her more than her sister."

"Oh! So do I," Caroline declared vehemently.

Lady Susan giggled, enjoying the idle talk on a rainy afternoon. "And so do I. No comparison." Then she began to tease her cousin, "But the men are all wild after Miss Elliot. Anne is too delicate for them. Is that not right, Buford?"

Buford Harding cleared his throat before offering up a defense. "Miss Elliot has a certain attractiveness—an unnamed captivation. Would you not say so, Wentworth?"

Frederick snapped out of the fog clouding his reason. "I am sorry, Harding, I missed what you said last."

"I just commented on how Miss Elliot possesses a certain winsomeness."

"Oh, I think," his oldest sister put aside her brother's opinions, "from what we observed in the last few minutes, Captain Wentworth would barely look at Elizabeth Elliot."

"Oh, really?" Lady Susan took up the taunt. "Whom would you prefer, Captain—Miss Elliot or her sister Anne?"

A thousand thoughts rushed through him. How could he stop the rumors these three would gladly carry forth? "I have known the Elliot family for many years—way back before I received my first ship. My older brother began his clerical career in Somerset, and, at present, my sister and Admiral Croft are letting the Elliots' estate. Our families are not necessarily on an intimate basis, but we have had a long-standing acquaintance—nearly a decade old. Miss Anne is the more agreeable of the three Elliot daughters if that is of what you speak, Lady Susan."

"Three?" Lady Amelia interrupted. "I understood there were only the two."

Frederick smiled, knowing he just scored a direct hit—very much like maneuvering a French ship in place for a kill. "Oh, no," he said slowly, savoring the moment. "The youngest sister is now Mrs. Mary Musgrove—the same Musgrove family into which Captain Benwick will marry. Her husband Charles will inherit the Musgrove estate at his father's passing. They reside less than three miles from Kellynch Hall. In fact, I spent much of October and November in the company of all the Musgroves and Miss Anne. Mrs. Charles suffers from a number of maladies, and Miss Anne tended her sister. I became a regular guest of the Musgroves because their son Dick served under me before his passing. The Musgroves felt a need to reconnect with that part of their son's life."

"So you really do know the family well?" Lady Amelia stammered, suddenly feeling very foolish.

Frederick would not normally add to the fodder, but today he wanted to dissuade any scuttlebutt about him and Anne, at least, until he confirmed she preferred Mr. Elliot instead. "I traveled to Lyme with the Musgroves and Miss Anne for a day trip in late November so they might meet my old friend Captain Harville and his family. It was on that trip that Captain Benwick, who took up temporary residence with the Harvilles, first met Louisa Musgrove. What you observed, Ladies, between Miss Anne and me, was a confirmation of what we both knew of the situation. Captain Harville related the news to me while Miss Anne received the tidings from Mrs. Charles."

"See, I told you," Buford Harding reprimanded his family. "I am afraid, Captain Wentworth, my sisters have vivid imaginations. We apologize if they pried into your personal affairs. I am afraid Bath does not offer them enough distractions to entertain them sufficiently."

"It is of no consequence, Harding. I am not ashamed of my admiration for Anne Elliot, nor would I ever speak poorly of her." Frederick sipped his tea before changing the subject. "What will you do now, Lieutenant, with Napoleon on Elba? Will you stay with the service or seek a buy out?"

Frederick sat back and pretended to be interested in Harding's schemes for bettering himself. He stifled the prattle of three mildly vicious young ladies—protecting Anne's reputation. Nearly thirty minutes later, he excused himself, claiming a prior engagement with Admiral Croft. Now, all he needed to do was escape to his room at Sophia's residence and regroup. Winning Anne Elliot would be his greatest reward, and what did he care if he had to move a few mountains in order to do so? Frederick was up to the task—all he needed was a way of seeing her again—a way to be in Anne's company. He would leave the rest to fate.

Chapter 14

In secret we meet—
In silence I grieve,
That thy heart could forget
Thy spirit deceives.
If I should meet thee,
After long years.
How should I greet thee!
In silence and tears.
—*Lord Byron from "When We Two Parted"*

Frederick spent a restless night, but he left Sophia's house on Gay Street with a new resolve. He hated that Mr. Elliot made inroads with Anne while he languished in Shrewsbury, but Anne was not promised to the man so Frederick still had a chance. Plus, he thought it positive she risked her family's censure by speaking to him—to actually leave her table and seek him out for private conversation. Likely, she spotted him prior to his entrance with the Hardings, and Anne waited to talk to him. At least, that was the imagined sequence of which he convinced himself. In addition, the situation at Lyme distressed her only as far as he was concerned. She cared whether Louisa's engagement destroyed a long-standing friendship. Finally, when she left yesterday, reluctance showed on Anne's face. She, evidently, wanted to remain with him. He almost wished he insisted on seeing her home; it would have caused a scene, but in some ways it would have been worth it. Of course, he would never embarrass Anne with such a public display, but the thoughts of walking through town with her on his arm offered a true temptation.

The only time he saw her that day was on Pulteney Street. He spoke to some of the Admiral's naval cronies before starting up the right-hand pavement, heading towards the main shopping district. "There she is," he mumbled to himself. Anne sat in an upscale coach. Seeing her there, Frederick, instinctively, walked in the same direction the coach traveled. Regularly, he turned his head to glance at her, while pretending to observe the busy street commerce. He wondered for a moment if he could wave down the coach somehow until he recognized Lady Russell's livery. At first, he thought Lady Russell must have seen him also, her eyes being turned exactly in direction for him, of her being in short intently observing him, but he noted the woman pointing to one of the houses along his side of the street. Anne nodded to her godmother in response to Lady Russell's attention. Perversely, Frederick stepped to the street at the cross section, taking a pose of interest. He hoped Anne saw him clearly; he prayed she recognized the smile of approval clearly displayed upon his face. Frederick stood his ground, seeking Anne's face for as long as the coach remained in sight, then he turned once more towards Gay Street.

Frederick did not see Anne anywhere, a day or two passing without producing anything. The theatre and public rooms where he was in attendance were, obviously, not fashionable enough for the Elliots, whose evening amusements, according to the society pages, were solely in the elegant stupidity of private parties.

His encounter with Anne at Molland's told Frederick where he would find her this evening though. Despite the dumbfounding surprise of walking into her that day, he did recall Lady Susan asking specifically about a special concert scheduled for this very night. It was a concert for the benefit of a person patronized by Lady Dalrymple, one of the Elliots' relatives. As he dressed, Frederick reasoned, "The concert was really expected to be a good one, and I am very fond of music." If he could only have a few minutes conversation with her again, he fancied he should be satisfied; and as to the power of addressing her, he felt all over courage if the opportunity occurred.

Attired in his full dress uniform, Frederick took a deep breath and settled his nerves before the door opened for him, and he strode into the octagon-shaped room, to be met immediately by the vision of the entire Elliot family—Sir Walter, his two daughters, and Miss Elliot's companion—stationed by one of the fires. A satisfied smile crept across his face, and he slowed his pace, trying to figure out a way to approach them in order to speak specifically to Anne. He could as he determined earlier pay his sister's respect to the family. The Elliots would disdain his familiarity, but speaking to Anne was what was important. Yet, a look of contempt from Miss Elliot made him question his choice, and he prepared only to bow and pass on.

To his pleasure, however, Anne, nearest to him, made yet a little advance and placed herself directly in his path. Despite the formidable father and sister in the background, Anne instantly spoke, "How do you do?"

Frederick touched her arm and led Anne out of the straight line to stand near her before responding. "Miss Anne, I am pleased to see you. I am well. May I assume you are too?"

"I am, Captain." Looking furtively over her shoulder at her family's glare, she said with some trepidation, "I was not sure you would remember my conversation with Lady Susan regarding the concert."

Frederick felt a rush of happiness. "I believe I told you years ago, Miss Anne, there is little about you of which I take no note. Plus, you remember my fondness for music."

"It should be very entertaining, Captain," she assured him. "Lady Dalrymple is a connoisseur of Italian opera."

"Then I shall be most pleased, Miss Elliot." He smiled down at Anne, just feeling content to be with her. "I experienced many such performances in Mediterranean port cities; from tonight's program I noticed some of which I became familiar in Romola, Italy, near Tuscany."

"It sounds so beautiful! Romola. Do you not simply adore the sound of the word?" she looked off wistfully before laughing lightly. "At least, you were able to come unarmed for Bath's weather. It is to be a star lit evening."

"My hand will seem empty," he teased. Standing before her, Frederick had a full view of her family over Anne's shoulder. "I assume your family is in health," he said when he could think of nothing else.

Sir Walther must have heard the inquiry because Frederick suddenly became aware of a whispering between her father and Elizabeth, and to his surprise, Sir Walter judged so well as to give him a simple acknowledgment of acquaintance while Elizabeth Elliot offered a slight curtsey. This, though late and reluctant and ungracious, was better than nothing, and Frederick dutifully made a distant bow in return. Their actions seemed to raise Anne's spirits, and for that, Frederick became grateful for what once seemed a chore on behalf of the Elliots.

After talking of the weather and of Bath and of the concert, the conversation began to flag, but Frederick was in no hurry to leave her. Just being next to her gave him contentment, and just seeing her renewed his spirit. With a little smile—a little glow, he said, "I have hardly seen you since our day at Lyme. I am afraid you must have suffered from the shock, and the more from its not overpowering you at the time."

She assured him, "Captain, the shock was minimal for me, and I did not feel anything more than concern for all involved."

"It was a frightful hour," said he, "a frightful day!" Frederick could not resist passing his hand across his eyes—the remembrance still too painful. Then realizing he wasted his time with Anne, in a moment half smiling again, he added, "As we briefly spoke previously, the day produced some effects—however—had some consequences, which must be considered as the very reverse of frightful." He would make sure one more time Anne knew he held no animosity about Louisa Musgrove's change of heart. "When you had the presence of mind to suggest that Benwick would be the most proper person to fetch a surgeon, you could have little idea of his being eventually one of those most concerned in her recovery."

She chuckled with the irony of the situation. "Certainly I could have none. But it appears—I should hope it would be a very happy match. There are on both sides good principles and good temper."

"Yes," said he, looking not exactly forward—"but there I think ends the resemblance. With all my soul I wish them happy and rejoice over every circumstance in favor of it." Then all the resentment he held for eight years trickled into his words. "They have no difficulties to contend with at home, no opposition, no caprice, no delays.—The Musgroves are behaving like themselves, most honorably and kindly, only anxious, with true parental hearts, to promote their daughter's comfort. All this is much, very much, in favor of their happiness; more than perhaps some."

Riled by years of frustration, Frederick nearly allowed himself to be carried away, but a sudden recollection gave him some taste of that emotion, which was now reddening Anne's cheeks and fixing her eyes on the ground, and he stopped—feeling her pain. Needing to protect her even from himself, he cleared his throat before proceeding thus, "I confess I do think there is a disparity, too great a disparity, and in a point no less essential than the mind.—I regard Louisa Musgrove as a very amiable, sweet-tempered girl, and not deficient in understanding, but Benwick is something more. He is a clever man, a reading man—and I confess I do consider his attaching himself to her, with some surprise. Had it been the effect of gratitude, had he learnt to love her, because he believed her to prefer him, it would be another thing. But I have no reason to suppose it so. It seems, on the contrary, to be a perfectly spontaneous, untaught feeling on his side, and this surprises me. A man like him, in this situation! With a heart pierced, wounded, almost broken! Fanny Harville was a very superior creature; and his attachment to her was indeed attachment. A man does not recover from such a devotion of the heart to such a woman!—He ought not—he does not."

Frederick stopped his tirade to look at Anne. Their eyes locked on each other, and everything else—the various noises of the room, the almost ceaseless slam of the door, and the ceaseless buzz of persons walking through—faded away. He watched her chest rise and fall with quick breaths, and, unconsciously, her tongue slid across her lips. He wanted to kiss her there in front of God and everybody; he wanted to whisk her from that room and take her to the nearest vicarage—to Edward or even to Gretna Green.

Finally, Anne found her voice. "You were a good while at Lyme, I think."

Frederick focused his energies to respond, but his eyes tried to speak things his words would not—he needed to convince her he regretted his actions at Uppercross. "About a fortnight. I could not leave it until Louisa's doing well was quite ascertained. I was too deeply concerned in the mischief to be soon at peace. It was my doing—solely mine. She would not have been obstinate if I was not weak. The country around Lyme is very fine. I walked and rode a great deal; and the more I saw, the more I found to admire."

"I should very much like to see Lyme again," said she.

"Indeed!" he exclaimed. "I should not suppose you could have found anything in Lyme to inspire such a feeling. The horror and distress in which you were involved—the stretch of mind, the wear of spirits!—I should think your last impressions of Lyme must be strong disgust."

"The last few hours were certainly very painful," replied Anne. "But when pain is over, the remembrance of it often becomes a pleasure. One does not love a place the less for having suffered in it, unless it was all suffering, nothing but suffering—which was by no means the case at Lyme. We were only in anxiety and distress during the last two hours; and, previously, there was a great deal of enjoyment. So much novelty and beauty! I have traveled so little, that every fresh place would be interesting to me." Frederick thought of telling her she could name the place, and it would be hers. To think he once debated whether Anne would take to his nomadic lifestyle. She continued, "But there is real beauty at Lyme." She reddened with a faint blush at some recollection, and Frederick smiled with delight. "In short, altogether, my impressions of the place are very agreeable."

"Anne," he stammered wanting to speak the long-lost words, "I need to say . . ." Before he could finish, the entrance door opened again, and the very party appeared for whom they were waiting.

He heard a footman calling out, "Lady Dalrymple, Lady Dalrymple," and to Frederick's horror, with all the eagerness compatible with anxious elegance, Sir Walter and his two ladies stepped forward to meet her. Lady Dalrymple and her daughter Miss Carteret, escorted by Mr. Elliot and his friend Colonel Wallis, advanced into the room. The others joined them, and it was a group in which Anne found herself also necessarily included, sweeping her from Frederick—dividing them.

Instinctively, they both reached for each other, but it was too late. Frederick stood glued to the spot; their interesting, almost too interesting conversation broken up, but slight was the penance compared with the happiness, which brought it on! He learnt, in the last ten minutes to feel hope.

Not realizing Anne would turn to him again, Frederick walked away into the concert room. He positioned himself in the back, not sure where the Elliot party would sit. He would like to sit beside her—to feel her warmth up and down the length of his arm. He nearly groaned with the image of it. He saw nothing, thought nothing of the brilliancy of the room; his happiness was from within. He thought only of the last half hour: their choice of subjects, her expressions, and still more her manner and look. Anne still felt something for him; on that, he would bet a year's salary. Anger, resentment, avoidance were no more, being succeeded, not merely by friendship and regard, but by the tenderness of the past—yes,—some share of the tenderness of the past. Frederick believed she could love him again.

Leaning against one of the columns, he smiled as Anne finally entered the room. She was beautiful! Her eyes were bright, and her cheeks glowed. He watched as she searched the crowd; hopefully, she looked for him. Once she was settled, he would move closer. He noted with some concern Lady Russell joined their group; some day he might be able to forgive Sir Walter, the man was bred for ignorance and disdain, but he was not sure he could ever forgive Lady Russell. Anne at nineteen turned to the woman for guidance, and her godmother betrayed the trust, destroying both their chances for happiness.

Her party divided, sharing two contiguous benches: Anne was among those on the foremost. To Frederick's chagrin, Mr. Elliot, with the assistance of his friend Colonel Wallis, maneuvered the seat by her.

Watching her closely, Frederick could not concentrate on the concert; his every fiber honed in to Anne's presence. From his new position along the right-hand wall, Frederick could see her face, and he delighted in watching her abandonment to the music. Anne sat mesmerized by the chords—lost in the melodic strains; it reminded him of her reaction to the sea. Her passion ran so deep—winning her hand would be her greatest gift to him.

As the first act came to a close, Mr. Elliot made a point of moving in closer to Anne, and they whispered intimately. Frederick stiffened as he watched Anne flush with color. Whatever Mr. Elliot said to her, she found embarrassing, and then she flipped back and forth through the concert bill, definitely flustered by his words. Whatever Mr. Elliot said definitely peaked her interest. She questioned him eagerly, but the man would not tell her of what he spoke. Frederick heard him tease, "No, no—some time or other perhaps," and then Anne visibly pouted with disappointment.

Her intimate conversation with Mr. Elliot made Frederick wonder, *What games did she play?* Frederick wondered. Not a half hour ago, her obsequious attitude towards him had his heart singing; now Mr. Elliot brought a flush to her face. The man was an obvious rake; he feigned regard with a practiced ease. Could Anne not recognize those qualities in him? Of course, she was an innocent—not used to the ways of a depraved soul, but she should listen to her instincts. He knew her to be intelligent. Why could Anne not see what was clearly in front of her? *Perfection* is not achievable in a man, nor in a woman, he reminded himself. Could she not remember how Mr. Elliot "played" the family when they sought his alliance years ago? A tiger does not change its stripes.

Watching the scenario playing out in front of him, Frederick hated the liberties the man took with Anne—with *his* Anne—for she would never belong to anyone else if he had anything to say about it. Elliot sat a little too close—laughed a little too loud—touched her hand or her arm or her shoulder a little too often. Each time he did, a jolt of resentment shot through Frederick. He was never a violent man, but a part of him would relish thrashing Mr. Elliot to an inch of his life. Just thinking of Anne caused his heart to pound in quick, hard *ka-thumps*—the same reaction he experienced in his dreams—those which haunted him for eight years.

Engrossed in his thoughts of seeing Mr. Elliot drawn and quartered, at first Sir Walter Elliot's words did not penetrate Frederick's imaginings. Seeing Anne flinch, keyed him into the critique between her father and Lady Dalrymple.

"A well-looking man," said Sir Walter, "a very well-looking man." Knowing Sir Walter's propensity for basing all opinions on looks, Frederick took what compliment he could get, but he knew it to be a second-hand one.

"A very fine young man indeed!" said Lady Dalrymple. "More air than one often sees in Bath.—Irish, I dare say." Frederick wanted to snarl at her for his own sake and for the sake of every Irishman. He served with many a fine man from the *Emerald Isle.*

"No, I just know his name. A bowing acquaintance. Wentworth—Captain Wentworth of the navy. His sister married my tenant in Somersetshire,—the Croft, who rents Kellynch."

Frederick wanted to scream at Sir Walter. *"I am more than that, you Idiot! I am the man who has loved your daughter for nearly nine years! You will know more than my name because I will soon be your son in marriage!"*

His heart raced with anger—first at Sir Walter and then at Mr. Elliot, and a little part even at Anne for not accepting him years ago. Trying to quiet his contempt, Frederick joined a cluster of men standing a little distance away. He seethed from the insults and from the uncertainty. *Maybe he should just walk away—accept the fact the barn door closed.* Thinking as such, he looked automatically at Anne, but she still spoke with Mr. Elliot. He wanted her attention on him—her gaze his. *Do not look at her anymore! You are being a fool once again!*

The next few minutes saw a shuffling of positions. The performance was recommencing, and the cluster of men restored their attention to the orchestra, so Frederick moved away. Surrounded by her family, he could not come near Anne even if he so chose. Consequently, as the first act was over, he waited impatiently trying to decide what to do. After a period of nothing amongst the party, some of them did decide on going in quest of tea. Anne was one of the few who did not choose to move. She remained in her seat, but so did Lady Russell. How could he approach Anne with Lady Russell close by?

When the others drifted back in, some further changes occurred as they resettled. Colonel Wallis declined sitting down again, and Elizabeth and Miss Carteret invited Mr. Elliot to sit between them. Eventually, Anne placed herself much nearer the end of the bench than she was before—much more within reach.

Now! He told himself as he moved forward a bit at a time, trying not to make a direct line to where Anne sat. He tried to look grave and seem irresolute, as by very slow degrees, Frederick came at last near enough to speak to her. With the others looking more intently, he found it hard to express himself with the same freedom they enjoyed in the octagon room. Although he tried desperately to recapture the magic, the difference was strikingly great.

"Are you enjoying the concert, Captain?" Anne searched his eyes, but although he chastised himself for doing so, he met her with the same gravity he offered when at Uppercross.

"In truth, Miss Anne, I am disappointed.—I expected better singing. In short, I must confess I should not be sorry when it is over."

"I am sad you feel so, Captain; I hoped we could share in the enjoyment of the music. I thought it right good, especially the Italian arias at the end, but I expect your having heard the pieces in Italy, you have a different perspective."

As much as he tried to stay aloof, Anne always touched his heart, and his countenance softened. "You are a true diplomat, Miss Anne."

"Do you think so, Captain Wentworth?" She gave him a beguiling smile. "Should I apply to the Central Office?" she joked.

The woman always affected him as no one else could. "May I offer you a letter of reference, Miss Anne?"

"Ah—a letter from a Naval Officer! Could I be so lucky?" Her voice softly taunted him in silliness.

Frederick looked down towards the bench, seeing a place on it well worth occupying. Just as he started to move and be with her despite everything, a touch on her shoulder obliged Anne to turn around.

"Miss Anne," Mr. Elliot leaned in close—too close, "I beg your pardon, but you must explain the Italian again. Miss Carteret is very anxious to have a general idea of what is next to be sung."

"Certainly," Anne bowed an apology to Frederick and turned towards her extended family. He despised the way Mr. Elliot took her arm and pulled her close to his side.

Noting their motioning to him, Frederick took a few steps to the left and held a stilted conversation with Lieutenant Harding and Lady Susan. Although they asked him repeatedly to join them, he declined. *Every time,* he thought. His gut twisted and turned in anticipation. *Every time I think we escape their societal pull, they suck Anne back in.*

As quickly as possible, he excused himself from the Harding party, promising to join them at the theatre one day next week. He could take no more of this evening; the emotional chaos ate at the back of his throat, and Frederick found swallowing a difficult task. He noted Anne finished her translations so he took his leave of her. He guarded his response to her closeness and bid Anne a hurried sort of farewell. "I wish you a good night, Miss Anne. I am going.—I should get home as fast as I can; Sophia will be expecting me."

Anne looked at him anxiously. "Must you, Captain?"

Frederick refused to look at her, knowing if he did he would betray his true feelings. "Unfortunately."

"Is not this song worth staying for? It is an Italian love song—a beautiful love song." Anxious to be encouraging, she nearly pleaded with him.

"No!" he heard himself say curtly. "There is nothing worth my staying for, especially a love song." He forced a bow and then spun on his heels and stormed from the room.

A pang of jealousy ricocheted through him as he slammed the door back far enough for it to resonate through the empty octagon room. "See how that sounds mixed with her love song!" he grumbled as he retrieved his greatcoat and hat. "Why with my luck, it will rain," he thought out loud, turning up the collar of his coat against the wind before pulling on his gloves. *Why was he so upset with Anne?* "Did she seek out Mr. Elliot?" He knew the answer before the words were out of his mouth. "Jesus! I am an idiot. What did you expect her to do? Ignore her family? She is still an Elliot for God's sake!" Frederick looked back at the concert hall he just left. *Should I go back in and apologize to her?* "Anne did not deserve your anger," he offered himself a reprimand. "I will call on her tomorrow at Camden Place. I made a big enough ass out of myself for one evening." He would go home and construct a proper apology—an earnest pledge. He would grovel if necessary, but Anne Elliot would accept his sincere regrets for tonight—for Lyme—for Uppercross—and for leaving nine years ago.

*   *   *

Frederick and Anne completed their first circuit of the deck. Today he walked without assistance, although a bit slow, he relished finally being on his own.

"Doctor Laraby says we should be in port late tomorrow afternoon or early the next morning, depending on the weather." Anne held his arm for her husband's sake, more so than his giving her support. She watched as he took each step, a gingerly move followed by a solid planting of his foot. "I will be happy to have you on dry land again." She squeezed his arm, feeling his muscles tighten in response. "Will it not be nice to have some solitary time together?"

"I must admit I look forward to resting in your arms—a repeat of the other evening." Frederick's words caressed her ear, just loud enough to bring a flush to Anne's cheek. He smiled down at her, knowing they shared like images.

"You, Sir," she started a reprimand, "are beyond reform."

"And you love me that way," he whispered softly—a wicked grin spreading across his face. "In fact, you love me very well. I am married to the most beautiful and passionate woman there is."

"Why do you tease me so?" Anne stopped to be sure he knew his taunt struck a cord.

Frederick became instantly serious. "My darling, Anne, you know I mean no harm; I would not embarrass you for the world. I suppose I sometimes just get carried away because it is unbelievable to me you are finally mine. Being able to take some liberties with my wife is such a pleasure—such a relief—after waiting for you for so long."

Anne laughed lightly, knowing she could never be angry with him. "Frederick Wentworth, if you want to keep my heart, those are the kind of words with which you should shower me. When you speak as such, I can never deny you. Speak the truth, my Love; please understand, false platitudes work only with my father and my sisters."

Frederick pulled her hand in closer to his side, holding her tightly to him. "Come, Anne, let us make another turn around the deck; we have drawn some attention thanks to our ardor," his voice only heard by her. They walked a third of the way on the starboard side before he said anything else, but again Frederick spoke only loud enough for his wife's ear. He did not look at her directly, but the intimacy remained. "For you, my Dear, to think of yourself not deserving of praise—of every declared compliment—is a blasphemy against nature. From the first moment I saw you in that shop nearly a decade ago, it is your face I desire, and, if you recall, your sister Elizabeth proceeded you into the room that particular day; yet, she held no power over me. Only your countenance—your eyes—haunt me." He knew Anne dropped her gaze; she watched her steps—her footing. "I know others would think your sister Elizabeth the beauty in the family, for she truly has a handsome face, but one only must spend a minute in her company, and he can see there is nothing but porcelain skin and striking features." Frederick paused before finishing; he cupped her hand with his. "However, along with those doe-like innocent eyes of yours, your face exudes pure beauty because your loveliness come from an inner charm—a goodness of spirit. Look at how quickly James Benwick came under your spell. Think about how even with Mr. Elliot's return to the family, he never named himself for your sister—never accepted her beauty. Did you ever ask yourself why? Because Elizabeth has nothing to offer beyond her vanity. You, however, my Sweetling, caught Mr. Elliot's attention before he even knew who you were. As much as I despise the man for his deceit, I cannot fault his taste in women."

Instinctively, Anne leaned her head against his arm—although just for a few seconds. "I love you, Frederick Wentworth," she whispered.

"Each day I tell myself how lucky I am to hear you say those words."

Again they walked in silence; words no longer needed to be spoken. Finally, to break the stillness, Anne lifted her chin and offered him a veiled challenge. "I am surprised, my Love; you actually said something positive about my cousin."

"Do not expect it to happen very often," he warned. "From the moment I saw Mr. Elliot look at you at Lyme, I wanted to introduce him to a set of chains in a rat-infested cargo hold."

Anne smiled brightly. "I savored your display of jealousy at the concert. The gratification was exquisite. My only concern was how to quiet such jealousy and how, in all the peculiar disadvantages of our respective situations, would you ever learn my real sentiments. It was misery to think of Mr. Elliot's attentions.—Their evil was incalculable."

"I have been reliving our romance since my injury. It began with the laudanum-induced sleep, but it continued throughout my recovery." He waited for her reaction, but Anne just nodded in understanding. "Last night I dreamed of finally winning your regard, but it was not how it actually happened. It was quite extraordinary though. I am not sure I did not prefer it to the actual event."

"How so?"

"For one thing, I was out of my misery the day after the concert instead of having to wait three more days to know my fate." He smiled down at her, leaving no doubt where his thoughts now rested.

"Would you tell me about your dream?" she taunted. "I would enjoy your version of how everything *should* have been resolved."

"Only if you will lay in my arms again when we return to my quarters." His voice became husky, murmuring his thoughts in undertones purely for her hearing.

Anne simply nodded her agreement, unable to express herself as easily as did he.

"I am becoming tired," he said loud enough for those close by to hear. "If you do not mind, Mrs. Wentworth, we will retire to my quarters."

"Of course, my Dear," she spoke her affirmation. "Let me help you on the steps."

Chapter 15

Your open heart,
Simple with giving, gives the primal deed,
The first good world, the blossom, the blowing seed,
The hearth, the steadfast land, the wandering sea,
Not beautiful and rare in every part.
But like yourself, as they were meant to be.
—*Edwin Muir from "The Confirmation"*

The candle burned down, leaving distorted shadows dancing in every corner. Anne snuggled into her husband's chest as he stroked the silkiness of her hair spread out across his arm.

"Now, my Love, I want to hear how things should have been between us." She caressed Frederick's jaw line with her fingertips.

He kissed her forehead as he pulled her closer to him. "You might find this amusing," he cautioned. "At least, the suspense was over quickly for both of us."

"Frederick, just tell me." Her voice displayed an annoyance with his stalling. "I will not scoff at or make light of what you say. Actually, I am most interested; I used to come up with multiple scenarios on how we would rediscover each other."

"An action for which I am eternally grateful." He raised her chin with his fingertips and kissed her gently.

"Tell me," she demanded once he withdrew.

"Yes, Sweetling," he said dutifully before settling her in his arms once more. "Well, if you recall, you visited Mrs. Smith at Westgate Building the morning after the concert. She kindly warned you about Mr. Elliot, but, of course, I had no idea you left her apartment altogether in a confusion of images and doubts—a perplexity, an agitation of which you could not see the end."

Anne sighed audibly and snuggled in closer. She kissed the underside of his jaw line before leaning back to lightly stroke the muscles of his chest. Frederick held her tightly to him, unwilling to release her closeness. "Oh, Anne," he groaned as he tried to force the desire away.

"I am waiting," she whispered.

Frederick knew Anne meant she waited for him to return to his story, but the sound of her voice was reminiscent of the dream, which haunted him all those years of separation. Unable to control his need, Frederick rolled her to her back and repeatedly drank of Anne's lips. "God, I love you!" His mouth rested just above hers. "You are everything to me."

Anne nibbled on his lower lip. "I suppose I will never hear your story's ending," she mocked.

"Oh, you will hear it," he whispered in her ear, "but not for a few minutes. I have a different story to tell you—one about a man who loves his wife beyond reason—about a man who worships his wife as if she was the center of his universe."

Anne snaked her arms around his neck, lacing her fingers through his hair. "I believe I heard this story before." She giggled as he kissed the sensitive spot between her neck and shoulder. "But," she gasped as his lips traced a line from her ear to the base of her neck, "I believe—it needs—retelling." She finally got the words out before succumbing to his more persuasive administrations.

Some time later, Anne sat tailor-style in the middle of the bed, her hair draped prettily around her shoulders. "So, I knew about Mr. Elliot, but you did not know how I felt about him," she prompted.

Frederick leaned against the backboard, pillows propping up his upper body—a look of pure satisfaction encasing his countenance. "All right, you win." He lowered his forearm from where he draped it over his eyes, but before he continued his tale he took Anne's hand and pulled her into closer proximity; he laced their fingers together.[1]

---

[1] The cancelled chapters of *Persuasion* were written from July 8-18, 1816. According to all accounts, Austen rewrote them, thinking the originals "tame and flat." The original draft is on display at the British Museum. This "dream" sequence is based on Edith Lank's translation found on the Republic of Pemberley's website.

"While you were speaking to Mrs. Smith about Mr. Elliot, I suffered from another version of the story from my sister and the Admiral. The Admiral heard from one of his cronies, who also attended the concert, that at the end, Mr. Elliot declared himself, and you accepted. I did not know what to believe; I could not accept the Admiral's words as the truth, but I knew how Mr. Elliot touched you with a familiarity I was no longer allowed."

"I am sorry," Anne stammered.

Frederick squeezed her hand. "It occurred to the Admiral, you and Mr. Elliot might want to return to Kellynch, and he and Sophia could speak of nothing else. My heart knew such pain, and my family did not recognize my angst. As the day progressed, I hid in the study, pretending to read, but envisioning the worst.

"Somehow, the Admiral and you met on the street. That part of the dream was not very clear. I suppose I just needed an excuse for your appearance at Gay Street. Anyway, I hid in the study, but much to my horror, I heard Benjamin outside the door."

"'I cannot stay' said the Admiral, 'because I must go to the Central Office, but if you will only sit down for five minutes, I am sure Sophy will come.—You will find nobody to disturb you; there is nobody but Frederick here.' The Admiral opened the door as he spoke.

"There was no time for recollection! For planning behavior or regulating manners!—There was only time to turn pale before you passed through the door and met my astonished eyes. I was sitting by the fire, pretending to read and prepared for no greater surprise than the Admiral's hasty return. Equally unexpected was the meeting, on each side. There was nothing to be done, however, but to stifle feelings and be quietly polite.

"The Admiral wanted to know the truth of the rumors so he began to question you. 'Why, Miss Elliot, we begin to hear strange things of you.' Benjamin smiled nicely while I cringed, awaiting your response. 'But you have not much the look of it,' the Admiral teased, 'as grave as a little judge.' His words brought a blush to your face, which to Benjamin confirmed his suspicions. 'Aye, aye, that will do. Now, it is right. I *thought* we were not mistaken.' He had no idea his words ripped a hole in my soul. 'My Sophy will be very happy to see you. Mind—I will not swear that she has not something particular to say to you—but *that* will all come out in the right place. I give no hints. Please sit down, Miss Elliot. Mrs. Croft will be down very soon.' You moved to one of the winged chairs, sitting on the edge and obviously being very nervous. I assumed from my observations you simply did not know how to tell me the truth. 'I will go upstairs and give Sophy notice directly.'

"You sprang to your feet. 'Please, Admiral, do not interrupt Mrs. Croft. I will call another time.'

"'I will not hear of it,' the Admiral used his best military tone, and like every man who ever served under Benjamin, you followed orders and reseated yourself. Then the Admiral made a quick bow and offered his excuses once again—taking his leave. You and I were to be left alone to deal with our quandary. However, at the door, he turned back to me and said, 'Frederick, a word with *you*, if you please.'"

"That sounds so like Benjamin," she observed. "What happened next?"

"I had no choice but to attend him. As Benjamin might do, he began the conversation before we were out of your hearing. 'As I am going to leave you together, it is but fair I should give you something to talk of.' I managed to close the door, knowing to where Benjamin's words would lead and because I did not wish to give you pain.

"Benjamin continued, 'I must know so if you please, I need you to speak to Miss Elliot.'

"I pleaded, 'I cannot do this, Sir. Please do not ask me.'

"However, the Admiral's agitation could not be contained. 'We have a lease for Kellynch, but Sir Walter has options to end it on proper notice.'

"'Have you not signed the lease?' I asked.

"'Yes—yes, of course, but I hate to be at an uncertainty.—I must know at once.—Sophy thinks the same. If Miss Elliot is to marry, Sophy and I will remove to another property.'

"The thoughts of asking if you were to marry Mr. Elliot nearly brought me to my knees, but Benjamin was oblivious to what he requested. I begged to be excused from the task; however, the Admiral was determined. 'Phoo, Phoo,' he shamed me. 'Now is the time. If *you* will not speak, I will stop and speak myself.'

"I agreed, although a firing squad would have been a more welcome occasion. I no more said, 'Yes, Sir,' than he opened the door leading back to you. There we were—alone—trying to overcome the impossible. I knew you must have heard part, if not all, of my conversation with Benjamin. He spoke without any management of voice, although I tried to check him."

"Poor Frederick," she cooed. "You actually dreamed such an awful state of affairs for yourself?"

In feigned serious, he spoke, "I am a real trooper."

Anne laughed lightly at his false bravado—a tender, romantic gesture. "You are a saint, my Husband,"

"Anyway," he began again, "I walked immediately to a window, irresolute and embarrassed. I longed to be able to speak of the weather or the concert. I stood looking out at nothing for, at least, a half minute. Then I forced myself to walk to where you sat. In a voice of effort and constraint, I followed the Admiral's orders. 'You must have heard too much already, Madam, to be in any doubt of my having promised Admiral Croft to speak to you on some particular subject—and this conviction determines me to do it—however repugnant to my—to all my senses of propriety, to be taking so great a liberty.—You will acquit me of Impertinence, I trust, by considering me as speaking only for another, and speaking by necessity.—The Admiral is a man who can never be thought impertinent by one who knows him as you do.—His intentions are always the kindest and the best; and you will perceive he is actuated by none other, in the application, which I am now with—with very peculiar feelings—obliged to make.'

"I knew I made little sense—rambling on, but when you refused to look at me, I could barely think. I stopped—merely to recover my breath—not expecting an answer, I proceeded, with a forced alacrity. 'The Admiral, Madam, was this morning confidently informed you were—upon my word I am quite at a loss—ashamed . . . ' Again I took a deep breath to settle my nerves and finished by speaking quickly. 'The awkwardness of *giving* information of this sort to one of the parties—you can be at no loss to understand me.—It was very confidently said that Mr. Elliot—that everything was settled in the family for a union between Mr. Elliot—and yourself. It was added you were to live at Kellynch—Kellynch was to be given up. This, the Admiral knew could not be correct.—But it occurred to him it might be the wish of the parties—and my commission from him, Madam, is to say if the family wish is such, his lease of Kellynch shall be cancelled, and he and my sister will provide themselves with another home, without imagining themselves to be doing anything which under similar circumstances would not be done for *them*.—This is all, Madam.—A very few words in reply from you will be sufficient.—That *I* should be the person commissioned on this subject is extraordinary!—And believe me, Madam, it is no less painful.—A very few words, however, will put an end to the awkwardness and distress we may both be feeling.'"

Wentworth heard Anne gasp. "Oh, Frederick, tell me I said something intelligible at this juncture. Please say I was not as tongue-tied as I usually am."

"I am afraid, my Love, I dreamed you as you really are—perfect—but often afraid to give offense to anyone." He continued his tale as Anne stared silently at him.

"Before you could answer, I added, 'If you only tell me that the Admiral may address a line to Sir Walter, it will be enough. Pronounce only the words, *he may.*—I shall immediately follow him with your message.'

"I stood transfixed, waiting for you to speak the words, which would doom me to a life of loneliness. Finally, you found your voice. 'No, Sir—there is no message.—You are misin—the Admiral is misinformed.—I do justice to the kindness of his intentions, but he is quite mistaken. There is no truth in any such report.'

"There we were—hearts beating madly—held in a moment of exquisite agony. I was a moment silent, and then you turned your eyes towards me for the first time since my reentering the room. I saw all the power and keenness that no other eyes possess. '*No* truth in any such report!' I repeated.

"You gave me an amused smile. 'No truth in any *part* of it?—None.'

"I collapsed in the chair I was standing behind, enjoying the relief of what you said. I drew a little nearer to you. We looked at each other with expressions that were silent but still a very powerful dialogue. On my side there was supplication, on yours, acceptance. Then I took your hand and said, 'Anne, my own dear Anne!'"

With this, he pulled her hand to his lips and kissed the inside of her wrist. "Was that the end of the dream?" She barely got the words out. His actions literally took her breath away.

"Not entirely . . ." Frederick's eyes lit up with mischief. "You, of course, ended up in my arms."

Anne rolled her eyes. "Of course."

"We kissed passionately until Sophia finally left her mantua maker long enough to make an appearance in the study. I am afraid my sister quite understood the situation even without our explanation. Your lips were swollen from my passion, and you looked quite thoroughly kissed." Frederick chuckled in remembrance. "Quite beautiful, in fact."

"You would enjoy embarrassing me so!" she chastised him.

Frederick pulled her even closer. "I enjoyed holding you in my arms. You were finally mine. How could I not kiss you blind?"

"Then what?"

"Well, it began to rain, and my sister astutely invited you to stay to dinner. A note was dispatched to Camden Place—and you stayed—stayed with me until ten at night. Sophia knew I once loved you so she contrived for her and the Admiral to be frequently out of the room together. Nature, or fate, took its course. The rest of the dream is very much like what happened in reality. I told you of my love, and we found each other—so rationally, but so rapturously, happy as any evening could be."

"I agree." Anne fell into his embrace. "Your version is nearly as romantic as the real thing. Now, I was wondering if you would care to demonstrate how well you kissed me during this romantic dream?" She stretched forward to where her lips met his.

"That, Sweetling, I will do most willingly—any time—day or night." With his hand behind her head, Frederick pulled Anne's mouth to his. Quickly, he deepened the kiss, hearing himself moan with the pleasure of it. "Perfect," he whispered, only a breath away from her lips. "Absolutely perfect."

Chapter 16

Love, faithful love, recalled thee to my mind—
But how could I forget thee? Through what power,
Even for the least division of an hour,
Have I been so beguiled as to be blind
To my most grievous loss!
—William Wordsworth from "Sonnet"

Frederick knew he could not escape Sophia's close examination when he returned, but he honestly wished he could simply slink off to lick his wounds and regroup for a new assault on Anne's regard. He handed his hat and coat to a waiting servant before heading upstairs to the Admiral's study.

"Frederick, you are home so early," the Admiral noted as Frederick stepped through the open door. "I thought you might join some friends after the concert."

Frederick walked to where Sophia sat, bending down to kiss his sister's upturned cheek. "I left before the concert ended." He crossed to the window to peer out at the darkness. *Just get through some civilities, and then you can withdraw,* he told himself.

"Was the concert not entertaining?" Sophia watched him to see his reaction.

Frederick clasped his hands behind his back. "I was disappointed—the singer was lacking."

"Really?" his sister sounded surprised. "I would have thought Lady Dalrymple would never lend her name to anything less than perfect."

Frederick paused before answering, not wanting to rehash the entire evening with his sister. "Some found the performance adequate."

"But you did not?" Benjamin seemed as amused as was his wife.

"Miss Anne says it is probably because I heard the arias—the songs—while I was in Italy. These were poor imitations." He tried to come up with an excuse that did not reek of jealousy, but he could think of nothing original.

Sophia sat down her book. "You spoke to Miss Anne at the concert?"

"Do not think as such, Sophia," he warned, looking over his shoulder at her. "Lady Dalrymple is a relative, and, of course, Sir Walter would want to preserve the connection. The whole Elliot clan was in attendance."

"I see," Sophia mused. "Were you received by the family?"

"Other than Miss Anne—the rest treated me only as a bowing acquaintance although Sir Walter thinks I am a very well-looking man." Sarcasm dripped from his every word. "And even though Lady Dalrymple agreed, she believes I have the air of an Irishman!"

The Admiral guffawed, nearly choking on his port, while Sophia stifled her smile. "That is better than being the best-looking sailor he ever met." Benjamin countered.

"When one puts it that way, I suppose I prefer my compliment to yours." He begrudgingly took the seat across from his sister.

"I am sure Miss Anne did not treat you poorly," his sister said the words softly, not sure whether Frederick wanted to hear them. "Miss Anne does not judge."

"No, she does not." Frederick allowed at last. His time with Anne this evening was superb; surrounded by concertgoers, he remembered none of them—only he and Anne existed in those moments. *Think about it!* He said to himself. *Anne faced the censure of her family and of society when she approached you this evening. And at the confectionary shop she did not move when you started past her. She avoided her family again that day to be with you. That should count for something.* Without realizing he did so, Frederick nodded his head in remembrance. "If the two of you do not mind, I think I will make it an early evening. After spending six weeks with Edward, I am accustomed to country hours." He shoved to his feet before offering them a quick bow. Then he headed towards the door; he needed time—time to figure out how to fix the mess he created.

The night seemed endless—little sleep came, and Frederick took some relief at leaving his bed, having had a thorough battle with the linens and pillows throughout most of the time he spent stretched out across it. Part of the time he thought it best to abandon Anne to Mr. Elliot. As much as he despised the man, Mr. Elliot could offer Anne things of which Frederick could only dream. If Anne married Mr. Elliot, she could assume her mother's position as the mistress of Kellynch Hall. She would be Lady

Elliot—call Kellynch her home again—her home forever. Mr. Elliot was to inherit everything.—Anne deserved everything.—Frederick thought there would be every possibility of their being happy together. A most suitable connection everybody must consider it—but he thought it might be a very happy one also.

Yet, the thought of Anne sharing her life with anyone but him ripped his heart from his chest. Anne—*his Anne* was so incomparable—so beautiful—so intelligent. His fascination for her began years ago, and it never waned—not one day, even though he tried repeatedly to put her behind him. He spent too many nights wondering what it would be like to hold Anne in his arms in a moment of ecstasy—of pure desire. He saw her disdain the social proprieties thrust upon her by her family; he knew she was made of sterner stuff than how she appeared. *He was a wishful fool—hoping against hope something would change before Anne accepted Mr. Elliot's troth.*

*   *   *

To make matters worse, Frederick spent the day after the concert walking about Bath in hopes of a sighting Anne. He visited the Pump Room, Victoria Park, the Royal Crescent, the shops, and Sydney Gardens; yet, he found her not. Panic set in!—Could Mr. Elliot be applying for Anne's hand as Frederick searched fruitlessly for her? His skin itched in anticipation; he was foolish last evening. He left her in the company of Mr. Elliot although she, obviously, wanted him to stay—to join her, even, on the bench. She asked him to listen to a love song, and he refused. To his sorrow, Frederick heard the words he spoke to her: *There is nothing worth my staying for.* What idiotic words those were! He should have told Anne she was worth staying for and then seated himself next to her. But he allowed her family to turn him away—to question his own worth—to retreat before being snubbed. What did he care if the likes of Lady Russell or Lady Dalrymple or Sir Walter Elliot did not approve of his relationship with Anne? *Evidently, more than you thought you pompous ass! How could you let them ruin your chances to see Anne or call on her again?*

That evening he took a tray in his room, unable to hold a civil conversation with his sister or Benjamin. Totally discommoded, Frederick felt a prickling along the back of his neck and spine, telling him his time was shorter than he expected. If he did not reconnect with Anne Elliot by the next afternoon, he would call, unannounced, on her at Camden Place and plead for her to receive him. He would immediately pledge his love for her and ask Anne to make him the happiest of men—giving her complete control of their fate.

He could not rely on the inspiration of the moment; he needed to carefully construct what he would say to Anne when he discovered her. He failed a golden opportunity at the concert; now he must formulate a plan. He would prove himself, most especially to her. At least, this gave him a focus for the evening—to pass away the hours until he could search for Anne again. *If only,* he thought.

*   *   *

"Wentworth!" Frederick heard his name. Turning quickly to search the stream of faces rushing by him on the busy street, he finally saw the smiling countenance of Thomas Harville followed closely behind by Charles Musgrove.

"I say, old man," Charles laughed lightly as he extended his hand in friendship, "I never expected to find you on the streets of Bath."

"Neither did I," Harville joined in the meeting, "but I am pleased to see you, Frederick. You are looking well. How long have you been in Bath?"

"Only for a week." They stepped to the side to let the onslaught pass them by. "I came to join Sophia and the Admiral; he is here to take the water for his gout. What brings you two to Bath?"

Charles supplied the answer. "Captain Harville wanted to come to Bath on business."

Thomas interrupted, "I wanted to see some of the offerings at the better shops—to inspect the workmanship. It would give me an idea of what Rushick might need." Frederick nodded with understanding.

"Anyway," Charles continued, Harville began to talk of it a week ago; and by way of doing something, as shooting was over, I proposed coming with him, and Mrs. Harville seemed to like the idea of it very much, as an advantage to her husband; but Mary could not bear to be left, and made herself so unhappy about it that, for a day or two, every thing seemed to be in suspense, or at an end. But then, Papa and Mamma took up the cause. Mamma has some old friends in Bath, who she wanted to see; it was thought a good opportunity for Henrietta to come and buy wedding clothes for herself and Louisa; and, in short, it ended being Mamma's party, making it easier on the captain here. Mary and I came too—Mary to help Henrietta with the shopping."

Frederick looked pleased to see them. "When did you get in?"

"Late yesterday evening," Thomas added as he shifted his weight to his cane hand.

"You must come say hello to Mamma," Charles insisted. "She would have my hide if I let you slip away without her renewing the acquaintance. You know, you are as good as family as far as my parents are concerned."

"That is very kind of you." Frederick looked towards his best friend. "Milly's last letter gave me the impression you were to return to Lyme."

Thomas met Frederick's eyes; they would have a conversation in front of him to which Charles would not be privy. "*I assumed* we would travel," he stressed the words, "but the Musgroves *were insistent* we stay. Plus, the children developed friendships with Charles's youngest siblings. Milly stays behind with *all* the children and Mr. Musgrove. Of course, James tends Miss Musgrove."

"I see," Frederick answered, very much the captain, listening to a report from his second in command. "How *fortunate* for all of you!" He noted the humor flash in Thomas's eyes.

"Then come," Charles started ushering them forward. "We took a suite of rooms at the White Hart." He led the way as the two sailor friends took up companionship. "Mary and I called on her father earlier today. Miss Anne came back with us; she may still be with Mamma. Have you seen her since you came to Bath, Wentworth?"

"We spoke at a concert a few nights ago." Frederick knew his heart leapt with the news. He would see Anne today, but now with the possibility, he found his resolve faltering. Maybe he would observe how she reacted to him—to make sure he did not misconstrue her looks of renewal the other evening. If she seemed friendly today, he would approach her with his pledge.

"Good—good," Charles added in reply. "It will be just like last autumn—all of us together again."

They walked the few streets needed to bring them to the White Hart. Charles hustled both of his friends into the room. "Mamma, look who we found," he called.

The wrinkles in Mrs. Musgrove's face increased as she broke into a full smile. "Captain Wentworth! For heaven's sake, how perfect is it to have you among us again. You were sorely missed, Sir."

Wentworth gave the room a proper bow and then took Mrs. Musgrove's outstretched hands in his. He brought one chubby set of knuckles to his mouth and grazed them with his lips. "Thank you, Ma'am, for receiving me."

Mrs. Musgrove teased him about his formality, and then led Frederick full center into the room. Frederick did not look directly at Anne since coming through the door, but his whole body knew she was there even before Charles led them across the portal. Although he prepared himself for the prospect she might be among the party, the surprise of the moment at looking at her, after pining for her approval the last two nights, still took his breath away. *Stay calm. Observe.* He warned himself, needing to be in control in front of their combined party. He made a quiet comment or two to the group at large and then took up a position behind one of the larger wing chairs peppering the room.

Frederick tried not to make it obvious he watched Anne, but try as he may, his eyes remained on her. He attempted to be calm and leave things to take their course, trying to dwell much on being rational. He thought, "Surely, if there be constant attachment on each side, our hearts must understand each other ere long." And yet, a few minutes afterwards, he felt as if their being in company with each other, under their present circumstance, could be exposing them to inadvertencies and misconstructions of the most mischievous kind.

Mary's call to Anne broke Frederick's concentration. Standing close to the window, Mrs. Charles seemed pleased to announce to the whole room, "Anne, there is Mrs. Clay, I am sure, standing under the colonnade, and a gentleman with her. I saw them turn the corner from Bath Street just now. They seem deep in talk. Who is it?—Come and tell me." But before Anne could obey, Mary gasped, "Good heavens! I recollect.—It is Mr. Elliot himself."

"No," cried Anne, and Frederick watched as she blushed. "It cannot be Mr. Elliot," she offered in explanation. "I assure you he was to leave Bath at nine this morning and does not come back until tomorrow."

How does Anne know Mr. Elliot's traveling plans? he wondered. *How intimate are they?* The thoughts vexed him to no end; Frederick was near the point of ordering everyone from the room, except Anne, and demand she recognize his need for her. If it was his room, he might seriously consider it if it would end this madness. *Could Anne have stressed the times for Mr. Elliot's coming and going to let him know she would be alone? God!* He hated all this uncertainty.

Mary, resenting she should be supposed not to know her own cousin, began talking very warmly about the family features, and protesting still more positively it was Mr. Elliot. She called for Anne to come and look herself.

Frederick delighted in Anne's stubbornness in relenting to Mary's wishes. He prayed she did it for his sake, but those moments of hope vanished on perceiving smiles and intelligent glances between two or three of Mrs.

Musgroves' friends, as if they believed themselves quite in the secret. It was evident the report concerning Anne—Frederick's suspicions about Mr. Elliot—spread; and the short pause succeeded in ensuring it would now spread farther.

Reluctantly, Anne moved to the window to satisfy all the eyes now falling upon her. Frederick cringed as she stepped forward and drew back the drape. "Yes, it is Mr. Elliot certainly," she announced to the room. "He changed his hour of going, I suppose, that is all—or I may be mistaken; I might not attend." Frederick's eyes followed her back to her chair. Anne seemed composed, and it irritated him to think others in the room thought she must acquit herself to them.

After a few more excruciating minutes, Mrs. Musgrove's friends finally departed, much to the relief of everyone else in the sitting room. Then Charles revealed, "Well, Mother I did some thing for you while I was out today that you will like. I went to the theatre and secured a box for tomorrow night. Am not I a good boy? I know you love a play, and there is room for us all. It holds nine. I am sure we can engage Captain Wentworth, and Anne will not be sorry to join us too. We all like a play. Have not I done well, Mother?" Frederick actually liked the idea of being with Anne without the rest of the Elliots looking on. It could be the opening he needed.

"Charles, how thoughtful," Mrs. Musgrove good-humoredly began. "I do so love a play, and it would be a wonderful evening if Henrietta and all the others can join us. You will come will you not, Miss Anne?"

Mary eagerly interrupted the exchange. With delight at being the center of attention, Mrs. Charles delivered a reprimand to her husband with a large dose of Elliot pride. "Take a box for tomorrow night! Have you forgot we are engaged to Camden Place for the same evening? We were most particularly asked on purpose to meet Lady Dalrymple and her daughter and Mr. Elliot—all the principal family connections—on purpose to be introduced to them? How can you be so forgetful?"

Frederick and Thomas Harville traded a knowing look—they both held the same opinion of Mary Musgrove. No wonder Charles spent so much time out of the house. Frederick could not imagine being married to such a woman. He thought Charles would happily turn back the clock and press Anne harder if he could.

Being called out in front of everyone, Charles Musgrove had no choice but to be contrary, declaring his renewed intention to see the play. "Your father might have asked us to dinner if he wanted to see us. You may do as you like, but I shall go to the play." He added the last line for good measure.

Thus began a heated discussion on both sides. Frederick witnessed more than one of these arguments during his time with the Musgroves. In the beginning he found them amusing, but now he thought it a pathetic situation. It came from marrying without love—marrying without respect. If he did not win Anne, he may never marry; he did not believe he could tolerate such a life just for the sake of an heir. He could leave any of his fortune to Edward's and to Sophia's children.

"Please, Charles, there was always such a great connection between the Dalrymples and ourselves," she pleaded. "We are quite near relations, you know—and Mr. Elliot too, with whom you ought so particularly to be acquainted! In time he will be our nearest neighbor. Every attention is due to Mr. Elliot. Consider my father's heir—the future representative of the family."

"Do not talk to me about heirs," cried Charles. "I am not one of those who neglect the reigning power to bow to the rising sun. If I would not go for the sake of your father, I should think it scandalous to go for the sake of his heir. What is Mr. Elliot to me?"

Frederick gave Anne his full attention, looking and listening with his whole soul. The last words brought his inquiring eyes from Charles to her. *Will Mr. Elliot be Charles's new brother? Tell me, Anne. Deny your connection to the man.* He tried to will her to bring their love together.

Finally, Mrs. Musgrove interceded. "We better put if off. Charles, you had much better go back and change the box for Tuesday. It would be a pity to be divided, and we should be losing Miss Anne too, if there is a party at her father's; and I am sure neither Henrietta nor I should care at all for the play if Miss Anne could not be with us."

Frederick realized Mrs. Musgrove would prefer Anne to attend to serve as a buffer to Mary's pretensions, but he was thankful because the woman provided Anne with the opportunity to set everyone's assumptions straight. *Say it, Anne,* he silently pleaded.

Frederick listened intently as, trembling noticeably, Anne spoke. "If it depended only on my inclination, Ma'am, the party at home, excepting on Mary's account, would not be the smallest impediment. I take no pleasure in that sort of meeting and should be too happy to change it for a play and with you. But, it better not be attempted, perhaps."

Frederick let out the breath he did not realize he held. Anne did it! She made it clear she wanted nothing to do with the structured lifestyle to which her family clung. Automatically, he moved from the seat he took with the ladies' earlier departure. He walked as inconspicuously as possible to the fireplace, pretending to warm his hands with the flame before taking a station with less barefaced design by Anne. As the others continued to speak of the pros and cons of the party and the play, Frederick spoke directly to her. "You have not been long in Bath," said he, "to enjoy the evening parties of the place." He demanded she confirm what he hoped to be true.

With a beguiling smile, she turned her full beauty on him, and Frederick felt his knees go weak. "Oh, no! The usual character of them has nothing for me. I am no card player."

A smile of his own turned up the corners of Frederick's mouth; strings of a love song took flight—swelling as his lungs filled with a scent of lavender so close he could touch it. "You were not formerly, I know." He thought, *I know you better than anyone.* "You did not used to like cards, but time makes many changes." Their words spoke of cards, but their hearts spoke of love.

"I am not yet so much changed," she protested, and then she stopped.

Frederick feared she did not want him to mistake what she said, but he could no longer contain the emotions coursing through him. As if it were the result of immediate feeling, he declared, "It is a period, indeed! Eight years and a half is a period!"

Before Anne responded, Henrietta interrupted their private moment, totally unaware of the magic building between them. Frederick felt the air sucked from him; he still had no answer—strong suspicions—but no answer; and he watched in dismay as Anne, obviously reluctant, spoke of being perfectly ready to retire the room.

More vexing was the entrance of Sir Walter and Miss Elliot. Having moved away unwillingly from Anne, Frederick noted the general chill hanging over the room. Anne, disquieted by her family's grand entrance, appeared oppressed, and wherever he looked, he saw symptoms of the same. The comfort, the freedom, the gaiety of the room was over, hushed into cold composure, determined silence, or insipid talk, to meet the heartless elegance of Anne's father and sister.

"We came to issue everyone an invitation for tomorrow evening," Elizabeth declared. Then she turned to Frederick, offering him not only an acknowledgment but also a flirtatious smile. "Oh, Captain Wentworth, I especially hope you will be available to join us." Frederick flinched with her attention—a shiver shooting down his spine. *What was Anne thinking with the change of situation?* He often wished for such acceptance but never at this cost. "Tomorrow evening," he heard Miss Elliot saying the proper nothings, "to meet a few friends, no formal party."

It was all said very gracefully, and the cards which she provided herself, the "Miss Elliot at home" were laid on the table, with a courteous, comprehensive smile to all, and one smile and one card more decidedly for Frederick. A definite twist in his stomach sent his earlier meal rising to a sickening awareness. He fought back the urge to run from the room. *Lord knows,* he thought, *no such alliance would satisfy him!* Elizabeth pointedly slid her card across the table to Frederick before she and Sir Walter disappeared.

He knew all eyes fell on him, and although Frederick saw the offering as atonement for all the insolence of the past, he knew only surprise rather than gratitude—polite acknowledgment rather than acceptance. Disdain filled him as he held the card in his hand after they left. He seriously considered accepting the invitation, but never for Elizabeth. If he ever entered Sir Walter's drawing room, it would be to claim Anne as his own.

The interruption was short, though severe; and ease and animation returned to most of those they left, as the door shut the Elliots out. Frederick stepped to the side, deep in contemplation, wondering how Anne perceived all that just happened.

Mary moved to her sister's side and audibly whispered, "Only think of Elizabeth including every body! I do not wonder Captain Wentworth is delighted! You see he cannot put the card out of his hand."

Frederick wanted to toss it into the fire, as if the card was a live spark burning his fingertips. Anne caught his eye, and he felt his cheeks glow with embarrassment. His mouth formed itself into a momentary expression of contempt before he turned away in vexation.

"Wentworth, Harville and I plan to check out some of the shops in the trade district. We would be pleased if you joined us." Charles picked up his hat to head for the door.

"Certainly, Musgrove," Frederick stammered, preferring to stay behind in hopes of speaking to Anne but unable to do so. "Are you ready, Harville?" Thomas grabbed his cane and followed the others out.

Both he and Thomas remained quiet, deep in their own brooding. Musgrove rattled on about the possibility of taking up falconry or some other such sport, but neither of the other two men heard much of what he said. When they reached the trade shops, they agreed to separate for a while. Frederick called off to join Harville, claiming his friend might need his help in maneuvering the crowded stores.

"You must be put out by all this," Frederick noted as they stepped through the doorway of a cramped furniture shop.

"What brings you to say that?" Harville stopped to look carefully at the intricate carving on a grandfather clock.

Frederick chuckled lightly. "You did not object when I used your injury as an excuse to avoid Musgrove right now. You would never accept any such offer otherwise."

Harville pulled up, leaning heavily on his cane. "Do you have any idea what Benwick requested of me?" Anger hung on every word.

"Tell me," Frederick's lips barely parted—his jaw clenched in anticipated contempt.

"That pretentious ass wants me to commission a portrait for Louisa Musgrove. He gave me this to use as the model." Harville thrust a small miniature painting into Frederick's hand. "Damn him! He had it made for Fanny—remember at the Cape—he met with a clever young German artist at the Cape, and in compliance with a promise to my poor sister, sat to him, and was bringing it home for her. And I have now the charge of getting it properly set for another!" And with a quivering lip he wound up the whole by adding, "Poor Fanny! She would not have forgotten him so soon!"

Frederick stared at his best friend's countenance. "You should not be put in this position; I brought my folly upon your home."

"I do not hold you responsible any more than I do James. But who else is there for him to employ? Yet, I cannot easily accept this. Fanny was my dearest sister—the playmate of my childhood." Harville walked away, needing to distance himself from his own words.

After an extended moment, Frederick followed. "Leave it to me," he told Harville. "I will take care of the commission. That is the least I can do for you. You must cherish Fanny's memory.—I will not have it tarnished."

Harville swallowed hard. "Thank you, my Friend."

Frederick did not acknowledge the thanks—no need existed between them. A person cannot stand beside another in times of war and not develop a deep unexplainable connection—a brotherhood in arms. Instead, he pointed to the elaborate design of a nearby table. "Do you suppose you can duplicate such artistry?"

"I expect I can; I made some preliminary drawings. Seeing all these pieces gives me some ideas of how I can make my mark." With his fingertips, Thomas reached out and traced the edges of a small table. "I love the feel of the wood," he confided. "The smell of the oil as it stains the grain." For a brief moment, he existed in another realm. "I know all that probably sounds deranged."

"It would take more than that to make me ever think you mad." Frederick moved up beside him. "It is time to meet Musgrove—let us hear more about shooting and sport."

Harville laughed—a deep belly laugh. "He does go on, does he not?" They started for the shop's door.

Frederick spent the evening with the Musgrove party. He would not abandon Thomas to the group's continual talk of wedded bliss. Secretly, he hoped Anne might rejoin them, but she did not come, although Mrs. Musgrove relayed how she earnestly begged Anne to return and dine—to give them all the rest of the day, but she was promised to come again for breakfast on the morrow. Frederick vowed he would be there; he and Anne would finish this.

Chapter 17

Yes yours, my love, is the right human face.
I in my mind had waited for this long.
Seeing the false and searching for the true,
Then found you as a traveler finds a place
Of welcome suddenly amid the wrong.
—Edwin Muir from "The Confirmation"

Anne did not keep her appointment to break fast with the Musgroves. Of course, the weather took an unfavorable turn, and Frederick knew she would walk to the hotel, but it did nothing for his state of mind. They feasted on a hearty fare; yet, he ate little of what he placed on his plate. Frederick hungered for something totally unrelated to food; only Anne's acceptance could fill him.

Late morning, she made her way to the proper apartment, and Frederick breathed at last. The aura of the room radiated from the moment Anne walked through the door, and, ironically, her arrival signaled a clearing from the earlier downpour.

Their eyes met immediately. Being close to the door, having positioned himself to greet her upon her arrival, Frederick stepped forward and took her proffered hand and raised it to his lips in greeting; then he forced his legs to move, placing himself at the desk and beginning to separate the papers and prepare the pen.

"Ah, Miss Anne," Mrs. Musgrove ushered her forward towards a chair at the table, "we are so glad you came. Henrietta and Mary feared you would not—what with the weather and all. The ladies could not wait once the sky began to clear, but they will be back again soon. They gave strict injunctions before they left; I am to keep you here until they turn back."

Out of the corner of his eye, Frederick noted how outwardly composed Anne appeared, and he wondered how he must look to the others. From the moment she walked in the room, he felt himself plunged at once into all the agitations which he merely anticipated tasting a little before the morning closed. There was no delay—no waste of time. He was deep in the happiness of such misery or the misery of such happiness, instantly.

Clearing his throat and trying to take on the guise of non-interest, Frederick spoke to his friend, "We will write the letter we were talking of, Harville, now, if you will give me the materials."

"They are on the side table." Thomas gestured to a small table to Frederick's left. With materials all in hand, he went to it, and nearly turning his back on the gathered party tried to appear engrossed by writing.

His sister Sophia spoke to Mrs. Musgrove, and he listened carefully to their conversation, trying to gleam any words spoken by Anne. Mrs. Musgrove informed Sophia about the changes taking place at Uppercross, and his sister heartily agreed that young people should not dwell in long engagements. Frederick found himself agreeing in principle with Sophia's sentiments. He knew she spoke from experience; she and the Admiral married in a little over a month of their meeting. As he pretended to draft the letter, which he composed in his head overnight, Frederick thought about how quickly he could marry Anne after she accepted him. He would not be willing to wait any longer than necessary.

Sophia declared, "To begin without knowing that at such a time there will be the means of marrying, I hold to be very unsafe and unwise. People should not delay their coming together."

Instinctively, his pen ceased to move, his head raised, pausing, listening, and he turned round the next instant to give a look—one quick, conscious look at Anne. She flushed with the recognition, but neither of them looked away. The two ladies continued to talk—to urge again the same admitted truths and enforce them with such examples of the ill effect of long engagements as had fallen within their observation, but Frederick heard nothing distinctly; it was only a buzz of words in his ear, his mind in confusion. Finally, Anne succumbed to the need to break the connection, and she diverted her attention towards Thomas Harville, who motioned her to join him by the window.

Frederick pushed the longing back down in his gut while returning to the task at hand. He began writing the letter in earnest.

Scratching out the order for the artist he would commission, Frederick heard Thomas talk to Anne regarding the miniature. His friend explained to her why Frederick took up the charge of the letter. He thought it ironic Thomas spoke so openly to Anne when he refused to share his frustration with anyone else in the party besides Frederick. When their words turned to a light-hearted debate on which sex loved best, Frederick heard only their musings; his sister's conversation no longer existed. With every nerve in his body tuned to Anne—only she existed in *his* world, and he *must* know how she felt.

"It would not be the nature of any woman who truly loved," she protested against Harville's assertion that men never forsook the women they loved. Frederick would never forsake her—of that he was sure. Her soft voice brought him back. "Yes, we certainly do not forget you so soon as you forget us. It is, perhaps, our fate rather than our merit. We cannot help ourselves. We live at home, quiet, confined, and our feelings prey on us. You are forced on exertion. You have always a profession, pursuits, business of some sort or other, to take you back into the world immediately, and continual occupation and change soon weaken impressions."

Frederick swallowed hard. *Was that how it was for Anne? Did she believe he did not suffer from their separation?* She must think because he threw himself into his work, he forgot her—that he did not leave his heart behind in Somerset. He must tell her; only her love gives him comfort.

Needing to respond immediately, he took another sheet of foolscap from the desk drawer and began to address her with a passion he could no longer control.

> I can listen no longer in silence. I must speak to you by such means as are within my reach. You pierce my soul! I am half agony—half hope. Tell me not that I am too late, that such precious feelings are gone forever. I offer myself to you again with a heart even more your own than when you almost broke it eight years and a half ago. Dare not say that man forgets sooner than woman, that his love has an earlier death. I have loved none but you.

Realizing Anne's voice now spoke with a fervor he was long to remember, Frederick jerked his head up and clumsily knocked over the blotting jar, sending it scattering dust across the carpet. His pen followed. He quickly retrieved the items, embarrassed at being so obvious in his intent.

"Have you finished your letter?" called Captain Harville.

Frederick stammered, "Not quite, a few lines more. I shall have done in five minutes."

Harville smiled at Anne. Frederick should have known Anne would win Thomas's loyalty; he and Harville both understood the qualities of a fine woman. "There is no hurry on my side," his friend shared. "I am only ready whenever you are.—I am in very good anchorage here—well supplied and wanting for nothing.—No hurry for a signal at all." As he rearranged the items on the desk, he heard Harville lower his voice to speak to Anne further. They talked of inconstancy, and Frederick's heart went out to his friend as Thomas spoke with compassion and with insights into how sailors feel about the women they love. "I speak, you know, only of such men as have hearts!" Thomas ended with pressing emotions.

"Oh!" cried Anne eagerly; "I hope I do justice to all that is felt by you and by those who resemble you." She offered his friend empathy, and Frederick smiled, knowing it to be her true nature. "No, I believe you capable of every thing equal and good in your married lives. I believe you equal to every important exertion, and to every domestic forbearance, so long as—if I may be allowed the expression, so long as you have an object." Frederick leaned forward, hanging on Anne's every word. "I mean, while the woman you love lives and lives for you. All the privilege I claim for my own sex is that of loving longest when existence or when hope is gone."

Frederick ached to touch her. Possibly his friend understood because out of the corner of his eye, Frederick watched as Thomas put his hand on her arm quite affectionately.

Hearing his sister stirring behind him, Frederick returned to his letter.

> Unjust I may have been, weak and resentful I have been, but never inconstant. You alone brought me to Bath. For you alone I think and plan.—Have you not seen this? Can you fail to understand my wishes?—I had not waited even these ten days, could I read your feelings, as I think you must have penetrated mine. I can hardly write. I am every instant hearing something which overpowers me. You sink your voice, but I can distinguish the tones of that voice, when they would be lost on others.—Too good, too excellent creature! You do us justice indeed. You do believe there is true attachment and constancy among men. Believe it to be most fervent, most undeviating in
>
> FW

"Here, Frederick you and I part company, I believe," Sophia spoke loud enough to recall him from his task. "I am going home, and you have an engagement with your friend.—Tonight we may have the pleasure of all meeting again at your party." The last line she directed to Anne. "We had your sister's card yesterday, and I understand Frederick had a card too, though I did not see it—and you are disengaged, Frederick, are you not, as well as ourselves?"

As she spoke, Frederick scratched out his postscript.

> I must go, uncertain of my fate; but I shall return hither, or follow your party, as soon as possible. A word, a look will be enough to decide whether I enter your father's house this evening, or never.

He managed to answer his sister, although a bit incoherently. "Yes, very true; here we separate, but Harville and I shall soon be after you, that is, Harville, if you are ready, I am in half a minute. I know you will not be sorry to be off. I shall be at your service in half a minute."

Sophia nodded her farewell to each of them, and he and Thomas began to make their leave also. Frederick sealed his letter with great rapidity. Having made the decision to write it, he wanted the words in Anne's hands; Frederick needed to be finished with this part and to start his life with Anne if she would just have him.

With a definite plan in mind, he slid Anne's letter under the blotter pad, having sealed it and marked it with her initials. "Let us be off, Harville," he encouraged. Frederick picked up his gloves—laying them purposely to the side of the desk—then his hat before walking to the door. He could not speak to Anne—nor even look at her. His impatience to be gone creating a new agitation—a hurried air as he exited the room.

Frederick heard Thomas offer a kind "Good morning. God bless you" to Anne. He regretted not being able to speak his goodbyes, but if Anne were to refuse him, he wanted no pity from those who saw their departure.

He and Thomas made it to the outside door before he spoke again. "Harville, wait for me a moment; I seemed to have left my gloves in the Musgroves' quarters."

"No problem—I shall remain here." Harville shifted his weight, allowing the cane to support him.

Making his unexpected entrance, Frederick took delight in seeing Anne's beseeching eyes fall on him. "I apologize, Mrs. Musgrove," he spoke as he crossed the room, "I left my gloves behind."

Mrs. Musgrove stood by the window, looking out for the rest of their party. "It is quite all right, Captain Wentworth." The woman did not even turn around.

However, Anne stood close by, and she watched his every move. Stepping beside the desk, Frederick purposely slid his fingers along the edge of the scattered paper. He locked eyes with Anne, assuring him she recognized the intent of his actions; and then he drew out the letter, placing it before Anne with eyes of glowing entreaty lasting an elongated moment. With the slightest of nods, he hastily collected his gloves and was again out of the room—the work of an instant!

Everything was, literally, in her hands. Frederick found Harville where he left him, and they started towards the portrait studio to meet with the artist. They walked two blocks in complete silence—Frederick's vexation clearly evident.

"Do you want to tell me to whom you wrote the second letter?" Thomas asked softly, never looking at his friend.

Frederick hesitated, not sure how to respond. "You saw that?" he finally answered with his own question.

"Obviously," Thomas taunted. "Was it a love letter for Miss Anne?" His friend chuckled at seeing Frederick flinch, but when Frederick did not answer, Harville gasped a little too loud, "It was a love letter for Miss Anne!"

Barely audible, Frederick moaned, "Yes—yes, it was for Anne."

"Anne?" Thomas continued to respond in a mixture of disbelief and pleasant surprise. "How long has she been *Anne*?"

"From the first day I laid eyes on her."

"In Somerset over eight years ago," Thomas finished the sentence for him. "I knew it, you sly fox!" He slapped Frederick on the shoulder.

"Do not congratulate me, Thomas; I know not my fate. The letter professes my love, but will Anne accept a renewal of my regard?"

Frederick looked distraught, and Thomas took pity on him. "May I ask why you are with me? Give me the miniature and the letter; I can well do this without you." Frederick started to protest, but a wave of Thomas's hand stopped him short. "Go—go back to the White Hart and win the woman you love. Do not leave there until she is yours!"

"Dare I risk it?" Frederick looked back the way they came, unsure what to do.

Thomas gave him a full grin. "Do you truly love this woman?"

"Most whole heartedly," Frederick whispered.

"I never knew you, my Friend, to allow anything to keep you from what you most desire. This would be a first."

"No," Frederick shook his head. "It will not be a first." Anxiety increased as he looked away once more. "I must go—I am sorry, Harville, but I must go!" As he strode away, he heard Thomas chuckling.

Turning the corner at Bath Street, he noted she and Charles crossed to Union. He quickened his step to catch up, but when Frederick reached them, he paused. Knowing within a few minutes he would speak what was in his heart, he froze—irresolute whether to join them or to pass on, saying nothing, after all. He stared at her—agape—wondering what to do! Each heartbeat infinitely long! Then Anne, sensing his approach, turned suddenly; she blushed—the cheeks, which were pale, now glowed, and the movement, which hesitated, was decided. Frederick stepped up beside her, and they were lost to each other. Eyes danced in happiness, and they were as before—united—hearts interlocked, needing no words to declare their love.

"Say, Wentworth," Charles implored him. "Which way are you going? Only to Gay Street or farther up the town?" Charles appeared most anxious to leave.

An element of surprise played through his voice, although Frederick never diverted his eyes from Anne's countenance. "I hardly know," he replied.

Charles continued without taking note of what transpired between them. "Are you going as high as Belmont? Are you going near Camden Place? Because if you are, I shall have no scruple in asking you to take my place and give Anne your arm to her father's door. She is rather done for this morning and must not go so far without help. And I ought to be at that fellow's in the market place. He promised me the sight of a capital gun he is just going to send off; said he would keep it unpacked to the last possible moment, that I might see it; and if I do not turn back now, I have no chance. By his description, a good deal like the second-sized double-barrel of mine, which you shot with one day, round Winthrop."

Frederick tried to wipe the silly grin from his face, but he gave up the effort when he saw a like one on Anne. "It is fine, Musgrove. Go see the gun. I will be most honored to escort Miss Anne home; she will be safe with me."

"That is superb news," Charles gushed. "I am in your debt." Then he disappeared, hurrying along Union Street.

"Which way, Miss Anne?" Frederick's voice remained husky with emotion.

"Some place quiet, Captain—you may choose." Anne placed her hand on his proffered arm, and Frederick pulled her close to his side. Relief rushed through him as they turned away from the crowd.

As they entered the park, Frederick led her to a nearby bench. "May we sit for a time?" They spoke little over the last few blocks other than small talk about the weather and such. When he properly seated Anne beside him, Frederick took up her hand in his, clutching it to his chest. "Anne," he whispered, "my hearts beats again because of you—with the hope you will receive me—that you understand how ardently I adore you." He brought her palm to his lips and planted a kiss on the inside of her wrist. "Please say I am not too late."

Anne released her hands from his, but she did so to trace the outline of his lips. "Yours is the face I see every time I close my eyes. It has always been so—nothing you could say or do will every change that."

Frederick physically gulped for air. The passion rose in her eyes, just as he remembered it, and it took all his control not to clutch Anne to him. "May I be so forward as to presume there is hope for us?"

"There is more than hope, Frederick. I give you my assurance." She did not look away. "I am no longer that foolish green girl; I am not so persuadable. If God gives us a time once more, I will never turn from you. You will be my life if that is truly your desire."

"Say it, Anne," he demanded. "Say the words you know I need to hear."

She raised her chin to look him directly in the eyes. "I love you, Frederick Wentworth; I have loved none but you."

Frederick's fingertips traced the line of her cheek from her temple to her jaw. "You have no idea," he began, "how much I love you." He took her hand once more and pulled Anne to her feet. "Come, my Dear, let us walk. It will not do for me to take you in my arms in the midst of this busy park, and I fear if we sit her any longer, I will ruin your reputation with that or more."

Anne laughed—a light tinkling of bells drifting on the breeze. "You would never break with propriety, Captain," she teased.

He leaned towards her, letting his breath tickle her ear. "Do not tempt me, Miss Elliot," he taunted in return. "When it comes to you, I have little control."

Redness spread across her chest and warmed Anne's face. "I recall vividly," she murmured.

Frederick knew instantly he liked the more mature Anne. She still blushed with his words, a fact in which he took great delight, but she, too, spoke more boldly and accepted his *seductive* ways. "I plan to give you new memories," he whispered.

They retired to the gravel walk, where the power of conversation would make the present hours a blessing indeed. There they exchanged again those feelings and those promises, which once before seemed to secure every thing, but which were followed by so many, many years of division and estrangement. There they returned again into the past, more exquisitely happy, perhaps in their reunion, than when it was first projected: more tender, more tried, more fixed in a knowledge of each other's character, truth, and attachment; more equal to act—more justified in acting. And there, as they slowly paced the gradual ascent, heedless of every group around them, seeing neither sauntering politicians, bustling house-keepers, flirting girls, nor nursery maids and children, they could indulge in those retrospections and acknowledgements, and especially in those explanations of what directly proceeded the present moment, which were so poignant and so ceaseless in interest. All the little variations of the last week were gone through and of yesterday and today there could scarcely be an end.

"Admit it; you were jealous," Anne spoofed.

They walked into a secluded area; a row of hedges blocked their view of the finely worn path. Instinctively, he pulled Anne to him, taking her into his arms; she snuggled into him—her head resting on his chest. Finally speaking, Frederick feigned being offended, "Were you trying to make me jealous, Sweetling?" His hands moved slowly up and down her back, keeping her tight in his embrace.

Anne tilted her head back to look up at him. "If I did, you deserved it, you know." A smile turned up the corners of her mouth, and Anne's eyes twinkled with enjoyment.

Frederick outlined her lips with his fingertips, pulling gently on her bottom one. His smile matched hers—his being lost to her closeness. "I believe, Sweetling, I did; but you have no idea how I suffered this past week."

"I would think you would know me well enough to realize Mr. Elliot was not to my liking." She moved in closer, wrapping her arms around his waist and relaxing into him.

Frederick swallowed hard, shoving his overwhelming desire down. "Oh, Anne,—but you know not the misunderstanding—the doubt—the torment." He held her to him until he heard someone approaching at a distance. "We should walk again, my Dear."

"Frederick," she began softly as she fell into step beside him. "I would like for us to be honest with each other. When we were together before neither of us spoke the whole truth. For me, it was because I did not want to disappoint; I so desperately feared losing your love. I suppose it was my age or my lack of life experience; I had no idea of what I should expect.—Sometimes, the feelings were so foreign to me, and I wondered if other women felt as I did. For you, I believe you tried to protect me. Unfortunately, because I did not know what to expect, my fears surfaced too quickly."

"I do not understand, Anne. What do you desire of me?"

She paused, trying to find the right words. "What I suppose I am trying to convey is my need to know how you feel—what you felt—whether it was jealousy or anger or humor or desire. I want something different from what I see every day. I once told Mr. Elliot my idea of good company is the company of clever, well-informed people who have a great deal of conversation; of course, he shunned my ideas, but the point I want to make is I desire the same type of relationship I observe in your sister and the Admiral."

"Then you wish to know of my anguish?"

"I would never ask of you to do so, especially if it was a painful experience; yet, if we are to really know each other, we must speak our hearts." Anne looked up at him, trying to explain the unexplainable.

Frederick just nodded. "I agree. Over the past few months I observed love in the eyes of my brother and Christine—in Thomas and Milly—and in Sophia and Benjamin. With each, I knew I could settle for nothing less, and in doing so, I realized I could settle only on you. I came to Bath to win your regard, and when I saw you in the company of Mr. Elliot, I lost all reason. I tried to tell myself you offered me signs of returning my affection, but my mind was not sensible. Jealousy began to operate in the very hour of first meeting you in Bath; it returned, after a short suspension, to ruin the concert; and it influenced me in every thing I said or did or omitted saying and doing in the last four-and-twenty hours. It gradually yielded to the better hopes, which your looks, or words, or actions occasionally encouraged; it was vanquished at last by those sentiments and those tones which reached me while you talked with Captain Harville. Listening closely and feeling so much, I could hear no more without responding."

"It was a beautiful letter," Anne gushed. "I could not believe my eyes; it was as if my dream came to life."

"Every word was true," he insisted. "I have loved none but you; no one could supplant you in my life; I never saw your equal, my Love. I tried to forget you and believed it to be so; I imagined myself indifferent when I was simply angry at your actions. Because I suffered from our separation, I tried to deny your merits; but your character is perfection itself. Only at Uppercross did I learn to give you justice, and only at Lyme did I understand myself."

They returned to the main course way. Frederick led her to another bench. "When Mr. Elliot reacted to your presence on the steps at Lyme, I wanted to throw the man into the sea; I had no right, but I admit to such violent thoughts. You mesmerized me as I watched you on the Cobb—the way the ocean played at your feet; you were like a water sprite. Finally, your superiority shone through at Harville's: your empathy for James and the way you handled the crisis on the beach."

Anne dropped her eyes and pretended to straighten a seam on her dress. Frederick took her chin in his palm and raised it once more. "Anne, I am a foolish man—very foolish. I wanted to punish you for not loving me enough." Anne started to protest, but he silenced her with a touch of his finger to her lips. "I know you love me—I knew it then, but my pride would not let me admit it, so I tried to attach myself to Louisa Musgrove, although I soon realized we had nothing upon which to build a relationship. By Lyme, I tried to distance myself from her; I planned to approach you before we boarded our coaches to return to Uppercross, but fate twisted those plans. Louisa could never compare with the excellence of your mind or the perfect, unrivalled possession it has over mine. At Lyme, I learned to distinguish between the steadiness of principle and the obstinacy of self will. I exalt you in every way, and I deplore the pride, the folly, and the madness of resentment, which kept me from trying to regain your love the moment I returned to Somerset and found you unattached."

"It was a terrible time for both of us. I knew we could still be friends from the moment you took Little Walter from the room; I believed you no longer hated me when you secured the Admiral's carriage for my comfort." She slid her hand under his cupped one, and Frederick tightened his grip, guaranteeing she could not change her mind and withdraw. "Of course, I would have preferred not to listen to the Admiral speculate on which Musgrove you would marry."

Frederick chuckled. "Do I detect a bit of jealousy in your tone? I would relish in knowing so."

"Then fancy yourself satisfied; I wanted you for myself, and as much as I esteem Louisa Musgrove, I could never picture you with her." Anne's voice did not falter.

"I was so pleased when Louisa began to recover, thinking I could wait a reasonable amount of time and then present myself to you. I no sooner began to feel alive again, than I began to feel, though alive, not at liberty. I found Harville considered me an engaged man! Neither Harville nor his wife entertained a doubt of our mutual attachment. I was startled and shocked. To a degree, I could contradict this instantly; but when I began to reflect others might have felt the same—her own family, nay, perhaps herself, I was no longer at my own disposal. I was hers in honor if she wished it. I was unguarded. I had not thought seriously on this subject before. I had not considered that my excessive intimacy must have its danger of ill consequence in many ways; and I had no right to be trying whether I could attach myself to either of the girls, at the risk of raising even an unpleasant report, were there no ill effects. I was grossly wrong and must abide the consequences.

"In short, at precisely the time I became fully satisfied my not caring for Louisa at all, I regarded myself as bound to her, if her sentiments for me were what the Harvilles supposed. Therefore, I chose to weaken whatever feelings or speculations existed by removing myself to Shropshire, meaning after a while to return to Kellynch and act as circumstances might require.

"I was six weeks with Edward and saw him happy. I could have no other pleasure. I deserved none. He enquired after you particularly—asked even if you were personally altered, little suspecting to my eye you could never alter." Anne squeezed his hand and offered a little smile. "I remained in Shropshire, lamenting the blindness of my own pride until at once released from Louisa by the astonishing and felicitous intelligence of her engagement with Benwick.

"Here," said he, "ended the worst of my state; for now I could, at least, put myself in the way of happiness; I could exert myself; I could do something. But waiting so long in inaction was dreadful. Within five minutes I said, 'I will be at Bath on Wednesday,' and I was. Was it unpardonable to think it worth my while to come? And to arrive with some degree of hope? You were single. It was possible you might retain the feelings of the past as I did; and one encouragement happened to be mine. I could never doubt you would be loved and sought by others, but I knew to a certainty you refused one man, at least, of better pretensions than myself: and I could not help often saying. 'Was this for me?'"

"Yes, I overheard Louisa tell you about Charles's proposal." Anne added, "Charles is very amiable, and as much as I respect him as my sister's husband, the thoughts of spending my life with a man who rarely reads or who prefers sport above all else was not tolerable. Besides, my heart was engaged elsewhere." She offered him a flirtatious smile.

"You are so beautiful when you smile." Frederick stroked the inside of her wrist with his thumb.

"Then you, my Love, must give me more reasons to smile."

"How about this?" He brought her wrist to his lips and placed a kiss along her pulse.

Anne leaned into him, entranced by the moment. "Finding my thoughts when you do that is impossible." Her voice held that breathy pause, which told him her affections remained strong.

"Your appearance so suddenly on Milson Street was exquisite torture. You were in front of me—all I saw was you, but horror in the guise of Mr.

Elliot broke that splendor. Then you stepped forward in the octagon room to speak to me, and I was again lost to you. No one else existed at that moment. But again, your family whisked you away."

"I turned back to you after acknowledging Lady Dalrymple's entrance, but you were gone," she protested.

Frederick's face showed his regret. "I did not suspect," he mumbled. "It was such a time—to see you," cried he, "in the midst of those who could not be my well-wishers, to see your cousin close by you, conversing and smiling, and feel all the horrible eligibilities and proprieties of the match! You could be Lady Elliot, just as your mother was! To consider it as the certain wish of every being who could hope to influence you! Even, if your feelings were reluctant or indifferent, to consider what supports would be his! Was it not enough to make the fool of me, which I appeared? How could I look on without agony? Was not the very sight of the friend who sat behind you, was not the recollection of what had been, the knowledge of her influence, the indelible, immoveable impression of what persuasion had once done—was it not all against me?"

"Oh, Frederick," Anne sympathized, "I am sorry you suffered because of me. I assure you from the beginning, there was a sensation of something more than immediately appeared in Mr. Elliot's wishing to reconcile with my father. In a worldly view he had nothing to gain by being on terms with my family. In all probability he was richer, and the Kellynch estate would as surely be his here after as the title. At first, I thought it to be for Elizabeth's sake."

"How could any man consider your sister Elizabeth once he met you?" Frederick leaned back against the seat.

Anne looked around quickly as if worried someone might overhear. "I cannot explain everything at this time, but believe me when I say Mr. Elliot's intentions were not fully to seek my regard. He was more concerned with preventing my father from taking up with Mrs. Clay."

"Now, I see," replied Frederick, leaning forward in awareness, knowledge evident on his face. "If your father would have another child—a boy, perhaps, Mr. Elliot would lose his title."

Anne confirmed, "Exactly."

"Yet, I had no idea at the time. All I could see was the benefit of your connection to your cousin and my fear of being too late!" he exclaimed.

"You should have distinguished," replied Anne. "You should not have suspected me now; the case so different, and my age so different. If I was wrong in yielding to persuasion once, remember that it was to persuasion exerted on the side of safety, not of risk. When I yielded, I thought it was to duty; but no duty could be called in aid here. In marrying a man indifferent to me, all risk would be incurred, and all duty violated."

"Perhaps I ought to have reasoned," he replied, "but I could not. I could not derive benefit from the late knowledge I acquired of your character. I could not bring it into play: it was overwhelmed—buried—lost in those earlier feelings, which I smarted under year after year. I could think of you only as one who yielded, who gave me up, who was influenced by any one rather than by me. I saw you with that very person who guided you in that year of misery. I had no reason to believe her of less authority now.—The force of habit was to be added."

"I should have thought," said Anne, "that my manner to yourself might have spared you much or all of this."

"No, no! Your manner might be only the ease, which your engagement to another man would give. I left you in this belief; and yet—I was determined to see you again. My spirits rallied with the morning, and I felt I had still a motive for remaining here."

Anne laughed lightly. "We certainly misconstrued each other!"

Frederick stood at last; he reached out his hand to her. "Yes, we have, but no more. There will be no more misconceptions—no one else between us." Anne took his hand and allowed him to pull her to her feet. "You must know, Anne, it is my intention we will be married as soon as the banns can be read. I will not spend one more minute than necessary without you in my life." He held both her hands grasped tightly to his chest where she might feel his heart beating for her. "Although we do not need his permission any longer, if you will agree, I will speak to your father this evening after the party. I have fortune enough for us to live comfortably, and I have plans for ways to secure your future. Please say you will be my wife."

"Need you ask? I have been yours since we met all those years ago. I appreciate your addressing my father, but I will be your wife no matter what my family may say. We will make our plans tomorrow."

Frederick brought one of her gloved hands to his lips. "Tomorrow," he murmured. "I suppose I must see you home," he said after a long pause, "although my heart hates the idea of leaving you even for a few minutes."

"You will accept *Elizabeth's* invitation for the evening?" she teased.

"I never realized, Sweetling, you were such an *evil* woman; I may need to rethink my offer." He turned her towards the park entrance. "Should I give your sister my attention this evening?"

"Only if you wish to be alone on your wedding day," she warned.

"I will be with you, my Dear, tonight—and on my wedding day—and on every day for the rest of our lives. Is that understood?"

"Giving orders so early on, my Captain?" she mocked in a joking manner.

"As if," he laughed, "you would allow me to order you about or you would allow me to think you would obey. I expect from this moment on, I will contentedly walk the plank for you daily."

Anne tightened her hold on his arm. "I promise it will be a pleasant walk."

Frederick cupped her hand in his. Leaning in, he whispered, "I can barely wait for it to begin."

Chapter 18

My face in thine eye, thine in mine appears,
And true plain hearts do in the faces rest,
Where can we find two better hemispheres,
Without sharp north, without declining west?
Whatever dies, was not mix't equally;
If our two loves be one, or, thou and I
Love so alike, that none do slacken, none can die.
—John Donne from "The Good Morrow"

Back on Gay Street with Sophia and Benjamin, Frederick found it difficult to contain his happiness, but he and Anne agreed they would not announce their engagement until he spoke to Sir Walter. Even though they no longer needed her father's permission, Frederick felt it best to, at least, inform Anne's father of their intentions. He anticipated less resentment on Sir Walter's part this time, but he still assumed the worst in dealing with the man—such prideful vanity was unpredictable.

"Your sister says Miss Elliot personally gave you her card," Benjamin noted as they took a light meal prior to the Elliots' party.

"She did," was Frederick's simple response.

Yet, the Admiral did not abandon his thoughts. "Are we then to presume our family is now acceptable to the Elliots' standards? It would be pleasant to be referred to as something more than a *tenant*. It is not as if Sophy and I are simple cottagers on the estate. The man lives off the money I pay him for the use of his house."

Frederick pointedly put down his soupspoon. "If I was to conjecture as to Miss Elliot's change of heart in my regards, I would suspect she was apprised of the amount of prize money I bring to the table. Yet, I am aware she is the same Miss Elliot who served as Kellynch's mistress since her late teens; she contributed to Sir Walter's current financial loss of status. Even if I were interested, I cannot imagine I have enough funds to satisfy Miss

Elliot's need to spend; I would soon find myself without financial soundness, and unlike Sir Walter, I may not live off my aristocratic name. However, I do not attend tonight with any desire to earn Miss Elliot's attentions. She is handsome, but rather long in the tooth."

Sophia looked up with his last words. "One might say the same of Miss Anne."

Frederick knew to where his sister's thoughts led; the fact she did not share her suspicions with her husband pleased Frederick. He guarded his words as much as possible, even though he would prefer to shout his love from the rooftops. "Anne Elliot is three years younger than Miss Elliot, and I think you will agree a comparison between the two is without merit. Anne is far superior to either of her sisters in intelligence and character."

Sophia smiled at him with her 'I thought so' attitude before saying, "The man who earns Anne Elliot's hand, I suspect, will be remarkable. Do you suppose she is really intended for her cousin Mr. Elliot? He seems a bit too perfect to be true, if you ask me."

"I have no idea of Mr. Elliot's plans." Frederick realized his sister wanted to know why his mood changed so suddenly today; Sophia suspected his feelings for Anne, but he wanted everyone to be surprised by their announcement. "I promised Thomas I would call on him before the Elliot party; I will bring him along with me."

"Then we will see you there," Benjamin declared, laying his napkin on the table before standing. "Come along, Sophy, we *tenants* should not be late."

*   *   *

Frederick swore Thomas to secrecy, knowing his friend would be happy with the outcome of the evening. They had little time for an explanation with the entire Musgrove party around, but Frederick managed to tell him not to say anything just yet. So, when they stepped into the Elliot's drawing room, Frederick's nerves reached a peak. All those who only a few nights ago would oppose his pledge to marry Anne—Sir Walter; Lady Russell; Mr. Elliot—sat before him; the difference was the look on Anne's face. He gained confidence just looking at her laughing eyes, which reminded him the evening would include exchanging compliments with a pack of self-absorbed, overdressed aristocrats. The thought was laughable—actually ludicrous,—and Frederick could not help but return her smile with one of his own. Frissons of excitement coursed though him as he finally stepped in front of her.

"Miss Anne," he said courteously as he raised her offered hand to his lips. Their eyes spoke of the desire coursing through both of them—created by the touch of a hand and a pronouncing of a name.

"Captain Wentworth," she spoke with husky overtones, "we are pleased you could join us for the evening. May I show you to one of the tables or perhaps offer you some refreshment?"

Frederick looked around the room; he would be unable to concentrate on a card hand this evening. "A drink would be nice, Miss Anne," he said loud enough for others to hear.

"This way, Captain." Anne motioned to a table preset with port, wine, lemonade, and champagne. Frederick followed her there, the closest he would come to being alone with her for the next few hours. "Champagne, Captain?" she said as she handed him a glass and took one for herself. "To us," Anne mouthed the words.

Frederick turned his back to the room, blocking her view and preventing the others from observing their exchange. "You are exquisite, Sweetling," his voice barely audible. "Such beauty easily unmans me."

"Frederick," she laughed softly, before taking a sip of the bubbly mixture. "You are such a flirt."

"It is not flirting, my Dear, if I speak the truth." He leaned in as close as he dared without raising suspicion. "Are you as happy as I?"

Anne smiled up at him with indulgent, romantic assignation. "Ecstatic."

"Excellent, Miss Anne." Again he spoke for the room and not for her ears alone. He offered her a crisp bow and moved away to where Thomas joined Charles Musgrove over a glass of port. Musgrove spoke of the gun he rushed off to see today, but Frederick heard only bits and pieces of the conversation; only one person's presence wielded power over him.

The planned evening—nothing more than a simple card party was a mixture of those who met before and those who met too often—a common place business, too numerous for intimacy and too small for variety. Frederick's gaze followed Anne as she made her way around the room. Glowing and lovely in sensibility and happiness, she had cheerful or forbearing feelings for every creature around her. Judiciously, she avoided Mr. Elliot, sparing Frederick any qualms at observing their interactions. She displayed restrained amusement with Mr. Elliot's friends, the Wallises, and with her innocuous cousins Lady Dalrymple and Miss Carteret. Anne, obviously, disdained Mrs. Clay and by her father's protestations embarrassed her.

With the Musgroves, there was the happy chat of perfect ease; with Captain Harville, the kind-hearted intercourse of brother and sister; with

Lady Russell, attempts at conversation, and with the Admiral and Sophia, every thing of peculiar cordiality and fervent interest.

She was making her way towards him, and he pretended not to anticipate her approach. Frederick turned slightly away but not before hearing Miss Elliot reprimand her. "Do not monopolize Captain Wentworth as you always do. Others would like his company too."

"I believe the Captain is capable of choosing his own company, Elizabeth. I will not avoid him because it is your wish that I do so." Anne gave her sister a curt nod and moved on.

To make things less obvious, he moved to the far side of the room and pretended to admire a fine display of green-house plants. Sensing her approach, Frederick turned to meet her. "I wondered when you would make your way back to me," he whispered.

"I felt your eyes on me, Sir. Did you not will me to return?" She obviously loved the power she held over him, and Frederick chuckled with her boldness.

"You are a vixen in disguise as a demur lady. How could I not take note of such before?"

"It is odd." Anne shook her head as if to clear it. "With my family—with everyone—I take the role as the quiet, unassuming sister, but when I am with you, my tongue says things I never realized were part of my thoughts."

"It is because, my Love, I see you differently from the others. With me, you are the other half of my heart. There is little you could say that would offend me. In reality, I rejoice in seeing you allow me such insights."

He watched as she bit her lower lip; then she looked back to the gathering before speaking again. "I was thinking—thinking over the past and trying impartially to judge of the right and wrong, I mean with regard to myself; and I must believe I was right, much as I suffered from it; I was perfectly right in being guided by the friend whom you will love better than you do now. To me, she was in the place of a parent. Do not mistake me, however. I am not saying she did not err in her advice. It was, perhaps, one of those cases in which advice is good or bad only as the event decides; and for myself, I certainly never should, in any circumstance of tolerable similarity, give such advice. But I mean, I was right in submitting to her, and if I did otherwise, I should suffer more in continuing the engagement than I did in giving it up, because I should suffer in my conscience. I have now, as far as such a sentiment is allowable in human nature, with which nothing to reproach myself; and if I mistake not, a strong sense of duty is no bad part of a woman's portion."

Frederick looked at her, looked at Lady Russell, and looking again at Anne, replied, as if in cool deliberation, "Not yet. But there are hopes of her being forgiven in time. I trust to being in charity with her soon, but I too was thinking over the past, and a question has suggested itself, whether there may not have been one person more my enemy even than that lady? My own self. Tell me if, when I returned to England in the year, eight, with a few thousand pounds, and was posted into the *Laconia*, if I then wrote to you, would you have answered my letter? Would you, in short, have renewed the engagement then?"

"Would I?" was all her answer, but the accent was decisive enough.

"Good God!" he cried, "you would! It is not that I did not think of it or desire it, as what could alone crown all my other success. But I was proud, too proud to ask again. I did not understand you. I shut my eyes and would not understand you, or do you justice. This is a recollection which ought to me forgive every one sooner than myself. Six years of separation and suffering might have been spared. It is a sort of pain, too, which is new to me. I was used to the gratification of believing myself to earn every blessing I enjoyed. I valued myself on honorable toils and just rewards. Like other great men under reverses," he added with a smile, "I must endeavor to subdue my mind to fortune. I must learn to brook being happier than I deserve."

"We will speak no more of this," Anne declared. "We—you and I—knew sadness in our separation, but we will let no such impediment keep us apart ever again."

"For you, my Dear, I will temper my dislike for the lady." He glanced around the room again. "Anne," he spoke softly for only her ears, "I want nothing more than to spend the rest of my days with you by my side and the rest of my nights with you in my arms. After tonight, you may be sorely plagued by my presence, but I will not hear of our parting ever again."

"That would please me, Frederick. I will relish each of those moments."

Their conversation ended as Elizabeth insisted he join the group to whom she would show the house. The group included Mrs. Musgrove, Henrietta, Captain Harville, the Admiral, and Sophia. Bowing to leave Anne, he reluctantly followed the others to the hallway.

When Sir Walter briefly stepped from the drawing room to offer his own anecdotes, Frederick took the opportunity to approach the man. "Sir Walter," he blocked Anne's father from trailing after the others, "may I speak to you for a moment, Sir."

Sir Walter looked a bit annoyed at losing his audience to his daughter, but he accepted the interference with as much grace as he was known to give to anyone. "Certainly, Captain." He gestured towards an open door. "Perhaps the library will do." Frederick followed the man into a dimly lit room. When he turned to look at the furnishings, the number of books, which filled the shelves, surprised him. Besides Anne, he felt confident few other Elliots regularly opened a book purely for the pleasure of reading it. However, two huge mirrors hanging on opposing walls did not surprise him. "Well, Captain," Sir Walter's voice brought him to the moment at hand, "what may I do for you?"

Frederick cleared his throat. "This will seem a case of déjà vu," he said nervously. "Today, I renewed my proposal to your daughter Anne, and she accepted my offer."

Sir Walter looked on, discommoded by the news. "But Mr. Elliot," he stammered.

"I understand your surprise, Sir, but I assure you Miss Anne does not take Mr. Elliot's attentions seriously. We will marry; Anne is of age, and we no longer need your permission or your blessing, although I pray for the sake of family accord, you will not withhold either. As I told you eight years ago, the Navy would allow me to make my fortune in the world. I accumulated nearly thirty thousand pounds to date. I plan to purchase a small estate so Anne may be the mistress of her own home. She will want for nothing as long as I live."

"Captain, your continued devotion to my daughter amazes me. It is only of late I noticed Anne's appeal for some men. Mr. Elliot took to her quite quickly." Frederick flinched with the words. "Yet, if Anne chooses to attach herself to you, then I have no objections. Even the Prince Regent prizes the accomplishments of men such as you. It would be well for my family to align itself with a man of service to our country. Anne, as justly due her, will receive her share of ten thousand pounds upon my death."

Frederick just nodded, afraid to think how much the situation changed, but still remained the same. Sir Walter valued Anne only as a means for her father to advance his own place in society. Frederick was now esteemed quite worthy to address the daughter of a foolish, spendthrift baronet, who had not principle or sense enough to maintain himself in the situation in which Providence placed him. Sir Walter, indeed, though he held no affection for Anne to make him really happy on the occasion, was very far from thinking it a bad match for her. "We would prefer to announce our engagement this evening, Sir, as we have both family and friends in attendance. If you would do the honor, Sir Walter, I am sure Anne would be most appreciative of the gesture."

"I hear the others returning, Captain. Why do we not join them? We may address this before people begin to retire for the evening." The baronet ushered Frederick towards the door. "Did you know, Captain, my cousin Lady Dalrymple found you to be a very fine young man."

"Really?" Frederick feigned his surprise. "Then I hope her Ladyship will approve of our connection."

"I am positive she will." Sir Walter instinctively stepped in front of Frederick, checking his appearance in the nearest mirror.

When they reentered the drawing room, Anne, who stood beside Sophia, looked up in anticipation. He smiled at her as he strode across the room and took her hand in his. He heard Sophia gasp in delight as Sir Walter cleared his throat loudly enough to draw attention to where he stood by the open door. "My friends and family," he began in his most pretentious tone, "it is with pleasure I announce that our simple card party has become a momentous occasion. My daughter Anne has this day accepted the proposal of Captain Wentworth, and they wish you to share in their happiness."

Everything remained silent for a heartbeat, and then they were surrounded by well-wishers. Sophia, with tears of happiness streaming down her face, hugged Anne tightly to her.

Harville, who moved behind Frederick during Sir Walter's speech, was the first to reach him. He gave his friend a male hug. "You did it," he congratulated his friend. "I knew nothing could stop you once you put your mind to it. At last, you will be happy; you will have the one thing you missed."

"The one thing I always needed," Frederick assured him before the others interrupted.

"Miss Anne!" Mrs. Musgrove caught her at Sophia's release. "How you kept us all in secret! None of us ever suspected over the last few months you and Captain Wentworth developed an affection for each other."

Frederick wanted to set the record straight and not let it appear Anne accepted Louisa Musgrove's cast offs. "Mrs. Musgrove, I am sure you are not aware I lived in Somerset for a short time with my brother years ago. I fell in love with Miss Anne at that time, but she was too young. Although I tried to forget her, when I returned to the area, I found she still owned my heart."

"That is so romantic," Henrietta gushed.

Thankfully, no one reminded him that for a while it appeared he set his sights on Louisa.

Lady Russell made her way to them, and with his hand resting lightly on her back, ready to offer her protection, he felt Anne stiffen. "My dear

Anne," the older friend took both Anne's hands in hers, "let me wish you happy."

"Thank you," Anne murmured. Then straightening her shoulders she added, "Will you not acknowledge my future husband?" Her remarks, demanding recognition for him, surprised Frederick.

Lady Russell's jaw twitched with something he suspected to be disdain, but she graciously turned to him. "Captain, you won a jewel; cherish her and protect her as such."

Frederick offered her a polite bow. "I will do nothing less, Lady Russell." With that, she stepped to the side to allow others their moment with them.

He noted out of the corner of his eye that Mr. Elliot and Mrs. Clay conversed intimately on the far side of the room, nearly unseen behind a large palm. Beaming with happiness, Anne, he was sure, did not observe how shortly afterwards, Mr. Elliot took his leave. Neither he nor Mrs. Clay offered them words of congratulations.

For Frederick, the rest of the evening was perfection. He walked about the room with Anne on his arm, sat with her on a secluded settee for nearly an hour, and openly declared his affection for her. At one point Anne motioned Sophia to join them. "Mrs. Croft," she began, "I have a boon to ask of you."

"Of course, Miss Anne, how might I serve you?" Sophia shot a look of approval at Frederick.

Anne slipped her hand into Frederick's before speaking. "Your brother and I wish to marry as soon as the banns can be properly called. Although I am sure Mary and the Musgroves will wish to assist me, their party will return to Uppercross soon. I hoped you would go with me to a proper modiste to secure my bride clothes. I am afraid I would not know to whom to turn in Bath."

"Oh, Miss Anne, what a delight! I know just the person; I will not disappoint you. Plus, it will give us time to learn more of each other. Having two brothers, I always wanted a sister. Did you hear, Frederick?" Her voice was breathy with excitement.

"I believe my future wife gave you the perfect excuse to spend more of the Admiral's money," he teased her lovingly.

She protested, "Benjamin will not care, and you know it."

"This is true, Sophia, and I will be pleased to escort the two of you if you are in need of my protection," he conceded.

"Let us say, the day after tomorrow, if that is acceptable to you, Mrs. Croft," Anne added quickly.

"It is most acceptable except for one thing. If we are to be sisters, I am Sophia, and, hopefully, I may call you Anne."

"I would prefer that." Anne leaned against Frederick's shoulder for a few brief seconds. "It is all so sudden, and it just occurred to me I will be part of a different family—one with brothers and new sisters."

"The Wentworths are very close," he warned. "Sometimes you may wish they did not want to know your business, but you will find no stronger allies when you need them." He gave Sophia an affectionate look and a pat on her hand.

"Unfortunately, the Elliots are not so devoted to their loved ones." Anne's face fell with the disclosure.

He assured her, "I have the *best* of the Elliots; the others are insignificant to me."

"You deserve better than what I offer you. You give me a family and friendships in which to share." She finally met his gaze with hers.

"I *deserve* nothing, but I *need* you." He kissed her fingertips. "Now, no more regrets. Let us return to our wedding plans. Do you suppose Edward could officiate?"

"Do you want to marry out of Bath or out of Uppercross?" she asked.

Frederick smiled with the question. "It would be best if we did so in Bath. As much as it would please me to marry you in the chapel on Kellynch, the place where this all began, it would be awkward for your father and sister and Lady Russell to celebrate our union there. Let us choose some place here where Edward might be part of the service. I will make it my mission to find such a church tomorrow. I will ask your father for the nearest services."

"The Admiral and I will see if the Pump Room Assembly Hall is available for the breakfast. I am sure Miss Elliot will not mind if I assume some of those responsibilities. I did not attend Edward's joining with Christine because the Admiral and I were still at sea. This will be a pleasure to plan."

"Thank you, Sophia. I would not wish to subject either Frederick or his family to the type of celebration my sister might choose."

"I will include the obligatory echelon from Bath's society, but I insist on Frederick's fellow officers being present." Sophia's excitement continued to grow.

"Definitely," Anne confirmed. "I wish to meet Frederick's friends."

"Then it is settled," Sophia began to plan even before she took her leave of them. "I will call on you tomorrow, and we will come up with a tentative list. This is most exciting!" She took several steps in retreat.

"Make it before noon," Frederick called to his sister. "I plan to spend the afternoon with Anne."

"After services then," Sophia turned to say. "Anne, we will wait until Monday and spend time together. That way you and Frederick may attend services together and speak to the vicar about calling the banns. I will send a note around tomorrow to confirm. Welcome to the family, Anne."

*   *   *

Happy to recognize the union of a member of the titled gentry in his parish, Mr. Osgood readily agreed to share the services with Edward Wentworth. Although a bit rushed, the first reading of the banns occurred that day; the official announcement would appear in the society pages the next morning.

"Can you believe this is happening at last?" Anne sat beside him as Frederick addressed a note to Edward and Christine, telling his brother of his plans and asking him to participate.

Although a chaperone should be with them, they were left to their own devices. Frederick leaned towards her and brushed his lips across hers. "Nothing matters but our union; I am afraid I have become quite singular in my thoughts. We waited long enough for this. If I could convince you to leave with me for Gretna Green, I would; but since I cannot, I am putting all my energy into making sure this comes off without any problems."

"May we call on my friend Mrs. Smith this afternoon? I wish to share my news with her; she is a widow now."

"Who is Mrs. Smith, my Dear?" Frederick sealed his letter with wax and wrote the directions on the outer side.

Anne, close enough to touch him freely, placed her hand lightly on his knee, and Frederick forced himself to breathe. Her innocent touch sent heat radiating through him, and without realizing his response, he placed his free hand behind her neck, pulling her mouth to his. This time he tasted her lips fully, quickly deepening the kiss before releasing her—with the sounds of the servants in the hall. She sat, staring at him, eyes glazed over with desire, and he chuckled before moving back. Despite finding it more than a bit distracting, he left her hand on his leg; it was a splendid sort of torture. "Mrs. Smith?" he repeated, his voice a bit raspy.

Anne shook her head to clear it. "Mrs. Smith," she stammered. "Mrs. Smith is my old school friend Miss Hamilton. I told you of her years ago;

she was my most dear friend when I attended school here after my mother's death."

Frederick nodded in recollection. "And she is in Bath now?"

"She lives in Westgate Building—a widow of little means. She suffers from rheumatic fever and cannot go about." Anne continued to set too close for propriety, but she innocently took no note of it. With Frederick every thing seemed so natural she took and allowed liberties she would never consider with anyone else.

"Is it important to you we see her today?" Frederick asked in all seriousness.

If anyone else asked Anne whether the visit might be postponed, she would consider doing so, but with Frederick, Anne knew he would not judge Mrs. Smith's condition or lack of connections. "I would like for you to meet her." Anne could not explain it to him—would not say the words because they were too personal. She felt her own inferiority keenly.

Frederick saw the angst spread over her countenance. "What is it, Sweetling? Is it something to do with Mrs. Smith? You may tell me anything."

"I need for you to meet Mrs. Smith; it was she who warned me off from Mr. Elliot, but that is not my concern. I have no words to make this sensible."

"Whatever it is, Anne, we can address it together."

"My Love," she spoke haltingly, "I—I am—I am ashamed how little I bring to our union." Frederick wanted to interrupt and tell her he wanted nothing but her, but Anne needed to work through this so he listened quietly. "I spoke of it before; it is a real concern for me. I do not speak of the disproportion in our fortunes—although great, it does not give me a moment's regret because you would have it no other way. But to have no family to receive and estimate you properly—nothing of respectability, of harmony, of goodwill to offer in return for all the worth and all the prompt welcome, which met me in your brothers and sisters, is a lively pain. I have but two friends in the world to add to your list: Lady Russell and Mrs. Smith."

"As I said last night, I will do my best with Lady Russell; I decided I will not dwell on her former transgression, but will judge her based on here and now." He traced lines up and down Anne's forearm with his fingertips. "And as for Mrs. Smith, if she helped turn you from Mr. Elliot's attentions, then she is in my favor already."

"Oh, Frederick, I cannot comprehend what my cousin did to Mrs. Smith. It is so terrible! I am horrified he is our relation," she exclaimed.

Frederick felt her anxiety and immediately wanted to conjure a way to alleviate it. "Tell me what you know. Is there some way we may help your friend?"

"Mr. Elliot was an associate of the late Mr. Smith," she began to explain. Frederick leaned back in his seat in full concentration. "That is how Mr. Elliot knew so much of me—my friend spoke often of our times together. He took a dislike to my father and sister years ago, but with me, he had a new 'in' with our family, and he had a double motive to his visits: Mrs. Clay gave a general idea among my father's acquaintances of her meaning to be the new Lady Elliot, and, unfortunately, despite my warning months ago, my sister was blind to the fact. Mr. Elliot returned to Bath to fix himself here for a time, with the view of renewing his former acquaintance and recovering such a footing in the family, as might give him the means of ascertaining the degree of his danger of losing the title and of circumventing the lady if he found it material."

The knowledge Anne came close to aligning herself with Mr. Elliot still bothered Frederick, and the less said on the subject the better; therefore, he directed Anne's thoughts to her friend. "You said as such yesterday; I can guess the rest. But what of your friend? How did Mr. Elliot betray her?"

Anne allowed him to divert the subject, knowing how he still smarted with jealousy. "As I said earlier, Mr. Elliot and Mr. Smith were long standing friends. The Smiths often loaned him money prior to Mr. Elliot's marriage. His wife was wealthy—from the trade class—but wealth was the source of Mr. Elliot's wooing game. Even after my cousin's marriage, they were as before, always together, and Mr. Elliot led his friend into expenses much beyond his fortune.

"From his wife's account of him, Mr. Smith was a man of warm feelings, easy temper, careless habits, and not strong understanding, much more amiable than his friend, and very unlike him—led by him, and probably despised by him. Mr. Elliot, raised by his marriage to great affluence and disposed to every gratification of pleasure and vanity, which could be commanded without involving himself, and beginning to be rich, just as his friend found himself to be poor, seemed to have no concern at all for that friend's probable finances, but, on the contrary, prompted and encouraged expenses, which ended in the Smiths being ruined.

"The husband died just in time to be spared the full knowledge of it. It was not until his death that the wretched state of his affairs was fully known. With a confidence in Mr. Elliot's regard, more creditable to his feelings than his judgment, Mr. Smith appointed him the executor of his will; but Mr. Elliot refused to act, and the difficulties and distresses, which this refusal heaped on Mrs. Smith, in addition to the inevitable sufferings of her situation, brought on such anguish. I find myself quite indignant!

"She showed me letters to which she applied to Mr. Elliot for assistance and his hard-hearted indifference in his response. In my opinion, no flagrant open crime could be worse! Mrs. Smith related incident after incident, creating a dreadful picture of ingratitude and inhumanity."

Frederick thought out loud. "It is beyond reprehensible that a man—a gentleman, no less—should treat a woman as such!"

"There was one circumstance," Anne continued, "in the history of her grievances of particular irritation. She has good reason to believe some property of her husband's in the West Indies, which was for many years under a sort of sequestration for the payment of its own encumbrances, might be recoverable by proper measures, and this property, though not large, would be enough to make her comparatively rich. But there was nobody to stir in it. Mr. Elliot did nothing, and she can do nothing herself, equally disabled from personal exertion by her state of bodily weakness and from employing others by her want of money. She has no natural connections to assist her even with their counsel, and she cannot afford to purchase the assistance of the law. She really ought to be in better circumstances! Just a little trouble in the right place might do it! I fear the delay might be even weakening her claims, and that is hard to bear!"

"Anne," he grabbed her hand to draw her attention, "I may be able to help, Mrs. Smith."

"How, Frederick?" She sat now on the edge of the seat.

His smile grew larger by the second. "I did not serve twice in the West Indies without connections. If your friend's property claim is legitimate, I know to whom to apply for retribution. She may sell the property for there are many in the Americas seeking such land opportunities, or we may find her the proper overseer to handle it for her. I will help Mrs. Smith know to whom to write; if she will permit it, I can act for her and see her through all the petty difficulties of the case."

Before she thought what she did, Anne threw herself into Frederick's arms, and he instinctively pulled her onto his lap. "Oh, Frederick," she cackled with glee, "I knew you would make it right! You always do!" Her arms went around his neck, and Anne gave him a full mouth kiss of passion.

When she withdrew, Frederick mumbled, "So nice . . ."

"May we go see Mrs. Smith now?" Anne started to stand, but Frederick pulled her back into his embrace.

"In a few minutes, my Love," he whispered. "Let me hold you while I can. These moments will have to sustain me until our wedding day." He held her tightly to him, and Anne lay back in his arms, resting her head on his shoulder. "I love you more than life," he spoke softly. He twisted a strand of her hair around his finger. "Your hair is like silk," he murmured against the side of her face as he kissed her temple. "I dream of it down and spread across my pillow."

Anne turned slightly in his arms and looked deeply in his eyes, never breaking contact. Then she lifted her arms and pulled pins from the loosely roped chignon. Frederick gulped for air, ablaze with her forwardness. *His Anne* hid a passion, which she showed only to him. When she released her hands, auburn locks cascaded down from the twisted knot, which once held them. They draped over her shoulders and hung loosely down her back.

"My God, you are gorgeous!" he uttered, unable to say much more.

"Then you approve?" her voice sounded as throaty as his.

Frederick laced his fingers through her hair, twisting handfuls of it and releasing it to repeat the action. "I need to adjust my dreams," he stammered. "They do not even come close to defining your beauty." He used her hair to force her face to his, and then Frederick kissed her in earnest. It was a dream of eight years: her slightly parted lips, the silky texture of her hair, the lavender emanating from her every pore. The kiss began sweetly and gently, taking more effort at self-control than he imagined. His embrace tightened when her body arched towards him. His tongue teased her lips apart, and he deepened the kiss, tasting Anne's sweetness fully. *Stop this!* he told himself. *You waited this long—do not ruin everything—she is an innocent who depends on you to do the right thing. Damn!* Frederick broke abruptly from the kiss and pulled Anne back, seating her on his knees, trying to breathe again. She licked her lips, creating a new fissure of desire in his groin. *If she knew,* he thought. He stammered, "I apologize, Anne; I shall try to keep my desire for you in check until we are wed. I did not mean to frighten you."

Looking suddenly aghast, she choked out the words, "I should not have acted so impulsively. What you must think of me." She turned her head to hide her embarrassment and her tears.

"Anne," he lifted her chin to make her look at him. "The fact you want me and trust me is a heady feeling, which I do not wish to abuse. You must believe me when I say, you were not acting wantonly. Our problem is we have known each other so long it seems natural to be in each other's arms; yet, because we waited to know each other intimately, we could easily anticipate those moments. It is only a few more weeks, and I wish our first time to be perfect—with no regrets. There is nothing more I want than to love you throughout the night, but I will not seduce you now even though my body screams for me to do so. We will do this properly."

Her bottom lip trembled as she acknowledged the truth in what he said. "Maybe we should go to see my friend."

Frederick touched her lips with his fingertips. "Sweetling, you are quite beautiful when you have been thoroughly kissed," he teased.

"I feel quite beautiful, and I never felt as such before," she whispered.

"Then our taste of sweetness was not insignificant. We learned we are strongly suited, and you saw something in yourself I saw from the first day in that mercantile years ago. Now, my Love, let us straighten our disheveled appearances and go see your friend Mrs. Smith."

Frederick sat her on her feet beside his chair and then stood himself. Anne pulled her dress back into place and smoothed the wrinkles in her skirt, as Frederick did the same with his waistcoat and jacket. "Here let me help you." He took the pins from her hand and inserted them carefully back into the sleek twist of hair resting at the nape of her neck. Unable to resist, he kissed the curve of her neckline as it led to her shoulder. "Soon, I will kiss every inch of you," he caressed her ear with his lips. "And I will not stop until you call out my name." Anne relaxed back into him as he held her by the shoulders, the warmth of his body all up and down her back. "This will be a long three weeks," he uttered in frustration before he moved away, leaving her as discomfited as before. Frederick moved to the door, trying to breathe deeply with each step he took. At the portal, he turned and extended his arm to her. "Come, Love, I believe we both need a long walk and the company of other people."

"Yes," she muttered, "the company of other people." Trancelike, she moved to him, taking comfort in the feel of his hand around hers.

Frederick brought the back of her hand to his lips. "I love you, Anne Elliot," he said boldly, loud enough for anyone nearby to hear.

"And I love you, Frederick Wentworth," she responded just as brazenly. Then she took his proffered arm to leave the study behind.

*   *   *

Frederick, Sophia, and Anne worked studiously on wedding plans and the invitation list in the Admiral's study on Gay Street. The trio decided to move their planning to the Crofts' house to avoid the cold and unconcerned looks Elizabeth Elliot now gave her sister.

"Father will want Lady Dalrymple and Miss Carteret on the list." Her tone told Sophia and Frederick Anne cared not for the company, but Sophia dutifully recorded the names.

"What of Mrs. Clay?" Sophia asked.

Anne looked surprised. "Have you not heard?"

Frederick added, "I did not see where I should spread the rumors."

"Sophia is your sister, Frederick," Anne reprimanded him. "She will be my new family, and I see no reason not to tell her."

"Then tell her." He laughed as Anne pulled herself upright as if delivering an important message. In some ways, she was still so childlike—and adorable.

"The announcement of our engagement deranged Mr. Elliot's best plan of domestic happiness—his best hope of keeping my father single by the watchfulness, which a son-in-law's rights would give him. He quitted Bath, and Mrs. Clay did likewise. Because Frederick observed them talking intimately at the party, and earlier my sister Mary observed them as such on the street, we assume they are together, even now." Anne delivered the news with some perverted delight. "At least, that is how your brother sees it."

"I said no such thing," he protested. "I simply noted that if Mrs. Clay could not become Lady Elliot by marrying your father, then possibly she could do so by becoming involved with Mr. Elliot."

"You are just happy not to have to welcome Mr. Elliot to our celebration," she said definitively.

"That is where you err, my Love," he taunted. "It would give me great pleasure to see your cousin's face when I make you my wife. The agony I felt the past few weeks would be displayed on his face, and I would take comfort in that."

Anne chastised him, "You are unforgiving, Frederick Wentworth!"

Frederick smiled wickedly. "And you are beautiful when you are angry, Sweetling."

Anne blushed with the intimacy of his words in front of his sister, but Sophia did not look at either of them. She seemed engrossed in adding names to her list. Frederick started to offer her an apology for his teasing, but before he could express his feelings, the appearance of a distraught looking Benjamin Croft entering the room interrupted them.

"Admiral!" Anne called and was immediately on her feet, but Frederick got to his brother before her. He supported the man to the nearest chair. Anne rushed to a table for a glass of water, while Sophia collapsed at her husband's feet.

"Benjamin?" Sophia patted his hand and stroked his face. "What is it? Tell me, Sweetheart."

Her husband smiled slightly, contented to be with her. "I am afraid, Sophy, I bring bad news," he said haltingly.

"What do you mean, Dear?" she coaxed, as Anne moved into Frederick's embrace.

The Admiral looked up at Wentworth. "Frederick, my boy, you are being ordered back into service. You must be in Plymouth in ten days."

"What?" Frederick stammered. "I do not understand, Sir."

The Admiral forced himself to his feet. "While we were all enjoying the blessings of the Lord yesterday, Bonaparte escaped the island of Elba."

Sophia gasped, "How?"

"The damn Frenchies!" His thoughts now animated the Admiral. "They barely guarded the man! He assembled several hundred followers and a flotilla of seven vessels. He appears to be headed for Cannes!"

"No!" Anne protested, burying her face into Frederick's chest. He pulled her tightly to him.

Frederick demanded, "Admiral, how do you know I am to be called back up for service?"

"I went to get a paper to see your announcement in print." The Admiral now stood and paced the room, trying to organize his thoughts. "The papers are full of speculation on the French emperor so I went to the Central Office to learn more. That is when I found out they were organizing those to be recalled."

"How do you know I only have ten days?' Frederick prodded.

Glancing back at his brother in marriage, the Admiral stopped in his tracks. "I do not know for sure, Frederick, but you will have ten days, at most, from the time they find you. Did you not report to the Central Office when you came here?"

"Yes, Sir." By now, he stroked Anne's back, trying to comfort her.

"Then it is only a matter of time before you receive orders. It may be you have twelve days instead of ten, but it will not be three weeks. I am sorry, Frederick." The man collapsed back into the nearest chair.

Sophia realized what he said. "But the wedding?" she pleaded.

Anne raised her head to look at Frederick. "What will we do?"

"I do not know, my Love. We do not even have time to go to Gretna Green." He began to think out loud.

Sophia began to brainstorm. "A common license?"

Benjamin reasoned, "Frederick has not lived here long enough to qualify for such consideration. What of you Miss Anne?"

"I have been in Bath long enough if the archbishop will allow it. Usually, he prefers it to be the man's residency rather than the woman's, but we can try."

"Even securing a common license may take too much time. I could be made to report before the end of week. We need to marry immediately."

"What of a special license?" Anne followed suit.

Frederick reminded her, "I am not of the aristocracy."

"But I am," she protested. "My father is titled and so is Lady Russell and Lady Dalrymple. Surely their names can help us."

Frederick traced the outline of her face with his thumb. "As you said moments ago, we will try," he assured her.

"You and I will go see my father immediately." She moved to find her things. "I will not let you leave without me."

"Anne." Frederick did not move. "We must realize our plans may not come to fruition."

She turned on him, unable to control her anxiety. "I will not hear of it, Frederick Wentworth! Do you hear me? I will not let Fate bring us together again and then pull you away! I will not have it!" Nearly hysterical by this time, she sank to her knees, swaying with the energy draining from her.

Frederick knelt in front of her, lifting her into his arms and carrying Anne to the nearest chair. He sat her in his lap, cooing words of love and devotion, rocking her as one might do a child. He nodded to both Sophia and Benjamin as they slipped from the room, but he never ceased his loving ministrations.

"Sweetheart," he coaxed as he dabbed her tears with his handkerchief, "please let us figure out what we must do."

Anne took the handkerchief and wiped her eyes and cheeks. Still sniffling, she pulled back where they might talk. "I will go with you even if we are not married." Her determination did not falter.

"Anne, I cannot allow you to risk your reputation by taking you with me. I will not broker such an idea." He kissed her forehead to let her know he still wanted their life together; Frederick preferred to kiss her properly, but their emotions wavered too close to the surface. "If I must leave before the banns are called the third time, I will only be gone a few months—a year at most. We can wait."

"Frederick, I want children. Do you not want children too? I am near eight and twenty; another year and I may not be able to bear a child!" Tears began to stream down her face again.

Frederick closed his eyes; images of Anne holding their child came easily to him. "Of course, I want children—our children, but I want you more than even the possibility of a child. If I do not marry you, I will not marry at all." This time he kissed her lips, slowly drinking in the taste of her. "If I must leave before we marry," he began again, "I will send for you the first time we make port. You will need to be wherever it is a fortnight before I arrive; I will have Sophia travel with you, and as soon as I make land, we will marry. It will only be a matter of months at most."

"May we, at least, ask my father for help?" she pleaded. "I have never asked for such preferential treatment before; I am sure he will make things right."

"Anne, your father agreed to our marriage because Prinny is all aglow with praise for the military. I am sure the Prince Regent will not be happy to have the resurgence of this war thrown into his face. Your father may choose to distance himself from our union. It is a fact, my Love, we must face."

"That may be, but I insist we try." She began to release herself from his clasp. "Will you come with me?" she asked as she stood.

"Of course, I will come with you." Frederick followed her to his feet.

*   *   *

"Captain," Sir Walter called out as soon as Frederick and Anne entered the room. "How will the latest development with the French affect your plans?"

Frederick led Anne to a nearby chair before answering. "I cannot say, Sir Walter; the Admiral believes I will be called to command a new ship as the *Laconia* was to be dismantled."

"We are unsure, Father," Anne interrupted, "how soon that will be."

Lady Russell, who sat to the left of Sir Walter's desk, rolled her eyes in exasperation. "Maybe this is Providence's way of saying this union is not meant to be."

"Do not—do not let me ever hear you say such a thing again if you expect to remain in my favor," Anne warned her long time companion.

"Anne, I am sorry if I upset you; I just meant Fate may be speaking to you." Lady Russell's feigned consideration shot through Frederick; but he must let Anne be her own person, although it took every ounce of control not to respond for her.

Anne returned the fake smile with one of her own. "Lady Russell, I always assumed when you separated Frederick and me years ago, it was because you loved me as a surrogate mother. Now, it is apparent you did so because you wished to keep me as a way of playing at a loyal friend. If I leave, what will be your connection to this family? You will have served my mother's memory and will no longer be needed."

"Anne," the woman flustered, and Frederick beamed with pride at Anne's new resolve. "I always wanted to protect you from your romantic heart."

"Do not protect me; I have Frederick to do that." Anne took his hand as he stood beside her chair. "I need you to be that substitute mother and to help me marry the man I love." Anne held the woman's gaze, challenging her to do the right thing.

Sir Walter rejoined the conversation, "What do you expect us to do, Anne?"

"We would wish to marry before I leave for Plymouth." Frederick explained. "It is definite; I must return to service before the third time the banns are called. If we are to marry, we will need a special license. We considered a common license, but even that may take too long."

"That may be a problem," Sir Walter observed. "The bishop is particular about whom he issues such privileges. Plus, a baronetcy is not a peer of the realm; it is purely an hereditary title."

"We know that, Father. That is why we are here to beg for your assistance."

Sir Walter stammered, "My help? You expect my help with this? I am afraid, Anne, that is impossible. I will not allow the public to think you *must* marry. Besides, this match is still with a man of no connections. If I place the Elliot name on the line, I would prefer to do so for a title. The Captain has admirably risen in society, but if you were the first daughter rather than the second, I would not consider the match as acceptable."

"Then why, pray tell, did Elizabeth so blatantly flirt with Frederick prior to our announcement? Would you accept him then? Would all his money be enough for acceptance in this family?" she challenged.

Sir Walter held his ground. "At the time we thought you were to marry your cousin. None of us expected such a turn of events."

"Anne," Frederick's resonant voice broke into the confrontation, "I suspect I should take my leave. It is as we suspected—a moot point. I will see what else the Admiral learned and call for you later. We are to dine with the Musgroves this evening."

"I will go with you now." She stood and hooked her arm through his.

Sir Walter stood, planning to assert himself as her father. "It would be best, Anne, if you did as the Captain suggested."

"That is the difference, Father; Frederick makes *suggestions;* he does not demand *obedience.* There are a few things you should consider over the next few hours. First, I will marry Frederick, or I will not marry. I already turned down Charles Musgrove and Mr. Elliot—that is money and a title.

If I do not marry, you will have two spinster daughters—both long in the tooth, so to speak. What will that say about Sir Walter Elliot? You never considered Mary's match appropriate. You, Sir Walter Elliot, will have three daughters—none with a match you would want to recognize." Frederick saw Sir Walter clutch the edge of his desk in anger. "What will you write of the Elliot family in the Baronetage, Father?"

Lady Russell warned, "Anne, that is enough!"

"No, it is not enough!" She left Frederick's side, and he suddenly felt naked. He would never suspect Anne to have so much mettle. It was as if she saved up all her frustrations and now allowed them all to escape. She leaned across the desk to speak to her father directly. "Either you help us get a special license and weather the gossip of how we anticipated our marriage *or*," and at this she paused and waited for her father's full attention, "we *will anticipate* our marriage for real. How will you explain a grandchild that is less than nine months in its conception, Father? Or perhaps I will simply leave with Frederick without the sacrament of union."

"Anne!" Lady Russell exclaimed. "You cannot mean what you say! See what an influence this man has on you!"

Frederick started to object, but this was Anne's show—her step to freedom, and he savored every moment. She would make him a splendid wife; how he ever thought otherwise amazed him. She withstood her family's wishes for her to marry Charles Musgrove when all other offers seemed foreign. Likewise, she thwarted their plans for her union with Mr. Elliot. When they needed a voice of reason in Lyme, they all turned to her for guidance. Everyone saw her as weak and pliable, but Anne Elliot had a backbone of steel.

"That is where you are in error, Lady Russell." She turned to face him. "This man is honorable; he said he will not ruin my reputation, but I will do my best to change his mind because I will have him above all others. Even if he keeps his honor, I will swear I lost mine, and you, Father, will have no choice but to protect me and help us purchase a special license to salvage what is left of my reputation. We will return early for your decision." She turned on her heels and headed toward the door. "Are you coming, Frederick?"

He smiled after her. "Yes, my Love." Frederick offered her father and Lady Russell a proper bow and strode from the room. He caught her in the front foyer just as she accepted her cloak from the waiting servant. "You were magnificent," he whispered to her as he put on his great coat.

"Not so magnificent," Anne's trembling voice caught Frederick by surprise. "If you could see how my legs wish to buckle, you would offer me the support of your arm immediately." She began to slump, and Frederick pulled her to him, wrapping his arms about her waist.

He laughed and then twirled her around under his arm before stepping into an impromptu waltz. "What are you doing?" she gleefully gasped.

"I am celebrating our upcoming marriage." He said as he maneuvered her around a table and back into the main entranceway.

"Then you believe it will happen?"

Frederick slowed their steps where they just swayed together. "You left your father no choice." He pulled her to him. "And me no choice."

"Frederick, do you mean?" she murmured.

"Anne, I will have you as my wife and as my lover." Even though several footmen lurked in the shadows, he kissed her briefly. "Now, you are thoroughly compromised, my Love. Before we return to Gay Street, half of Bath will hear of how I held you too close, waltzed you around the floor, and kissed you shamelessly in front of your household staff. You will have to marry me."

She laced her arms around his neck. "May I be just as shameless?"

"We are a perfect pair." With that, she returned his earlier kiss and then walked purposely out the door. He smiled with the knowledge he unleashed a passion no one knew was there.

Chapter 19

Then you rose into my life
Like a promised sunrise.
Brightened my days with the light of your eyes.
I've never been so strong,
Now I'm where I belong.
—*Maya Angelou from "Where We Belong: A Duet"*

It was not Bath Abbey as Sophia hoped; however, Frederick paced the front of the church waiting as patiently as possible for Anne's appearance. Dressed in his full military regalia, he cut a fine figure of a man. The morning crept by at a snail's pace as the enormity of what was to come created butterflies dancing in his stomach. In a few minutes, Anne would be his; the reality of the day came full force as he let his fingers trace the pages of the *Bible* laying open on the table.

After Anne delivered an ultimatum to her father, things changed quickly. Lady Russell overcame her initial shock from her goddaughter's actions, and then the woman began her own assault on Sir Walter, culminating with Lady Russell manipulating Lady Dalrymple's good opinion of both Anne and Captain Wentworth. With Lady Dalrymple's stated approval, Sir Walter's determination to ignore Anne's demand melted with the desire to stay in her Ladyship's favor, and for a tidy sum, the needed license was procured.

Anne thought it all quite humorous, the power of having her family members do as she said for a change being an intoxicating feeling, but Frederick felt like a puppet—strings tangled in a knotted mess. Of course, neither he nor Anne would follow through on the threats, a few intimate kisses the most in which they partook. Frederick respected her too much to possess Anne without the bonds of marriage; his orders would force them to wait—and wait they would.

It was a week of "what ifs" for both of them. What if the church could not be secured? What if Edward and Christine did not arrive in time?

What if the same fate happened to the rest of the Musgrove party still at Uppercross? What if Anne's dress was not finished when ordered? And the list went on and on; yet, somehow with Sophia's tenacity and the Admiral's churlishness, even the surly manager at the White Hart, who finally agreed to book the breakfast in the hotel's large dining room, succumbed to the fact this wedding would happen.

The stain-glassed windows fractured the early spring sun streaming through the color prisms, every face highlighted with flecks of the rainbow. Somehow they were all there—family and friends. Besides Benwick and Harville, the Admiral managed to locate many of the officers with whom he served over the years. Those seasoned sailors filled the pews of the church—most of them amazed to see their captain, a man of decision and of action, in obvious perturbability; however, Frederick did not care; only Anne's appearance mattered.

"Relax, Wentworth," Thomas Harville leaned in to whisper his admonition, "Miss Anne will be here."

"Probably her father," Frederick grumbled. "Heaven forbid my future wife should outshine Sir Walter on her wedding day."

Thomas chuckled before observing, "He is quite a dandy."

A stir at the rear of the church brought their attention immediately to the small group gathered there. A bevy of females started making their way down the aisle, many of them already dabbing away the tears coming to their eyes, among them Mary Musgrove, Lady Russell, and Mrs. Musgrove. Elizabeth Elliot, looking surprisingly young in a dark green gown, with matching accessories more appropriate for an evening soiree than a wedding, entered with Lady Dalrymple and Miss Carteret. Several of Frederick's fellow officers followed Miss Elliot with their eyes.

A sharp breath escaped his chest when Frederick finally saw her—*his Anne*—coming toward him on Sir Walter's arm. Surprisingly, her father toned down his appearance for the occasion, choosing a more traditional look, except for his lace trimmed cravat and sleeves. Then Sir Walter turned, and there was Anne, beautiful in white with rubies at both her neck and dangling from her ears. Deep red roses and white lilies, streaming with ribbons, held tightly in her grasp finished the effect. His eyes rested on Anne's countenance—a short veil blocking his view of her returning gaze, but Frederick knew from the full smile creating dimples in her rosy cheeks that Anne's eyes were full of warmth and eagerness. His heart raced with passion, but, unexpectedly, he felt calm, as if he prepared for this day his whole life.

When she reached him, Frederick vaguely heard Sir Walter announce he would give Anne's hand in marriage, and then, even though gloved, he felt the warmth of her hand slide into his. Anne gifted him with a dazzling smile, and the hectic pace of the last four days melted into insignificance.

Behind him, he heard Milly shush one of the Musgrove children, probably Little Walter, as Edward delivered the opening lines of the service: "Dearly Beloved, we are gathered here in the sight of God to join this man and this woman in the bonds of Holy matrimony."

When it came time for him to pledge his love and devotion to Anne, Frederick forced a clearing of his throat before finding his voice to repeat his vows. Then he slid the ring, a symbol of their never-ending love, upon her finger.

Before he knew what happened, Edward, who stood silently as the local vicar read the ceremony, delivered the final line: "With Mr. Osgood's blessing, as well as mine, I pronounce that Frederick James Wentworth and Anne Gabriella Elliot be man and wife together, in the name of the Father, and of the Son, and of the Holy Ghost. Amen."

Frederick turned her to him so he might lift the veil, rolling it back to drape over the brim of her bonnet. If he had a choice, Anne would be in his arms right now, but instead he placed her hand on the crook of his arm and led her up the aisle and into the vestibule where the registry laid waiting for their signatures.

"Are you happy?" he whispered near her ear as Anne wrote her name with a flourish.

Wide bright eyes met his question. "Absolutely—so intensely happy it resembles pain."

"Then are you ready, Mrs. Wentworth?"

The words brought tears to Anne's eyes as she blinked back the natural response, and Frederick, instinctively, tightened his grip on her hand. "I thought I would never hear those words," she gasped. "I am Anne Wentworth now!" She laughed nervously.

He gently pulled their joined hands to his lips before kissing the back of hers. "You most certainly are Anne Gabriella Wentworth—forever—that will be your name, my Love."

"Then let us meet our well-wishers, my Husband." She laughed again, watching him fill in his signature next to hers. "Husband," she repeated. "I believe that is the most beloved word in the world."

"Next to the word *wife*," he teased, before leading her outside to the cheering crowds waiting in the churchyard to pelt them with rose petals.

"Run for it," she happily ordered as she turned her head into his shoulder, avoiding a mouthful of flower parts thrown with accuracy by Harry Musgrove, the youngest of Mr. and Mrs. Musgrove's brood.

Frederick wrapped his arm around her and began to hustle Anne towards their waiting coach. She lifted the skirt of her dress; trying to match his long strides; she nearly skipped along beside him towards the bow-decorated carriage. He lifted her easily into the waiting landaulette.

"From where did this come?" she asked, noticing the lushness of the finely upholstered seats.

"It is yours," he said, climbing up beside her. "It is not a barouche, but it is your wedding present, my Love."

"Frederick—you did not?" she gushed as she lightly ran her fingertips across the thickly padded cushions.

"My *wife*," he emphasized the word, "will have the best I can afford."

She wrapped her arms through his, clutching tightly to him. "It is not necessary." Her eyes rested on his countenance.

"You, Anne, are my beloved; you touched my heart in a way no one else can. Love is *necessary*—your love is necessary for my survival." He leaned down and kissed her gently, much to the delight of the gathering throng. "Let us make it through the wedding breakfast, and then I plan to spend the night showing you how much I love you and how very essential you are to me." As he expected, his words made Anne blush, but Frederick also saw something else in Anne's eyes: a desire to know him as intimately as he wished to know her. "Do I embarrass you, my Love?" he asked as he picked up the reins.

Anne flushed again with color, but her voice held a calmness he did not expect. "In my heart I waited for this night; I am afraid of the unknown, but I welcome it just the same." She raised her hand to his cheek, and he turned his lips to kiss her palm. "I love you, Frederick James Wentworth."

"As God is my witness, I am not sure I can wait until this breakfast is over," he said seductively.

Anne looked up at his laughing eyes. "Just a few more hours." She rested her hand on his. "Let us go while we can." With that, he flicked the reins, lunging forward into their future.

Hand-in-hand, they entered the large dining room to a thunderous applause and even a few catcalls. Voices and laughter followed as everyone pushed forward to either shake his hand or to kiss Anne's cheek. "You make a beautiful bride, Mrs. Wentworth," Lady Susan Lowery praised her as she stepped in front of the couple.

"Thank you, Lady Susan," Anne responded without thinking.

"And you, Captain," she spoke louder to be heard over the din, "my family sends its regards and wishes you happy."

"Are your cousins not here, Ma'am?" He steadied Anne's stance by edging slightly behind her.

"No, Captain, I am afraid they are not. My cousin Lieutenant Harding received his orders. He is to report to Bristol today, but he sends his undying devotion to you and Mrs. Wentworth. Buford regretted not getting an opportunity to meet Captain Benwick's betrothed."

"You may present the lieutenant's regard to Benwick." Frederick paused in contemplation. "Lieutenant Harding will be safe; Napoleon cannot hope to succeed," he tried to offer comfort.

Lady Susan displayed a courageous smile. "Now, listen to us; this is a day of happiness. I am pleased to be found right all along, Captain. You did favor Miss Anne."

Frederick looked down at the profile of the woman he loved. "All my protests to the negative found me out."

"It will gratify me to send my family word of the day and all the beauty and love found in this room." She moved on as the last of the well-wishers nearly crushed them in their anxiousness to be remembered to the couple.

Sophia clapped her hands loudly, bringing some order to the celebration, and everyone found a place at one of the tables, while Anne and Frederick made their way to the central setting. As much as he hated such formal occasions, Frederick took some perverted pleasure in knowing Anne's family would be expected to offer their blessings in a very public way.

Once everyone was seated, Edward rose to his feet. "I am Edward Wentworth and will represent our family this morning. With this marriage my brother Frederick closes our family circle. Our Sophia found love with her husband Benjamin. I am blessed with my Christine. Now, Frederick finally has the love of his life. Raise your glasses please and with me wish Frederick and Anne happy."

Mumbled "here-here's" were heard scattered about the room, and to recognize his brother's sentiments, Frederick raised Anne's gloved hand to his lips and kissed the back of it.

Sir Walter Elliot stood next, and the room fell quiet. Frederick leaned back, content to be amused at watching the man say what he did not wish to say. "The Elliot family is an ancient and respectable one, first settling in Cheshire and being listed as part of the nobility by Sir William Dugdale in 1675 and honored by Charles II with a baronetcy. Today it gives me great pleasure to write into the Baronetage by my daughter Anne's name: married 3 March 1815, Frederick, son of Edward and Cassandra Wentworth of Herefordshire, Captain and war hero, the British Royal Navy." Her father paused before going on. "Captain," Sir Walter addressed the couple, "our Anne will undoubtedly make you an excellent wife." He lifted his glass in a salute to his daughter and Frederick and then took his seat on Anne's right.

The toasts continued for nearly a half hour, many of them coming from the men with whom he served in various expeditions. Their words of genuine devotion to him as their leader in moments where death came close to claiming them spoke of his character, and Frederick found himself choked up with more than one declaration. Although words of war seemed inappropriate for a wedding, Bonaparte's influence on the British public invaded their celebration. It seemed natural because without the resurgence of the war, Frederick and Anne would wait, but duty called many of these men back to their fleet, and to acknowledge that life awaited them—love awaited them seemed ever important.

"I am sorry your special day was colored by the war," he whispered close to Anne's ear after Thomas Harville's toast.

Anne turned her head slowly to look at him. A single tear cascaded down her cheek. He used his thumb to wipe it away. "Do not be afraid stories of your bravery will ruin my day, my Love. How could they? They speak of the man I have loved for nearly a decade—a compassionate man of determination. I was thinking how much you changed the lives of these people and countless others, and although we suffered in our separation, God needed you where you were, because without your leadership, many men in this room would no longer be with us. God knew we would find our way back to each other after you did what you must for others." She laid her head on his shoulder. "I am honored to be your wife."

Frederick swallowed hard, nearly overwhelmed by her words; he kissed her forehead. "Why do we not circulate about the room and greet our guests?" he spoke softly, trying not to let her hear the emotion in his voice. She nodded, and they stood to speak to each of the tables of family and friends.

After greeting Lady Dalrymple first, as well as several other members of the *ton*, generally acquaintances of Lady Russell or Sir Walter, they made their way to the Musgroves congregated at several adjoining tables.

"Captain," Mr. Musgrove stood to greet him as they approached, "my family wishes you and Mrs. Wentworth the best marriage can bring. Who would think in September we would be celebrating three marriages among those who spent many happy hours in our company throughout October and November." The other men at the table rose to their feet as the family patriarch spoke.

"Gentlemen, please be seated." Anne gestured to the party.

Frederick tightened his grip on her hand when they came to Louisa Musgrove and Captain Benwick.

Anne took the high road as would be typical for her. "Miss Musgrove, my husband and I are pleased to wish you and Captain Benwick happy on the announcement of your engagement."

"Mrs. Wentworth, you are most gracious," Benwick spoke up first. "You won the love of a fine man in Captain Wentworth. I am blessed to count him among my friends."

"Thank you, Captain." Anne looked lovingly at Frederick.

Louisa leaned forward to add her own observation. "We were surprised to learn of your speedy engagement, Mrs. Wentworth. Little did any of us, including your sister, realize your regard for Captain Wentworth. In fact, I believe some thought before I found my James, that the good Captain might be my choice. How could we know when dear Frederick upon first seeing you again, said you were so altered he should not have known you?"

Frederick flinched, and he felt Anne stiffen with Louisa's *sweeten* gaucherie. Benwick gave his betrothed a reprimanding look. Frederick was not about to let Louisa expunge Anne in any way. He retorted, "Miss Musgrove, I apologize if I led you to believe I might choose a woman fresh out of the school room; it was my trying to become friends with the family of a man, who once served under my command and trying to make myself amiable to my sister's nearest neighbors, which you misinterpreted. Mrs. Charles was away at school when I first declared my love for Anne in '06. Do you not remember my stressing those years in my dinner conversation? I hoped Anne might remember what we once were to each other. Do you recall how I placed Anne in my sister's carriage when we all walked out together? I could never see her suffer and not respond. She has always owned my heart. I returned to Somerset with the pure purpose of seeing Anne again. I did not know whether she would renew her regard, but I could never move on until I knew for sure. My comment about my dear Anne was nothing more than my conceit and pride speaking, for I feared she chose not to see me with her excuses for tending Little Charles. I did not give Anne credit for being the kindest woman God ever created." He pulled Anne closer to him as he slipped his arm around her waist. "Now, if you will excuse us, we have other guests to whom to attend." He made a quick bow and led Anne away.

"Another thing for which I will spend my life in apology," he said close to her ear as they walked towards some of his naval buddies.

"You were perfect," Anne offered her praise. "You made Louisa question what she thought she knew about you." She glanced back over her shoulder to see a look of puzzlement plastered on Louisa's face. "I almost believed it myself."

"It is your fault, Sweetling." His voice sounded seductive again. "When I am near you, I do the most uncharacteristic things to get your attention."

Anne openly laughed at his out and out lie, knowing what, in reality, happened with Louisa. "I think from now on your version of our resurging connection will be what I repeat on every occasion where confabulation is necessary."

"You may embellish it as you see fit, Sweetling. I give it to you to do with as you please." He wrapped his arms around her, moving the two of them together in an embrace, and then kissing her in front of everyone gathered there. Instead of being embarrassed by his actions, she reciprocated by encircling his waist with her arms and laying her head briefly on his chest. Laughing at their open display of affection, they caught hands and moved among his comrades.

"Captain, none of us at this table ever thought we would live to see the day," Peter Laraby said as they approached. All three men stood as Wentworth stepped in front of them.

"Anne," Frederick placed her safely in the comfort of his body, outlining hers with his. "May I present three of my fellow officers? These are Lieutenants Avendale and Harwood." He gestured to each man as they bowed to her. "And this rascal is our ship's doctor Peter Laraby—one of the finest physicians found aboard a vessel. They will join me when I return to Plymouth." As the Admiral predicted Frederick received his orders yesterday. He was to command a new ship—*The Resolve*. "Gentlemen, this is my wife, Anne Elliot Wentworth."

Peter Laraby continued to be the spokesman for the group. "Mrs. Wentworth, we are pleased to meet you. Our good Captain kept his regard for you a secret. We will hope to wield the details from you; the man is a virtual steel trap when it comes to sharing his personal life."

"You should be aware, Mr. Laraby, my husband taught me subterfuge before he would agree to marry me." Frederick laughed as Anne's face straightened in all sincerity, and as her words amazed his three shipmates. "Yet, you will be happy to know he just bequeathed me a story which I may repeat to my heart's desire."

"Do not forget, my Love, you have my permission to *embellish* said story, especially where these three are concerned." Frederick rested his hands on her shoulders.

"Did you hear that, Gentlemen?" Anne's voice took on an idolized, coquettish tone. "My *esteemed* husband gave me his *permission*. Am I not blessed among women?"

The three took up her tone, heartily enjoying her flaunting of her and Wentworth's courtship. "We look forward to it, Ma'am," Laraby acknowledged. "Do you intend to travel with the Captain, Mrs. Wentworth?"

Frederick looked down at her; the question brought back the reality of their rushed marriage. "It would be my wish never to part with Mrs. Wentworth." Frederick's eyes delve deep into the chocolate-gray ones looking back at him.

Anne returned her attention to the three men. "I will see you aboard ship, Gentlemen. It has been my pleasure to make the acquaintance of men with whom my husband serves his country." With that, she curtsied before stepping away to the next group. Frederick bowed too and then followed her.

"Thank you," he said softly, "for agreeing to come with me." He tightened his hold on Anne's hand.

With her other hand, Anne gripped his arm. "I can be nowhere else," she spoke with defiance. "I did not test my father's wrath to be left behind."

Frederick melted with her sentiments. How often he misjudged her! Even though it hurt her to do so, Anne set him free because she thought she would hold him back in his career. Who was to say whether she might have? Some of his captures required risks he wondered if he would take if Anne traveled with him. He assumed for years her persuadable temper to be a weakness, but he learned at Uppercross and Lyme a resolute character possessed weakness in its absolute determination when reason should prevail.

"Let us make our final farewells," he said, once more consumed by his desire for this woman. At last, they came to Lady Russell. "How may we ever thank you for what you did for us?" Frederick made the effort to place former transgressions in the past.

Lady Russell took Anne's hand in hers. "Elizabeth Stevenson was my best friend, and I grieved greatly at her passing; but she left me you—my sweet Anne, the perfect image of your mother. I loved you, Child, as my own, and when I offered my advice I did so as I thought Elizabeth might. I do not regret what I did, but I see now I denied you time with this man because I misjudged your resiliency. That is my real regret; I never saw your full worth until you withstood both your father's and my censure. I forgot that Elizabeth, despite being both sensible and amiable, possessed a streak of stubbornness also. She became infatuated with your father, and she would broker no one denying her the man she loved. I should have remembered that about her. When you demanded our help, I suddenly pictured my dear Elizabeth standing there saying she would have no one but Sir Walter Elliot as her husband. It was at that moment I knew I must be Elizabeth Stevenson's true friend and help her daughter be with the man she loves. I used the same argument on your father. With Sir Walter, Elizabeth humored and softened and promoted his real respectability. He could deny her very little."

Anne fell into the woman's arms, crying tears of happiness. "You served me well," she assured Lady Russell. "I loved and respected you, and that will not change. I only ask you to allow Frederick into our circle."

Lady Russell sat Anne away from her—the display of emotions very uncharacteristic of the woman. "Captain Wentworth will have my devotion as your husband. I assure you, Anne; this will be so."

"Thank you—thank you for everything." Anne clutched Frederick's hand, and he led her away to the last of their good-byes: their individual families.

"Father, we will be leaving soon." Anne waited for Sir Walter to finish expounding on the lack of beauty among members of the *ton*.

"Then we will part, not knowing when we might meet again." He stood to address his middle daughter. "You will, of course, maintain your family heritage in all your dealings. First and foremost, remember you are an Elliot."

"Yes, Father, I will remember." Anne became docile with her father's charge to her. To combat this, Frederick moved up behind her, allowing Anne to feel his strength radiating all along her back. Reinforced by his thoughtfulness, she raised her chin and straightened her shoulders. "You and Elizabeth will be careful. Do not allow those with false faces to seek out your generous natures." The warning pleased Frederick. Possibly, Sir Walther might not succumb to flattery so quickly in the future. "Father, you are still a relatively young man, and no one maintains his appearance as you do." Her father actually began to preen right in front of them. "I would like to see you find someone to bring joy to your life. Start a new family; foil Mr. Elliot's plans for the baronetcy. I, for one, would welcome a younger brother and a new Lady Elliot. Think of it, Father: Kellynch would remain in our line of the family."

Frederick added his own insights. "As for me, I agree with my wife. The Admiral is likely to be needed in a supporting role for our services. He and my sister would then have to quit Kellynch. I would not wish to see your ancestral home, Sir Walter, fall into the hands of someone who does not love it as much as you. A man should grieve for his wife, but twelve years is sufficient in society's eyes."

"Thank you, Captain. I will consider your words. Maybe I will spend some time in London when the Season begins anew. I would not need someone so young the lady had no life experience—possibly a young widow—a war widow even or a woman of independent means. The lady would just need to be young enough to give me a male heir. It is a thought." Sir Walter's gaze came back to Anne. "Take good care of my daughter, Captain; she is her mother in every way. You will, therefore, be a fortunate man; my Elizabeth was a remarkable woman, one I did not appreciate enough until she was gone."

"I will, Sir Walter."

Next came Sophia and Edward. "Anne, you will do well onboard ship," Sophia guaranteed.

"I will learn from all you told me; it will be a great adventure—my first adventure," Anne gushed.

"You sail with the best," the Admiral confirmed what Anne gleamed from the various conversations she overheard today. "Your Frederick is highly esteemed by those with whom he sails and by the British Navy's high command. You will be safe with him. I am proud to be called his brother."

Frederick looked away, a bit embarrassed by such high praise from the Admiral. "My wife will probably be more in control than I." He teased to break the tension. "I have seen the ocean play lovingly at her feet as she stood on an outcropping at Lyme. While the others ran from the tide, Anne stood and welcomed it, and the sea responded by kissing her with a delicate spray. I saw that reaction only a few times; Anne is meant to be near the ocean."

"It sounds like how I felt when I first saw your sister standing along the shore at North Yarmouth. I knew she had to be mine." Admiral Croft draped his arm around Sophia's shoulder.

Sophia patted his hand. "I knew you by character long before."

"Well, and I heard of you as a very pretty girl. And what were we to wait for besides? I do not like having such things so long in hand." Benjamin Croft kissed the tip of his wife's upturned nose. "Now, Frederick brought us a gem, Sophy."

"I have, Admiral," Frederick interrupted, trying to get a moment with Edward. "And you, my Brother," he continued, "how do I give you my gratitude?"

"You do so, Frederick, by returning to us safely. My child needs his uncle and his new aunt. Our prayers will daily be with you and your men on the

Resolve." Edward gave him an embrace before saying, "Now, the two of you get out of here. You waited long enough to start your life together."

"On that we will easily agree." Frederick's smile grew by the second. "Are you ready, Mrs. Wentworth?" He turned to take Anne's hand in his.

She blushed but nodded her agreement. However, before they could escape the room, they were beset once again by women trying to bid Anne farewell. Mary Musgrove and Elizabeth Elliot led the way.

Frederick stood patiently to the side and let the women have their way, but when it appeared their exit might never occur, he gallantly stepped into the milieu. "Excuse me, Ladies," he said as he moved up to face Anne, "but I seemed to have misplaced my wife. I am sure you will understand when I now lay claim to her once again." With those words, he scooped Anne into his arms, and holding her close to his chest, strode from the room. A gaggle of female voices followed him as he placed his totally shocked wife into the front seat of their carriage. "Wave goodbye to our families, my Love," he told her as he sprang to the seat to take up the reins.

Frederick glanced back to see women waving handkerchiefs and men holding their glasses high in a salute as he maneuvered his team into the coach traffic of Bath Street. Anne swiveled around to look at him after offering their party her own farewells. "Frederick Wentworth, you, Sir, are incorrigible," she reprimanded.

"This is of what you used to say of me years ago, Sweetling. Why would you think I might change?" he teased. "I am of the persuasion to not want our marriage to wait any longer for its beginning. Even you cannot fault me for that, I think."

Anne tried to look stern, but the effort was useless; she loved him too much to fault him anything. "It was quite romantic," she gave him "to be carried off by the man I love."

Frederick lost all reason; he knew nothing else but her, and he lowered his head to kiss her lips. Although only a brief interlude, everything changed at that moment. They traveled to a private inn outside of Bath to spend their wedding night. Frederick secured the best rooms and ordered a private meal for them. Footmen delivered their bags this morning. They both knew what the night would hold, and all teasing dropped away. Anne sat as close to him as propriety allowed, and Frederick dropped one of his hands into her lap. Turning his palm up, he waited for her to place her hand in his. "I love you," he whispered in her ear, "more than life itself."

"And I love you," Anne whispered back. "Always have—always will."

Chapter 20

Light, so low upon earth,
You send a flash to the sun,
Here is the golden close of love,
All my wooing is done.
—*Alfred Lord Tennyson from "Marriage Morning"*

By the time they reached the inn, it was late afternoon. The earlier sunny day became overcast and threatened rain. Frederick put up the roof on the landaulette, but they were quite chilled by the time they reached their destination. Frederick loosened his coat and wrapped Anne in it, forcing her into his embrace to keep warm. "I will not have you catch your death of cold on your wedding day," he insisted. Both lap blankets became tucked around her also.

"What of you, my Love?" she asked as she snuggled into his chest.

"First, I am more used to the elements, having spent years fighting all sorts of weather aboard ship. Secondly, my coats are much heavier than your muslin and cloak. But, more importantly, to have a legitimate reason to hold you in my arms and feel you pressed to me, I would suffer the worst winter has to offer. A temperamental spring day means nothing. If you will just kiss me occasionally, I will stay as warm as on a summer day."

"You are so not what you appear to be," she noted as she wrapped her arms around his waist. "I would venture to say most people see you as the disciplined sea captain, ever observant—brave to the end."

"And you do not see me that way, Sweetling?" He kissed the tip of her upturned nose.

She sprayed kisses along his chin line before answering. "I see that man; in fact, I have heard the inculcation in your voice when things do not go your way, but there is another man inhabiting your body—a man who loves to tease—who protects those he loves—and who is passionate about everything in his life."

"I am passionate about you, Sweetling." They rode in silence for a few minutes. "Anne?"

"Yes, Love."

"I will be gentle tonight."

She paused before answering. "I know.—I am not afraid."

"Promise me," he began again. "Promise me if anything bothers you—if you are uncomfortable—you will tell me. I will not have you lie there and be only a vessel for my pleasure. That is not how love is to be." He kissed the top of her head. "I know I should not be talking to you about this; it is something a mother should tell her daughter, but I assume you had no one to whom to speak."

"I did—I did speak to your sister. Truthfully, much of what she said was shocking, but I am glad Sophia was so direct. For many times you kissed me, I did not understand why my body reacted to you as it did. Even though I am older, I have known no one but you. I let you kiss me from the beginning because it felt as if that is the way it is supposed to be, but I never felt that way with anyone else. I saved myself for you." She blushed with the open intimacy she felt with him.

"I never doubted that," he said. Pulling up the carriage, they overlooked the makeshift town. "I suppose we should separate before we enter the village. We would not wish to scandalize the residents with our behavior." Anne began to shift away from him, but he pulled her to him one more time, kissing her properly. Lips posed above each other, he nearly growled, "Of course, I promise scandalous behavior in the privacy of our own room."

"I will be counting on it." She leaned in for another intimate kiss, actually taking Frederick by surprise.

When they separated, he was breathing hard. "You, Anne Wentworth, are a dangerous woman." Then he laughed. "Let us go, Love. I need to get to know my wife a bit better." He flicked the reins across the horses' backs, and the carriage sprang forward.

They took a light meal as soon as they arrived. Having eaten very little at the wedding breakfast, they were both quite famished; then they took a walk about the village. Anne bought some ribbon to trim one of her day dresses and a couple of men's handkerchiefs that she planned to monogram with his initials as a present for him. He bought a couple of bars of lavender scented soap so Anne might have them aboard ship. Frederick already packed a bag of essentials—luxuries on a ship—so Anne would not have to do without many of her favorite toiletries. He sent them ahead to Plymouth in preparation for their departure.

"When do we need to be in Plymouth?" she asked as they strolled along the wooden walkway.

"Benjamin will send one of the coaches for us on Monday. A groomsman will drive our carriage back to Kellynch for safe keeping while we are away." Frederick lifted her over a sizable mud hole before continuing. "I need to be at the ship by Thursday, but I would prefer to actually take possession and walk its decks on Wednesday. By leaving early Monday morning, we should arrive by late afternoon, soon enough for me to inform the Central Office of my change in marital status. I thought on Tuesday we might attend the performance at the Theatre Royal II before we set sail. Would you like that?"

"That would be pleasant to spend an evening on your arm."

Frederick spoke with some regret. "I am so sorry, Anne. You deserve a wedding trip to the Continent instead of a few nights at a country inn before I drag you off to a crowded ship and an uncertain war."

"Oh, Frederick, do you really think I care about those things? I will spend three glorious days and nights in your arms, with us getting to know each other. Then I will visit a bustling sea port for the first time—shipyards and battleships everywhere. I am most anxious to see it."

After a few elongated seconds, he said, "I do not deserve you."

"But you love me," she finished his thought.

"That I do," he whispered. "I love you more than you will ever know."

After dinner, the time came for their night to begin, and Frederick took her in his arms. "I will join the men downstairs for a drink, but I shall have the maid bring you up a bath first. I return in an hour. That should give you plenty of time to prepare."

"I will be ready." Anne went up on her tiptoes to kiss his mouth again. Knowing what the night would bring, Frederick closed his eyes to push desire away for just a little longer.

Slowly, reluctantly, he let her go. "I will be back soon." He squeezed her hand and then quickly strode from the room before he changed his mind.

Frederick sipped on a tankard of ale and pretended to listen to the men talk of crops and of the weather, but all his mind really dwelled on was the innocent passion of Anne's kisses and what he was likely to encounter when he reentered their room.

Heart pounding erratically, Frederick slipped back into the room, securing the lock behind him. Needing a deep breath before stepping forward, he actually flexed his hands several times to relieve the tension building quickly in his limbs. The room was warm thanks to the fire burning in the hearth, and he needed a few seconds for his vision to adjust to the dim light.

"Frederick?" Anne's soft voice brought his eyes to her. She stood in the middle of the room, hair draped over her shoulders and hanging loosely down her back. The glow from the fire picked up the auburn highlights, giving her curls an inner shine. Barefoot, she stood innocently staring at him, her white dressing gown clinging to her shapely body.

Frederick swallowed, trying to say the words he wanted her to know. "You are exquisite," he murmured. Then he crossed the room in a couple of strides, taking her in his arms.

The feel of her body without corsets and chemise and layers of dress nearly did him in. He forced himself to go slow although his body demanded immediate action. He stroked her hair, allowing his fingers to trail down to the ends and then rested them on her slim waist. Beginning with slightly parted lips and then using his tongue to coax her mouth to respond to his, he bent to kiss her. Anne pressed closer to him, snaking her arms around his neck. "Ah, Anne, I thought this night would never come."

"I love you," she whispered near his ear. "No, I did not mean that," she stammered as his eyebrow rose in surprise. "I do love you, but, more importantly, I am *in love* with you."

It took no other enticement to convince him. Frederick scooped her into his arms and headed towards the bed, already turned down for the night. Carrying her close to him, he asked, "Can you hear my heart? It stop beating years ago; now, you are the other half of it—and it can take up again." Frederick laid her gently across the bed; seeing her hair spread out across the pillow completed the picture from his dream.

Looking down at her, he began to unbutton his jacket. "I cannot believe how beautiful you are," he spoke reverently, enthralled by her appearance.

Anne stretched her arms out to him, and Frederick's dreams came to life. He leaned over and blew out the single candle—only the glow of the fire showed in the room. Then he slid into the bed with her. "I love you, Anne Wentworth. I have loved no one but you. You are my life."

"This is our first night together," she whispered in his ear. "The first night of thousands to come. This is the night I become a real woman—your woman." She kissed him after, and no more words were needed. They knew from the first day they met—from the first time they danced—from the first time they kissed. This was where they were meant to be.

*   *   *

On Saturday they took the landaulette out for a ride about the countryside, taking in the beautiful vistas. Frederick ordered a picnic lunch packed by the innkeeper's wife and laid claim to extra blankets for the drive. The sun shone brightly although the air still held a brisk coolness.

Choosing a rocky outcropping overlooking a panoramic glade and orchard, he spread the blanket on the flatten ledge and then he helped Anne settle there. She sat with her knees pulled up and her arms wrapped about them. Watching her intently, he relished the image of Anne tilting her face up to the sun. "It is such a beautiful day," she said.

Frederick leaned over to kiss her upturned lips as he sat the picnic basket beside her. "Perfectly beautiful," he murmured while offering her a wicked smile. He laid the extra blanket to her left in case she needed the additional warmth, and then he stretched out his full length, lying on his back and covering his face with his hat.

After ten minutes of pure silence, Anne's voice broke through his quiet time. "Did you bring me all the way out here so you might catch up on your sleep?"

He removed the hat and rolled to his side, propping himself up on one elbow. "I enjoyed the warmth of the sun, and I admit it could easily lull me to sleep. I got little rest last night."

"Neither did I," she asserted.

Frederick laughed before taking her hand in his. "I recall." His smile grew by the minute. "Would you like a repeat performance?" He moved up to kiss her earlobe. "I would be willing to serve your needs, Sweetling."

Anne joined in his banter. "Why do you not serve the food instead?"

"Ah, Sweetheart, you wound me greatly, but I am here to please you." Frederick sat up to open the basket. "Now, let us see what Mrs. Francis created for us today." He sat roasted chicken, hard, dark bread, cheese, and some fresh fruit on the plates. "What do you think, Love? Is this not a grand meal?" He poured them each a large glass of wine.

"It is, Frederick." Anne leaned in to kiss his wine-touched lips. "It is the best meal ever served to me."

He wrapped his arms around her. "Do you love being married as much as I?"

Anne turned to sit back against him after feeding Frederick a mouthful of cheese and bread. "Married life is very satisfying." She wiggled up next to him, and he automatically began to kiss the nape of her neck. The freedom to touch each other became more intoxicating with each new exploration. "Will it always be this way?" she asked as she leaned back further to feel his warmth along her body.

"I would hope it will be so," he spoke next to her ear. "Yet, I am sure some day we will seek comfort in other ways. Twenty years from now it will not be so adventurous, but I guarantee the passion and the desire will still be there."

"Can you imagine us twenty years from now?"

Frederick traced his fingers up and down her arm. "I see us in a small estate—near the sea, of course, where we will entertain our neighbors. Our children will be strong as their father and as beautiful as their mother, and they will accept only love matches—the same as their parents." This was a defining moment; he and Anne actually had a future. Speaking of children and of a home out loud seemed very prophetic—almost mystical.

"How many children?" She kissed his cheek and then under his jaw line.

He encircled her in his embrace. "Two—maybe three."

"Two," she decided.

"Two it is."

The afternoon passed too quickly, but the time spoke of commitment—to something greater—something beyond them. They planned their life—talked of where to live, how to arrange the house, how to treat the cottagers, how to positively impact the community, what qualities to instill into their children, and what role they would each play. They learned about each other intimately the night before; they learned how to make the marriage work during that impromptu Saturday afternoon picnic.

On Sunday, they joined the villagers at the local church to give thanks for their love and to pray for the safety of all the men with whom Frederick would sail.

When the Admiral's coach rolled into the inn yard early Monday morning, they came to grips with the reality of what would change when they reached Plymouth. "Frederick, I am frightened," she whispered once they were on their way.

He took her hand in his. "I would be telling a lie if I told you there is no danger. Of course, in war there is always danger." Frederick lifted her chin to force Anne to look at him. "There are dangers even when there is not a war. Women die regularly in childbirth. Poverty claims hundreds daily.

Men lose their homes and property to gambling and overspending, sending their families into bankruptcy. A gentleman can easily greet death simply by stepping into a busy street and meeting a speeding milk cart. We cannot control our fate, Anne; all we can do is exercise caution and reason. I am known for those qualities. I will never put you or the men on my ship at risk simply to win a government prize. I value human life too much."

"I know," she spoke the words softly but with a degree of determination. "Change is frightening, though."

"I understand, my Love. It is more of a change for you as a woman than it is for me. You are giving up a lifestyle—your way of life, all you knew. You must promise, just as you did on our first night together, you will tell me when things are too much—too much change at once. There is *nothing* you can say to me that will lessen my love for you or that I will find reasons for which to censure you."

"I promise." Anne brought his hand to her mouth. She kissed his palm and then followed his lifeline with her index finger. "You will have a long life," she said as a way to break the tension.

Frederick took the glove from her hand and then he aligned their palms so their life lines touched each other. "We will have a long life, and your life line matches up perfectly with mine." His fingers interlaced with hers. "As our hands are linked together, so is our fate. We belong to each other—you and I."

"You and I." A smile turned up the corners of her mouth, and desire glowed in her eyes. "Our fates predetermined."

"Yes, our fates brought us full circle to each other." He wrapped his other hand around their two and squeezed them together. "We are bound together, and nothing will pull us apart. I need you near me, Anne, and then I can do anything."

*   *   *

"Captain, we are coming into the Sound." Harwood brought the message.

His assistant helped Frederick finish dressing. "Thank you, Lieutenant; I will be ready."

"The crew is pleased to have you up and about, Sir." Harwood began to straighten the quarters.

"It was tenuous for a while, and I do thank you and the other officers for your part in my recovery; I am doing well. Yet, four and half months at sea are long enough. I do not know about you, Harwood, but I am ready for some dry land." Frederick straightened the cuff of his uniform's sleeve as his assistant brushed down the back of the coat. "Are the prisoners ready for the transfer."

"They are, Sir. Our men sail the French sloop into the Bay behind us. That one, plus the frigate we captured earlier should serve us all well."

"I am not usually worried about the financial rewards as long as we all make it back safely, Lieutenant, but I admit to looking forward to this pay out. I promised Mrs. Wentworth a place of her own when this action is over." Frederick wrapped the belt from his saber around his waist.

"How much longer do you think we will be, Captain?"

"The war, you mean?—It cannot last much longer. When we took on supplies at Gibraltar, Wellington had Napoleon on the run. That was nearly a month ago: I cannot imagine Bonaparte can hold out much longer. That is one of my first tasks when we are in port—we need an update as to if we go back out again." By now, Frederick slid on his gloves.

"What will we do with the American—the one who shot you?" Harwood opened the door for Frederick.

"I will turn him over to the Central Office as soon as we dock: I am sure they will be most anxious to question him." Frederick nodded to both men. "Let us greet England." They followed him to the main deck.

Anne stayed in the background, allowing Frederick to lead his men home to England. His was the most serious injury of their journey, but they made it home safely because he trained them to operate efficiently without him. A month into their orders, they captured a French frigate, which was already disassembled and the prisoners on one of the many ships anchored off Plymouth's coast. Today, they brought in the sloop as a second prize.

"You will wait on board with the men until I return for you. It may take several hours to turn over all the records to the Central Office." Frederick led Anne to one of the railings, not allowing his officers to hear what he said to her, needing to apprise her of naval protocol.

"I understand. It will give me time to finish packing."

"Shall I send one of the men to help you?"

"No, my Love, I can handle it. I would be mortified if one of the crew saw some of my private papers or even worse some of my clothing."

He smiled at her. "Only I am allowed to make you blush."

"That is your prerogative," she taunted. "Now, go about your duties; I will be fine," she assured him.

"We will dine at the Royal Hotel tonight. You enjoyed staying there when we first came to Plymouth."

"That sounds delightful. Now, off with you." To emphasize her point, Anne walked briskly away towards her quarters. Frederick's eyes followed her—if she only knew how essential she was to him!

Returning to his officers, gathered on deck, he addressed them. "Gentlemen, without your devotion to duty, we could be coming home to England with news of our losses; instead, we enter this port with everyone safe and sound. I salute your efforts. It will be a part of my official report. I take Avendale and Harwood with me. The rest of you see to securing *The Resolve*. I will return with our new orders and leave for everyone."

"Yes, Captain." The men dispersed to do his bidding, knowing in a few hours they would see loved ones again.

Strolling down the gang plank, Frederick, surprisingly, found Benjamin waiting for him. "Frederick, my Boy, Sophy will be so happy to know you are safe; she was so worried. As soon as I heard it was *The Resolve* coming in, I hurried down to see for myself." He started to give Frederick a warm hug, but Frederick backed away.

A look of dismay crossed Benjamin's face. "I suffered an injury in our last encounter, Admiral. I am well now, but still a bit sore. Is Sophia in Plymouth too? Anne will be happy to see her."

"Your sister is still at Kellynch. I am traveling back and forth, mostly between Bath and here, occasionally to Bristol in support of the Central Office. I am only at Kellynch a few days a week, but I cannot leave Sophy there alone for very long. I should wait for your sister to tell you, but I will not. Sophy, after all these years, is with child. Once I found out I could not subject her to a return to the sea; that is why I am acting as an advisor to these various groups."

"Sophia? You are to be a father, Benjamin? How magnificent! And what of Edward?" Frederick's mind rushed through the many things he wanted to ask his sister's husband as they walked briskly towards the Central Office for Naval Affairs.

"Christine is in her confinement. Our brother is a mess if his letters are any indication. Of course, in six months Edward will be able to return my ridicule. Let us get you clearance, and then I want to see that wife of yours. We have not laid eyes on either of you since you rode away from your wedding breakfast. How did Mrs. Wentworth take to the sea?"

"As if she was born aboard a warship," Frederick assured him. "Truthfully, Benjamin, if Anne was not with me, I am not sure I would have survived. Doctor Laraby says she tended me for over three days straight while my fever raged on. Benjamin, Anne was of all I thought.

Only when I opened my eyes and found her there, did I have a will to go on. If this happened years ago . . . ." They stopped walking when Frederick touched the Admiral's arm.

"Then I am pleased you and Miss Anne found your way back to each other. I would never want to be in a position to tell Sophy or Edward of your demise. Did you lose any men?" They began their walk again, followed closely behind by Frederick's two lieutenants.

"Not a one, Admiral."

"Excellent! The high command will be pleased to hear it." Benjamin patted him on the back. "Here we are." The Admiral indicated the door to a small store front office. Frederick and his men followed Benjamin into the darkened room.

"Wentworth!" Pennington, a Vice-Admiral of the Red, came forward to meet them. "You returned. That means we have all our ships back but two. We are certainly glad you made it in safely. Have a seat, Gentlemen." He gestured to two chairs at the end of the table. "Sit here, Wentworth, I want to hear all the news before you write up your report."

Benjamin took the seat next to Frederick to lend his support. "I am not sure, Sir, where you want me to begin; I assume you read the report of our earlier capture—the frigate."

"Certainly, Captain, but what of this latest prize? My spies on the dock tell me you brought in a French sloop."

"My men, Sir, did the *bringing;* I am afraid I was severely injured when we made our assault. As we prepared to board the sloop, an American took me into his sights and unloaded into me. If it were not for the men of my crew and the ship's doctor, I would not have survived. Fortunately, we had no other serious injuries and no causalities."

"An American, you say?" Admiral Pennington questioned.

"Yes, Sir; the last I remember, the man shouted out some curses directed to the King." Frederick turned to his two lieutenants. "Might either one of you give the Vice-Admiral more facts on the American prisoner?"

Lieutenant Harwood spoke up first. "The prisoner surely was not happy with our take over of the French ship; he put up quite a fight. Needless to say, many of our men were upset with his attack on the Captain; he suffered the wrath of several of them before we could secure his safety. He shouted his curses for several days, but as we came closer to English soil, he became more docile—accepting his fate. It appears that the ship, as noted in our log, was a private one, sailing under the French flag—mostly mercenaries onboard."

Benjamin turned to Avendale. "Did the American give any indication as to why he was on this ship?"

Avendale shared what he knew. "In the last few days, the American was more open with his information. One of our men speaks French, and he managed to hold several conversations with him. The prisoner's father, evidently, was of French extraction, having settled in a predominately French community in what is known at New Orleans in the Americas. He said he was sent by a group of French sympathizers to help Bonaparte. We thought that to be ridiculous. I mean, what would Bony do with an American? How could America play into this crazy French war? They cannot surely be still fighting the War of 1812? It was three years ago, after all."

"Some do not end their fights with the cessation of the war," Pennington remarked. "And it may not be so bizarre what the American said."

"What do you mean, Sir?" Frederick stopped filling the water glass he sat before him and turned his attention fully on Admiral Pennington.

Pennington instructed, "Tell us what you know of Bonaparte."

Frederick told Pennington pretty much what he said to Harwood earlier. "We found out at Gibraltar that Wellington defeated Bonaparte at Waterloo. That was in the middle of June. We know little else of the scope of the war since that time. We have not been in port for a month. The men on *The Resolve* carried on after my injury, but towing the French sloop slowed down our return."

"Then you do not know Napoleon surrendered to the *Bellerophon's* captain two days ago? Bony tried to make his escape: He planned to take refuge in the United States. Two French ships anchored off the Atlantic coast prepared to receive Napoleon, but the *Bellerophon* blocked the port and his escape. It is rumored there was to be a third—maybe even a fourth ship, each with American sympathizers to aid in the Emperor's escape."

"Are you suggesting?" Frederick stammered.

Pennington reasoned, "It is possible, Captain. It would make sense as to why the American chose to make you his target. If you take out the head, the rest of the body often crumbles."

"Not with Captain Wentworth," Harwood interjected. "He taught us our duty comes before everything."

Pennington closed out the subject. "That is the British way; we would expect nothing less than from the commander of one of our ships." Yet, even Pennington knew how unusual the situation was to have men so well trained and so devoted to their commander. It spoke volumes of the type of man Frederick Wentworth was.

"Let me summarize what I understand you to be saying, Sir." Frederick tried to clear his thinking. "First, the war is essentially over, and very soon my men and I will be returning to civilian life." Pennington nodded his head in agreement. "More importantly, for the immediate future, my crew quite possibly captured a French ship transporting an American sent to relay Bonaparte to safety in the United States."

"That is what it sounds like, Captain Wentworth," Pennington confirmed.

Benjamin began to laugh. "If this plays out, Frederick, you and your men will be national heroes. You will have foiled part of Bony's plan to leave France behind. It is said he missed his first means of escape, and the *LaSalle* was Bonaparte's last hope." Frederick sat silent in disbelief. "You have to admire the man," Benjamin continued. "Bonaparte's rise to power came as a result of his ability and his ambition, not as a man of rank or privilege. He had no noble title—actually from a poor family of Corsica. He was trained as an artillery officer and now is a symbol—a product of the new France."

"He sounds like you, Captain," Avendale said out loud what Benjamin thought. "Unlike lots of our officers, you have no title, but I would rather follow you into battle than anyone under which I ever served. You were trained as a naval officer. Your lives have parallels, do you not see it?"

"It will make a great story for the War Office." Pennington knew how it would play out in the newspapers.

Frederick protested, "I want no parallels to Bonaparte."

"Let us get all the particulars on paper," Pennington encouraged.

Frederick turned to his brother by marriage. "Admiral, might I impose on you to return to *The Resolve* and to gather Anne and take her to the Royal Hotel. I promised her we would stay there for a few days—at least, until this is complete."

"It would be my pleasure. Mrs. Wentworth is an exceptional woman. Wait until you meet her, Pennington." Benjamin Croft stood to take his leave.

Pennington called to the Admiral's retreating form. "Croft, see if Mrs. Wentworth will join us for dinner? I will bring my Miranda along; she will enjoy the company of another lady."

"Admiral," Frederick interceded, "after you have Anne settled in one of the hotel rooms, be sure to advise the hotel dining room of our party."

Benjamin just waved his hand in recognition of what the men said. He knew exactly how to arrange the evening; the Admiral would make sure Anne understood her husband, under subtly worded orders, would dine this evening with one of his commanding officers. Frederick needed her support tonight; a good naval wife could make or break her husband's career. Frederick probably planned an intimate meal, but that would have to wait. Her husband's career came first this evening. Besides, if Anne Wentworth could entertain the supercilious people who populated her father's drawing room, Frederick had no cause for alarm; yet, Benjamin Croft would guarantee Frederick's success with gentle hints to Sir Walter's second daughter.

Chapter 21

My Luve is like a red, red rose
That's newly sprung in June:
My Luve's like the melodie
That's sweetly played in tune.
—Robert Burns from "A Red, Red Rose"

They spent six weeks in Plymouth waiting for something to change. Although pressed repeatedly by the allied armies, the French continued to hold out, not accepting their defeat. The Wentworths let a small cottage on the outskirts of the town for privacy and to economize. Between them, Frederick and Anne decided to save his prize money to purchase their own home. Despite never having once prepared her own meal or taken care of her own home, Anne became quite adept at improvisation. Used to fending for himself, Frederick helped her, and some of their memories came from disastrous attempts in the kitchen. Such moments usually culminated with their collapsing hysterically into each other's arms, normally leading to a passionate night of lovemaking.

At the beginning of August, he received word from Edward that he and Christine welcomed a son, Edward Oscar. Frederick promised in his return that he and Anne would visit as soon as the Navy released him from his duties.

In September, the story of the action taken by *The Resolve* and of Wentworth's injury became well known in Plymouth, and he and Anne retreated to Kellynch to stay with the Admiral and Sophia. Frederick worried how the move would affect her—returning to her childhood home, but as a guest. Yet, Anne reasoned she should be there for Sophia, before his sister's lying in. "We can revisit the lake," she whispered in his ear as Frederick took Anne into his arms.

He settled her next to him. "Have you ever made love in the open?" he teased, as he trailed a line of kisses down Anne's neck.

"Frederick!" she protested, trying to shove away from him by placing her hands firmly against his chest.

He raised his eyebrows, feigning innocence.

Finally, she burst out laughing. "You know full well I never made love anywhere but in your bed."

"Then how about your bed?" he asked in all sincerity.

"My bed?" Anne looked confused. "From the first day of our marriage we shared the same bed."

He offered in explanation, "Your bed chamber—the one in the east wing."

"My old room?" she whispered.

"When I returned to Lyme—the time I left you the note regarding Louisa's progress . . ." Anne looked at him intently, trying to understand the emotions behind his words. "I went to your room and spent time there—alone. I imagined you there—touching your favorite things. My heart felt heavy—I accepted the fact you would never be mine; I would never know happiness. I laid across your bed trying to recall the smell of lavender on your pillow—hugging it to me, imagining you in my arms—and feeling my chest contract around the loneliness consuming my soul."

Anne understood; she knew how she would feel if she found herself in the house where Frederick grew into manhood. "We would have the wing all to ourselves," she started.

"As if we were alone in our own house," he murmured.

"Kellynch would feel like home again." Her eyes lit with excitement. "Would you mind?" she asked, hope playing in her words.

Frederick pulled her closer. "Would I mind making my wife happy? Would I mind having you entirely to myself—hearing you fully cry out my name in ecstasy? I assume those are rhetorical questions." This time he made a full assault of her lips. I will have Ned move us into your room this afternoon," he said huskily when he came up for air.

"Thank you, Frederick." She kissed his ear as she inched closer to him. "You are the kindest, most considerate man . . . ."

"Do not tell anyone else." He turned her chin so she faced him. "Kind and considerate are not qualities for which the Navy looks in their captains." By then, they were lost to their combined desire. Frederick pulled her down with him as he leaned back on the chaise. "I love you," he gasped as Anne moved across him. "I love you—forever."

*   *   *

The news of his commendation shocked the household but gave everyone a reason for celebration. "A Rear Admiral of the White!" Anne danced around the room waving the letter through the air as if it were a butterfly's wings. "How many bars and medals is that on your dress uniform?" she laughed as she spun around him one more time.

"Enough to even impress your father, I suppose." Frederick smiled with seeing her so happy. "Of course, it is not as many as Benjamin."

"You, my Husband, will be the best looking Rear Admiral in the whole British navy," Anne declared as she went up on her tiptoes to nibble on his bottom lip.

"Now, you do sound like your father," he teased.

She chuckled with the irony of what he said. "Well, my father cannot be wrong all the time."

Frederick snorted, choking back the laughter bubbling in his throat. "Sir Walter Elliot speaks the truth. What a novel idea that is!"

"Let us take the landaulette and visit Mary and Charles. I will take pleasure in sharing your advancement with my younger sister." Anne wrapped her arms around his neck. "My sister always appreciated the fact you were richer than either Captain Benwick or Charles Hayter."

"And that is important because?" Frederick sat Anne away from him, interested in this new side of his wife.

"It is important because Mary is an Elliot, and she will rush from whatever sick bed in which she now *thinks* she occupies to share her news with Charles's family—to let Charles's family know I am now married to a Rear Admiral of the White and . . ."

"And Louisa is married to retired Captain Benwick." Frederick finished her sentence. "I am surprised, my Love; I never knew you to be so revengeful."

Anne dropped her eyes from his. "I suppose, like Mary, I too am an Elliot; I should be ashamed for having such thoughts."

"But you are not?" Frederick mocked.

"No," she shook her head vehemently. "No,—I am not. Since our wedding breakfast, I keep hearing Louisa's voice saying, *'I believe some thought before I found my James, that the good Captain might be my choice.'* If I am taking Louisa Musgrove's leftovers, I perversely want her to realize she threw away the wrong man."

Frederick kissed her forehead. "Wear your heavy cloak, my Love." He laughed as he headed towards the door. "If you wish to turn green with jealousy, I do not want you to turn blue from the cold as well. The colors are complementary, after all."

"Thank you, Frederick," she said to his retreating form.

He spun around to face her. Giving Anne a very exaggerated bow, he declared in his most military-sounding voice, "That is Rear Admiral Wentworth to you, Ma'am." Then he disappeared through the open door.

Laughing loudly, Anne called to his departing footsteps. "Yes, Sir!"

*   *   *

In late November after a night of difficult labor, Sophia delivered a beautiful baby girl, whom she immediately named Cassandra Rose after her late mother. Benjamin Croft paced the floors for hours, waiting impatiently, for his child, but no baby would have a more doting father.

"She is quite the most adorable child God ever created," the Admiral said softly as he bundled the sleeping baby to him. "Is she not beautiful, Frederick?" He gently pushed the swaddling blankets away from the child's face to give his brother a look at his daughter.

"Cassandra Rose will break many hearts, Benjamin." Frederick looked lovingly down at the child. "You will need a military escort wherever she goes."

"I never knew—I mean, Sophia and I never thought this could happen. Maybe all those years at sea kept Sophy from . . ." Benjamin lightly touched his daughter's face.

Frederick placed his arm around the Admiral's shoulder. Still looking down at the sleeping child, he barely whispered. "Your and Sophia's time at sea had nothing to do with my sister waiting until she was six and thirty to deliver her first child. It is just simply God's plan. The same as it was God's plan that I return to the service alone all those years ago—because I needed to be there for my men when we were at war—the same as Anne needed to be with me on my last voyage or else I would have died. God decided you and Sophia needed a child, and I will bet a year's wages He thinks you need more than one. Sophia will look grand with a crew of little Crofts trailing along behind her, and you, my Admiral—my brother in marriage—will have your proverbial hands full."

The Admiral chuckled with the image. "Words from your mouth to God's ears! I hope God is listening to those prayers."

*   *   *

"We will take a house together close to Mayfair," Benjamin Croft said as they all sat relaxing in his study at Kellynch. "Edward and Christine will join us there."

Frederick sat back in his chair. He turned over and over again in his hand the invitation, which came that morning. With France's signing of the Treaty of Paris in late November, actually about the same time Sophia gave birth to Cassandra Rose, the country went crazy for anything military. The war, now at an end, demanded a celebration, and the Prince of Wales knew exactly how to do so. He and his inner circle would recognize the most prestigious of the British war heroes at Carlton House, while all those who served the country well would receive military honors with parades and such. Those invited to Carlton House would spend the evening, along with Prinny, with leaders of the Allied countries and other dignitaries: Field Marshal Gebhard Blucher, Prussian General Gneiseneau, the Grand Duchess Catherine and her brother the Czar of Russia, Prince Frederick of the Netherlands, Francis I of Austria, Levin August, better known as Count von Bennigsen, the King of Prussia, and William II of the Netherlands, who reportedly would marry Princess Charlotte of Wales.

Sophia took the card from Frederick's hand and read it aloud: "The Prince of Wales requests the pleasure of the company of Rear Admiral of the White Frederick Wentworth and Mrs. Anne Wentworth at an evening of celebration."

"It reads the same as the one Benjamin received," Frederick assured her as he took back the card.

Anne sat quietly spellbound with the news. "We are invited to Carlton House," she spoke slowly trying to synthesize the information. "The Prince of Wales and the Queen will both likely be there."

"Yes, Love," Frederick, although a bit discommoded by the situation, thought Anne's reaction rather amusing. "You and my sister each read the cards."

"Frederick, we cannot," she started her protest, but realized the effort was fruitless.

Frederick crossed to where she sat, joining her on the settee. "Of course, Mrs. Wentworth, I will send our regrets to the Queen of England. I suppose you do have her personal address in your ledger," he chastised her sarcastically.

"But, Frederick," she stammered, "I never had a Season or was presented at court."

"Anne, you are a married woman; you need neither of those in this case. We will not even be speaking to any of these royals; there will be hundreds of people there. It is a State dinner; Benjamin and I will be part of the pomp and circumstance of the evening—that is all. We are likely to be seated at one of the back tables; yet, we will be able to tell our children we were part of history. Besides," he whispered in a conspiratorial tone, "think how jealous Mary and Elizabeth will be."

Anne's countenance turned to one of delight. "They will, will they not?"

He whispered even lower. "Mrs. Benwick will not be invited."

"I love you," she giggled as the words burst from her mouth.

He laughed as he took her hand in his and settled back into the furniture. He stretched out his legs to their full length. "How could you not? I am, after all, a Rear Admiral of the White."

"Now, who is mimicking my father?"

Frederick looked sharply at Anne. He took on a serious mien and pretended to be offended, applying a sharp tone. "I take your words to heart Mrs. Wentworth. You are right; I will not speak thusly again."

Immediately, tears formed in Anne's eyes. "Oh, my Love, I apologize. I never meant to criticize you." Tears flowed freely down her face. "I would never censure you so. You must believe me."

Frederick instinctively took her in his arms, ignoring the fact they sat in a room with Sophia and Benjamin. "Sweetheart, I teased you as I always do; I never thought criticism to be a part of your words."

Although she fought to control them, still the tears streamed, leaving trails of wet powder on her face. "I do not know why I am crying; I feel like such a fool. Sophia—Benjamin, I never meant to make you uncomfortable," she called out to them.

"You are just nervous, Anne," the Admiral assured her. "You are to meet the reigning monarchs of our country. Who would not be nervous? I am nervous. Are you not, Sophia?"

"But the three of you are not moved to tears. What is wrong with me?" Sobs began all over again. This time they came because she knew she was the only one acting out of sorts.

"Come, Love," Frederick coaxed her onto his lap. "You are one of the strongest women I ever knew. If you were not afraid of armed French ships, you will easily win the approval of any dignitary we might meet." He wiped away her tears with a handkerchief and soothed her with the comforting sound of his voice. "You are incomparable."

Anne snuggled into his chest as she encircled his neck with her arms. "Thank you for loving me even with all my insecurities," she whispered in his ear.

Frederick would love to kiss her—to make love to her—to prove to Anne the power she had over him. Instead, he simply pulled her closer and stroked her hair. Out of the corner of his eye, he noted Sophia and the Admiral slipping from the room, but his ministrations did not cease. The day Frederick won her hand after waiting to love Anne for all those years, he committed himself to meeting her needs over everything else in his life—no propriety standards would exist between them.

"You are tired," he said softly. "Let me take you to our room; you need to rest." He easily lifted her to carry Anne to their quarters.

"Will we sleep?" she said dreamily.

Frederick chuckled. "You are a tempting one, Sweetling, but I will insist you sleep. At least, initially," he added as an afterthought.

"Initially," she murmured, nearly asleep already. "I love you, Frederick. You are too good to me."

"Nothing is ever good enough for you, Anne—nothing could match your love." Frederick kissed the top of her head as he carried her down the long deserted corridor to their room. "I will spend my life loving you completely."

*   *   *

"You are not eating this morning?" Sophia asked as Anne shoved her plate away. They prepared to leave for London today nearly a month before the celebration at Carlton House. The four of them would take a house together on the edge of Mayfair.

Married nearly a year, Anne looked forward to seeing her father and sister again. Evidently, Sir Walter took her and Frederick's advice. He gave up the house in Bath and took one in a fashionable, but not top of the *ton* area of London. From Lady Russell's last letter, Sir Walter actively wooed a war widow—a Mrs. Bradley. Elizabeth, from whom Anne had not received one letter since the day she hugged Anne at the wedding, attempted, at first, to sabotage the relationship, but Sir Walter selfishly denied his eldest daughter's wishes. After his having catered to Elizabeth for nearly thirteen years, the eldest Elliot suddenly found herself supplanted by a woman two years her junior. Anne would see for herself at the end of the week when she and Frederick dined with her family.

"I did eat," Anne nodded her thanks to the footman who removed the plate. "I will get something at the posting inn; I am sure we will stop several times today." She took a sip of her tea. "Besides, I am so nervous my stomach is in knots."

"Have you had to use your chamber pot?" Sophia held her teacup to her mouth, but she did not drink. Instead, she watched Anne carefully over the rim of the cup.

"Yes—but only yesterday and today. You do not suppose I am coming down with something? That would be unforgivable; this is Frederick's big moment." Anne now looked concerned.

Sophia put the cup down, fully interested. "How long has your stomach been bothering you?"

Anne thought back—trying to give an accurate answer. "About a week, I suppose. It is worse in the morning—dry toast usually does the trick, though."

"Anne, when were your last courses?"

Anne's head snapped around. "What do you mean, Sophia? I cannot be!"

"Morning nausea—emotionally crying for no real reason—exhausted all the time. Think about it, Anne; it says 'with child' to me. Why can you not be carrying Frederick's baby? Do not tell me it is your age; I am nearly seven years older than you, and Cassandra Rose says it is possible." Sophia summarized what Anne already suspected but never allowed herself to consider the prospect.

Panicking, she begged Frederick's sister. "I will not tell Frederick until I am sure. Please, Sophia, you will say nothing. I cannot bring up Frederick's hopes only to have them dashed. These next few weeks are too important to let my nerves be mistaken for the possibility—the reality of—a child."

"I will say nothing for now," Sophia assured her. "But you must watch carefully. The next few weeks, as you just said, will be filled with ceremony after ceremony. Do not let the demand of Frederick's obligations risk your health and that of your child. My brother would *never* allow harm to come to you. His career—everything—is secondary to the love Frederick feels for you. I never saw him act thusly; Frederick unconditionally loves you, Anne."

"I will be careful until I know for sure, and then I will tell your brother if our suspicions prove true." Instinctively, Anne's hand slipped to her abdomen where it remained while she sat silently contemplating their conversation.

*   *   *

"Anne," Sir Walter scrambled to his feet as a footman announced her and Frederick. "My, do you not look well! Your complexion glows, and you look less thin in your person and in your cheeks. Have you been using Gowland's as I suggested?"

"No, Father—nothing at all," she replied as she offered him a kiss on the cheek.

"Certainly you cannot do better than continue as you are; you cannot be better than well." Her father moved past her to greet Frederick, who stood to the side, amused by what Sir Walter considered to be the first thing to say to his daughter after nearly a year. "Captain," the man offered his hand, "it has been a long time, Sir."

Anne jumped at the opportunity to correct her father's misstep. "Father, remember I wrote—Frederick is now a Rear Admiral of the White?"

"Of course, you did," Sir Walter looked differently at Frederick. "How could I make such a faux pas?"

"It is perfectly understandable, Sir. I am afraid I too am unaccustomed to the title." Frederick took Sir Walter's hand, vowing to be civil to the man.

"Come, I have someone I wish you to meet." Sir Walter gestured to a woman of approximately Anne's age. Raven-haired with astonishing blue eyes, the lady was taller than Anne by at least three inches. A bit on the lanky side, she notably had a small waist and a well-developed bust line, which she displayed quite fully with the cut of her gown, a lavender one usually indicative of a widow after her mourning period. "This is Mrs. Amelia Bradley. Mrs. Bradley, this is my second daughter Anne Wentworth and her husband Admiral Frederick Wentworth."

Frederick and Anne offered the lady in question a proper bow and a curtsey, which Mrs. Bradley returned in a like manner. "Mrs. Bradley," Anne took the lead, "it is pleasant to meet you, at last. We heard much of you from Lady Russell."

"I hope the report from Lady Russell spoke of my good qualities," the woman seemed unsure of how Sir Walter's family might view her.

"I assure you, Ma'am," Frederick led Anne to a nearby chair, "we heard nothing but a glowing account."

Mrs. Bradley nodded to a winged chair for Frederick's use. "I am pleased to hear it," she uttered. "Your father speaks often of your union, Admiral Wentworth; Sir Walter became quite enthralled by stories of your recent captures; I cannot imagine the dangers, Sir. And you, Mrs. Wentworth," she continued, "traveled with your husband?"

"I did, Mrs. Bradley," Anne became quite purposeful in her response. "A woman should follow her husband."

Frederick interrupted, "My wife is very adamant about the possibility of our separation, as am I. We waited many years to share our life." He cleared his throat with the emotion building in his words. "You may be unaware, Mrs. Bradley, how close I came to death's door in this last journey; if Anne had not traveled with me—to tend me—I could likely have succumbed to my wounds."

"Really, Wentworth?" Sir Walter questioned, "I never supposed Anne tenacious enough to handle such a crisis!"

"Then you, Sir, misjudge your daughter. Anne is sensible, emulous, compassionate, intelligent, and, often times, a bit stubborn, although I find those moments most endearing. I have heard many of her family and friends compare Anne to the former Lady Elliot, may God bless her soul. I cannot say whether that is a true evaluation of my wife, but all who know her know there is no one more capable than Anne."

"Well," Sir Walter stammered, "I suspect I still see Anne as the little girl always with a book in her hand—lost in her world of make believe."

Anne, always the diplomat in the family, added quickly, "I suspect I am a combination of both the fanciful girl and the sagacious woman."

Mrs. Bradley joined in again. "I imagine you would be, Mrs. Wentworth. Most women are, although the men in our lives sometimes see us as one dimensional."

Frederick took the woman's words to heart; he imagined she spoke from first hand experience when dealing with Sir Walter. "I understood, Mrs. Bradley," he returned his attention towards the woman seated before him, "your late husband served in the Iberian campaign?"

"He did, Sir." Amelia Bradley paused in remembrance. "My Stephen lost his life trying to break Napoleon's tenuous military hold on the rest of Europe."

"Did you follow the drum, Ma'am?" Anne asked quietly.

"No—No, Mrs. Wentworth, I do not possess your determination. I wish I was there when Stephen . . ." she paused and took a deep breath. "But, I suppose, it would not matter."

"What I know of men who served in both Andalusia and in Portugal is they dealt Napoleon a major blow, but they suffered unbelievable losses." Frederick did not know what else to say. "Your husband, Ma'am, was very brave to meet his duty in such a way."

"Thank you—you are most kind, Sir."

Anne wanted to change the subject, knowing her father held an interest in this woman, and speaking of her late husband in such "intimate" terms probably wounded Sir Walter's ego. "Father, where is Elizabeth this evening? I hoped to see her."

"Elizabeth is out with Mr. Stitt and his family at the theatre."

"Mr. Stitt?" Frederick questioned in an amused tone.

"A nobody," Sir Walter noted. "Mr. Stitt made his own way—he has his wealth, although he has no title. Owns a silver mine or some sort of hole in the ground—near Cornwall, I believe. Of course, I dare not object; the man is your sister's first serious suitor in several years. At least, he can afford her tastes; if he presents himself, I will agree most readily."

"Father!" Anne protested, but the damage was done. Sir Walter aired their family's "laundry" for all to hear.

Before anyone could respond, a footman announced dinner, and they retreated to the dining room, Anne taking her father's arm and Frederick escorting Mrs. Bradley. Mrs. Bradley sat opposite Sir Walter at the ends of the table. Anne and Frederick made up the center guests. Four courses served as the dinner, and the conversation remained cordial throughout.

"And you will be in town through the end of the month?" Sir Walter asked after motioning for the last course to be removed from the table.

"We will, Sir." Frederick placed his cutlery to the side of his setting. "We took a house with the Admiral and Sophia; my brother will join us after a fortnight."

Mrs. Bradley noted, "That is quite a household."

"You and I, my Dear," Sir Walter directed his attention to his lady friend, "will need to call on the Admiral and Mrs. Croft. They are my tenants at Kellynch Hall."

"As are Frederick and I, Father. We have been in Somersetshire since last September." Anne would not allow her father to paint Frederick's family in a subservient light.

"Of course, Anne," Sir Walter placated.

Mrs. Bradley stood, acting as the lady of the house, obviously, with Sir Walter's consent. "Mrs. Wentworth, why do not we retire to the drawing room and leave the men to their cigars and port?"

"Thank you, Mrs. Bradley." Anne followed the woman to her feet, as did Frederick and Sir Walter. "Frederick—Father, we will see you in a few minutes." And with curtseys, the ladies left the room.

"Well, Wentworth, what will it be?" Sir Walter led Frederick into his study.

Frederick settled in a chair opposite Sir Walter's desk. "A brandy or a glass of port will be fine, Sir."

Elliot handed him a brandy, and Frederick took the obligatory sip. "I am glad we had this time alone, Wentworth. I have something I need to discuss with you."

"Certainly, Sir Walter. What might that be?" When Anne's father treated Frederick as an equal, suspicions arose quickly.

Sir Walter came around the desk to sit next to Frederick. "As you and my daughter might surmise, I plan to offer for Mrs. Bradley soon. She is an attractive woman and young enough to bear me additional heirs. I find her company most pleasant, and, I believe, we will get along well together. She has her widow's pension and an unentailed piece of property left to her by her father, as well as a good living from her husband's investments."

"I see," Frederick mused. "Of course, Anne and I wish you happy. But how does your offer to Mrs. Bradley affect us? What do you need of me, Sir Walter?"

Elliot swished the brandy around in his glass. "When I offer for Mrs. Bradley, I would prefer to take her to Kellynch as my wife. I will be terminating your sister's lease on the estate when the terms are up in September."

"And you expect me to deliver that message to my family?" Frederick hated being put in the middle—in such a position.

Sir Walter pretended to be offended. "I would never place my daughter's husband in such a role; I can speak for myself, Wentworth." Elliot took a large gulp of his drink before going on. "I have done nothing to date because you and Anne are also at Kellynch. I cannot turn my daughter out, but I also cannot bring my bride into a household predisposed to taking orders from both your sister and your wife."

Frederick paused—extending his thinking time before responding. "Then you would like to know when I will be a husband and give my wife a proper place of her own?"

"That is not the way I would have put it, Sir, but it is the crux of the matter."

Frederick stared at his wife's father, disbelief filling his every pore. "I have two prospective homes, appropriate for Anne's station in life, which meet our other criteria for where we wish to live. Like you, I did nothing—other than to make enquiries—as my recent promotion delayed my governmental paperwork." Frederick began to check off the details in his head. "I assure you, Sir Walter, once this month of celebration is complete, your daughter and I will make a choice in earnest. We are most anxious to have a place of our own and raise our own family. With the war finally over, my services will no longer be needed; I remain in an advisory position, but go on with my life. I will take a half pension, if necessary, but Anne and I will soon vacate Kellynch, and you and Mrs. Bradley can live there in wedded bliss."

"I did not mean to offend you, Wentworth," Sir Walter started.

"Sir Walter, you did nothing but insult me for the past ten years. I know I am a disappointment in your estimation, but I tolerate even you for Anne's love. Here, however, are the facts. As a Rear Admiral of the White, I possess nearly as much social clout as do you. You have a position in Parliament I will never have, but it is I, at this time, who have the fortune. You foolishly ran through yours and now must marry a woman of independent wealth in order to save your name and your estate. I, on the other hand, married the woman I love. Although I supported Anne when she encouraged you to reclaim your family's name, it never occurred to me you would do so by besmudging mine. Marry for convenience; marry for money; that is the way of the aristocracy!"

Sir Walter flinched with the tone of authority radiating through Frederick's voice, but he managed to speak again. "And what of your sister and the Admiral?"

"You pompous prat!" Frederick cursed under his breath. "With Sophia's recent delivery, I seriously doubt she and the Admiral wish to remain long at Kellynch. When she starts walking, Cassandra Rose will want to actually touch things—not live in a museum! I will tell my sister of your intentions. If you are finished, Sir Walter, I think, I would prefer to return to my wife's company." He sat the glass down hard on the table, sloshing some of the brandy onto his hand.

"How long have you known my father, Mrs. Bradley?" Anne helped herself to a cup of tea before taking a seat on one of the settees in the drawing room.

The woman took up her seat in one of the thickly cushioned winged chairs, sitting her cup and saucer on an end table. "A little over three months."

"And I am to assume from what I saw this evening, yours is an understanding?" Anne sipped slowly letting the aroma of the brew fill her senses.

"I cannot speak for Sir Walter, but I am confident we are moving in that direction." She straightened the seams of her dress as it draped over her lap. "Do you object to our possible union, Mrs. Wentworth?"

Anne took her time before answering. "If my father is satisfied, then I have no objections."

"Your sister Elizabeth is not so accepting," Mrs. Bradley confided.

"When our mother passed, my father foolishly turned all his attention on my eldest sister. Since she was seventeen, Elizabeth acted as the mistress of Kellynch. She would not be happy to be supplanted by anyone; it is her identity, after all. Mary is Mrs. Musgrove, and Elizabeth was the mistress of Kellynch. Until Frederick came along, I had no identity; my perspective is different from theirs. Why do you not tell me more about yourself, Mrs. Bradley?"

"May I call you Anne, Mrs. Wentworth?" The woman searched for a way to make a connection.

Anne half smiled, trying to assess what to value. "As long as I may call you Amelia."

Mrs. Bradley nodded in agreement. "You know of my previous marriage. I married Stephen at nineteen and was a widow by two and twenty. I am, from what I know, only a year older than you and two years Elizabeth's junior. I am independently wealthy—a gentleman's daughter, but I would like a title to go along with my wealth. Many men find me too old; it is not as if I can have a Season at my age and marital status. I want a family, Anne. Your father wants a second family, possibly an heir to save his estate. Sir Walter says you sent him here with just that purpose. I am not a foolish woman, Mrs. Wentworth. Neither am I overly emotional. Your father and I get along well together. Ours will not be a love match, but I hope it will be more than one of convenience; yet, if it is not, both of us understand that relationship. Your father and I both married for love the first time. At least, I assume Sir Walter married the late Lady Elliot out of love; he speaks of her fondly."

"To answer honestly, Amelia, my father can be difficult. He is not known for his business sense; you will need to practice economy in the home. Like my mother, you will need to find a way to humor him and even to soften bits of his personality. You must help him to conceal his failings and also to promote his respectability if you wish harmony in your home."

"I see," Amelia said as if Anne shared the secrets of the universe.

"Am I to assume you wish to move into Kellynch upon your marriage?" Anne needed to know the truth of the situation. "I ask because Frederick's sister, her husband, and child lived there some eighteen months. Frederick and I will move out soon—after these celebratory events, but Sophia and the Admiral remain. They should be given proper notice."

"As you indicated moments ago, Sir Walter could economize more in a place other than London; it is expensive to live here—to maintain a lifestyle here. The purpose of marrying your father is to assume the position of his wife—his title and his estate. Otherwise, the relationship might not seem so promising. I have a small estate—one not entailed—given to me by my father, but I cannot imagine Sir Walter would wish to live there. As I want a title, your father, likewise, wishes to save his estate and family line. I planned to sell my property and use the money to make Kellynch Hall solvent."

Anne asked out of curiosity. "Where is your property?"

Amelia took up her teacup again. "Oxfordshire—it is in Oxfordshire. It is a small affair with a decent house—repaired recently as I anticipated selling it—around fifty tenants—about three thousand per year annual clearance, if my man of business keeps accurate books. I have a reliable steward who maintains it while I am away."

"It sounds very pleasant," Anne said wistfully.

Amelia turned her head sharply to look at Anne. "Would you and Admiral Wentworth be interested in it? I would not mind keeping it in the family."

"As much as it sounds to be a smart investment, I am afraid Frederick and I seek something close to the sea. I do not think my husband could tolerate being totally land locked."

"That is too bad; it seemed like a perfect solution for all of us." Amelia looked towards the open door. "I believe I hear the men coming this way."

"Amelia . . ." Anne lowered her voice, trying to make sure Frederick did not hear. "Would you consider the Admiral and Sophia as being family? Might I discretely mention your estate to Frederick's sister? Since the birth of their child in November, they both seem more intent on putting down roots. Kellynch thrives under their care, but I do not believe they need all that room."

"If you would like to speak to the Crofts, I would gladly entertain their inquiries if they are truly interested. It will be our secret until your husband's family chooses to make it public."

Nothing more could be said as the men reentered the room. Anne could tell immediately from the tension in Frederick's stature, he and her father argued. After thirty minutes of strained conversation, she feigned a headache to curtail the evening.

As Frederick led her to a waiting coach, he guided her along with a rough hand on her elbow. Nearly pushing her into the carriage, all at once he realized how preoccupied he was. "My God, Anne, what am I doing?"

"I suspect you are reacting to something stupid my father said." She settled herself into the warmth of the coach.

Frederick climbed in after her, still frowning from the encounter, but, more so from how ungentlemanly he treated her. "The man knows how to make me lose reason!" He took her hand as he settled himself next to her. "But you do not deserve my wrath; I beg your forgiveness."

"What is there to forgive? Did you not defend my honor this evening?" She kissed his cheek as the coach lurched forward, ending up in his responsive arms as they swayed into the night carriage traffic. Despite his recent annoyance, her presence softened his demeanor instantly. "Now, this is the perfect way for you to beg my forgiveness," she mocked.

Frederick wrapped her in his embrace, tightening his hold. He began to drape kisses along her face. "Forgive me," he whispered with each kiss.

"Say it again," Anne joked as he hit one of her sensitive spots. "Again, please," she gasped when Frederick kept up his assault. Her moan told him he was forgiven although that fact did not stop him from finishing what he started.

Chapter 22

So we'll go no more a roving
So late into the night,
Though the heart be still as loving
And the moon be still as bright.
—Lord Byron from "So We'll Go No Move a Roving"

"Where are we going this evening?" Frederick's secret peaked her interest. They spent every evening over the last fortnight at one event or another—one evening, a ball, another, a soiree, still another, a musical interlude—but, tonight it would be different. They were on their own; Sophia and Benjamin begged off to spend the evening with Cassandra Rose.

"You will see."

Frustrated, Anne sat back in the carriage with a huff; Frederick sat across from her, staring out the coach's window, pretending to be interested in the increasing darkness. "How long will you make me wait before you share our destination?"

Anne's pleading pleased him; he loved to surprise her—to see the pure joy in her eyes when she experienced something new. "It is our anniversary, my Love," was all he divulged.

Finally, the coach halted in front of a concert house—actually, the best concert house in London. For a moment, she sat mesmerized by the impressive façade of the building before asking, "A concert?" As he helped her from the carriage, Frederick still made no attempt to answer her; instead, he took Anne's arm on his and led her into the hall.

In a private box overlooking the stage, he seated her and then secured champagne from a server before closing the curtain, sealing them away from the crowded hallway. "May I say you look very beautiful tonight, Mrs. Wentworth," he whispered close to her ear. Even in the dimly lit theatre, he laughed lightly to see her blush.

"Frederick," her voice came out all breathy, "what is all this?"

"Why do you not read the playbill, my Love?" Smiling largely, he sat back firmly into the cushioned chair.

Dutifully doing what he asked, Anne began to thumb through the pages. "Madamé Tresurré!" she whispered loudly.

"I heard from those more in the know than I the lady is exceptional." His grin grew with the look of bewilderment on Anne's face.

She stumbled, trying to respond in a like manner, but, eventually she composed an appropriate taunt. "I heard, Sir, from those who experienced Italian arias in their natural setting, the performance may be a disappointment."

"What a foolish person to think so," Frederick mocked himself. "I would imagine whoever told you such lies must have been preoccupied with something else rather than truly listening to the performance."

"Then we will enjoy the music together." She moved closer to him—as close as propriety would allow. "Do you suppose love songs are on the program?"

"I am sure they are, Sweetling." He took her hand and returned it to his arm. "Will you translate the Italian for me?"

Anne tightened her grasp. "What makes you think I speak Italian well enough to translate for a man who traveled as you, my Husband?"

Frederick grew serious for a moment. "I want what Mr. Elliot and my conceit robbed of me that evening. I want to experience the music the way it should be—with a person so in tune with herself she becomes part of the music. That concert in Bath was nearly the end of our relationship; I came close to giving up. I walked away from the most important person in my life. In retrospect, it was a low moment—a memory I would just as soon forget. Therefore, I propose we replace the anxiety and the depression felt that evening in Bath with a new memory, one where no one else exists but you and me—nothing but us and the music."

"It amazes me a man who has known the savagery of war can be such a sentimental romantic." Anne slid her gloved hand into his, allowing Frederick to pull it to his lap.

"Because I faced death's mask and came away only scathed, I seek out the joys life brings. For me, the most joyful moments are those I share with you; only with you am I made whole again." The lights began to dim throughout the theatre, but their eyes remained only on each other. Neither spoke words, but devotion ruled their thoughts. Only when the acclaimed soprano took the stage did they return their attention to the performance. Yet, even as the music took them into its folds and carried them to magical realms, their personal connection did not depart; Frederick and Anne traveled together.

*   *   *

They would leave London at the end of the week after experiencing a whirlwind of rituals—a carousel of celebration. Edward and Christine joined them ten days prior, bringing young Edward with them. The couples set up a nursery, and Sophia noted how often Anne snuck in to hold the babies.

"You should be getting dressed," speaking softly, Sophia stood in the doorway.

Anne shifted young Edward in her arms. "Is he not beautiful?" Anne's light touch traced the outline of the child's face. "I could look at him for hours and never tire."

Sophia stepped into the room, peeking in the crib at her own Cassandra Rose. "God knows everything else pales when one looks into the face of a child." She walked to where Anne sat. "Here, let me take him. You cannot be late tonight; the Prince Regent and the Queen await."

"I suppose I should be about it." Anne stood, but she did not make a move to leave the comfort of the room. Sophia handed the sleeping Edward to the nursery maid, and then rejoined her brother's wife. She wrapped her arm around Anne's waist to urge her to move. They were nearly to the door when Anne said, "I have not had my last three courses."

"I know." Sophia turned Anne towards her. "I can tell by the shine of your hair and the glow of your complexion. Women know these things without being told. Are you not happy?"

"Yes—yes, it is of what I wished for years."

Sophia looked concerned. "Then what, pray tell, is the matter?"

"Have you noticed Frederick never comes in here unless someone insists? What if he does not want children—I mean, we spoke of it before we married, but it has been a year, and my husband seems oblivious to the fact he has no child."

"Oh, Anne." Sophia pulled her along, seeking the privacy of the hallway. "You really do not think Frederick might not want children? Do you believe he will not be happy with the news?"

"I do not want to lose him, Sophia. What if he turns from me—from our child? I could not bear it! When you and I first suspected my condition, I was sure he would be happy with the prospect; yet, now I am not so confident. Frederick has all these plans for a house and an estate and . . ."

"Anne," Sophia chastised, "for a woman of such great intelligence, you know so little of life. If Frederick feigned disinterest in children, it was for your sake. As small children, the three of us used to play at knights and Celtic warriors and everything imaginable for a child, but in each play, we always imagined these heroes with their families. We feared a separation when our parents passed, and the three of us swore staying together as a family would be the most important ideal in our lives. Frederick would be content with a household of children, one child, or no children if he has your love, but, I guarantee, my brother will be ecstatic with your news. Has he not the most loving heart?"

"Yes—yes, he is the most romantic man under that stiff exterior." Anne sounded almost wistful.

Sophia smiled with the knowledge her brother finally found happiness. "Do you not think he possesses the capacity to love his own child? I would suspect his heart is large enough to love all those in his life. The man is built to love and protect. How can you doubt him?"

"I never doubt my husband," Anne spoke with determination. "I doubt myself often, but never Frederick. I simply fear disappointing him; I did so all those years ago."

"Trust me," Sophia said as she walked Anne towards her chambers. "Frederick would rather have your news than all the recognitions he will receive tonight."

Anne smiled that Madonna-like smile commonplace among mothers and mothers-to-be. "I will tell him this evening when we return."

"I anticipate hearing shouts of joy coming from your chambers," Sophia teased.

Anne turned red with the wanton thoughts going through her head. She offered up a different smile, one of the knowledge of thoroughly knowing a man. "Yes," she chuckled. "I anticipate my husband's happiness this evening."

*   *   *

Being announced, the Wentworths and the Crofts walked proudly into the dining hall at Carlton House, the depth of importance on their being firmly impressed upon them by the Central Office itself. A naval attaché to the court called upon them specifically two days ago to review protocol expected by George IV at such dinner occasions.

The light of hundreds of candles flickered off the gold plated trim of the ceiling, creating a breath-taking experience. Chandeliers hung low, their light shimmering over the gold-trimmed place settings and goblets, preset upon the while linen-lined tables. Wall scones, every few feet, added to the brightness; it was as if one stepped into the bright of day. Bouquets of fresh flowers perfumed the air, while patrons crushed dried rose petals and lavender under their feet as they walked.

Women in gowns of various shades of the rainbow, some wearing plumes arching high out of their hair,—a virtual kaleidoscope of colors—moved about the room on the arms of handsomely dressed gentlemen. The shimmer of the material and the sparkle of their jewels added to the glow of the evening.

Anne wore a custard-tinted white empire waist gown of satin, and Frederick thought her the most beautiful woman he ever saw. A white pearl necklace adorned her throat, and beaded pearl pins held the complicated upsweep of her hair in a sleek design. Frederick, in full dress uniform looked very masculine—large and powerful and perfectly in control. Together, they were a striking pair, and more than one head turned upon their entrance.

The Crofts chaired one of the many tables dedicated to the navy, while Frederick and Anne found themselves at a table led by Vice-Admiral Pennington. Lieutenants Harwood and Avendale, along with Doctor Laraby represented *The Resolve*, while like officers from the Bellerophon also occupied the table.

"So, Wentworth, did you share your news with your wife?" Pennington called from his end of the table.

Frederick looked up suddenly, seriously discomposed by the question. "Unfortunately, I arrived home too late to fully give it my attention, Admiral."

"Then will one of you tell me?" Anne's curiosity peaked.

Frederick cleared his throat. "I am sure, Mrs. Wentworth, you will find this quite amusing." Actually, he expected to be bombarded by barbs from his fellow officers once word got out. "The Navy Board chose to release five sets of captain's logs as books to the public—tributes to the war. My log from the last months of my service—the capture of the two French ships and the American traitor will be the first one released. The book publisher asked that I review the entries and add additional facts—embellish, so to speak."

Anne offered one of her beguiling smiles, and he knew immediately where her mind would go. "Embellish?" she laughed. "They will allow you, my Husband, to embellish your log? The publisher must have heard of your storytelling prowess."

Avendale's new wife Margaret gushed, "So, you will be an author?"

"I do not expect, Mrs. Avendale, to compete with Mrs. Ratcliffe, if that is what you mean," Frederick teased.

Anne laughed, although she tried to stifle it. "No, Mrs. Avendale, I cannot see Admiral Wentworth competing with the new Gothic writers—no castles and strange prophecies or damsels in distress aboard a ship."

Frederick loved her taunt; her quick wit never ceased to amaze him. "Maybe I will be able to compete with your favorite writer, my Love. What is her name?"

"We readers are unsure. Her first book *Sense and Sensibility* simply reads 'by a Lady.' The second reads 'by the author of *Sense and Sensibility*.' Hers are novels of our time, speaking of the social classes and the economic structure, which paralyzed our efforts for independent thinking. But they are books of hope because one can see the changes coming whether those in charge choose to recognize it or not."

Mrs. Avendale took on a quizzical look. "I thought they were simply love stories."

Frederick smiled at the woman. "My wife is a great believer in crossing cultural lines, but I am sure she enjoyed the romance part of the book, as well, for she has a very tender heart."

"If it is the Captain's Log, then we shall all receive a mention," Doctor Laraby observed.

Admiral Pennington confirmed, "I suspect you will. When Admiral Wentworth was disabled, others filled in the report—the log—it will reflect the two captures and the Admiral's struggle to survive. The British public will be enthralled by the drama involved. We jumped the gun, so to speak; the Army has not deployed its high rollers, as of yet. The Battle of Copenhagen and probably that of San Domingo, as well, of course, as the Battle of the Nile will also be released. Did you not see action in some of those, Wentworth?"

"I did, Admiral"

"Then maybe we can tie the logs together that way. Your story leads to another one in which you play a different role. Excellent idea! I will run it by the higher ups tomorrow." He returned his attention to Anne. "Mrs. Wentworth, your husband's log will be the first one released; you must be very proud."

"I assure you, Admiral Pennington, I am proud of my husband in so many ways, but I am positive this will complement his other talents."

"I thought," Frederick whispered privately, "I might persuade you to help me; you seem, my Love, to have a gift for words."

Anne smiled at his blatant flattery—a full smile, which spoke of her undying love. "I am not so persuadable as I once was," she mocked.

"I will use one of my *talents,* of which you are so proud," he responded.

"For that, I am most thankful."

The attaché, who attended them previously, appeared at the table, interrupting their conversation. "Admiral Wentworth, his majesty George IV wishes to speak to you and Mrs. Wentworth."

"Speak to us? Now?" Frederick stammered.

The man nodded, and Frederick stood quickly, reaching out for Anne's trembling hand. As they walked the long aisle between the tables towards the head table the man instructed him. "You are quite tall, Admiral. His majesty prefers to meet someone over whom he can dominate. You will be asked to sit in a chair to create that image; try to look comfortable in doing so."

Frederick nodded his understanding and then steadied Anne as she rushed along beside him. Touching her elbow, he balanced her as they wove their way between tables and serving staff. "Are you all right, Sweetling?" he spoke through gritted teeth to the side of her head as he guided Anne behind the attaché, hurriedly leading the way.

"We have been summoned to meet the heir to our country's throne. How should I be?" Anne sounded frightened. Frederick was not sure her teeth were not chattering, although the room to him suddenly became very stuffy and warm. Unconsciously, he ran a finger around his collar, feeling it tightening on him.

Anne nearly swooned as they came within sight of the Prince Regent. "My legs," she hissed to Frederick.

"I am here," he murmured.

Despite what she knew he must be feeling, he looked more confident than she ever saw him, and for that, Anne was suddenly grateful. They were together—she and Frederick could do anything together. She took a few quick breaths to relax her stomach and then straightened her shoulders. "I am ready," she told him as he directed her the last few feet before being presented to George IV and his special guests.

"I never thought otherwise, my Love." He placed her hand on his arm as they stepped in front of their future king.

"Your Majesty," the attaché spoke once the Prince Regent turned his head to look in their direction. "May I present Rear Admiral Frederick Wentworth and his wife Mrs. Anne Wentworth?" Both men made a proper bow as Anne dipped into a deep curtsy.

No one raised his eyes or spoke until the Prince spoke. "Admiral Wentworth, would you and your wife care to join us for a few minutes?"

"We would be honored, your Majesty." Frederick's voice changed in timbre. He handed Anne into the nearest chair, purposely taking the one set at an angle from the Prince to hide his height as the Naval consultant suggested.

"Are you enjoying yourself, Mrs. Wentworth?" the Prince asked nonchalantly.

Anne swallowed hard before answering. "It is a magnificent gathering, your Highness."

"Then you approve, Madam?" He seemed amused by her innocence, and his tone spoke volumes. "Have you not been to Carlton House previously?"

"No, your Highness. I mean, I have not been to your home previously." A tone of disapproval crept into her voice; she did not like being the object of his entertainment. "As far as approving of the dinner, one would be foolish to disapprove of what his monarch offered." Anne actually looked a bit angry at being placed in such a position.

A long pause added to the tension before the Prince laughed. "A woman with spunk, Wentworth. You may have your hands full." He motioned to the man on Anne's left. "This is Prince Metternich of Austria, Madam."

Anne dropped her eyes, but did not stand to curtsy. "It is with pleasure that I greet you, Prince Metternich."

"Mrs. Wentworth," the Austrian spoke in heavily accented English, "we understand we owe your husband a great debt."

"I am sure my husband does not feel worthy of such accolades, Prince Metternich."

The Prince Regent broke in, "Is that true, Admiral Wentworth? Does your wife speak out of turn?"

Frederick spoke with as much dignity as he could. He never realized how often he used his height to establish control. "My wife is extremely loyal; she would never speak falsely where I am concerned. My men—my crew—were as much a part of the success of our campaign as was I. In fact, they carried on most admirably once I became injured."

"Then you give them the credit for the captures?" the Austrian prince questioned.

"We are a crew, Prince Metternich; we live and survive together. Like a chain, we are only as strong as our weakest link." Anne stared at him in disbelief; her softhearted husband appeared a rock of granite.

George IV laughed heartily, followed closely by his minions. "A lesson we are pleased Bonaparte never learned. Tell me, Wentworth, from where you hail," Prinny demanded.

"From Herefordshire, your Highness."

"And your parents?"

"Edward and Cassandra, your Majesty, of simple birth if that is your question, my Prince." Frederick would not cower simply because of the grandeur of the situation.

"Was I misinformed?" Prinny looked about concerned to appear foolish. "I thought you from Somerset, Admiral."

Frederick did not flinch. "My wife and I reside in Somerset with my sister and her husband Admiral Croft. We are at Kellynch Hall, your Highness."

"At Kellynch?" the Prince Regent now seemed completely interested. "Sir Walter Elliot's seat?"

"The very one, your Highness. My wife is Sir Walter's daughter." Frederick's confidence grew with the twist of the conversation.

Prinny now directed his comments to Anne. "Your father, Mrs. Wentworth, is a known pompous ass!"

"As you say, your Majesty. Often times, I, unfortunately, must agree." Anne, thankfully, did not crack a smile. The rest of the Prince's table, however, burst into laughter again, as if on cue.

"Then are you not Lady Wentworth?" The woman to the Prince's right, someone neither Anne nor Frederick recognized, asked.

Anne allowed an amused smile to turn up the corners of her mouth. "My husband has no title, Madam."

The Prince Regent leaned forward and took Anne's hand affectionately in his while Frederick fought the urge to snatch it out of his grasp. Prinny knew exactly what he was doing—a test, so to speak, of the Wentworths' reported devotion to each other. He brushed his lips across Anne's knuckles. "Tell me, Mrs. Wentworth, when did you meet the Admiral?"

Anne blushed with all eyes now on her. "Your Highness, my husband and I fell in love when I was but nineteen, and he just received his first command. We never loved another or considered another worthy of our attention, although we spent many years apart."

"Not even a prince, Mrs. Wentworth?" Prinny prodded her. Frederick bit back the anger swelling in his chest.

Anne looked lovingly at her husband. "Your Majesty, although you have the world to offer, I never wanted the world; I turned down money and a title previously to marry Frederick. I do not regret my decision."

"Mrs. Wentworth, you are incomparable!" the Prince exclaimed. "I do not know when I last so enjoyed a conversation." He purposely placed Anne's hand in Frederick's. "You are a lucky man, Wentworth."

"Thank you, your Highness; it is a fact of which I am well aware." Frederick tried to control the tone of his voice so as not to give offense.

Anne recognized the Duke of Mayfield at the table earlier so when he asked of her father she expected it. "Mrs. Wentworth, am I not mistaken? Is not Sir Walter set to marry Mrs. Amelia Bradley?"

"He is, your Grace." Anne squeezed Frederick's hand, glad to have his support so close.

The Duke continued, "Then will he not return to Kellynch when he marries?"

"My father—Sir Walter," Frederick began, "will return to Kellynch Hall soon—at the end of the Season. Having recently begun their family, my sister and her husband are considering a place of their own in Oxfordshire. My wife and I seek a like estate of our own now that the war with France is at an end."

"So, Sir Walter marries Mrs. Stephen Bradley, the war widow," the Duke said sarcastically, "for her money and her for his title. Then he displaces his own daughter, as well as two men who served this country for nearly three decades between them." The alcohol gave the Duke courage he might not possess otherwise. "It seems a shame, your Highness; we have this evening to celebrate men like Wentworth here, only to find out we displace them in other ways."

"My wife and I appreciate your concern, your Grace," Frederick added with a nod of his head to those at the Prince's table, "but we encouraged my wife's father to remarry. He has only daughters and will lose the estate to a man who may own the title but not care for the position it gives him. I earned enough from my service to provide for Mrs. Wentworth."

The Prince rejoined the conversation. "Your consideration speaks well of you, Admiral Wentworth. You reflect estimably on our country's Navy, as a gentleman of reason and of vision. Your country and your future King thanks you for your service."

Realizing their time with Prinny and the inner circle came to an end, Frederick rose to his feet and helped Anne to hers. They both acknowledged their positions by bowing out to the company. "Your Majesty," Frederick said as he lowered his body in a proper bow. "Mrs. Wentworth and I thank you most graciously for the honor."

"Admiral" is all the Prince said before turning his head back to his guests. Frederick and Anne took steps backward, as coached by the attaché, bowed again, and then turned quickly to leave.

"Nothing like an inquisition," Frederick chuckled as they approached their own table once more.

Anne swayed against him, feeling all the adrenalin drain from her. "I never realized the Royal Court cared so much for gossip. I felt like I should have provided a family tree as a parting gift."

"Do you believe what just happened?" Frederick took hold of her arm before they returned to their seats. "I would prefer not to have to relate even half of that conversation with our tablemates. May we simply tell them Prince George wanted me to describe the boarding of the French sloop and you to describe my recovery?"

Anne glanced quickly at his fellow crewmembers, waiting in anticipation for his retelling. "I agree; telling your men the Prince wanted to gossip about my father and wanted to make you jealous is not my idea of pleasant dinner conversation."

"Our Monarch succeeded in one way; I seriously considered planting him a facer if he held your hand much longer. That hand belongs to me," he whispered close to her ear. "That hand—the arm to which it is attached—the body to which the arm is attached . . . ." Shall I go on, my Love?"

"Thank you, my Husband, for showing restraint. Finding you in a cell at the Old Bailey tomorrow morning is not how I wish to end my time in London." Anne took his arm to return to the table.

They convincingly told their "little white lie" to everyone who would listen. The captain of the *Bellerophon* told a similar tale. Anne and Frederick wondered if he "lied" also or whether the Prince's party actually spoke of Bonaparte's capture to him.

As the party's entertainment began to die down, Frederick and Anne prepared to take their leave and rejoin Sophia and Benjamin for the ride home. However, before they could make their goodbyes, the attaché reappeared at the table. "Admiral Wentworth," the man spoke softly, "his Majesty requests to speak to you again." Frederick laid his napkin on the table preparing to stand, when the man spoke in more confidence. "Come alone, Sir."

"Frederick?" Panic laced her voice, and Anne reached for him instinctively.

He helped her to her feet. "Go wait with Benjamin and Sophia, my Love. Whatever it is Prince George wants, I will handle it." Uncharacteristically, he kissed her cheek before turning to follow the court's messenger. Frederick had no idea what to expect. Prince George earned a reputation for his magnanimous character, as well as his frivolous one. With the turn of the earlier conversation, Frederick had no idea what to expect when he approached the table again. For all he knew, the Prince might demand Anne's company; it was not beyond him. Then what would he do? Frederick certainly would not look the other way, no matter what it cost him.

He waited with the court's emissary for nearly ten minutes before the Prince chose to recognize his presence. "Admiral Wentworth," the Prince called out, "you returned." Frederick could hear the slur of the speech and knew he dealt with a powerful man in his cups. As a ship's captain, he handled more than one insensible man, but Prince George was his country's leader.

Frederick made his bow. "As you requested, your Majesty."

"Come closer, Wentworth." He gestured to the same chair, which Frederick occupied earlier.

Frederick guarded his words. "May I be of service, your Highness?"

"Actually, Admiral, I decided to be of service to you," he said pretentiously.

"I beg your pardon, your Majesty, but I do not understand."

The Prince gestured to the other side of the table, and Mayfield took up the disclosure. Frederick noted how they all stared at him—silly drunken smiles plastered on their faces as if they all shared some perverted secret. "According to our sources—Sir William Dunlap, to be precise," the Duke's speech was more slurred than the Prince's, "your wife's father's family was granted its title by Charles II."

Frederick tried to stay composed. "I believe, your Grace is correct in this matter."

"Of course, I am correct," Mayfield asserted.

"Charles," Prince George laughed at what he would say before he said it, "was a two. Charles two. I am a four; that makes me twice as powerful. Is that not right, Admiral?"

Frederick wanted to smile; Prince George was a lousy drunk. "Four is twice as strong as two, your Highness," he said as seriously as he could.

"Charles the two gave the Elliots a baronetcy. I am a four; I will give you more. That rhymes," he cackled as did the rest of his table. The Prince snapped his fingers, and one of the footmen placed a folded document shield in his hand. "Admiral Wentworth, I need you to stand, but I think I will not stand. We will do this seated. Sir Walter Elliot is a nincompoop, but you are a sensible man. England needs sensible men, Wentworth. Your wife's father is a mere baronet, but from this day forward you and your children will have a title greater than that man. I give you this!" He held out the document, and Frederick tentatively took it.

Gingerly, he unfolded the paper and began to read.

"What do you think, Wentworth?" the Duke puffed up like a bantam rooster.

"It is phenomenal, your Majesty; I do not know what to say except to offer my devotion and my appreciation." Frederick began to read the paper again. A royal proclamation—containing the King's seal and the Queen's signature under that of George IV.

"My man will call on you tomorrow morning, and all the details decided then. He will tell you of the property and of your duties to the Crown. I suspect you should return to Mrs. Wentworth, Admiral. As loyal as the woman is, she is likely to be missing you."

"Yes, your Highness." Frederick got to his feet and began his obligatory bow out of the group's sight. "Your kindness will never be forgotten."

As he backed away, Frederick wondered of what just occurred. No one would believe it; he was not sure even he did, although he clutched the proof of it tightly in his hand.

When he reached Anne, her curiosity clearly bubbled over, but he told her nothing. "In the carriage," is all Frederick said as he hustled her from the room, followed closely by Benjamin and Sophia.

Finally settled in their coach, Anne could contain herself no longer. "Tell me," she demanded.

"I considered it, and I may wait until tomorrow. Our Prince George may change his mind, after all." He leaned back into the cushioned upholstery and pretended to close his eyes for sleep.

Anne noted the amused smile, however, and she took up a similar pose, allowing herself the liberty to recline against his shoulder. "I suppose I will wait to tell you what I know." Anne snuggled into his arm, relaxing her weight against him.

"You have no secrets from me," Frederick mumbled, trying to sound sleepy.

Anne yawned before saying, "If you say so, my Dear." She shut her eyes and sighed heavily, totally comfortable.

"Will either of you tell Sophia or me?" Benjamin asked, too curious to stifle his anticipation.

Anne chuckled lightly, but she did not open her eyes. "I swear Sophia already knows my secret," she mumbled dreamily.

Frederick sat up now, suddenly aware Anne might not be mocking him. "What is your secret, Anne?" he shoved her to a seated upright position.

"You first," she stated.

Frederick turned to his sister. "Sophia?"

"Leave me out of your domestic squabbles." Instead, Sophia draped a leg over Benjamin's knee. He removed her slipper and began to massage her foot.

"Anne?" Frederick's attention reverted to his wife.

She looked away—out the coach's window. The lantern reflected off her profile. "It is nothing, Frederick; I only wanted you to share what Prince George said."

Frederick turned her chin to face him. "You are a terrible liar, Sweetling, but I will share with you my news; then you must share as well. Prince George or Mayfield or someone at that table dislikes your father profusely. The more they drank, evidently, the more they mulled over what the group asked about our life together. In short, Prince George bestowed a title on me, on you, and on our children."

"A title?" Sophia gushed. "What kind of title?"

"I am now Frederick James Wentworth, Viscount Orland of Hanson Hall in Dorset."

Frederick waited, but no one moved; suspended in disbelief, they stared at him, suspecting he offered up a joke of some kind. "Viscount?" Sophia laughed, but with a suspicious overtone. "My brother is a viscount?"

"Yes." Frederick never took his eyes off Anne. "I am Viscount Orland. Anne is a viscountess. Did you hear me, Anne?" She still did not move, barely blinking—barely breathing. "Anne?" He patted her hand. "Say something, Anne."

She swallowed down her incredulity; her lips moved, but no sound came out. Finally, after several failed attempts, she stammered, "Frederick, this is not amusing."

He gathered her into his arms, placing the proclamation in her hands. "It is so dark in here, you probably cannot read the paper you hold, but it says, you are married to a viscount. Prince George's man will call on us tomorrow with specific details."

Benjamin began to laugh heartily, and Sophia soon joined in. "A viscount and a Rear Admiral before you are forty; you are one lucky man, Frederick!"

By that time, Frederick too laughed; his speech peppered with bursts of air. "Prince George . . . said he was . . . was a four . . . made him . . . made him stronger . . . stronger than Charles . . . Charles the two . . . Charles II." The laughter came easily now to all four of them as they each succumbed to his obvious joy. "Charles gave . . . gave your father . . . a baronetcy . . . . George gave me twice . . . twice a baronet . . . a viscount."

Anne collapsed into his arms, trying to stifle her laughter, burying it into his chest. "My father," she got the words out. "My father will have to bow to you."

Her words brought a loud burst of laughter from Sophia, who buried her fist in her mouth to smother what now was uncontrollable happiness emanating from the coach's passengers. "Both your sisters will have to bow to you, Anne. Will not Elizabeth love that?"

"Elizabeth!" Anne shrieked. "Poor Mary!"

"Mrs. Charles will be green with envy, Anne," Benjamin added. "She will probably go to her bed for a month."

Frederick became more serious. "I could give Edward a better living if he wants it—on my estate."

"Let us wait for that," Anne became the voice of reason. "We do not know the condition of the estate. It could be run down—near ruin." She wiped the happy tears from her cheeks.

"Even if it is, we will make it work—you and I, Anne; it will be ours. I promised you years ago, I would give you all you deserve. We will have a house in London; I will sit in Parliament; I may be the voice of those men coming home to England and encourage England to protect them, rather than the other way around."

"I knew you would find an altruistic reason for our good luck. You may continue to protect your men." Anne stroked his cheek with the back of her hand. Without thinking, she added, "Our children will have the best of fathers."

"Children?" Frederick latched onto the word.

Again, everything in the carriage grew stone quiet. Sophia whimpered with expectation.

The light from the lantern suddenly seemed very strong. "Yes," Anne managed to say. Staring deep into Frederick's eyes, she repeated, "Yes."

"Say it, Anne," Sophia whispered.

Anne's hand reached out to him. "Child . . . our child will have the best father."

Her words were so soft, Benjamin and Sophia strained to hear her, but Frederick heard her as if a trumpet announced what she said. "When?" he needed to know.

"Late summer," she murmured. "I felt the quickening begin earlier in the week."

"You feel our child move?" Instinctively, Frederick's large palm covered her stomach. "Will you tell me when it happens next?"

"Yes," but Frederick's mouth smothered Anne's words in a deep kiss.

"I love you," he cooed to her ear. "I have always loved you."

"Forgive us," Anne blushed, although no one in the carriage could see, nor would they have cared if they could. These couples lived together; besides their marriage partners, they knew each other better than anyone else. "We should not share such intimate moments in front of you." She begged their excusal.

"What is there to forgive?" Benjamin started. "You just learned the most perfect news—you are to be parents."

"Say it again—make it so," Frederick demanded of no one in particular.

Anne clutched at his hand. "We are to have a child, my Love."

Sophia chided in, "A baby of your own, Frederick."

"Maybe a son to inherit your new title," Benjamin teased.

Anne joined in the taunt. "Or a daughter who will wrap you around her finger."

"I do not care which," Frederick declared. "A child! What was it you said, Benjamin? The future is a place for dreams, and those dreams lie in our children." He turned to his wife. "Thank you, Anne. Despite what we earned from the Prince this evening, your gift is greater than any wealth or title. Even if we were in a simple cottage, I would be a rich man at this moment." He pulled her into his embrace, holding Anne's head to his chest where she might hear his heartbeat. He kissed the top of her head.

Sophia resisted the urge to tell Anne "I told you so." Instead, she switched her position and swiveled into Benjamin's arms. "We are a happy foursome tonight. The Admiral and I confirmed earlier today Mrs. Bradley accepted our offer for the Oxfordshire property."

Benjamin pulled her closer. "My man of business saw the property last week and assures us it meets all our needs. We gave him a list of what we desired, and he confirms our expectations will be exceeded with this estate. It is about half the size of Kellynch, but it will be roots for Sophy and me and for our daughter."

"And maybe some day for your son," Anne whispered.

Benjamin chuckled lightly. "The Wentworths have settled down, Miss Anne, and we will reap the benefits."

Anne snuggled in closer as she slid her arm around Frederick's waist. "Admiral, we married into the best."

"We did, Miss Anne; we certainly did."

Chapter 23

It is not while beauty and youth are thine own,
And they cheeks unprofaned by a tear
That the fervor and faith of a soul can be known,
To which time will but make thee more dear.
—Thomas Moore from "Believe Me, If All Those
Endearing Young Charms"

When the footman announced Lord Wallingford, Frederick greeted him in the rented study. The rest of the household prepared for their departure on Saturday. Benjamin and Edward supervised the packing, making sure the belongings, recently merged, separated along property lines. The three ladies paid a final call on Bond Street, securing the latest gems of London fashion.

"Viscount Orland," Wallingford bowed to Frederick upon his entrance.

Frederick laughed lightly. "You are the first to call me as such, Lord Wallingford. I am afraid the name still sounds foreign to me. I am barely adjusting to my new rank—a new title may come more slowly." Frederick led the man to matching winged chairs in front of the hearth. "May I offer you refreshments, Sir?"

"I believe, I will decline." Wallingford settled into the chair, laying his papers across his lap. Once settled comfortably, he addressed Frederick again. "It seems I have the dubious honor of bringing you up to snuff on the property bestowed upon you by our Prince."

"Mrs. Wentworth, the voice of reason in this household, convinced herself and me, to a certain extent, this gift from our Prince Regent has some sort of catch. The estate, for example, she believes to be in ruins, and I will spend all my prize money bringing it back to life."

"Your wife, obviously astute, is half right, but not about the estate or the title. I assure you the title is sound and the property is in repair and productive; it will bring you a comfortable living. The house is immaculate;

Mrs. Wentworth will love it immediately. You will be the third-highest ranking family in the area. His majesty would never put you in the position of having to pull rank on some of the older members of the aristocracy. You would never be accepted in the community in such a case."

After years of reading between the line of military orders, Frederick recognized a stall. "And it is important to his Majesty that I be accepted in the community?"

"Yes, Admiral, it is," Wallingford acknowledged at last.

Frederick's grin spread slowly. "Then I was *chosen* for something other than a gift from my future king?"

Wallingford gave him a brief nod. "You wish me to be honest?"

"Preferably."

Wallingford rifled through his stack of papers before beginning. "The gift of which you speak is as I described—the house, the land, the title—they are all yours. They will remain yours for generations, but for such an honor the Crown expects some sort of reimbursement."

"Would you, please, Lord Wallingford, simply get to the point."

"All right, Admiral." Wallingford became all business-like. "You and a few select others were *chosen,* as you say, based on your military careers—on the report of your loyalty to England—but, more importantly, on the report of your leadership—your men's training—the way they respect you and respond to your expertise. One thing to which you should be privy is George IV does not laugh 'hysterically' when he is drunk; last evening was a ruse. Many of the honorees who spoke to the Prince and his guests simply talked of their military experiences."

"My audience dealt with my wife's father," Frederick mused.

"Part of the ruse," Wallingford assured him. "The Central Office for Naval Affairs has a plan, approved by the Crown Prince. During this war, a system of smugglers, as well as traitors, many French sympathizers, increased in numbers. Unfortunately, without a war to peak its awareness of the dangers, the public will look the other way; the conspirators will thrive without censure. We cannot allow that to happen. That is where you and those others *chosen* come in. We need our own system of people in place throughout England to combat whatever is thrown at us.

"Each of those the Central Office identifies will become part of communities where we need them to be our eyes and ears. Some chosen are already established in their home counties. Each recruit to our cause receives *payment* catered to his needs. One, for example, needs front money to make his business solvent; another needs a brother saved from transportation to

Australia. With you, we needed a point man, a person to coordinate our efforts along the Channel. What better way than to reward a war hero with what he desired, a title and an estate for his wife?"

Although he knew the answer, Frederick could not resist asking, "How much does the Central Office know of my personal life?"

Wallingford laughed, recognizing Frederick's solitary temperament. "Probably more than you care for them to, Admiral. They monitored your career since before your taking control of the *Laconia*—probably as far back as your first meeting with Anne Elliot."

Frederick sat forward suddenly. "I will not endanger my wife and our child—not even for a title and an estate," he asserted vehemently.

"Then you are to be a father?" Wallingford noted.

"I am, Sir; please understand Anne is the only person—the most important person in my life." Frederick's voice brokered no doubts. "Loyalty to Anne and our family comes before even loyalty to my country."

"We never doubted that, Lord Orland. In fact, we are counting on your willingness to give Mrs. Wentworth what you expressed openly on more than one occasion—the title and the house."

Frederick asked suddenly, "How does this work?"

"It is uncomplicated, Sir. You and Mrs. Wentworth take possession of Hanson Hall and make it your home. You insert yourself into the local society and become the person everyone trusts—to whom everyone talks freely. We will help you establish connections to our trusted assistants. Dorset was chosen specifically for its location—close to Cornwall and its strong smuggling business, but not Cornwall, where strangers are never accepted on face value. Orland's demise without an heir left us the perfect opening to establish a presence in the area. Your capture of the American gives the Crown a logical excuse, one people will easily accept, to reward your efforts with a moderate-sized property and a title."

Frederick had to know. "How dangerous is this?"

Wallingford smiled again, and Frederick recognized the half-truths he would receive. "Not dangerous at all in comparison to what you experienced over the years."

"Honesty, please, Lord Wallington," Frederick demanded.

Wallingford's genial nature allowed him to insinuate himself easily into a person's trust; secretly, he admired Frederick for not capitulating to these practiced charms. "Anytime, Admiral, a man faces those who wish to overthrow our government or who wish to defraud our commerce, there is danger, but you will not be fighting in hand-to-hand combat; you will be facing down some of the most manipulative people in our realm. You need to depend heavily on your intuition to recognize those scheming. We have others in place to capture those involved or to help a person escape. What we do not have is a 'captain,' a manager, so to speak. We strongly believe you are that man."

"What if I refuse?" Frederick charged.

Wallingford picked up his papers. "Then you go on with your life; you draw your half pay until the country calls you to service again. You tell Mrs. Wentworth the Prince took back what he gave you in a drunken stupor."

Frederick summarized, "If I want the title and the estate for Anne, then I do what is asked of me."

"That pretty much epitomizes the situation. So, what will it be, Admiral Wentworth?" Wallingford offered up another obviously fabricated smile.

Frederick sat in deep contemplation and total silence for nearly five minutes—so long even Wallingford's practiced confidence took a hit. "May I see the papers you brought?" Frederick finally uttered.

"Let us move to the desk, Admiral. We may spread out the map I possess of your new property. It has renovated stables and barns and even a system in place for indoor running water. It is very close to the shoreline. Did I mention that before?"

"No, Lord Wallingford, you did not." Frederick accepted the decision he just made.

As Wallingford spread out the map on the desk, he added, "You may not, Wentworth, tell anyone of your arrangement. Not Admiral Croft—and, especially, not Mrs. Wentworth. I will serve as your contact. You will report to me in most of your endeavors; I will apprise you of whom you will need to know."

Frederick ironically commented, "Then, you Sir, are my new best friend."

"We will, Wentworth, get along well." He spread out the rolled paper and began to point to the topographical elements of interest on the map. "The parkland drops down to the sea at this point."

After being sequestered for nearly an hour reviewing the legal papers involving the Prince's gift and Frederick's service to the Crown, he straightened from his stance upon hearing Anne return to the house. "I believe I hear Mrs. Wentworth, my sister Mrs. Croft, and my brother's wife, Christine Wentworth. I suppose I should introduce you to my wife. If we are to be acquaintances, Mrs. Wentworth should become familiar to you."

Wallingford began gathering his papers. "That will not be necessary, Lord Orland."

Before Frederick could respond with the obvious question of 'Why not?' Anne lightly tapped on the door and entered without waiting for her husband's bidding. "Frederick," she started, but then froze, not expecting him to be with someone else. "I apologize; I did not realize you entertained."

Frederick crossed the room as she spoke and took up a position in front of her. "No, my Dear, I am happy you came in when you did; I would like for you to meet someone." He placed her hand on his arm to walk Anne towards the desk. Wallingford still had his back to them, gathering the last of the papers dealing with Frederick's service to the government. "This, Anne, is Lord Wallingford; he brought the papers from the Prince regarding the estate. We were just going over them."

Wallingford straightened his stance and slowly turned, the usual smile plastered on his face. "Hello, Anne," he said casually.

"Marcus?" she gasped and then declared, "It is you! Marcus Lansing! You assumed your father's title?" She left Frederick looking shocked and offered Wallingford a quick embrace.

Annoyance laced Frederick's next words. "I was unaware, Wallingford, you were intimate with Mrs. Wentworth."

Anne, realizing his propensity for jealousy, returned to Frederick's side as she offered an explanation. "Marcus attended the boarding school outside of Bath before going off to study at the university. The girls' school I attended often joined Marcus's school at social functions, trying to teach us the niceties of life. As our fathers were classmates at Cambridge, we were often thrust together at such socials."

"I see," said Frederick, suddenly wary at having trusted his governmental contact to tell him the whole truth. It was a lesson he would not forget.

"Miss Anne is too kind. I was a gangly boy with two left feet. Your wife, Lord Orland, took pity on my inability to count music." Wallingford smiled pleasantly at Anne. "She was always of a kind heart."

As if he needed to stake his claim to her, Frederick took Anne's hand and brought the back of it to his lips. "My wife's heart is still the kindest of them all; I am blessed to have earned her regard."

"Oh, Frederick," she gushed. Then Anne focused on what else her former friend said. "Did Marcus say Lord Orland?"

"I did, Mrs. Wentworth." Wallingford gestured to the open map. "I was showing your husband the property. Would you like to see for yourself?"

"Certainly, if you would not mind." Frederick led her to the desk. "Is our new estate close to yours, Marcus?" Anne asked as she leaned over the paper to analyze it.

"Your estate?" Frederick tried to sound casual, but he seethed with anger at how much Wallingford withheld.

Marcus Lansing pointed to the shoreline so Anne might see for herself where the property lay before he answered. "You recall, Wentworth, I mentioned two others in Dorset would outrank you in title and size of their estates."

Frederick responded warily, "Yes."

"I would be one of those two." Wallingford said softly as he pointed out the location of the house in relationship to the parkland for Anne's inspection. "My estate borders Somerset on the other side of the county. As you are now both Wentworth and Orland, I am both Marcus Lansing and Wallingford."

"And would you be number one or number two on the list?"

"Marcus is an earl," Anne interrupted. "His father left the title to him after a long illness."

"An earl?" Frederick said incredulously. "Is there a Countess Wallingford?"

Marcus, instinctively, laughed again, realizing his and Frederick's relationship hinged on the next few minutes. "I was pressed into service by our Prince until of late. Dorset has an expansive coastline, and the government needed me to help in Lyme and Bath and Swanage. So, unfortunately, I neglected my duties to my private life. Maybe Mrs. Wentworth will have a soft heart and introduce me to someone as kind as she."

From what Frederick could tell Wallingford's compliments worked effectively on Anne. She patted Marcus's hand as she said, "I will keep an eye out for someone special." Then she turned to Frederick. "You will assume the title being offered here?"

"I told Lord Wallingford I would." Frederick shot the man a look of circumspection. "Unless you have an objection, my Dear."

"Oh, no, Frederick; it looks wonderful. May we visit the property one day next week?" Anne rushed to his side again; she looked up at him with those doe-like eyes, which mesmerized him years ago.

"Anything you want, my Love," he whispered softly to her. "Welcome your newest neighbors, Wallingford," he declared as Anne slid her arms around his waist and rested her head briefly against Frederick's shoulder.

"Great!" Wallingford looked confident. "Your Prince will be most pleased with the news."

*   *   *

Although Wallingford offered to escort them on their first trip to their new property, Frederick judiciously declined. Besides not wanting to throw Anne and the affable Marcus Lansing together until he knew the full extent of their previous relationship, he wanted time to see the area for himself. Lyme and Bath and even Plymouth outlined the county, but he was as unfamiliar with this part of England as she.

"It is beautiful, Frederick," Anne clutched at his hand as they stood looking out over the bay from one of the highest vantage points above Swanage. They traveled through hay meadows and wooded areas and natural countrysides; now, they stood braced against the wind looking out over a coastal cliff and limestone down land.

Frederick rented a coach, and they spent each of the past few days visiting the sights about the county. They spent much of this day exploring the ruins of Corfe Castle, a medieval castle, which came to prominence during the time of William the Conqueror. A Royal residence during the medieval period, King Edward II was imprisoned there, and King John kept his crown jewels there. Henry VII gave the castle to his mother, but Henry VIII reclaimed it when he came to the throne. His daughter Queen Elizabeth I sold the castle to one of her favorite courtiers, Sir Christopher Hatton, who fortified it during England's defense against the Spanish Armada, a fact which greatly impressed Frederick. Sir John Bankes, the Lord Chief Justice to Charles I owned it during the Civil War in the mid-1600s, but the Parliamentary forces left it in ruins. It stood in silent testament to the grandeur of English history. At the bottom of the hill leading to the shell, picturesque stone houses peppered the village where Anne bought gifts in the local shops for the Admiral and Sophia.

Swanage Bay, four and half miles southeast of the remains, offered the current view. "King Alfred fought a fierce naval battle against the Danes in that very bay in 877," he shared as he wrapped his arms around her and pulled Anne to him. "They say Ballard Cliff is very dangerous—the sea quite treacherous in those parts, although I do not know that first hand for I never sat anchor in these waters."

"You know so much of the world," she whispered near his ear as she willingly turned in his arms. "I feel so protected when I am with you."

"Do you, my Love?" he asked as he used his finger to tilt her chin upward where he might kiss her.

Anne knew, instinctively, he still brooded over her recent meeting with Marcus Lansing; she would give him what he needed in terms of reassurance.

She snaked her arms around his neck. "I never felt safe any place else; I never felt love any place else. Frederick, you are the only man I could ever love; you must know that."

"I do know, Anne, but I am conceited enough to want to hear it from your mouth." He kissed her again. "What a deliciously beautiful mouth it is." Frederick's lips lingered over hers, running his tongue teasingly along her bottom lip and teeth. "I love drinking from your lips."

"Frederick," she stiffened in his arms, "give me your hand." Not fully understanding, he complied with what she asked. She took his palm, kissed it gently, and then placed it on her abdomen. "Feel."

The sensation spread through him. "Our child?" he murmured, stunned by the love he felt for this unborn baby. Anne's eyes grew in intensity as she nodded her agreement. "It is God's work," he whispered. "To think our joining—our love—grows within you."

"You sacrificed much, my Husband, to reach the pinnacle of your success. You will never know how very proud I am of you because words cannot express such depth of feelings. This baby will know a man of strength, but also a man of love." She kissed his palm once more.

"Come, Sweetling," he said at last. "Tomorrow we see our new home. I sent word to the staff to expect us in the afternoon."

"What will we do in the morning?" she teased.

Frederick scooped her into his arms and carried Anne back to the carriage. "The same thing we will do this evening," he whispered close to her ear.

"Sounds heavenly," she giggled. Then Anne rested her head on his shoulder and lay comfortably in his arms as he approached the waiting coach. "Our child and our home—I thought the day would never come."

"The day is here, Sweet Anne; you will have everything you desire."

*   *   *

The parkland surrounding the house stretched out for a half mile before the well tread road dipped down to a wooden bridge crossing one of the many creeks leading to the River Stour, and then climbing once more towards the romantic-looking house with rows and rows of windows facing the noon day sun. The sunlight danced on the panes and turned the streaming rays to fractured colors of the rainbow. The red brick with gingerbread trim made it look like something out of a fairy tale.

"Welcome to your home, my Love," Frederick announced as the coach crossed the wide cobbled curve leading to the house's entrance. Purple-clad servants hurried down the entry to greet them. The coach's steps were lowered, and Frederick climbed out to stand on his own property. He reached in and took Anne's hand, guiding her to his side. "Viscountess Orland," he spoke softly "your new house awaits."

"Marcus was right," she returned his tone, "it looks sound."

"At least, it is not a skeleton," he murmured close to her ear. "Hopefully, the rooms are not gutted on the inside."

"Viscount Orland," a stately butler in black came forward. Making a proper bow, he gestured towards the house. "My name is Mr. Smythe; I am in charge of the household staff. If you and the viscountess will follow me, I will show you about the house."

"Thank you, Mr. Smythe," Frederick acknowledged several of the other waiting staff with a nod of his head. "Lady Orland and I appreciate your attention to detail." As they followed the man closely through the entrance, Frederick continued, "Today, simply, we want to become familiar with the house and the immediate grounds. Tomorrow, I would like to get down to business. Is the steward available?"

"I will send word, Lord Orland." The butler paused before speaking, "May I say, Sir, we are happy to have a new viscount in residence; it has been nearly a year, Lord Orland. We understand you are a decorated military man."

"My husband is a Rear Admiral of the White," Anne instructed. "You may tell the staff their new master is a national hero—a man who served England for over a decade. They have much of which to be proud."

"My wife," Frederick half laughed as he handed his outer coat to one of the waiting footmen, "is my staunchest admirer."

Mr. Smythe indicated the opening foyer. "As one can see, the house is in good repair. Would you like me to show you the rooms, Sir?"

"I hope it will not offend you, Mr. Smythe, but I think my Viscountess and I would prefer to explore on our own. We are both very hands on types; we will want to know each room thoroughly. Please—you and the others—go about your regular duties. We are not here to censure—only to learn what our new home has to offer."

"Very well, Sir; I will have the luggage brought in and placed in the master chambers. If you need anything, simply ring the cord." With that, the butler disappeared although several other servants scrambled to their stations.

Frederick asked with a smirk, "Are you ready, Mrs. Wentworth?"

Anne gave him her most beguiling smile. "I prefer the name Wentworth to all the other names to which I have been addressed in my life." She took his proffered arm as they walked to the first room on their right.

"It is the name you were born to share." His breath caressed her cheek as they entered the room—their first look at what would be their abode for the rest of their lives. "And this, Sweetling, is the place we were born to share."

"Our child will inherit this estate, Frederick. It is our future; the Wentworth name will be a part of England's history, its present, and its future. Your dedication—your determination—created the opportunity for us to shape our identity. Let us make the Wentworth name stand for all that is best in English society."

In the room alone, he gently guided her into his embrace. "We will act with decorum, with compassion, with empathy, and with kindness. You, my Love, will be the model of English grace and womanhood. I will try to live up to your image of the man to whom you gave your heart."

"You have no one above you, my Husband; you are already the best man I ever knew. You deal with people honestly and honorably; that is a very rare quality." She stroked the underside of his jaw line with her fingertips. "Now, your child and I," she teased, "wish to see our new home. I, my Love, need to set up a proper nursery. This is a very active child." Anne gently touched her stomach. "I have a feeling he will hit the floor running, and I shall not have a chance to catch up if I procrastinate now."

"He?" Frederick masked the amusement in his voice.

Anne turned to take his hand. "He," she paused, "or she." Taking a few steps away from him, she looked back over her shoulder and added, "or they," before bursting into peals of laughter.

"No *they's*, Anne Wentworth," he warned. "One crew member at a time, do you hear me?' Then he burst out laughing before grabbing her and spinning Anne around. When he sat her down again, Frederick beamed with happiness. "I love you, Mrs. Wentworth," he said as he bent to kiss her lips.

When they separated, Anne whispered, "Let us find the master bedroom."

He chuckled, "It probably would not be a good first impression if the servants found us sharing an intimate moment, would it?"

"A good impression—probably not." Anne straightened the lines of her dress. "Let us go and claim this house as our own."

Chapter 24

And in Life's noisiest hour
There whispers still the ceaseless Love of Thee,
The heart's Self-solace and soliloquy.
—Samuel Taylor Coleridge from "The Presence of Love"

Over the next two months, they established themselves in the community. Raised in such a fine house as Kellynch Hall, Anne instinctively knew how to run a household. It amazed Frederick how Sir Walter managed to find himself in financial straits with Anne in his family. The man must have worked at ruining his name because Anne sensibly ran Hanson Hall with the authority of an army drill sergeant and the compassion of a combat nurse. If Sir Walter allowed Anne to run Kellynch instead of elevating Elizabeth to that status, he may never have had to leave. Of course, that would have meant Sophia and Benjamin would never come to Somerset, and he would never have returned to claim Anne. In retrospect, Frederick thanked his lucky stars to have a father as inept as Sir Walter.

For his part, Frederick managed quite well on land. Although he spent most of his adult life on the sea, Frederick understood hard work and how to command men without domination. He learned quickly in whom he could place his confidence in dealing with supplies—with materials—with construction. To complement his education as a landowner, Frederick, judiciously, placed men he knew he could trust in positions around him. When Edward and Christine decided they would remain in Shropshire, he offered the living to Lieutenant Avendale, who jumped at the chance to be closer to his wife's home of Bristol. Lieutenant Harwood joined his staff as an apprentice to the estate's steward. Mr. Lawrence, informed Frederick the first day they met he wanted to pension out soon, and as Harwood's father held a similar position in West Sussex, his former lieutenant had a working knowledge of the responsibilities involved.

Two of his former able seamen became Cottagers on his estate, and he found a like situation for another on a neighboring property. As news got out how he tried to help those who served with him previously, Frederick regularly received pleas from men who returned from service to find themselves with nothing. As often as he could, he located places for shopkeepers, farmers, or tradesmen, especially if they served valiantly. Occasionally, a lackey would beseech him for help; in those cases, he politely replied he knew of nothing available for the man at the time. He would not help those who shunned their duties aboard ship. He now had more than a dozen men strategically positioned throughout the county in whom he could place his trust implicitly.

With each placement, when his former crewmember professed gratitude and offered Frederick his allegiance, he gave them the same speech: "I may be Viscount Orland to everyone else, but to you, I am still your *Captain*. All I ask is for you to help me become a part of this community. As a titled gentleman, I am responsible for the lives of many people in the area. If you hear of anything out of the ordinary, I ask you to let me know, no matter how insignificant it may seem. If you learn of a tradesman who cheats his customers, I want to know. If you find a group of men up to no good, please send me word. If you do this, you repay me for my kindness. You will make my life on land as productive as you did with my tenure on the sea." The men understood his sentiments because they knew how their captain felt about responsibility and about preparation by anticipating problems. Each of them readily agreed—his was a small price to pay for the respectability and the manhood he gave them.

Wallingford called upon them several times and gave Frederick tours of the area, introducing him to people in place to aid the British government's cause. Frederick listened carefully and made his own evaluations. Since the day Wallingford revealed having known Anne previously, Frederick held back in believing Marcus Lansing completely, possibly out of jealousy, but something more he could not explain. Wallingford appeared to have Frederick's best interest at heart, but he knew appearances could be deceiving.

*   *   *

Frederick and Anne hosted the community picnic for the village of Hurn's annual May Day celebration. At the picnic, they would meet many whom they did not know. People would judge them by how the Wentworths performed on this particular occasion. Frederick held no doubts Anne would excel in every manner—the woman possessed a way about her. Anyone who ever met *his Anne* fell in love with her gentle nature. He worried more about his own acceptance. At sea, Frederick understood the natural practice of taking orders from those above and giving orders to those of lower ranks. In local issues, a man had to know on whose side to be found; those in power were more ruthless than any pirate or mercenary he ever met. The business of politics required him to be genial and pleasant to people for whom he cared little. Idle banter drove him crazy; Frederick considered himself a man of action, not social tedium; the game played by those in power certainly tried his patience.

Since he agreed to Wallingford's proposition, Frederick spent many hours analyzing his own disposition. Essentially, he was a loner; maybe that was why he was so successful as a naval officer. He learned the proper way to handled most situations—the naval way, but with strangers, he, generally, held back. That is—with all strangers, except with Anne. With her, he knew no façade—only with Anne did he feel comfortable from the beginning. Self-sufficiency highlighted his life—his haven of strength. When he looked at Edward and Sophia, he saw the same "stubbornness" of spirit—to mold Fate—to cheat it, actually. He knew his siblings to be very amiable, downright loving with friends and family, but making small talk with total strangers was mediocrity. Like his brother and sister, for Frederick, such situations were exquisite torture. So, he did not anticipate the hours of playing the perfect host.

Anne suddenly appeared before him, clasping the bodice of her dress to her bosom. "Would you lace me?" She caught his attention by snuggling her backside into his chest.

Frederick laughed at her playfulness. He feigned chastising her, "Where is your maid?' As he said so, he took up the ribbons and began to slip the ends through the eyelets.

"I married you. Why do I need a maid?" She glanced lovingly over her shoulder at him, and Frederick, instinctively, gave her a quick kiss on the lips.

He continued to crisscross the laces and pulled the bodice tighter. "You are looking well, my Love." He kissed the nape of her neck before tying off the ends of the ribbons.

"I am looking pleasingly plump is what you mean," Anne corrected.

Frederick smiled a wicked one before adding. "Pregnancy becomes you, Lady Orland. In fact, I may see what I can do about keeping you with child for awhile." He pulled her into his embrace. "I like all the extra curves of your body."

"You like resting your head on my very ample bosom," she teased.

Never tiring of her closeness, Frederick bent to kiss her. Holding only inches from her mouth, he continued to nibble on her bottom lip. "I never previously complained about the size of your breasts, my Love. I found them quite enticing, in fact."

"You are such a cad, Frederick Wentworth!" Anne went on her tiptoes to partake of his attention once more before drawing away from him. "You look very handsome today, my Love."

Frederick pulled at his shirt's neckline. "I thought full dress uniforms were uncomfortable!"

Anne laughed at his adjustment to civilian life. "Although I adore you in all your military regalia, I find you look quite well-formed in your waistcoat and white cravat—very masculine and strong in your turn out."

"Are you flirting with me, Mrs. Wentworth?" he asked as he reached for his handkerchief and watch fob.

Anne twirled once to let the movement of her dress catch his attention. "I might be, my Lord. Is it working?"

Frederick's eyes followed her as she made her way to the door. "If you, my Viscountess, wish to know whether your feminine charms still have power over me, let me show you up close and personal." He strode towards her before coming up short, posing over her, forcing Anne to look up in his eyes. "You, Anne Elliot Wentworth, have only to smile at me or raise your eyes to mine or even walk into a room, and I am yours completely. I lost my heart to you long ago." His finger traced a line from her temple to her lips. "I will come to you more often than you may want—yet, I can do nothing less for you possess me body and soul."

"I choose to take my comfort in your arms, my Husband; I never suspected love required such complete surrender, but I gladly run the white banner up the flag pole of life and turn over my whole self to you. This child and I are blessed to find the love in your heart. My present and future are forever bound to you."

Frederick forced himself to breathe. It struck him how terribly lonely he was all those years without her. "It is a shame we have a party awaiting us," he spoke hoarsely. "I can think of a much better use of an afternoon." Knife-cutting tension hung in the air. Finally, he pursed his lips before offering her his elbow. "Let us go meet our neighbors, Lady Orland."

She lightly placed her hand on his forearm. "Of course, my Lord."

The earlier overcast skies cleared by noon, and the hope for fine weather proved possible. People from all walks of life peppered the lawn with blankets and games, content to enjoy the lovely weather and to view the new Viscount and his wife personally. Linen-lined tables were heaped with all sorts of foodstuffs. Although each family contributed at least one dish to the assortment, the bulk of the offerings came from Hanson Hall: roast beef, cheese, fresh fruit, roasted rabbit and pheasant, dark bread, boiled carrots and potatoes, seed-cakes and berry tarts, along with lemonade. Anne even hired a quartet of fiddlers to provide music throughout the day.

"Lady Orland." One of the Cottagers approached her as Anne made her way down one of the slopes. The woman offered up her version of a proper curtsy, definitely hard to do on the incline. "Me name be Mrs. Miller. Me family it lives past the second hedgerow."

Anne reached out and touched the woman's arm. "Mrs. Miller, the Viscount and I are pleased you are here. I hope you find everything satisfactory. As this is our first May Day celebration, we were unsure as to the traditions."

Mrs. Miller flushed with the fact the estate's mistress hoped to please her. "No, Ma'am, it be one of the best we seen." Anne's eyebrow shot up, waiting for the woman's next remark. "Me family just wishes to say we be happy you and Lord Orland come to stay. Me be a midwifin' if you need me for the babe."

"Thank you, Mrs. Miller." Anne started on her way, but the woman had one more thing to say.

"We be hearin' the new Master he be a hero. That be true."

"Lord Orland is a Rear Admiral in the British Navy. George IV awarded him this title because of his actions in the war." As she spoke, Anne's eyes automatically searched the crowd to find Frederick. "My husband is an honorable and brave man." Her gaze rested on Frederick's back.

"The Master be a hero makin' a difference to some," Mrs. Miller continued. "We be judgin' how he treat us—those who work for him. He deal honestly with me man—first time in many years. We be glad you and he and this babe come so we have a place. None of us be wantin' to leave the land. We be workin' hard for him; you tell your man—the Master—that."

Anne looked humbled by the woman's words. "I assure you, Mrs. Miller, Lord Orland will be moved by your sentiments; he is a man who accepts responsibility seriously. You tell Mr. Miller and the others if we make mistakes or if there are things we need to address, they need to speak to Lord Orland. He will listen; he may not always be able to solve every issue, but my husband will deal with each fairly."

"Yes, Mistress Orland." The woman made another awkward curtsy and then moved on to her family.

Frederick walked the grounds for the third time, stopping to speak to as many people as he could: Cottagers, shopkeepers, tradesmen, and landed gentry. With each he tried to learn something about the person—names, especially; he learned long ago being able to call people by their names meant something in this world. He watched his wife orchestrate the food and the games. At the moment, he planned to catch up with her and insist Anne find her own patch of shade. Going on six months of pregnancy, she had no business overextending her energies. On his last pass through the crowd, he recruited Mr. Harwood and Mrs. Avendale to take over some of the responsibilities.

"Captain," Mr. Avendale cornered Frederick as his former commanding officer circumnavigated the terrace, "may I speak to you?"

"Certainly." Frederick walked back into the house where they might talk privately. Once alone, he asked, "What may I do for you, Lieutenant?"

"When you gave me this position, Sir, you asked me to keep my ears open and to let you know if I heard of anything unusual."

Frederick stiffened, concerned with what he might hear next. "Do you have something for me?" He motioned Avendale to a nearby chair.

"Day before yesterday, Mrs. Thomason came to see me. Her brother Jatson Laurie fell in with some men who Mrs. Thomason believes are quite unsavory characters. Anyway, she wanted me to intervene with Mr. Laurie. From what I understand, Laurie is involved in some kind of smuggling ring. Many of these small time smugglers sold brandy and cigars and the such taken from French ships during the war. The local law officials looked the other way for much of this trade, but Laurie appears to be involved in something bigger. If my limited sources are correct, something big is going down in a warehouse outside of Studland this evening. Most people in this part of the county travel from here to Wimborne Minster for the celebratory fireworks. The ports and the warehouses are likely to be deserted."

"Do we know in what these men are involved?" Frederick steepled his fingers as he tried to come up with a plan.

Avendale squirmed a bit, the same as he always did when reporting to his captain. "Mrs. Thomason seems to think her brother may be involved in something dangerous. He was told to bring a gun. No one is going to shoot someone over some cigars, no matter how fine they may be. That is penny ante dealings; it has to be something more than that, Captain."

Frederick hesitated, needing to define what choices he would make—whom he would trust. "Avendale, I need for you to do something for me. I cannot be seen contacting our men, so I want you to find Mr. Harwood and tell him what you just told me. I want all our former crewmembers to meet me at eleven tonight on the north side of the Studland Bay warehouse district. If they need horses, have Harwood make arrangements to use cattle from my stable; tell each of them to come prepared to fight."

"Yes, Sir." Avendale moved to follow Frederick's orders.

"Michael," Frederick called after him, "you are not to come with us. I need someone the locals will trust, and I will not ask you to go against your religion and pick up a gun again."

Luckily for Frederick, the picnic zapped much of Anne's liveliness, so when the suggestion to retire early for the evening came, his wife offered no objections. She fell asleep quickly—nearly an hour ago, but Frederick lay wide awake, the importance of the choices he made this evening thudding through his mind.

He made a commitment and sold his "soul" for an estate and a title for Anne, but he would do so on his own terms. Tonight, he would lead his men into the unknown; he never felt so uncertain—not since his first naval command mission. What if someone died? It was likely he asked these men to do the impossible. Did he have that right?

He slipped out of the bed some time later. Now, he stood looking down at the reposing figure of the woman who owned his heart. "I love you, my Anne," he whispered, before quietly leaving her chamber for his dressing room. He uniformed himself in casual attire—breeches, boots, a cambric shirt open at the neck, and a great coat.

With the help of Matthew Harwood, he left the estate via horseback in time to reach their meeting point long before his men. After serving under him for several years, Harwood knew Frederick *needed* to assess the scene prior to the others' arrival. Riding in silence for nearly a half hour, Harwood finally asked, "Do we have any idea what we face tonight?"

What the man really wanted to know was if Frederick had a plan. Of course, he had a plan; he just was not sure whether it fit the situation. "If you ask have I thought this through, I assure you I did, Lieutenant." That is all he said because the specifics of the plan were nowhere to be found. Tonight he would learn first hand how to be an agent for the government. He wondered now if he should have contacted Marcus Lansing, after all. "Will the others join us?"

"The men will be there, Captain—I guess I should say Admiral or even Lord Orland." Harwood's voice betrayed his nervousness.

Wentworth flinched with the knowledge his men would put their lives on the line simply because he asked them to. "I prefer Captain to the other titles; it seems a more comfortable fit."

Finally arriving in Studland, Frederick and Harwood made their way along the deserted streets and alleys surrounding the warehouses. They left their horses tied up in the wooded area outside the village and moved through the shadows. As predicted, villagers throughout the county celebrated during the day so anyone who legitimately might be out at this ungodly hour had long since gone to bed. However, when they located the warehouse in question, several men buzzed about it. Two stood guard at the entrance while the others unloaded barrels from wagons, evidently cargo from the ship sitting in Studland Bay.

"Are they armed?" Harwood whispered from their vantage point between two buildings facing the warehouse.

Frederick nodded slightly, putting away the spyglass he instinctively brought with him. "The two out front are. We should assume so are the others." He paused ever so slightly before continuing. "I need for you to sneak back to the horses and meet the men. I am going around to the back to see if I can get a better look. If I am caught, you are not to stage a rescue; I will not have men's lives put in danger to save me. You will ride hard to find Lord Wallingford and tell him what I did, and he will know what to do. Do you understand me on this, Harwood?"

"Yes, Sir—I understand." Frederick heard the man's breath catch in his words.

"If I think we have a chance to stop this, I will follow you to meet the men. Now, move out, Harwood."

Hesitating briefly, Harwood turned to leave. "Be careful, Captain. Your missus needs you."

"I am fully aware of that, Lieutenant—now hurry."

The ease with which he managed to find his way through the back of the warehouse surprised Frederick. He expected it to be better protected, especially considering the cargo was likely to be illegal, but he assumed the gang foresaw no trouble. The men separated the items into four distinct areas—very much as someone might in dividing furniture for individual rooms of a house.

He worked his way through the shadows. Not a short man, he found it difficult to secure places to hide as the cargo was not stacked. He nearly crawled from one area to another, trying to get close enough to survey the unloading. He wanted to know what the thieves moved and how much resistance his men might face. Yet, afraid to get any closer, Frederick hid behind some barrels near steps, slipping back into the orifice beneath the stairs.

Hearing the planks above his head creak with the weight of someone walking on them, Frederick moved flush against the back wall, pulling his dark coat about him to make himself more invisible in the dim shadows. Then people—three from what he could tell—began to descend the steps slowly—first one and then another.

Not even breathing, he demanded silence, although his pulse thrummed in his ears, and Frederick wondered how the men could not hear it. He wanted desperately to know who these men were, but he forced himself to remain patient and just watch and listen.

"The pictures go to my special client," a man in a dark grey coat spoke as he stepped to a lower level. "He pays well, and we can use the money to buy additional hulls."

"What of the brandy?" Another man posed on the upper steps. All Frederick could see of him was his boots. He sank further into the wall, trying to make himself as small as possible. He could not confront these men alone; he must learn as much as he could before going for help.

A local, speaking in a Dorsetshire accent, descended next. "The brandy be for sale to pay me men."

"Is everything else in place?" The first man now stood so close Frederick feared he would turn to see him hiding in the shadows.

"Lord Cochrane understands we do this for him. He sent specific instructions." With that, the men began to walk towards the warehouse's main opening, and Frederick slowly uncurled and loosened his muscles, preparing to move out the way he came in. He wished he knew more, but he could not risk staying any longer. He scuttled from one cluster of barrels to another, pausing only long enough to allow guards or workers to pass close by. Finally reaching the door, he edged it open, barely wide enough to slip his body through. Yet, he did not relax until he was well away from the action going on inside the building.

Frederick circled the area, coming out on a different pathway, before setting out to the meeting place on foot. Proceeding through the wooded farmland surrounding the village, he followed the hedgerows rather than cutting directly across the fields. A clear night, even with the lack of a full moon, he was able to see quite clearly. Coming near the copse of trees hiding his men, he let out the prearranged whistle before entering the wooded circle.

All the men—his men—stood around casually waiting for him. Harwood rushed forward, clearly thankful to see Frederick. "What did you find, Captain?" The other men closed ranks to hear his story.

"First," Frederick began, "I want each of you to know what I am asking you to do is dangerous. It is not like when we took ships and shared prize money. With this mission, you simply get the thanks of a grateful nation and what little I can give you so if you want out, no one will consider it a shame for you have served your country and me most faithfully."

"We follow you, Captain." Harwood spoke first, but the others echoed his sentiments.

"Then this is what I know. A group of smugglers move cargo into a warehouse, evidently to separate it before dispersing it to different interested parties. There must be four distinct types of commodities—for they divide the containers as such. I overheard some men speaking of pictures, and I observed large wooden crates, which must contain framed artwork, probably smuggled out of France to satisfy a member of the aristocracy. They also spoke of brandy, and I noted appropriate-sized casks in which, I suspect, the brandy can be found."

"What of the other items, Captain?" John Langley, a former quartermaster, offered up the guarded question all of them thought.

"Truthfully, Langley, I do not know. Barrels of some sort were being unloaded, but no markings showed. Yet, I know I missed something. It was like I could smell rotten fish or rotten eggs, but that makes no sense. They could not sell something rancid for a profit."

Harwood needed to know. "How many men?"

Deep in thought, Frederick remained silent for a few moments, as if mentally counting the men he saw. "There was a half dozen moving the supplies in and out; I counted four guards—two front and two on the sides; and there were three others—those are the ones I overheard speaking about the brandy and the crates."

"A dozen men then!" George Shipley, a lately minted midshipman, replied, his tone more forceful than his words.

Frederick looked them all directly in the eyes to assure they each understood what he said. "Again, what I ask of each of you is not a requirement to maintain the position in which I placed you. I will *not* force anyone to become a part of this. These men we seek betray our government, making a quick profit at the expense of hard working people like yourselves. They set themselves above the law. My interference will make some enemies—those who wish to forge an alliance with France being among them. If you come with me tonight, you will be a part of something great. We have left our ship, but the battle for a free England still remains. Yet, each of you must decide for whom you fight and whether they are worth it. I fight for Mrs. Wentworth and my unborn child; I want them to live in an area where such crimes are not the normal—are not tolerated by a titled man nor a tradesman nor a farmer." Frederick's expression grew grim.

There was silence, then John Langley asked, "How do we proceed, Captain?"

"First, we need a distraction to entertain the guards in front while the majority of us slip in the back of the warehouse."

"Drunks are common along the docks and the warehouse district," a mast captain added. "One of us could be obnoxiously drunk."

Langley thought out loud. "We need to recruit some women to help us next time. A woman could easily pretend to be a lady of the evening and distract the guards."

Frederick raised a brow, dealing with his new responsibilities were becoming unbelievably complicated. "Next time," was all he said, before summarizing, "then who among you can be the most obnoxious?"

All eyes immediately fell on Christian Hollmes, a tall, broad-shouldered, lean, but muscular, man, with rough calluses on both hands from hard work and a dark skin, tanned by a life in the sun. "I guess I am your man, Captain," he said jovially as the others slapped him on the back.

"Good," Wentworth commented. "You are large enough to handle any trouble once we are discovered. We are counting on you Hollmes."

"I have your back, Captain," he assured.

"Gentlemen, we set sail in unknown waters—very dangerous waters. Think of your first boarding of an enemy ship. None of us knew what to do the first time. It will be the same tonight. Be safe—take no undue chances. Capture whom you can, but do not follow a man into the night—into the unknown. I want all of us out of there as we were on *The Resolve*—no casualties. None of us has spent much time battling the enemy on land. Let us learn from tonight's encounter."

As he led the men back along the hedgerows towards the warehouse, Frederick tried to decide what it was that now drove him to take this action. He desired a proper home for *his Anne* and their child. He made a promise to the British government, and he was a man of his word. He *hated* being under Wallingford's watchful eye. He took responsibility as Viscount Orland. All seemed logical reasons—rationalizations for his actions—but were they the whole truth? In reality, he did not know.

Chapter 25

Now thou hast loved me one whole day,
To-morrow when thou leavest, what wilt thou say?
Wilt thou then antedate some new-made vow?
Or say that now
We are not just those persons which we were?
—John Donne from "Woman's Constancy"

When they signaled being in position to enter the back of the warehouse, Hollmes, shirttail out of his pants and face smudged with soot and smelling of splashed on ale secured from a flask Shipley carried, staggered forward out of the shadows, greeting the two men standing guard. Everyone else seemed to be inside. "Hey, Boys, what be here?" Hollmes called out as he lunged against the wagon, pretending to be barely able to stand.

The two guards searched the darkness to see if he came alone. "Nothin' for your concern. Be gone with ya'," they warned while bringing up their guns, prepared to deal with an obvious drunken intrusion.

"Ya' got drink in there, Boys?" Hollmes staggered closer.

"We be tellin' ya' no more. Ya' need to be leavin'," the man's tone became more demanding.

Hollmes plastered on his silliest smile as he stepped forward one more time. "Share ye drink with ole Toby. I be needin' a drink bad."

One of the guards reached out to steady Hollmes' movements. Chuckling lightly, he spoke a little less intimidatingly, "Ye be drunk enough, ole Toby."

Realizing the opportunity would never be better, Hollmes moved quickly. Grabbing both men by the neck, in one swift, powerful thrust, he clanged their heads together, dazing them both. He let the smaller man slide to his knees while he turned and delivered a well-placed upper cut to the larger of the two. A sharp crack of the guard's jaw told Hollmes he had no more worries from that encounter. The smaller man now staggered to his feet, preparing to turn his gun on Hollmes' back. Used to hand-to-hand boardings, where the enemy came from all directions at once, Hollmes spun, leg extended, to take out the second guard's footing. Hauling the man back up against the warehouse wall, as a way to protect himself from other assailants, Christian began to apply a profound pressure to the man's neck. The chokehold took only a few seconds to achieve its purpose—the guard's limp body now slumped against him. Quickly, he moved to drag the bodies out of the light in case someone else came along.

In the front of the warehouse, as Christian Hollmes stepped from the shadows, Frederick, Harwood, Langley, Shipley and three others slipped through the rear door. Frederick placed a man at each entrance to prevent anyone escaping, and then he sent Timothy Smallridge and Lucas Kendrick to the building's roof to work their way down from the upper floor. They were his best climbers on board *The Resolve*—no rope or ladder stopped either of them.

Hearing the commotion in the front, several men rushed for the main entrance, but Hollmes managed to swing the door shut just as they reached it. Confused in the commotion of escaping, they did not check to see if the door was bolted closed; instead, in mass, they immediately turned towards the other exit, running to find safe refuge.

From his vantage point behind a cluster of barrels, Frederick waited until the group was center court in the warehouse before signaling his men, and then they all stood, guns pointed at the retreating thieves. "Stand and deliver," Shipley demanded, as the cluster skidded to a halt and prepared to defend themselves.

A few of them foolishly reached for their weapons before realizing men with guns, loaded and cocked, surrounded them. A man near the front slowly edged his hands into the air. "Who be ye?" he demanded, although he evidently planned to surrender without a fight. Frederick recognized the voice as being the "local" he heard on the steps.

"Interested citizens," Shipley responded as they edged from behind the barrels to take the guns held by those they surrounded.

The man leading the group motioned towards the cargo. "Interested in what?" He grinned; a flash of movement in his eyes told Frederick he planned something. Without speaking, he motioned ever so slightly with his head, and Harwood nodded in response. They both stepped to the back of the group and took up positions holding hostages to persuade those to the front to abandon any thoughts of a fight. When the group leader noted their changed stances, he shoved his hands a bit higher. "How 'bout some Frenchie brandy, Boys?"

Shipley by silent consent, still spoke for Frederick's men. As much as possible, Wentworth did not wish to appear to be in charge. "We will help ourselves, but, first, where are the rest of your men?"

The same man spoke for the smugglers. "What other men?' He kept his eyes noncommittal.

Shipley knew now the man spoke half-truths. They stood facing one another—sizing up each other—waiting for a deeper understanding. Shipley shot a glance towards Frederick; he caught it, raised a brow. Then Frederick placed the gun he held next to the temple of the nearest member of the gang and pushed it forward as if he planned to pull the trigger.

The man swallowed hard before he gulped out the words, "Upstairs."

"Shut up!" The gang's leader ordered.

"Ye shut up!" The scruffy-faced thief shot back.

Frederick motioned with his gun for Harwood to follow him, and they both began to edge their way up the stairs. Meanwhile, Shipley motioned for the others to tie up the ones they caught. Moving cautiously forward, Frederick's mind remained alert although his chest felt tight with dread—one small step at a time, closer to the upper levels. He knew by now Kendrick and Smallridge had to be in place and were probably herding those remaining in the warehouse towards him.

Letting his gun hand lead, Frederick should have expected something, but when the attack came, it took him by surprise. A club came down hard on his forearm, and the gun skittered across the floor as he released it automatically. With his other arm, Frederick reached up to grasp his opponent's jacket to pull the man off balance. In doing so, they became entangled and began to wrestle as they tumbled down the short flight of stairs. He sensed, rather than felt, Harwood jump clear of this struggle, as well as a perfectly tossed cask of brandy smashed and dripping onto the packet dirt floor. Banging first against the wall and then against the railing, Frederick held on until they came crashing down in a heap of bones and muscles, slamming into the hardened ground serving for the floor of the building. Somehow, he ended up on top of his attacker, and he heard the air rush from the man's lungs as Frederick's weight hit him full force. Jostling to gain the advantage, Frederick pulled his knee up to first strike the man between his outstretched thighs and then to kneel on the man's chest, the packed weight of his body pushing down as his knee came under the man's chin and cut off his air supply. "Move, bastard, and I will kill you," he growled close to the man's face.

Sounds of gunfire from above sent Harwood scrambling up the steps, but moments later he reappeared, leading at gunpoint another of the gang of smugglers ahead of him. Kendrick and Smallridge followed, and Frederick gave a silent prayer all were well. The rest of his men appeared; Hollmes shoved his two captures towards the others. "Are you all right, Sir?" Harwood spoke close to him.

"Yes," he whispered, aware of his skittering pulse. "Let us lock these men up until we see what we have." Frederick rolled off the man, literally landing in the puddle of brandy.

They pushed all twelve into a small tool shed inside the warehouse. Barely enough room to stand, the men complained, but Frederick's crew turned a deaf ear. Prisoners secured at last, his men began to survey the accumulated goods. Breaking open one of the casks of brandy, they found cups enough for all of them to share before taking an inventory of what they recovered.

Frederick and Harwood moved to a table to find any paperwork associated with the haul. His arm throbbed from the pain of the blow, but Frederick simply gritted his teeth. He buttoned his greatcoat to chest level and slid his arm through the opening, bracing the arm to his body, like a sling.

Harwood teased, "You remind me of Napoleon."

"No Bonaparte jokes if you please, Mr. Harwood," Frederick warned. "I keep telling you I am too tall."

Frederick poured himself one drink; tossed it off and poured another to steady his nerves before returning to the task at hand. After a celebratory toast, his men went to work examining what they found. As he suspected, a smooth brandy was a hot commodity in these parts. The men reported the number of casks at fifty, counting the one from which they already partook and the one sloshed on the floor. Opening the crates, Frederick recognized the works of the Jacques-Louis David. the dazzling costumes and jewelry fashionable at the court of Napoleon Bonaparte clearly evident in each portrait. Another crate held work from François Gérard, known for his portrait of Madame de Tallyrand. "I prefer landscapes," Harwood commented when the man held up the painting for Frederick to see. "What will we do with those?" he asked as Frederick indicated for the men to replace the piece in the crate.

"Maybe I should make a contribution to my Prince—a payment for my gift."

Finally, the men came to the barrels at the far end of the warehouse. "Whew! These surely stick, Captain, even before we take the lids off," Shipley sang out.

"What is in them is all I want to know," Frederick responded. "Leave them capped after that."

They found metal bars to break the seals. Frederick and Harwood ambled over to take a look at the first one opened by John Langley. "What the hell is that?" Harwood mumbled as he dipped his finger into a black liquid with the consistency of a thick pudding.

"Coal tar." Cavton Harris touched the liquid.

Frederick turned on the man. "Are you sure, Cav?"

"Positive, Captain."

Langley wiped his hand on his pants. "Why would someone smuggle in coal tar?"

"It has lots of uses," Harris assured them, "but why steal it, and why such huge quantities?"

Frederick waved them on. "Let us see what stinks so bad."

They barely cracked the lid on one of the other barrels before they all reached for handkerchiefs to cover their noses and mouths. "I am afraid to ask," Frederick stammered as he backed away from the cylinder.

Tears coming to his eyes, Shipley quickly returned the lid to its place. "Pray tell, what is that," he gasped, coughing to clear his throat.

"Fire and brimstone," Tweed Swift, a former gunnery mate, stated flatly.

"Explain," Frederick demanded.

"Sulfur, Sir. I know the smell well. The *Bible* calls it brimstone; therefore, the phrase fire and brimstone. It was a favorite saying when we loaded the guns on *The Resolve*."

Harwood moved up beside him. "Again, why would anyone smuggle sulfur? It makes no sense."

"Harwood, did you ever hear of Captain Sir Thomas, Lord Cochrane?" With difficulty, Frederick tried to control his rapidly racing mind.

Harwood laughed good-naturedly. "Who has not heard of *le loup des mers,* the Sea Wolf? With the frigate *Pallas,* he alone earned seventy-five thousand pounds sterling in prize money. But Lord Cochrane is in gaol, Sir—part of the London Stock Exchange scandal, a little over a year ago—lost his knighthood—dismissed from the Royal Navy—everything."

"Then tell me why I overheard those men tonight talking of corresponding with Lord Cochrane?" Frederick murmured, exceedingly unsettled.

"A different Lord Cochrane—I do not know, Captain." Harwood looked concerned. "If the thieves know Cochrane, it has something to do with the sulfur and the coal tar. It is not likely a man in gaol has use for fancy portraits or French brandy."

Swift added quickly, a grim determination evident in his face. He clenched his fists trying to drive his point home. "A man could use the sulfur and coal tar if he wanted a big fire or a big explosion. Maybe they planned on breaking Lord Cochrane out of gaol."

"But why would they need so much?" Frederick reasoned.

Swift looked puzzled. "It beats me, Sir."

Harwood's tone grew much harder—more distant. "What do you want to do about all this, Captain?"

Frederick took up the plan he formulated when he was hiding in the warehouse earlier. "I do not want anyone to get his hands on what we have here, especially considering the dire consequences of mixing these two elements together. Could we load the sulfur and coal tar back onto the wagons and store them in the barn in the north pasture? No one goes up there this time of year. We will find a way of dispersing of the barrels—a few at a time. Harville could use some of each in his furniture business. Molten sulfur makes decorative inlays."

"We could spread some of the sulfur on the land. It is a slow-release fertilizer—best when it is wet, though."

"What else?" Frederick wondered.

"Me Ma uses pure powdered sulfur as a medicinal tonic and as a way to clean out a man's bowels," Kendrick thought out loud.

"Good," Frederick noted. "We will figure out ways to get rid of it little by little—make sure it is not used for gunpowder. What about the coal tar?"

"Besides being used in dye treatments for fabrics, a person can use it to seal roofs—makes a water tight seal."

The ideas came fast. "My grandmother used it for any skin irritation. The woman swore by it."

"Put some in paint. It helps to make the wall warmer. The Cottagers could use it before the winter comes to keep out the cold."

"All right," Frederick interrupted. "We have ideas; we do not need to settle it all tonight, but we do need to move these barrels before we turn those men over to the authorities. We will leave two of the paintings and some casks of the brandy as evidence. If the gang planned a jailbreak, they will not divulge the presence of the sulfur or the coal tar. Each of you take three casks of brandy. Sell it about the country or drink it. I will not ask what you do with it. However, you should be able to get a pretty penny for them at some of the inns if that is what you choose."

"Thank you, Captain," Shipley spoke for all of them.

Frederick's unnerving smile reappeared. "You might as well be paid for your work somehow. Now let us hurry; we should all be home in bed before dawn."

Two hours later, Harwood took the reins of one wagon and Shipley took the other. "We will all meet you at the north barn tomorrow before dusk to unload. Simply put the whole wagon out of sight," Frederick ordered. "Take five casks of brandy back to Hanson Hall for me, will you, Harwood?"

"Certainly, Captain." He and Harwood exchanged a glance. "Will you be all right, Sir? I mean getting home."

"I can still sit a horse, Harwood, but how I will explain my arm to Mrs. Wentworth is not something about which I care to think."

Harwood grinned with amusement. "You could claim in a nightmarish dream she kicked you out of bed, Sir."

"Mrs. Wentworth is not that gullible!"

"Good luck, Captain," Shipley called as they moved out.

Although the middle of the night, Frederick first made a call on the Harbor Master's office, leaving a note giving specific directions to the warehouse and the men locked in the shed. In the note, he told the Harbor Master that Jatson Laurie was the informant and to go easy on him, but make it look as if Laurie was as guilty as the others. That was the most he could do for Mrs. Thomason. After all, Laurie participated in the smuggling gang of his own free will.

Having set the door on latch when he left, at a quarter after four in the morning, he snuck back into his house. Frederick knew within an hour the servants would be up and preparing for the day. Exhausted, and more than a bit sore, he wove his way through the corridors to his chambers. Passing Anne's door, he hesitated, considering going in to face her, and wondering how he would explain everything, but a bit of a coward when it came to his wife, Frederick simply touched the door lightly before moving on. He turned the knob to his own door gingerly, trying to soften the sound as the door eased from the jam. Bathed in the early light of the increasing dawn, he could make out shapes of furniture, thanks to the dying embers of the fire.

Carefully, he unbuttoned his coat with his free hand and tried to shrug out of it without moving his arm. Halfway in and halfway out, he realized he would need to use his forearm and hand or forever be stuck partially clothed. Taking his left hand to move his right, he concentrated hard not to make any sound. In fact, Frederick so focused on the task he did not realize Anne stepped from his dressing room and stood behind him. When her hand touched his shoulder to ease the coat away, he could not control the catch in his breath he emitted—both out of pain and out of surprise.

"I will not ask why you were out all night, Frederick." She lowered the coat from his left arm before coming to face him. She walked to the nightstand and lit a candle and then finished removing the coat. "But you will allow me to tend my husband without complaint." Her voice sounded cold and detached. Tears streamed down her face, but she said nothing more.

"Anne," he started, but she shushed him and began to cut the shirt away.

"The shirt is ruined; we should not try to take it over your head. I have my scissors here." Her voice was barely audible, but Frederick stood and let her administer to him. "I will send to the village for Doctor Laraby."

Frederick nodded, but he said no more. She filled a basin with water and forced him to sit while she bathed his arms and then his face—his chest and his back. "You have bruises," she whispered as she sent the soapy rag across his shoulder blades. "Some scratches too, although they do not look deep. I will wash the dirt from you. You smell of brandy and sweat."

Frederick simply leaned back against the chair and watched her carefully. The tears still cascaded down her cheeks, and he took his thumb to wipe them away.

Still not speaking, she brought him a glass of wine. Holding it to his lips, he took a sip before setting it on the table. She stood by the fire, warming her hands. Her wrapper stood open, and he could see the outline of her body through the sheerness of her dressing gown. "You are beautiful, Anne," he whispered softly.

"Do not . . ." she hissed, but refused to turn around.

"Do not what?" he demanded. "Do not tell my wife I love her—tell her she is beautiful?" Despite the pain in his arm, he found himself beside her. "Do not tell her she is my world?" With his left hand, he turned her chin, forcing Anne to look at him. He pulled her to him, allowing her to sob into his shoulder. Her tears ran down his arm and chest. "Ask me, Anne—ask me where I was tonight," he pleaded into her hair.

"It is none of my affair. I am simply the mistress of your house; I know where men go when they no longer desire their wives."

Her words stunned him; Frederick expected her to be confused concerning his whereabouts—to be angry, even, because he did not tell her—but he never thought she might think him untrue. "God, Anne, is that what you think of me? I spend years celibate to come back to you, and you think I spread my seed elsewhere now?" He took her hand and forced it below his waist. "Does this appear as if I satiated myself elsewhere this evening?"

Anne withdrew her hand, but left it on his waistline. "Then where?" she whispered. "How did you come by your injury?"

"That is better," he said softly. "Send someone for Laraby, and then come join me in our sitting room." He kissed her forehead and walked through the door to the room they shared.

A few minutes later, she stood in the doorway. "I brought a blanket for your shoulders," she said as she entered the room.

Frederick leaned forward to allow her to drape the coverlet around his bare back. "Come sit with me," he demanded.

Anne seated herself beside him, but she made a point of not touching him, a bit ashamed for her accusation and still confused as to why he left her to roam the countryside.

"Do you wish to talk?" he asked as he pulled the blanket closer.

"I suppose we should; I do not like for us to be at odds." Anne slid her hand to his knee, needing to touch him. "If you are willing to explain, I will listen."

"Will you look at me, Anne?" he asked as he took her hand and raised it to his lips. He pressed her hand to his cheek, trying to think of a way to make her understand. In some ways, he almost wished he could keep the lie of a mistress, but he saw the hurt in her eyes and knew she became the Anne created by Sir Walter and her sisters—the one who lacked confidence; Frederick would face her anger from the truth rather than have her become that wallflower again.

"I want to tell you it all," he began, "but you must promise not to interrupt until I finish. Then I will answer your questions."

"I understand."

"You were right when you thought Hanson Hall held a catch. Marcus Lansing, as you know, brought me the details of the Prince's offer, but he also brought me the terms of my accession to the title. The Central Office recruited me to spearhead the search for smugglers and traitors working out of Cornwall and through the Channel." He saw her eyes grow wide with dismay, but as promised, she held her tongue.

"However, once I accepted the position, I began to question Wallingford, who is my governmental contact in Dorset. At first, I admit to being jealous of your former relationship with the man, but now, it is more than that, Anne. I cannot feel good about what he offers.

"So, I set up my own network. I have Avendale and Harwood and Shipley and several others. I asked them to keep their eyes and ears open and tell me if they took note of anything unusual. Today, during the picnic, Avendale brought me news I could not ignore.

"Harwood and I, along with ten others I trust, stopped a smuggling group in Studland Harbor. Unfortunately, I fought with one of the men after he struck my arm with a club. That is what you see on my body."

"Frederick," she gasped as she moved up to kiss him. "Oh, God, was anyone else hurt?"

He let out the breath he held; she did not respond negatively, at least, not initially. "No one. Just like on *The Resolve*, I took the worst of the encounter, but it was touch and go for awhile."

"Tell me," she insisted. "I need to know of what you were involved."

Frederick stalled, trying to decide whether to tell her it all, but he finally realized he would not build their relationship on half-truths. "Wallingford warned me not to speak of our deal with anyone, especially to you. I never wanted you to know of the danger, but, Anne, I can make a difference here. My men have a new life where they can keep their honor while providing for their families. You should have seen them this evening. I told each of them they did not need to prove themselves, but they came for me and for their own self-respect. They want to rid England of its traitors. How could they not? We fought for years to come home to enemies within our own borders."

"Of course, they would. It takes a special type of man to place his life on the line for his country." She stroked his bare arm as she spoke. "How could I have been so stupid to think otherwise? I am mortified by my ignorance. Can you ever forgive me?"

"For being jealous?" he taunted.

Anne blushed and looked away quickly. "Yes—I was so jealous—green with envy. I tried to make myself into the kind of woman who accepts her husband's appetites, but I could not. I was devastated to think you might choose someone else; I just could not fathom why you would leave our bed."

"You should know I would never leave you unless another person was in danger."

She suddenly understood what he was saying. He loved her—only her, but sometimes he must answer the call to help others. It was his nature. "God has a new path for you."

"For us," he corrected. "I need your support. God returned me to the sea when my men needed me, and then he brought me home to you. Now, he presents me with a whole new challenge. With this title, I can give honorable men a new start, and I can affect England's future. Yet, none of it means anything without you. I need for you to do what you did today—develop relationships—help me reach those I cannot reach. I do not possess your natural ease with people."

"What did you find tonight?"

Anne did not agree to help, but she did not refuse either; she simply accepted what he told her, and for that, Frederick was more than thankful. "Mrs. Thomason told Mr. Avendale her brother was involved with something dangerous. She was right, but it was not what I expected. We found French brandy, which made sense. We also found some paintings—portraits by François Gérard and Jacques-Louis David."

"Gérard and David! You trifle with me!"

"No, it is as I speak. Yet, we found something more bizarre in that Studland warehouse—barrels of coal tar and of sulfur."

Anne sat stupefied by his disclosure. "Coal tar?" she questioned. "Why would anyone want coal tar, or sulfur, for that matter?"

"It is not even that we found such an unusual haul; it is the large quantity of barrels with which we were surprised. According to Tweed Swift, we could blow up all of Whitehall and maybe even part of St. James."

"Why?" she stammered. "Why would anyone smuggle chemicals when they could simply use an explosive?" she reasoned.

"When I reconnoitered the warehouse before we went in as a group, I overheard some men talking of Sir Thomas, Lord Cochrane. Maybe you remember reading of him in the Navy lists. However, Harwood says Lord Thomas is in prison. We thought maybe they wanted to blow up his gaol—to release him." Frederick needed to make some sense of a senseless night; he hoped Anne would see something he did not.

She looked at him—but did not comprehend his unspoken question. "Why so much? I cannot imagine they would need more than a small portion to even bring down a wall. You said there were barrels."

"That there were."

"Did the captured men you say anything?"

Feeling a prickly uneasiness, Frederick tried to come to some conclusions. "We did not question the men; I left them locked up in the warehouse and sent word to the Harbor Master. He will question them. I left two of the portraits and some of the brandy as evidence, but we moved everything else to the barns in the north pasture. We will find ways to use the sulfur and coal tar. Harwood says we can use the coal tar for roofs and sealing and the sulfur for fertilizer. I gave each man three casks of brandy to sell or drink as they see fit. I thought it best not to be directly attached to the investigation."

"Will the thieves not recognize you? Will they not admit you have the barrels?" Anne seemed suddenly worried he would be accused.

"I thought of that. If they would say I have it, I would get Wallingford involved—turn over what we found, if necessary; but I do not believe that will happen. They planned something large, and these men probably knew little of the complete plan. I just wish I could find out more without involving Marcus Lansing." Frederick now stroked the inside of her wrist with his fingertips.

A light tap on the door ended their conversation. Doctor Laraby swept into the room. "Wentworth," he stated as he rushed through the door. "I hear you had an accident today."

"His horse was temperamental," Anne spoke for the servants standing in the background.

Laraby understood without being told something was amiss. "Let me take a look."

"Thank you, doctor; my husband tolerates my need to feel he is well." Anne appeared flustered, even though a moment ago she was perfectly calm. Frederick realized she performed for the staff; that is what she wanted them to think. Why else would she send for the doctor at such an hour?

Laraby moved the arm tentatively. "Rotate your wrist as much as you can."

Frederick did so through gritted teeth.

"You have a broken wrist and what appears to be a fractured bone in your arm. You must have tried to catch yourself with that arm." Laraby knew he covered for his captain; he did not know how Frederick really hurt his arm, but he did not need to know. He knew the man. "I will set it for you; you will heal nicely."

"Thank you for coming so quickly, Doctor. I wish I could have convinced my husband to see you before such an ungodly hour, but he did not want to disturb everyone's holiday." She continued to fuss over Frederick as servants brought in the supplies the doctor needed. "Next time, my Dear, please listen to me."

"I will, Sweetling." Frederick smiled at her. "I am still learning to be a proper husband."

Laraby went to work immediately and in a short time Frederick's hand was in a cast and his arm in a sling. "That should do you, Wentworth. I will check on you late tomorrow. I am sure you and Lady Orland would both like some rest now."

"Come by around three," Frederick stated, but Laraby knew it to be an order.

"I will do exactly that, Admiral. Until tomorrow." The doctor left, taking Frederick's service staff with him.

"Do you think you can sleep? The good doctor left some laudanum if you need it." Anne tended him for real.

Frederick rose and took her hand. "Will you lay with me as you did on the ship? I need you close."

She stood beside him, sliding into his one-armed embrace. "Come, let us make you more physically comfortable. We will use your bed; it is larger, and I am less likely to hit your hand. I will fix you a dose of the medicine Laraby prescribed."

Once they were contentedly settled, Anne snuggled into his back. Of course, her bulk kept her from truly outlining his frame, but Frederick still needed her reassurance. "Thank you, Anne, for understanding my need to do this my way. I know Lansing is an old friend, but I must make this mine." His words began to slur as he drifted off to sleep.

"Frederick, there is something you should know."

He caught her hand to his chest. "What is that, Sweetling?"

"Marcus used to brag of Sir Thomas's conquests when we were in school, and then again when I saw him a couple of times at parties and such; it must have been in '09 or so, and he could speak of nothing else. Marcus Lansing is Lord Cochrane's cousin. You were right to not fully trust Lord Wallingford."

"Neither should you, Anne," he warned.

She slid her arm up and down his chest. "I needed to know all this; do not leave me out again."

"Never, my Love," he mumbled. "You and I will see things through together."

Epilogue

And looking to the Heaven, that bends above you,
How oft! I bless the Lot that made me love you.
—Samuel Taylor Coleridge from "The Presence of Love"

Frederick rode hard, trying to reach Hanson Hall before dark. He took the last of the sulfur and coal tar to Harville and Rushick in Brighton. A week after the midnight raid on the warehouse, Wallingford showed up unannounced at the estate. He wanted to know Frederick's involvement. By that time, he and Anne discussed the best way to handle the situation. Frederick told Lansing, he and Harwood stumbled on the ring when he was trying to find the brother of one his Cottagers. When Lansing asked if he led the raid, he assured the man that he participated, but was not the spokesman for the group. His interest purely lay in the securing of Laurie's release. Later, when it became known through the aristocratic circles he possessed several of the portraits, Frederick claimed he bought them from an unknown seller in order to save them. To prove his point, he donated one of the paintings to the Royal Academy and sent another as a gift to George IV. Of course, Anne insisted on keeping one of the smaller ones to display in Hanson Hall. Frederick still wondered about Lansing's connection to the event. Was the man involved some how? Did he have prior knowledge of the thievery? In his astute questioning of Admiral Pennington and of Benjamin, he learned Lord Cochrane had some revolutionary ideas on how to win the war, but no one knew exactly what those ideas were. In addition, Frederick realized something else after the fact: The man in the gray coat was not among their captures. It took two months to dispense with all the barrels, but now each of his Cottagers had a sealed roof and walls. The fallow fields lay thick with sulfur, while Doctor Laraby claimed some of it.

Today, he rode for another reason. He spent the night with Thomas and Milly, but one of his footmen woke the household before dawn with the news Anne was to deliver their child. She was a few weeks early, and

Frederick worried for her health. He wished now he never left her. He changed horses several times, and he was not sure he should not do so again. Finally in Dorset, he doubted the one he rode would make it all the way to Hanson Hall.

"Wentworth!" Lucas Kendrick suddenly appeared on the road. Frederick pulled up his horse, tugging tightly on the reins.

"Got to hurry, Kendrick," he called. "Mrs. Wentworth delivers our child."

"I was sent to meet you. Take this horse; it is fresh, and you will get there faster. Shipley waits about twenty miles down the road with another."

Frederick slid from the saddle and hurried to the one upon which his friend sat. "Thank you, Kendrick. I cannot believe you thought of this."

"We did not. It was your wife; she says she needs you home." Kendrick called as Frederick rode away at a full gallop.

He traded horses with Shipley with seven miles to go. Horses from his stable held up better than the nags he secured at the posting inns across Hampshire. When he rode across the wooden bridge leading to the cobbled curve in front of the house, Frederick jumped from the horse as a footman reached for the reins. He nearly bolted through the door before Mr. Smythe could open it. Throwing his coat at one of the men, he demanded, "Where is she?"

"Lady Orland is in her room. Mrs. Miller is with her, and Doctor Laraby is standing by if he is needed." Smythe efficiently led the way as Frederick scrambled up the stairs.

"Then I am in time?" he nearly begged.

Smythe could not keep up with him, and so he called after Frederick's retreating form. "You are, Sir."

Skidding to a stop in front of Anne's door, he hesitated, wondering whether he should knock before entering, but hearing the distinct cry of a baby, he burst through the door, completely out of breath. Mrs. Miller and Harriet, Anne's maid, bustled about the room in a flurry of activity, but his eyes fell on the body reclining against the bed. Her hair plastered to her head in dampness, Anne's pale face looked exhausted—the veins in her neck and across her temple blue lines on white. His heart leapt at the sight of her—*his Anne*—so fragile—so vulnerable! She looked broken and twisted, and he moved to straighten her in the bed; then he saw the blood covering her legs and the linens. "Dear God, Anne!" he cried out in fright, as he dropped to his knees beside her.

Her eyes fluttered open and then closed again, but the makings of a smile took hold of the corners of her mouth. "You made it." Her lips barely moved, but he heard her.

Frederick gently kissed her forehead as he brushed the hair from her face. "I am here, my Love." He clutched at her hand, praying she was all right, but he never saw so much blood.

"Mrs. Wentworth," Mrs. Miller came forward carrying a bundle, "would ye be likin' to see ye' boy?"

Frederick's head snapped around; he heard the child's cry, but he forgot it all when he saw Anne. "A boy?" he whispered loudly, his voice raspy.

Anne's mind demanded her participation. "Let my husband see his heir," she told the older woman.

Looking at nothing but the bundle of swaddling clothes in Mrs. Miller's hands, Frederick reached out to carefully take the child into his arms. "Be holdin' his head just so," Mrs. Miller instructed.

Frederick nestled the child in the crook of his arm, and even before he turned back the blanket to look at the elfin face, his world rocked. In that moment, everything changed. "In all my life," he murmured as he slid back the blanket and touched the soft silkiness of his child's hair.

"Let me see," Anne's voice came from behind him.

Frederick bent low to lay the baby in her arms. "He is beautiful, Anne." The utterance rang in the silent room. "My, God, how perfect you both are!" He leaned forward and kissed the end of her nose. "I am sorry I could not get here any faster." He traced the outline of his son's face with the tip of one finger.

"And I am sorry," she spoke haltingly, "your daughter could wait no longer."

Frederick looked confused. "Daughter?" His eyes fell on the black curls of his child's hair. "Mrs. Miller, is this not my boy?" he asked, wondering why everyone now stared at him.

"Aye, Admiral, he be ye boy." Mrs. Miller went to the far corner of the room and picked up what he suddenly realized was another child. "This here be ye gal, tho'." She placed a second child in his arms. "She be little like her Mam, but ye should hear the gal cry."

Frederick rolled back the covering blanket. In his arms lay a miniature Anne—no doubt about it—the baby would be the spitting image of *his Anne*. "Perfection again!" He laughed as he returned his attention to his wife. "You did it all without me," he taunted.

"Next time." Her eyes began to drift closed.

"We be needin' to get ye cleaned up, Lady Orland. We let his Lordship take the babe to his room." Mrs. Miller began to shoo him away as she took his son and returned him to the makeshift nursery on the far side of the room. Frederick watched it all very carefully before bending to kiss Anne once more.

Standing slowly, he noted Anne's exhaustion taking over. "I will be back shortly, my Love," he whispered to her. "Take good care of her Ladyship," he ordered both of the women, even though he knew they would. "Come, Sweetling," he spoke to the child he carried. "Let me show you your new home." He left humming a sailor's song to the child.

Strolling casually through the house—his house—he took the newborn from room to room—cooing words of love as he went. "Would you like to see your nursery?" he asked as he walked into the room. "Is it not a fine room? Your mother prepared it well, and you my darling daughter will thrive in this room. It is made especially for you." He touched his daughter's hand, and the little fingers enfolded around his. "Your mother claims you will wrap me around these baby fingers." He touched the child's hand with his lips. "Your mother is a very smart person, and like me, my child, you are blessed to be loved by her." Frederick rubbed his cheek against the baby's hand. "I am sure they are finished; let us go find your brother."

By the time he returned his daughter to Anne's room, Harriet and Mrs. Miller cleaned up the bed and Anne. With a fresh gown and her hair combed, Frederick was happy to see her pale skin, less pallid, and some color returning to her cheeks. "Your daughter returns," he said jovially, coming to sit by Anne's bed.

"My daughter?" Anne accused. "I suppose our boy is *your son*? My daughter and your son? Is that how it will be?"

"No." He laughed lightly at her renewed playfulness. "They will be my daughter and my son when they are on their best behavior. They will be your children at the other times."

"That hardly seems fair," she countered. "I did all the hard work; I should reap the rewards."

Frederick touched her bottom lip with his fingertip. "Is not the fact that your husband loves you more than life reward enough?"

"It has its benefits," she teased. "Are you happy, my Husband? After all, you warned me about having more than one crew member at a time."

"Ours will be a houseful, but as long as you and the children are well, I will be content. I have a daughter to protect, and a son as my heir; plus, the other half of my heart serves as their mother. God gives me it all in one fell sweep."

Anne slid her hand into his. "Have you considered names for our children?"

"Not at all. I assumed we still had weeks to discuss it as you were not to deliver so soon." He brought her hand to his lips, rubbing them back and forth against her knuckles. "Do you have preferences?"

The corners of Anne's mouth turned up in delight. "I do have a thought for our daughter."

"Pray tell."

"You will think this insignificant, but it crossed my mind several times of late." She hesitated, not sure how to explain what she wanted to say. "Traditionally, I should name her after my mother Lady Elizabeth, but my sister dampens the 'enchantment' of that practice. Some would suggest we name our daughter after me, but that is not my wish. I always hated my name because it allowed my family to treat me as 'plain Anne.' I felt the name fit me quite well until you saw me—until I was no longer invisible. I do not want my daughter to be 'plain Anne.' I want her to have a name others will remember—a distinctive name."

Frederick hated the fact she once viewed herself in such derogatory terms. "Do you have a suggestion?"

"When we met again at the concert, you spoke of once being in Romola, Italy. I thought the place's name the most beautiful sound—the way the word rolls off the tongue. Could we name our daughter Romola? If we wish to follow the traditional route, we can use *Anne* as her middle name. Romola Anne Wentworth. What do you think?"

"Just like the child, I believe the name is perfect." Frederick would never disagree with Anne's decision. It was the ideal name for their beautiful daughter, and some day he would tell the girl of how her mother reasoned out the choice.

Anne smiled enormously, happy that he agreed with her suggestion. "What of our son? Do you want him to have the name *Fredrick*?"

"Like you, I would prefer something else. The name fits me, but as you once told me, it is a mouthful—Frederick James Wentworth. My grandfather was a *Robert*. Do you think that would be acceptable? Robert James Wentworth, the Honourable Lord Orland?"

"It is an excellent choice; your family will be pleased you honored your patriarch."

"Romola and Robert—our children, Mrs. Wentworth." He laughed as he bent to kiss the top of her head. "Can you believe all this? How we got to this point? In '06, would you have believed we would be married and live in this house and have these children?"

"We are living our dreams," her voice held pure sentimentality. "Your father and mother would be so proud of the man you became. This land will belong to Robert some day; Romola will make a good match, and it will be because of you."

Frederick bent to kiss the indentation of her neck and shoulder. Anne closed her eyes and relaxed. "You are exhausted, and rightly so, my Love. I will have the wet nurse take the children to the nursery for the night. You may see them in a few hours." He helped to adjust the bed linens about her as she settled back against the pillows.

"We will need to employ another wet nurse," she mumbled.

Frederick smiled down at her. "I will do so with tomorrow's light." He kissed her forehead. Frederick caught his breath on a sob of relief. "You and the children complete my life," he whispered. "Rest now; we will talk more in the morning."

"Come lay with me," she pleaded.

"I will bathe and join you," he assured her.

Some time later, Frederick slid his long frame under the blanket. Anne slept, so he simply warmed her backside by saddling up next to her. The fragrance of her hair wafted over him as he relaxed into the familiarity of her body. He removed the strands of hair from about her face; seeing the thick lashes resting on the rise of her cheeks, Frederick realized the impact of the moment: Impulsively, he fell in love with Anne Elliot, and, decisively, he won her. "The children are a testament to our love," he whispered to her sleeping form.

She rolled over into his embrace, snuggling into his chest. "Umm," she moaned.

"I look into your face," he murmured as his lips brushed against her cheek, "and I see God's plan at work. In His infinite wisdom, He brought me to your doorstep twice."

She snaked her arm up over his shoulder. "Do you plan to talk all evening?" her lips barely moved. "I am sleepy, and I hoped you would skip the adorations and go straight to the kissing part."

"I can be as silent as the lambs."

"Prove it," she challenged. "Just prove it."

Afterword

When the Treaty of Paris was signed on November 20, 1815, Napoleon was already in exile on the tiny South Atlantic island of Saint Helena. Forced to accept the defeat of his Imperial Guard at Waterloo, Napoleon fled first to France, leaving behind coaches loaded with gold and jewelry and his private papers—his personal fortune. Reaching Paris on June 21, 1815, he still refused to admit his failure; on June 22, the Chamber of Representatives demanded Bonaparte abdicate.

Even with his renunciation, Napoleon did not give up hopes of escaping the British and Prussian armies. Instead, on July 8, he tried to escape to the United States by boarding the French frigate, *La Salle*; however, the English warship *Bellerophon* blocked the French emperor's escape. Yet, the *La Salle* was not the only French ship with American allies hoping to aid Bonaparte's retreat. Napoleon contacted more than one ship and asked it to prepare to receive him. Still smarting from the War of 1812, French-born Americans reportedly sympathized with Bonaparte and tried to help him escape from the Duke of Wellesley's justice.

Captain Sir Thomas, Lord Cochrane, held radical ideas on how the British should have conducted their naval warfare. A decorated hero, Lord Cochrane advanced quickly through naval ranks. Napoleon himself dubbed Cochran "The Sea Wolf."

However, he fell out of favor when he first became consumed by the 1809 court-martial of Admiral James Gambier. Cochrane's inability to properly express himself in public played out during the trial. To complicate matters, he earned political enemies with his election to Parliament. A "tarnished star," Cochrane eventually went to jail following the London Stock Exchange scandal in 1814, "charged with illegal financial manipulations."

The most interesting fact concerning Cochrane's career was his plan to conduct a sort of chemical warfare. Even the Prince Regent approved of Cochrane's plan, and Whitehall considered the merits of it—only turning it down when they considered the enemy might reciprocate with a like technology.

In Cochrane's plan, a hollowed out ship's hulk would be layered with clay, scrap metal, a thick layer of powder, rows of shells, and animal carcasses. This "loaded" ship would be sent among the enemy vessels and then exploded—sending deadly mortar in a circular path. Other "empty" ships would be layered with clay—then charcoal—and then sulfur, creating a floating stink bomb. The "noxious effluvia" clouds would quickly subdue the opposition.

In 1818, released from jail, Cochrane left England and became a mercenary, not returning home until King William IV pardoned him in 1829. He continued to purport his ideas even to Queen Victoria during the Crimean War. The details of Cochrane's plans never became public, and with the end of the war, all thoughts of radical warfare were sealed away in the record rooms of Whitehall. Ironically, ten years after the files were unsealed, soldiers faced yellow sulfuric clouds of mustard gas during World War I.

Resources

"A-Z Contents." *The Encyclopaedia of Plymouth History.* Plymouth Data Website. Sponsored by Plymouth Local Studies Library and the Plymouth and West Devon Record Office. 25 Dec 2008. {http://plymouthdata. info/index.htm}.

"Battle of Aix Roads." *Everything2.* 2002. *The Everything Development Company.* 24 Jan 2009. {http://everything2.com/title/battle%2520of %2520Aix%2520Roads}.

"Battle of Copenhagen (1807)." *Nation Master.* 2003-2008. {http:www. nationmaster.com/encyclopedia/Battle-of-Copenhagen-(1807)}.

"The Battle of Rasheed 'Roseta' March 31, 1807." *Arabic News.* 31/03/2001. {www.Arabicnews.com/ansub/Daily/Day/010331/2001033134.html}.

"The Battle of San Domingo." *National Maritime Museum.* 2008. {http://www.nmm.ac.uk/collections/prints/listPrints.cfm?filter=maker &node=185}.

"British Royal Navy Crews." *Napoleonic Guide.* 2006. {http://www. napoleonguide.com/navy_crews.htm}.

"A Calendar for Persuasion." *The Republic of Pemberley.* {http://www. jimandellen.org/austen/persuasion.calendar.html}.

"The Cancelled Chapters of *Persuasion.*" *The Republic of Pemberley.* Posted by Edith Lank, 3 Mar. 1997. {http://www.pemberley.com/janeinfo/ pcanchap.html}.

"Children's Amusements in the Early Nineteenth Century." *Memorial Hall Museum.* 2008. Pocumtuck Valley Memorial Association, Deerfield,

Massachusetts. {http://Memorialhall.mass.edu/classroom/curriculum_6th/lesson13/bkgdessay1.html}.

"Cleric." *New Ådvent.* from *The Catholic Encyclopedia.* {http://newadvent.org/cathen/04049b.htm}.

"Copenhagen." *Napoleonic Guide.* 2006. {http://www.napoleonguide.com/battle_cope1801.htm}.

"18th Century Naval Ranks." *N. Cargill-Kipar.* 1999-2008. {http://www.kipar.org/piratical-resources/british-navy-ranks.html}.

"English Report of Trafalgar." *Napoleonic Guide.* 2006. from *The Hampshire Chronicle.* {http://www.napoleonguide.com/sailors_uktraf.htm}.

"George Gordon Byron, Lord Byron (1788-1824)." *Poem Hunter.* "Bride of Abydos, The." 2000-2008. {http://www.poemhunter.com/poem/bride-of-abydos-the/}.

"The Lady of the Lake." *The Literature Network.* 2000-2008. Jalic, Inc. {http://www.online-literature.com/walter_scott/2561}.

Malcomson, Robert. "During the Napoleonic Wars a British Naval Officer Proposed the Use of Saturation Bombing and Chemical Warfare." *Tripod.* 2009. *Lycos, Inc.* 9 Feb 2009. {http://members.tripod.com/EsotericTexts07/Brit.NapChemWar.xx.htm}.

"Napoleonic Naval Balance." *Napoleonic Guide.* 2006. {http://www.napoleonguide.com/navy_balance.htm}.

"Officer Ranks in the Royal Navy: The Naval Hierarchy Explained." *The Royal Naval Museum.* 2000. {http://www.royalnavalmuseum.org/info_sheets_nav_rankings.htm}.

"Pictures of Corfe Castle." *Pictures of England.* 2001-2009. Pictures of England. 31 Jan 2009. {http://www.picturesofengland.com/England/Dorset/Corfe_Castle/Corfe_Castle}.

"Pictures of Swanage." *Pictures of England.* 2001-2009. *Pictures of England.* 31 Jan 2009. {http://www.picturesofengland.com/search/}.

"Pictures of Wimborne Minster." *Pictures of England.* 2001-2009. *Pictures of England.* 31 Jan 2009. {http://www.picturesofengland.com/England/ Dorset/Wimborne_Minster}.

"Royal Navy." from *Wikipedia,* the free encyclopedia. "HMSVictory." {http://en.wikipedia.org/wiki/Royal_Navy}.

"Ship of War, 1650-1815: An Age of Conflicts." *National Maritime Museum.* 2008.{http://nmm.ac.uk/visit/exhibitions/on-display/ship-of-war-1650- 1815/*/viewPage/7}.

Streissguth, Thomas. *History's Greatest Defeats: The Napoleonic Wars: Defeat of the Grand Army.* San Diego: Lucent Books, 2003.

"Toys and Games." *History Lives.* a division of the Cooperman Fife and Drum Company. 2005.{http://www.historylives.com/toysandgames.htm}.

"What is Coal Tar?" *wiseGeek.* 2007. *Conjecture Corporation.* 16 Feb 2009. {http://www.Wisegeek.com/what-is-coal-tar.htm}.

LaVergne, TN USA
10 February 2010
172580LV00004B/367/P